FIVE DATES BETWEEN FRIENDS

ERIN THOMSON

FIVE *Dates* BETWEEN *Friends*

for anyone who believes in happily ever afters

1

CHASE

WE REALLY NEEDED a lock on the office door.

If there was a lock on the office door, I wouldn't need to use the large desk to barricade myself in. I was sweating with the effort—and I hadn't brought a change of clothes. Rookie mistake.

I'd considered other options to seal myself inside but nothing was substantial enough, even sitting on the small tower of crates I pushed to one side wouldn't have done it. It needed to be the desk. The desk that had to weigh close to a tonne. The desk that Mack and I had found on the sidewalk at four in the morning and dragged back to our, as yet, unfinished bar.

It was a regal desk, with dark timber and hidden compartments; a desk of queens and kings and other important people. It was immense and ridiculous and had no place in our office. And yet, after we managed to get it inside—through tenacity and Tetris-like maneuvering—I could almost hear it sigh with relief that it was home.

The door opened, not all the way because the desk limited its progress to a medium sized crack. Although if there was a lock this wouldn't even be an issue. Mack poked his head around the partially opened door.

"There y—whoa—what's happening in here?"

I straightened, huffing a little, and blew an errant strand of hair out of my face. "Nothing, nothing's happening. Why do you ask?"

"Only because the desk isn't usually on that angle, or obscuring the door quite as effectively," he said with a chuckle.

"Oh that? It's fine. I was just... testing something out." Because of course I'd be doing that in the middle of wedding preparations. Totally normal.

"Uh-huh..." His eyes swept over me, seeing far more than I wanted them to. "You want to put it back where it was so I can open the door?"

"No."

"No?"

"If the door can open then you can come in, and I can get out, and I'm quite happy here right at the moment, thank you very much." And I would continue to be happy here until the night was over. What the hell had we been thinking, taking on a wedding? We weren't geared for events. Until a couple of days ago we didn't even have a functioning kitchen. We were a bar. A cool bar, if I did say so myself, but a bar nonetheless. Not a wedding venue. This whole thing was a mistake, I saw that now. So I was hiding.

Mack tried to wedge himself further through the crack in the door, he didn't get far. "Is this about the plums?" he asked.

My stomach rolled. "I am going to strangle Nash with his own hair. How could he fail to mention that his sister—*the bride*—doesn't like plums?"

"There are other cocktails."

"That's the best one," I said, running my finger over a scratch on the desk.

"Better than the ginger fizz?"

"That one's good, too. It's very warming, good for this time of year..."

"A fact I can attest to after you made me drink three." He shoved on the door. The desk moved a fraction and his shoulders entered the room. "So, this is just about the plums?"

"Yes."

Another shove. "Chase."

"No," I admitted as I watched him push his way all the way in. I turned my back and perched on the edge of the desk. He dropped down beside me and bumped my shoulder with his.

"What's up?"

I shook my head. "Maybe I'm just realizing that we might have bit off a little more than we can chew."

"Ahh... and is this you, or is it Maureen?"

I huffed out a laugh. "So what if it is Maureen? She's not always wrong."

"Maureen is full of shit—always," he said, voice gruff. Usually, I would agree with him. Maureen—the name he'd given to my negative inner voice—was often out of line. Today, though, today I was pretty sure she had a point.

"We've been talking about getting into events for how long?"

"At least a year, I know, but we were talking about *small* events. Birthdays, maybe engagements. Not celebrity fucking weddings!" My voice cracked on the last word. Why did Nash have to be related to a social media darling, and one of the most successful influencers in the country? And why did she have to be marrying an actor who was on the brink of becoming the next Hemsworth? Why?

My shoulders slumped. I needed a drink.

Mack turned me so we were facing one another. "We've wanted to get into the event space, this is just a little nudge."

"Ha! This is not a nudge. It is a two handed shove. Off a cliff."

He took my face in his large hands. I ignored the way my cheeks fit perfectly in his warm, slightly scratchy palms. His eyes pinned mine, looking all the way into my soul. Or that was how it felt, anyway.

"Maureen," he growled and a small thrill danced up my spine. *What the hell was that?* I hid my unsettling reaction because that was not the way to react to your best friend, whether they were holding your face or not. He continued, oblivious to my internal squirming. "We don't need you right now. Tonight is going to be great. Take a hike."

"Take a hike?" It sounded a tiny bit breathy.

He squashed my cheeks, pushing my lips into a delightful fish pout. "I just went where the mood took me."

Evidently I was the only one having an emotionally confusing moment. "Are you enjoying yourself?"

"Yup." He squashed my face a little more and grinned. "Now get your shit together, Linden, Jemma is looking for you."

I swatted his hands off. "Me? Why?"

"She didn't say, just some wedding related issue that only you could solve."

Unlikely. I held his gaze, searching for the lie but couldn't find it. Well, if Jemma was looking for me then I couldn't hide in here forever, no matter how much I wanted to. I stood and Mack caught my hand, pulling my attention back to him.

"We've got this, Chase, *you've* got this." There was something about the conviction in his voice, the fierce look in his eyes, that made me believe it.

I squared my shoulders and wound my hair up into a knot. "I've got this."

"Atta girl. Now go get 'em." I slapped his offered hand, the crack filling the room.

I've got this.

WE DID IT. We actually fucking did it.

This afternoon I would have been happy to hide under our desk until the entire thing was over, but right now I was elated, ecstatic, buzzing.

When Jemma had stormed into our bar, I'd thought she was mad for suggesting she'd be able to pull together a wedding in three weeks. Of course, she'd gone and proven me wrong. She and Nash had proven me wrong. I couldn't quite wrap my head around the fact that it was actually done. That Dallas was now Mrs Prince. That we hosted our first event, our first wedding. We'd done it. And it was amazing. Mack was right, Maureen really was full of shit.

"What's this?" Mack asked, nodding at the four glasses lined up along the bar. He looked ruined, eyes dark and tired, hair droopy, and there was a growing layer of scruff coating his jaw. I was sure I'd slam into that wall of exhaustion eventually as well, but right now I was too high on the night to feel it. If I got to sleep before dawn it would be a miracle.

I jumped up onto the bar, legs swinging. "A toast. Where are Nash and Jemma?" For two people who didn't even know each other a month ago, I couldn't believe how well they worked together, like they shared brain cells or something.

"Having a moment out front," he said with a wry smile that lightened his eyes a touch. "She's good for him."

"She is. Much better for him than Nadia." I all but growled the name. Nadia had always been a long way from deserving Nash, and he'd been too blinded by his dick to see it. Not that it was an issue now, with Jemma lighting him up like I'd never seen.

"Be nice." Mack leaned against the bar, his arm brushing my thigh.

"I don't need to be nice, not anymore. Anyway, we're not talking about Nadia, we're toasting to our success." I handed him one of the whiskeys, and held mine aloft. "We did it."

"I told you we would."

"Yes, yes... I think, deep down, I knew it too. I just needed a moment to freak out, that was all." And I needed him to pull me out of it. My voice of reason.

"To us."

"To us," I agreed and he clinked his glass against mine.

"And we didn't just do it, we *killed it.* Your signature cocktails were outstanding. You might have even changed Dallas' mind about plums."

I laughed and took a long sip, enjoying the warm track the whiskey made down to my stomach.

"This could be it, you know?" he said, looking around the aftermath in front of us. When I'd walked in this morning and seen the florist at work, I'd been scared that when she finished the place would be unrecognizable. But it wasn't, it was still Rudi, but more; Rudi, but elevated. Boughs of greenery hung from the beams overhead and explosions of flowers and leaves covered the small tables. It was stunning.

Since we started Rudi Blue, things had always been pretty comfortable. There had been some low periods of concern here and there, but on the whole we'd found a loyal group of locals who kept us in the black. This, though—hosting a celebrity wedding—this could be the thing to take us to the next level. It had the power to change things considerably. It was exciting and terrifying all at once.

"I can hear your wheels turning." Mack nudged my knee with his elbow.

I bumped him back and had another sip. "We'll probably need to hire more staff."

"Extra security, too."

I nodded and circled the amber liquid around in my tumbler, my mind already putting together a to-do list to start on tomorrow.

"Stop making your list and just enjoy the moment, Chase," he said, shooting me a knowing smile.

I snorted into my glass. "I am enjoying the moment. I'm capable of enjoying the moment and making a list. It's called multitasking."

His chuckle rumbled in his chest as I emptied my glass. So much change just waiting to happen. What if I couldn't manage it all?

"Nope." He planted one large hand on my thigh and squeezed.

"Stop! No! Mack! No! No!" I squealed as his fingers dug in just above my knee and I fell sideways wheezing with laughter. "Stop!"

"You are not going to ruin this moment with your overactive brain!" he said, batting off my attempts to dislodge his hand from my leg as his fingers found the precise spot that nearly had me peeing my pants. "We helped to pull off a fucking wedding, Chase."

"I know!" I said between bouts of giggles. "I know, please stop!"

His hand disappeared and I took a gulping breath, which turned into a squawk as he swept me off the bar and planted me on a stool. I tried to wriggle away, not keen for more tickles, but he caged me in, arms brushing my shoulders and chest in my face.

He hinged forward until we were eye to eye. "No more listening to Maureen, no more second guessing, whatever comes we deal with it, together, like we always do. Because we're a team," he said, pinning me to the spot with a fierce look.

"We're a team," I agreed, meeting his look with one of my own. "We're the best team."

The moment stretched as we continued to stare at one another and then, in a blink, something shifted. The air between us turned hot, charged with some crackling energy that made the hairs on the back of my neck and down my arms stand on end.

My heart rattled against my ribs. What the hell was happening? I'd felt that weird charge in the office earlier, but it had just been me, hadn't it? It certainly didn't feel that way now.

Was he going to kiss me? Did I want him to kiss me? I swallowed, my tongue darting out along my lower lip, the answer was yes. I did. I wanted Mack to kiss me. *Holy shit.* My breathing was quick and shallow as we both stayed exactly where we were. My eyes darted to his mouth. His to mine. I felt that look all the way down to my toes and they curled inside my boots.

Without letting myself think too much about what the hell I was doing, and how I'd feel about it tomorrow, I leaned in, my eyes fixed on his lips. The scratch of his stubble on my palms sent heat rolling down my center. Then the last of the space between our mouths disappeared and I was kissing my best friend. And it was ... good. Really. Fucking. Good. My arms locked around his neck, pulling our bodies closer, and the low groan he made sent a fresh wave of want through me.

This should be awkward, shouldn't it? We'd been friends for too long for it to be this hot. To be this, *everything*. But it had been this way that first time, too, all those years ago.

My thoughts quieted as his tongue sought entry into my mouth. As soon as it touched mine, it was like a live wire ignited. What had started as slow, tender, and exploratory turned needy, messy, and raw as years of friendship crumbled in the face of whatever the fuck this was. My fingers tunneled into his sandy curls as his hands moved down to my hips and squeezed. We weren't close enough. We would never be close enough. I wanted to crawl inside his skin.

The sound of the front door slamming shook me out of my lust trance and I pulled back—chest heaving, lips warm and swollen. Mack's hands were still on my hips, gripping me like I was his anchor. We stared at each other, eyes searching for answers that I wasn't sure either of us had.

Then, I heard it—a hitch of breath. Our attention swung towards the door and Nash sitting on his haunches, his head in his hands. My heart dropped into my stomach and, without a word, I was off the stool and moving.

I approached slowly, feeling Mack a step behind me. "Nash," I said. He didn't move, didn't look like he'd even heard me. "Nash, hey, are you okay? What's happened?"

"She's gone," he said to the floor and I shot a glance at Mack, my own concern mirrored in the swirling depths of his eyes. Neither of us needed to ask to know who he meant. Jemma. Jemma was gone.

The sparks had been flying between the two of them for weeks, ever since they had been thrown together to plan the wedding. Granted, Nadia showing up couldn't have helped things; but what the fuck could have happened just now to send Nash into such a tailspin?

2

MACK

MY ATTENTION WAS TORN.

On the one hand there was Nash, finally asleep on my couch after hours of staring at nothing. Distraught didn't even begin to cover it. I'd figured something was going on between him and Jemma, but this implosion meant it was a lot more serious than I'd thought. He'd barely spoken a word since we'd got him back to my place, after he refused to go to his own. *"She's everywhere,"* he'd muttered, *"she's everywhere I look."* My heart was fucking shredded for him.

Then there was Chase, standing beside me at the kitchen island, her eyes glued to Nash's sleeping form. Even now, I could feel the space between us—it was alive, crackling. I still had no real idea what the hell had happened earlier. One second I was trying to give her a pep-talk, and the next her mouth was on mine. Suddenly I was lost and found and... I didn't even know. I'd kissed plenty of women, but that kiss— that kiss had been something else entirely. Even calling it a kiss felt woefully inadequate.

She'd barely looked at me since. Yes, she was concerned

10

about Nash, but it was more than that. Her shoulders were stiff, her jaw tense.

"I'm gonna go," she whispered and darted around the island, walking to the door.

"Don't go." I followed but she didn't pause. "Stay, please." My voice cracked as I reached for her but she sidestepped, my hand falling useless through the growing space between us. No more crackling tension, it was a yawning cavern, cold and wide.

She shook her head. "I'm wiped out. I need sleep. You look like you could do with some yourself."

She wasn't wrong, I'd been exhausted before, right until the moment she'd kissed me and I felt more awake than I ever had. "You could sleep here."

"The couch is already taken." She lifted her chin in Nash's direction.

"Not on the couch..." I barely recognised my own voice, coated with a longing I hadn't heard before. Her eyes dropped to my mouth but I watched her shoulders straighten a little more, watched the wall come down over her eyes, the gold flecks losing their sparkle.

"Mack..." Her voice was low, but sure, and I could see the wheels turning, see her trying to find the right way to let me down. "That's not—what happened, before, it was—"

"Please don't say it was a—"

"Mistake."

I flinched. Even knowing she was going to say it, the word still landed like a slap. A flicker of regret passed over her face, there and gone so quickly I might have missed it. But we were not doing this again. We were not missing this chance again.

"Let's just—we're both tired." I ran a hand through my hair, squeezed the back of my neck to ease the growing tension. "We can talk about it tomorrow."

Her eyes flashed. "There's nothing to talk about, let's just say it never happened."

"Just like junior year, huh?" I hadn't intended to say it but the hard look in her eyes snapped whatever leash I was trying to maintain.

Now it was her turn to flinch. We had never mentioned that night, not once in the last fifteen years. Memories came flooding back, the shock in her wide eyes as our kiss had broken, the way she drowned it—and her shame—out with so many jello shots we'd almost had to take her to the emergency room.

I'd been drunk, sure, but not drunk enough to forget kissing her, not drunk enough to not know what it meant. But she'd never mentioned it. So neither had I. I wasn't making the same mistake again.

"It was a mistake then and it's a mistake now," she said with venom in her tone.

"That's bullshit," I growled, anger rising. Why was she trying to push me away again? Why couldn't she see?

"It's not. It's reality. You and I would not work."

"Why the fuck not?" As far as I could see, we'd be incredible. It would be a challenge, sure—working together, being a couple—but we could do it.

"You mean, aside from the fact that every one of my relationships has ended in a blaze of glory after a couple of months and you've got a different woman in your bed every night of the week?" I opened my mouth to argue but she cut me off. "We'd be a fucking disaster, Mack. You'd get bored, like you always do—"

"I don't—"

"—and I don't want to be another woman you throw away." She held up her hand when I tried to cut in again. "I love you, you're my best friend, my business partner. But I don't want a relationship with you. I'm sorry for what happened earlier. I was excited and scared about the next steps for our business. I got carried away. But I—"

"Don't want me." I didn't know if she was lying because she was scared or if this was how she really felt. Either way, my chest was caving in.

"Not like that, no. I'm sorry."

It had been stupid of me to hope, stupid of me to think this time would be any different to the first. "You don't need to apologize, Chase." I pulled open the door, no longer looking at her. I couldn't—not as the hurt, shame, and embarrassment all collided in my gut.

"I'll speak to you tomorrow?" she said, edging out the door.

"Yep."

"Keep me updated on Nash."

"Yep."

"Okay, night, Mack."

"Night." The door closed and I stood there staring at it, eyes stinging.

Part of me hoped she'd change her mind, but I knew her well enough to know it was wishful—delusional—thinking. I stalked back to the kitchen and picked up my cell.

Me: *Text me when you get home.*

I stared at the screen for a full five minutes until her reply arrived.

Chase: *home.*

The three dots danced and disappeared, danced and disappeared. I could see her, leaning against her front door, lip trapped between her teeth as she tried to find the right words. But there weren't any. I shut off my cell and went to the refrigerator, yanking out one of my Thanksgiving tester pies. I didn't care that it was almost three in the morning, I didn't care that this was probably going to make me feel sick. I retrieved a spoon and dug the chocolate espresso filling right out of the center before shoving it into my mouth.

HOW LONG DID it take for muscles to go into atrophy? Logically, I knew it was more than a couple of hours and yet there was no denying the sluggishness in my quads and calves the longer I sat here. Nash and I had been in the same positions for what could have been hours or days. Side by side on the couch, him in sweats, me in basketball shorts, staring with unseeing eyes at the television. Lost in the mess of our heads. I hadn't even bothered to shower this morning, something I was paying for as my own stench mingled with that of fried chicken and whiskey. It wasn't a great combination. Not that I cared right at the moment, not that I cared about much of anything right at the moment, aside from—

"I kissed Chase." The words leapt off my tongue like a base jumper from Angel Falls, running on pure adrenaline. Despite not being able to get the memory of that moment out of my head, I hadn't intended on saying it like that. Or at all.

I kissed Chase. And I was changed. It had shifted my gravitational pull. It had rearranged my fucking DNA. How could I not have seen what had been right in front of me all this fucking time? It was Chase, it had literally always been Chase. Maybe I had known it, deep down, and I was too much of a chicken shit to actually do anything about it.

I'd barely slept, unable to stop myself thinking of the feel of her lips on mine, the small, breathy sounds she made, the taste of her tongue. It drove me fucking crazy. I'd seen the sun start to slant through the windows before I managed to quiet my mind long enough to get to sleep.

Nash's head turned, slow, exorcist style. He looked like shit, pale and drawn, though I probably didn't look much better. He scratched his cheek. "You *what?*"

"I kissed Chase. Maybe she kissed me. We kissed." And I sounded like an idiot.

"When?" He croaked.

"Last night." Right about the time your world was imploding. I didn't add that.

"Wow."

"Yeah."

"So, what now?"

She wanted to pretend it never happened, of course she did, but I was pretty sure that was going to kill me—eat me alive from the inside out. "No fucking idea. You got any suggestions?"

He laughed then, long and hysterical to the point of wiping tears from the corners of his eyes. At my obvious confusion, he said, "I'm probably not the best person to ask, what with being in love with one woman and married to another."

I winced. I'd had a feeling things with Jemma were more serious than they looked, but he was in love with her? He hadn't said too much since waking up this morning. He had coffee, took a shower (unlike me), then returned to his place on my couch. Now here I was talking about kissing our best friend. But I needed to say it. I needed to talk about it with someone. And it was clear I wasn't going to be able to talk about it with her.

I don't want to be another woman you throw away.

Did she really think I'd treat her that way? Did she really think I treated any of the women I slept with that way? And her, her of all women? Just the thought soured the contents of my stomach. Did she know me at all? Worse, did she know me better than I did myself? I needed to get the fuck out of my own head.

"I'm really sorry, man, I didn't know you loved her. You wanna talk about it?" I asked.

"Nothing much to say. I don't know if I realized I loved her until it was too late." He blew out a breath. "Despite everything, I don't know if I'd actually change any of it."

"You wouldn't?" I could think of plenty of things I'd change. Not having my almost-ex-wife turn up to my sister's wedding and ruin a good thing, for one.

He shook his head, ran a hand down his face. "Nope, I think it happened the way it was supposed to. But let's not talk about the mess I've managed to make of my life. Let's talk about you and the fact you kissed Chase. *Chase*."

"I don't know if there's much to say about that, either, to be honest."

He gaped. "How can there not be? It's Chase, and you. *Together*. That warrants a conversation, does it not?"

I certainly thought so. "That would be *not*, according to her, because—and I quote—she 'doesn't want to be another woman I throw away'."

He sucked in a sharp breath, confirming that it sounded as bad as I thought it did. "She said that?"

"She did."

"To your face?"

"Yup. Along with the fact she loves me, as a friend and business partner, but doesn't want to be in a relationship with me."

"Fuck."

"That about sums it up, yes." I took the bottle of whiskey sitting between us and tipped it to my lips, letting the liquid cut a trail down my throat and to my stomach.

We passed the bottle back and forth until there was nothing left. I got another, knowing that I would regret it in the morning but not giving a single fuck about it right now.

"You're in love with one woman and still married to another, and I kissed..."

"Chase."

"Chase," I echoed.

"I guess we're both fucked," he said with a low, rumbling chuckle.

"Cheers to that." I slumped further into the couch cushions and let my focus blur. I guess it was like she said, we needed to pretend like it never happened—just like before—but how was I actually supposed to do that? Every time I closed my eyes I saw her, cheeks flushed, lips swollen, eyes alight, the most beautiful thing I'd ever seen.

Fuck. Was I in love with her?

IT WAS NEVER a good sign to wake up after a big night and still be drunk. As far as I was concerned, it was worse than a hangover. I couldn't remember the last time it had happened, but it wasn't exactly a surprise given the ungodly amount of whiskey Nash and I had consumed yesterday. Even now, I could smell it leaking out of my pores; my stomach gave a roll. Eating should have helped the situation but, evidently, I canceled out any positive effect with more whiskey. And more whiskey. And more whiskey.

I pulled myself up, stumbling to the bathroom and into the shower, my head spinning. I just needed to stand under the spray for a minute, maybe an hour, and then I'd be okay. Or slightly more human at the very least.

Fragments of conversation came back to me as I dipped my head under the water, letting the flow soak my hair and run over my ears, drowning the world out. I was no closer to knowing what the fuck to do about the situation. Part of me said that I should forget, like Chase said, while another was sure that was a physical impossibility. I would never be able to scrub the feel of her from my mind. Even now the shape of her hips was a ghost against my palms.

Fuck.

Fuck. Fuck. Fuck.

How the hell was I supposed to see her today and count stock like everything was normal? When everything was so far from fucking normal. Would she have changed her mind? Would she want to talk about it today? I wanted the answer to be yes, but didn't feel confident it would be.

There was no sign of Nash on the couch, or anywhere else in the apartment, by the time I dragged my ass out of the shower. The only signs that he had been there at all was a clean kitchen, a full coffee pot, and a note on the counter saying that he'd be heading back to LA in a few days, and might be there a while.

After refusing to talk about the situation for the better part of the day, the whiskey eventually wore him down and once the words started flowing I didn't have a hope of shutting him up. Despite their shaky start, what with Jemma thinking Nash was married when they first slept together—well, I guess Nash *was* still married when they slept together, but they were separated. Anyway, they got past that and, from the sound of it, shit got serious real fast. But Jemma walked away because she didn't want to be the reason Nash didn't try and make things work with his wife.

Last night he'd said there was nothing to work out with Nadia and, yet, he was going back to LA and *might be there a while?* That didn't sound good but I had my own problems right now. I'd check in with him later.

Even with a gallon of water and Tylenol, I could still feel a steady drum in my temples as I let myself into Rudi Blue. The door gave a groan that was probably relatively quiet but in my head sounded like a thunderclap. I winced.

Chase was at the bar, propped on a stool, attention focused on the laptop in front of her. Was it the same stool? The one she'd been sitting on when we—*don't think about it.*

She turned, her dark eyes wide as they traveled down to my feet then back up in a swift perusal. "Jesus, are you okay?"

I ducked behind the bar and grabbed a bottle of water. "Fine."

"Mack, you don't need to be here if you—"

"I said I'm fine, Chase." I ignored the concern in her tone, in her eyes.

Her mouth opened, closed, opened again. "Okay. Great. You want the bar or store room?" We usually worked through both together, I guess that wasn't happening today. Good.

"I'll take the bar."

"Great," she said again and I wanted to tell her to fuck the stock count, that we needed to talk. But I didn't. I kept my mouth shut as I watched her jump off her stool and march off, head high, shoulders stiff. Maybe she was right, maybe Saturday night had been a mistake. It sure felt like it right now.

THE DISH TOWEL came out of nowhere and slapped me in the side of the face. I really hoped it was clean.

"What the fuck?" I growled, throwing the thing onto the crate beside me.

Chase snorted from her spot on the floor and my attention landed on her. And, like it had every time I'd looked directly at her today, my stomach bottomed out like I'd just gone over the crest of a roller coaster.

I was so royally fucked.

She made an impatient sound in the back of her throat. "I've been trying to get your attention for five minutes. You're lucky it was a dish towel and not a bottle."

"Charming," I deadpanned and she rolled her eyes. What would she say if I told her I was distracted, not only because of Saturday night but also because I could see right down her shirt and I did not need to know she had a pink bra on.

A pink bra that was hidden under her all black clothing. Black jeans with rips across both thighs, black boots made for crushing men's skulls, and that loose fitting black shirt, knotted near her navel, giving me a very much un-needed peek at that fucking pink-lace bra.

Naturally, my mind had wandered, pondering over whether or not it was part of a matching set. My guess was no, and the mystery of whatever was on her bottom half had been driving me to distraction.

"Mack!"

"Yes—fuck—what?"

Her brows pinched, a little pucker appearing between them. "I asked if you were done with the vodka?"

I squeezed the back of my neck. No more thinking about Chase's underwear, or the feel of her tongue in my mouth, not if I wanted to avoid a concussion when she clocked me with the closest bottle of tequila.

"Yes, done with the vodka."

She opened her mouth like she was going to say something, then closed it again. Her lips pursed as she tapped something into the iPad. It was an effort to not let my gaze fix on her mouth. I looked at a spot over her left shoulder instead. It didn't help. I should have taken longer counting out front, not let myself be squeezed into this glorified broom closet with her and the jasmine and lime scent that was soaking my sinuses.

"You can head out, I'll finish up," she said, not looking at me, tension coiled tight down her neck.

"There's still a lot to get through."

"And I can manage it alone." Her tone was sharp.

"I'm sure you can, but I'm not going anywhere." I didn't know why I was arguing when she was giving me an out... the thought of not being near her was as bad as being close.

Her shoulders rose and fell with an impatient breath. "Why don't you just say whatever it is that you need to?"

"I don't have anything to say." I shifted my attention to the rum shelf and felt her step up beside me. I refused to look at her.

"You clearly have something to say about"—pause—"*the other night*, so go ahead and say it."

I turned. She was close but I didn't back up, I just leaned against the shelf like everything was fucking fine. "There's nothing to say. It was a mistake. We're going to act like it never happened. You don't want a relationship with me. That about sums it up, right?" The words were bitter, caustic on my tongue.

"Mack," she all but whispered, her tough facade cracking. I did my best to hold onto my anger, I really did, but how could I when she was looking at me like that? Dark eyes wide and pleading. God I wanted to kiss her again.

"I'd never throw you away, Chase."

"Mack..." Her hand came up to my chest, her palm pressing over my heart, the warmth of it seeped through my shirt, past my skin, all the way through me.

"You have to know that."

She shook her head. "It doesn't change anything."

"We could make this work." I knew it, I knew it in my fucking bones.

"And if it didn't work? How do we go back? Because I'm not going to lose you," she said, tone fierce.

I covered her hand with mine, willing her to understand that, if she gave me a chance, I'd be all in. "You won't lose me, not ever."

"Your friendship, our business, they are more important to me than I can even put into words." Her voice cracked, eyes going glassy with tears. "I don't want that to change. I just—I can't risk it. Please can we—"

"Act like it didn't happen," I finished for her, even as it cracked a hole in my chest.

She nodded, her lip trapped between her teeth. If she cried I was done for. And I'd known her long enough to know when an argument was lost.

"Okay."

"Really?"

"If it's that important to you—"

"*You* are that important to me."

I nodded. "Then yes, really, it never happened."

3

CHASE

THE WIND CUT an icy path down Kingsland as I turned the corner. Weighed down as I was with my groceries, I couldn't do much about the fact that my coat was blowing around like a cape and doing little to insulate me from the buffeting northerly.

Winter was teasing us and it was still almost two weeks out from Thanksgiving. I was already thinking about my domination of Mack's sweet potato pie. Nash may have been the chef of our trio, but Mack was surprisingly proficient in the kitchen—particularly with baked goods. Having said that, I wouldn't be surprised if my all-time favorite pie was made with store bought pastry and canned filling. I didn't care. Not. One. Bit. He'd never shared the secret with me, had been downright cagey about it in fact, so the chances there was more than one shortcut involved were high.

But so long as he kept providing it, I wasn't going to argue.

I stumbled a step—would he still make my pie? Even after everything? Yes, I had to believe he would, because we were acting like the world's greatest kiss never happened. Far easier said than done, granted, but worth the effort if I wanted to hold onto my best friend and business partner.

He really was one of the most important people in my life. The thought of losing him made my stomach twist with something I wasn't even sure I could name. It was more than anxiety, more than dread, more than anything I had words for. I couldn't lose him. I wouldn't, not even for the world's greatest kiss that would logically lead to the world's greatest other things too. I definitely wasn't letting myself think about that.

My mind was still circling around the Mack situation as I let myself inside my apartment and dropped the bags on the floor with a thud. I didn't care how many times I had to mentally slap myself when I started thinking about the kiss. I would do it as many times as I needed to because a kiss was one thing, it could be ignored, swept under the proverbial rug. More than a kiss, though, when hands and bodies and skin were involved, so much more could and would change. I wasn't going to deal with that much change. It didn't matter that my body still remembered the feel of his hands, even through layers of clothing.

Relationships didn't work. Not in my experience anyway. My dad had bailed before I'd even been born and every man since had left. Except Mack (and Nash but I hadn't gone and kissed him). He was still here and I was not going to risk changing that.

The shrill wail of my mother's ringtone pulled me out of my head. I briefly debated screening the call and then answered because she'd only call again, and again, until I picked up.

"Hey M—"

"Chase darling!" she sang down the line. "What are you doing?"

"I'm at home, just catching up on some work," I lied. It

wasn't that Mom and I didn't get along, she was just a bit *much* some of the time. She was the blue skies to my generally gray clouds—which I loved about her—but, with my mind far too preoccupied with my best friend's mouth, I wasn't really in the mood for it. And there was also the issue of me wanting to tell someone to get it out of my head. But telling someone went directly against the *act like it didn't happen* strategy.

"You work too much, baby girl. And, as your mother, I'm saying you need a break."

"Is that right?"

"It is. Now open up, your buzzer is busted again."

"You're here?"

"I am, and I have egg rolls."

"I do love egg rolls," I said, a smile curling the corner of my lips despite my mood. Mom made a kissing noise before hanging up and I opened the door to find her loaded down with bags.

"Oh my god." I laughed. "Did you bring the Knicks' full roster, too?"

"I couldn't decide, so I just got one of everything," she said with an impish grin, her blue-green eyes twinkling. I'd been so jealous of those eyes as a kid, resentful that mine were brown—and as far as I was concerned, not at all twinkly—and didn't have the same wide, round shape, thanks to my Japanese father. About the only thing physically Mom and I had in common was the dusting of freckles across our noses and cheeks.

Aside from that, we were a study in opposites. Her skin was light porcelain, while mine held an olive tone. Her hair, once honey and now more of a silvery blonde, was a wild mass of waves. Mine was inky black and stick straight no matter what I did.

She had always been larger than life, thriving at the center of everything, while I was more serious and preferred the sidelines. Even though she drove me crazy a lot of the time, I still loved her fiercely and couldn't live without her.

As we unpacked the food over the coffee table, I could feel Mom's energy coming off her in waves, butting against my surly shore.

"Out with it," I ordered, because her silence had always been worse than her incessant chatter.

"DerrickandIgotmarriedyesterdayandI'msellingthehouse." The words tumbled out in such a rush that at first I wasn't sure what she'd said. Or maybe I was just hoping I heard wrong.

"You—you're—"

"Married!" She waved her left hand and the diamond adorning her formerly bare ring finger. Derrick wasn't fucking around.

"You're married. You got married. To Derrick." She always did this, met someone new and got swept away until her whole world revolved around him and their *love*. She was constantly chasing the high of it. Until that love inevitably dwindled down to nothing and she was left depressed, eating ice cream in front of *Steel Magnolias* and *Fried Green Tomatoes*. Right before she decided she needed a fresh start and we moved, again.

"That's right." She audibly gulped. "And... because his place is bigger and closer to the city, we figured it made more sense to sell mine."

"Ours," I corrected.

"Chase," she said, her voice wrapping around my name like a hug. I couldn't process this. Mom was married. And she was selling the house, the only house I had lived in for more than two years. The house we could only afford because of Aunt Peggy. No discussion. No warning.

Was this the universe playing some kind of joke on me? I was trying so desperately to keep all the strands of my life in my hands and yet they were all slipping away anyway.

Despite my appetite fleeing the scene, I kept forcing food into my mouth well past the point of being uncomfortably full. It felt like the only thing I could do to not focus on Maureen's voice in my head, and the spiral she was attempting to lead me down. *Too much is changing.*

And then there was the worry over Mom. Had she not gone through this enough? How long would it be before I had to pick up the pieces? Because I would pick up the pieces when Derrick was gone. I always picked up the pieces when they were gone.

Why did she do this to herself over and over?

SATURDAY TRAFFIC WAS A DISASTER. Mack and I had been in the car for too long already, on our way to his niece's fourth birthday, stuck in a permanent loop of start-stop-start-stop.

"Okay, now's your chance," Mack said.

"My chance to what?"

"To tell me what's up. Or are you just thinking about the kiss?" His eyes darted to me then back to the road as the car in front inched forward and I choked on my mouthful of water.

"Excuse me?" We were not talking about the kiss, and certainly not right now when we were stuck in a car together for almost two hours.

"Not thinking about the kiss then?"

I cleared my throat. "I thought we established that it didn't happen."

"We did, but the thing is, I don't want to act like it didn't happen."

"Mack—"

"Relax, I know how you feel about it, I'm just saying ..." He shook his head. "So come on, what's up?"

I should have been happy he was changing the subject, instead I really wanted to know what he was going to say. He didn't want to forget the kiss. Did that mean he still wanted something more, even though he wasn't saying it? It didn't matter. And we weren't talking about it, because I would not be sucked into that conversation by him teasing me with unfinished sentences. Moving on.

"Nothing's up, I'm fine." I forced a smile onto my face despite the fact my insides were squirming.

"Chastity Heather Linden, you did not just *fine* me." He nudged me with his elbow. I swatted him back.

"Milton Alfred Carmichael, you did not just full name me."

"Back atcha, although you missed the Kent."

"Four names is too long."

"Don't I fucking know it. So, come on, spit it out."

I dropped my head into my hands and groaned. Why couldn't he just leave it alone? I knew the answer, because he was him, and I was me, and we didn't leave things—we poked until the other person was so frustrated they wanted to throw a punch.

"You are stuck with me until we get to Pip's suburban mansion, so you might as well start talking."

I turned my nose up and looked out the window. "I don't want to talk."

"Which usually means you need to."

And we were there already. I wanted to punch him right in his perfect, smug face. I would, too, if doing so didn't endanger my life. And his nose. He had a really nice nose. Not perfectly straight, thanks to a rogue punch, and yet somehow symmetrical. I wanted to run a finger down the bridge. *Stop staring at his nose.*

"I finalised those interviews for Tuesday."

"As you already said, and I resisted making a comment about the fact you scheduled them on your day off."

"We can hardly afford to wait around. We need people now. We needed them yesterday. I shouldn't be taking tonight off."

"One: Greyson and Micky can handle one night without us. Two: you are a workaholic and will take literally any excuse not to have a day off. You can't come in Wednesday to make up for it."

"We've got the last of the interviews Wednesday," I fired back and he made a low growling sound that had me simultaneously smirking and clenching my thighs.

"Mom got married and she's selling the house," I said in a rush, because it was a solid distraction to the riot of *feelings* in my chest.

"That's—"

"If you say that's good news I will punch you, I don't even care that you're driving."

His laugh was more of an awkward bark. "I was going to say *that's a surprise*. When did this happen?"

"A few days ago." I picked at my thumb nail. "Went to city hall, found a couple of witnesses and boom, married. They didn't bother to invite me. Didn't even bother to *tell* me. And then decided that they don't need two houses in Queens and his is bigger, so bye-bye house. No discussion, just *it's happening*." I slumped low in my seat. I'd been trying to wrap my head around it since she dropped the bomb over egg rolls and kung pao chicken.

What stung the most was the fact she didn't talk to me about any of it before it happened. I tipped my head back, ignoring the tightness in my throat and the sting behind my eyes.

Mack's hand landed on mine and squeezed.

"I'm sorry she didn't talk to you about any of that before it happened." Because of course he knew what I was thinking.

Not crying. I was not crying. "Thanks. I know it's stupid, and probably selfish of me to even be upset about it. But—"

"You don't have to justify it to me, Chase, your feelings are valid, no matter what."

I rolled my head to look at him, a couple of hot tears tracking down my cheek. What the fuck would I do without him? This was why I couldn't—why I *wouldn't*—risk what we had. "I'm ridiculous."

"You are," he agreed and I gaped. "What part of this outfit says fairy to you?"

My snorted laugh was swift and thoroughly unladylike. "I'm a dark fairy, our wings are invisible. And what about you? This shirt isn't screaming fairy to me either."

He shrugged. "That's because my costume was hand picked by the birthday girl."

"Is that right?" I asked, wondering why he thought it was a good idea to let a four-year-old dress him.

"Yup." His eyes were softer when he looked back at me. "Are you okay?"

I shrugged, not sure of the answer. "I'll get over it."

"You don't need to get over it, Chase. Not in a hurry, anyway."

"It's easier than hashing it out with Mom, which I am absolutely not doing."

He nodded, I knew his advice would be to speak to her, not that he'd do it if the roles were reversed.

I WAS NOT A KID PERSON. It wasn't anything specific about them, I just didn't gel with kids. I didn't know how to talk to them. I didn't know about kid stuff. I wasn't morally opposed to having any of my own, but it seemed unlikely at this point. And I was fine with that. How would they even fit into my life? It's not like I'd be able to strap one to my chest and keep making cocktails.

Mack on the other hand? It was like part of his brain hadn't advanced past the age of ten and, as a result, he could relate to them on their own level. He just got them. It baffled me but, at the same time, made perfect sense because of course he was good with kids. He was good with pretty much everyone.

I was starting to squirm in my seat as we pulled up at Pip's home, with its sweeping front lawn, circular drive, and colonial facade. It didn't matter how many times I'd been here, my reaction was always the same: first overwhelm, followed by *I would not want to clean this place.*

Mack parked his black Range Rover (a ridiculous vehicle, especially when you lived in Brooklyn) behind a line of monochromatic suburban tanks that probably all cost more than my apartment. As we climbed out, the sounds of squealing children filled the air. I took a steadying breath and prepared myself for the madness while Mack grabbed the enormous box from the back seat.

"Aunty Cheese!" Savanna's squeal carried across the yard as she came barreling out the front door, her rainbow fairy costume billowing around her as she ran at us. She collided with my legs, throwing me back a step, her arms wrapping around hips and squeezing tight.

"Happy birthday Savvy!" I might not be a kid person in general, but this kid, this kid I loved. Her older brothers were okay, too, but the twins had crossed over into monosyllabic preteens, so it was nods and grunts from here until who knew when. The now four-year-old Savanna, on the other hand, was a pint-sized tyrant who ruled over her kingdom with a tiny iron fist. I respected it, mainly because I didn't have to live with it. She was going to be a badass adult one day, just like her mom.

"Come on, come on! Your costume is inside!" She was practically vibrating.

"*My* costume?"

"Did I not mention she had one for both of us?" Mack said with a grin so wide the corners of his lips were almost touching his ears.

"No, you failed to mention that," I hissed out one side of my mouth as Savanna took my hand and, with remarkable strength, started tugging me toward the house.

Pip gave us both apologetic smiles as her strong-willed offspring led the way upstairs to her bedroom. Once inside she showed us, with great pride, our costumes.

Our *matching* costumes.

Mine was a sparkling red leotard, with a red tulle skirt and green and white tights. It looked like Christmas had thrown up on a fairy. There were also red shoes with curled toes and bells. Lord help me.

Mack's had the same green and white striped tights with the smallest red waistcoat known to man, the thing would be lucky to cover half his torso. It was the middle of November, but Savanna clearly wasn't going to compromise her vision for something as inconsequential as a temperature in the low fifties.

"Um, Sav, is there a reason we're matching?" I asked, ignoring the fact I'd be able to take out a kid's eye with my nipples once I was in this get-up.

"Because you're married," she said with a tone that suggested I was an idiot.

"What!? No, we're—" I spluttered at her.

"Uncle Mack is momma's brother, and you're *Aunty* Cheese. So you're married." Again with the tone.

"Oh, honey, no, we're friends, just friends. We're not—*not* married." I tried to send the bat signal to Mack, this was his blood relative and therefore his responsibility to clear up her delusions, but he just stood there grinning at me.

Savanna frowned, and planted her hands on her hips. "Momma said that too, but she's wrong."

"No, nope, she's not."

"But..." Her lip dropped. "Does that mean you're not Aunty Cheese?"

"Oh! No, no, Savvy." I dropped down onto my knees in front of her, desperate to stop the tears before they started up. "I'm still Aunty Cheese, I'll always be Aunty Cheese."

"Really?" She said with a sniff.

"Really, really."

She nodded, satisfied. "Good, now get dressed." And that was that. She flounced out of the room without a backwards glance, leaving us to get changed.

Ten minutes later I was officially braless at a four year old's birthday party. It was a new personal low. I glanced down at my boobs. Granted, they weren't much—more than an A cup, not quite a B—but they suited me just fine. As comfortable as I was with them, however, I'd rather not have them and my nipples on full display in glittering red spandex.

Remarkably, the costume fit well. It wasn't riding up in the crotch and the tights were surprisingly warm. But when I needed to go to the bathroom I was going to have to get completely naked—such was the curse of the leotard and the jumpsuit.

Time to head downstairs.

Mack was nowhere to be seen on the landing as I opened Savanna's bedroom door. I growled. *Thanks for that, friend.* I calmed my nerves with the reminder that, if things were too awkward, I could always hit the bar. Because, although this was technically a children's party, Pip and Tim saw no reason for the adults to have a shit time. Every party I had ever attended at their home had involved a stocked bar and epic catering. Naturally, their baby girl's fourth birthday was no exception.

The kitchen was buzzing with chatter as I walked in and spotted Mack with Savanna. She was opening her present, the one that she had all but ignored in her single minded need to get us both dressed. Her squeal of excitement filled the room as she tore open the Barbie camper, complete with hot tub and mobile dance floor.

Then there was Mack. He looked ridiculous. His tights would put *Dirrty*-era Christina Aguilera to shame. Those things were riding low. Obscenely low. And, as expected, his waistcoat was more of a crop top, making his already long torso look comical. I refused to let my eyes linger on the muscular lines of his abs and they definitely did not stray to the trail of hair that extended down from his belly button. Nope, I was not looking at that hair, didn't even notice it was the exact same dirty blond shade as the hair on his head.

Savanna was on the floor at his feet, mesmerized by the enormous pink plastic contraption in front of her. Or I thought she was anyway. Instead she proved to be a fine multi-tasker because at a lull in conversation she yelled, "Uncle Mack I can see your penis in those pants, it's bigger than my Daddy's!"

Wow. Kids just really did not give a fuck.

Everyone in the general vicinity had stopped whatever they were doing and, whether they wanted to admit it or not, they were staring at Mack's junk. The only person who wasn't was Tim who had gone bright red and was attempting to shepherd his child outside.

"He's not married to Aunty Cheese," Savanna added as she was shoved out the door.

I was gnawing on my lip in an effort not to laugh as Mack snagged my hand and dragged me in front of him.

"What are you doing?"

"Trying to keep what little dignity I have left!" he whisper-hissed in my ear, closer than I was expecting. Hot breath tickled my neck.

Pip chose that moment to walk inside. Her sharp, blue eyes took in the scene of me plastered against Mack and the corner of her lips twitched ever so slightly.

"Your child is a demon," Mack said, one hand planted on my hip to stop me from fleeing.

"So I hear." She was barely containing her laughter. "How about we get you a little cover up, huh?"

I couldn't stop my snort as she disappeared. Mack pinched me.

"Ow! It's a compliment, if you think about it ..." Not that I was. I was not thinking about it.

He glowered as his sister returned with a red tutu. "What the fu—dge is that?"

"Your cover up." She grinned. They had the same smile in vastly different faces. Mack was the image of his mother with his high cheekbones and dimpled chin, whereas Pip took after their father with her dominating brow and chestnut hair. Even still, that smile marked them as siblings.

"I thought you were going to get a pair of Tim's shorts."

It would have been the more obvious choice.

"And compromise your ensemble? I think not." She tossed the bundle of tulle at him and, because it was either walk around in a tutu or have people staring at his dick for the rest of the day, he put it on.

For the next couple of hours I watched as pretty much every woman, and a number of the men, ogled my best friend. Ordinarily, this would not bother me. On the whole, he was a pretty oglable individual, so I got it. But today, today it was like some kind of creature had taken up residence under my rib cage. Every time another one of Pip's Stepford Wife friends looked at him like he was a piece of meat, the creature flexed its claws and I wanted to put them to use on eyeballs. Plaster myself to his side, maybe growl a little. It was ridiculous. Not to mention unsettling.

I was just feeling protective, that was all. It was normal, to feel protective of your best friend. The fact that, in all our years of friendship, I had never felt quite this territorial was of some concern. But it was only a week after the kiss, and he'd gone and brought it up in the car, so the memories were closer to the surface. Tender like a fresh bruise. And this display was like a constant *poke, poke, poke.*

Not that it mattered. I'd made my decision and I would stand by it. He was too important to me to risk it on something that was destined to fail. I wouldn't do it.

Time for a drink.

4

MACK

THE WOMAN WAS a complete unrepentant workaholic. Even now, when she was at a party, Chase had found her way to the bar and, from the look of it, was currently reorganizing the station to her very particular standards.

I sighed and dropped into the seat beside my sister, adjusting myself under the tutu. I didn't know what she was thinking with these outfits. She looked over with a wide smile and glazed eyes.

"They were Sav's idea," she said to my scowl.

"And you didn't think to, I don't know, talk her out of it?"

She laughed. "Even if such a thing were possible, no, I don't think I would have." She wasn't wrong. Talking Savanna out of anything once she'd set her mind to it was largely impossible. But Pip still could have tried to save me—and Chase—the embarrassment.

Not that Chase had anything to be embarrassed about. She looked phenomenal. Her red, spangly leotard was skin tight and dipped low in the back and, rather than don the bell-toed shoes, she'd stuffed her feet back into her heavy, black boots. It was alarmingly sexy. I wasn't the only person who noticed. Marco, who was currently beside her behind the bar, wasn't even trying to be subtle about staring at her tits anymore. He was flirting like a man who had zero intention of going home alone and Chase was just drunk enough to go along with it. Her laughter carried across the tent and I ground my teeth together. I wanted to punch him in the throat.

Pip made a sound that was somewhere between a laugh and a hiccup. "You know, if you just told her how you feel then you wouldn't have to watch other people flirt with her."

"Actually I would, half our customers flirt with her." Not that she noticed a lot of the time and, when she did, she shut them down hard.

"And do the other half flirt with you?" The answer was probably yes, not that I was about to admit it. "So is that a yes?"

"A yes to what?"

"Telling her that you've been in love with her for maybe ... ten years?" It was probably closer to fifteen, but there was no way I was going to say that.

"How much have you had to drink, Pip?"

She waved a hand in my general direction. "*Psh*, hardly anything. And I'd be saying the same thing even if I was stone-cold sober."

"Of course you would." Because she was incapable of staying out of other people's business.

My gaze tracked Chase behind the bar, mixing cocktails with smooth, well-practiced efficiency. She had the waiting crowd docile and purring in the palm of her hand.

Was I even good enough for her? Did I even deserve to be with her? I wanted to, but I doubted it all the same. She was this driven, remarkable, infuriating woman. I was where I was only because she allowed me to be next to her. Without her, god only knew where the fuck I'd be, or what I'd be doing.

When I came back to New York at twenty-four, after almost three years away, I had zero plan—much to my father's displeasure. I'd gone to college and earned a degree in Media and Comms that I had done nothing with. The only reason I even applied to college was because Chase forced the form on me and told me to fill it out.

So I came back from years traveling with little more than some killer bar skills. Chase was managing some high end spot full of snobby suits and wannabe models. She was too good for the place and her boss was a fucking dick, so the minute she voiced the idea of starting her own place I was all in, because that was the only way I was with her. All in. I would have followed her even if I thought it was a shit idea. Which, obviously, it wasn't.

It took us a year to get Rudi Blue off the ground, probably another two before things started running as smoothly as they could. It wasn't something I ever saw myself doing, but I couldn't imagine anything else either. There was also no one I'd rather be doing it all with than Chase.

I watched her pour three drinks from her shaker. She was smiling and pink cheeked. Drunk Chase was particularly fucking cute.

"Okay... say, hypothetically, you're right," I said as I rubbed my chin.

"Hypothetically, yes." Pip smirked.

"*Hypothetically,* what do I do?" Chase had been clear about not wanting anything more than what we had. As much as I respected that—and I did, I really did—I also knew that we could be so good. All I had to do was make her see it too. All I had to do was prove her wrong. A near impossible task, by all accounts.

My sister laughed. "You have got to be kidding me. How many women have you seduced?"

"Seduced? God, you make it sound so fucking seedy. But, to answer your question, I've..." The sentence drifted into nothingness because I wasn't sure I had the right words and I sure as shit wasn't trying to seduce Chase.

"Wooed? Courted? I don't care what you call it."

Wooed wasn't much better but it didn't make me cringe. "I've *wooed* plenty of women. None of whom were my best friend and business partner. None of whom were Chase." There was also the issue that, whatever I'd done in the past, I wanted more than that now.

"Fair point," she conceded and pursed her lips. I braced because anything she suggested would probably be ridiculous. But it wasn't like I had any other options.

An hour later, my sister was wild-eyed as she outlined her increasingly absurd plan on an invisible board behind her. I could imagine the torn newspaper clippings, the photos, and the red string connecting each seemingly unrelated items together. It was both frightening and impressive all at once. I'd really like to see what she could do with an actual murder board. It would be something, that's for sure.

"Should I be concerned you're so into this?" I asked and took a sip of whiskey.

"I'm invested, Mack, any member of our family who says otherwise is full of shit." In fact, I was confident she would be the only one. "Now, read it back to me."

"Read what back to you?"

"The plan," she huffed. "Please tell me you've been taking notes, I'm too drunk to be remembering all the genius I'm coming up with right now." Her hands circled her head in a flurry.

"Surely, if it's genius, it'll come back to you."

"Do not get cute with me, Milton."

I winced at her use of my given name. I still didn't

understand what the fuck my mother had been thinking. She had delusions of grandeur, and I was the one who wound up looking like an obnoxious prick with three names. Thank god one of my brothers started calling me Mack before I turned one and it stuck. I only got Milton when I was in trouble. Or when Chase was trying to piss me off, which I was happy to give right back to her because she hated the name on her drivers' license, too.

Pip snapped her fingers in front of my face. "Stay with me! Have another drink."

I was pretty sure we'd passed the point of alcohol being helpful three or four drinks ago. I took another gulp of whiskey all the same.

"Okay, tell me what we've got so far."

I blew out a breath and squinted at the note in my phone, the words dancing merrily across the screen.

"What are you two conspiring about?" Chase asked and I yelped as I buried my phone in the folds of my tutu.

"Nothing!" Pip and I answered in unison. Yeah, that wasn't suspicious at all.

Chase's eyes narrowed and her nose scrunched up as she scrutinized us. "You're up to something." She hiccuped. "I had too many martinis." This was the problem with knowing someone since you were fifteen, the problem with knowing someone as well as I knew Chase. I'd rather be clueless about the implications of her choosing martinis over her usual whiskey. I'd rather not know that she only drank martinis (dirty and with extra olives) when she was horny.

The pit of my stomach hollowed out. Did that mean she'd seen someone who'd inspired the feeling... in a room full of mostly married men? Was it Marco? Was it me? *Wishful fucking thinking.*

She hiccuped again and somehow managed to trip on her

own feet at the same time, sending her tumbling sideways into my lap. She landed with a squeak, her arms curling around my neck like this was perfectly normal and she often used me as a chair. She didn't.

I could feel my sister's amused gaze on the side of my face but I couldn't look at her. I wouldn't look at her. Because I knew what her look would say. *I told you so*, along with *just throw away the plan and kiss her already*. But that wasn't a good idea. I needed to get her on a date first.

"I think it might be time for bed," I said against Chase's hair, attempting to be subtle as I took a deep inhale of the fresh floral and citrus scent that had been imprinted as hers years ago. She nodded, or at least I thought she did.

"The room across from Sav's is all made up."

"And the others?"

"One has Connor's Christmas present in it and is off limits and the other is being... repainted." There was something about her hesitation that had me suspicious but I didn't argue.

"I didn't think you'd be staying," she added.

In her defense that was because I said we wouldn't be. I'd had every intention of having a couple of quiet beers and driving home. But then Chase had walked down the stairs in that fucking costume and remaining sober was no longer an option. And now I'd be sleeping on the couch as penance, because I sure as shit was not going to get into bed with a drunk and horny Chase. Not because I thought she'd make a move, but because I wasn't sure I could trust my unconscious self to keep things platonic. Just having her curled against my chest like this was torturous enough.

"Let's get you to bed, Cheese.'

"Yes please." The words were warm air against my skin, making the hairs along my arms prickle.

My knees had a moment of unsteadiness supporting both

our weights as I stood, but I managed to stabilize us as Chase shifted and wrapped her legs around my waist. It was both better and worse. *Don't think about it. Just get her to bed.*

"Ni-ight," Pip sing-songed as we left the marquee and crossed the cold slice of space between it and the warmth of the house. Chase's legs tensed against me as the wind hit us and I swallowed a groan. If she remembered this in the morning, she was going to be mortified. I'd like to be able to tease her about it, but I already knew that I'd be doing my best to forget how she felt. It was yet more information I didn't need to know about her.

We made it upstairs to the only available room with minimal staggering. Why the fuck did I drink so much? If I'd stuck to my two beers we'd be in my car and on the way home by now.

"You smell really good." Chase murmured and I froze two steps from the bed. Despite the fact she was clinging to me like a limpet, I had assumed she was close to passing out.

I didn't bother responding because what would I say? *Thanks, go ahead and take a big whiff.* I stepped up to the bed with one hand gripping her butt so I didn't drop her—*don't think about it*—and I pulled back the covers with the other hand.

Her head popped up. "What is it?"

"Uh—what is what?" I asked, pleased my voice didn't betray the effect she was having on me.

"Your smell." She pressed her nose under my ear and breathed deep. She was huffing me. She was huffing me and I was doing my best to talk down my cock that very much liked where this was going. No. Nope. No way.

"I can't put my finger on it," she continued, her voice muffled. It was a challenge to ignore the graze of her lips as she spoke. I deserved a mother-fucking medal for this self control.

"Are you done, perv?" Seeing as she was now awake, I had no problem throwing her onto the bed—which would have been a lot easier had her legs not been locked tight around my waist.

"Ha! Nice try!" she howled, tightening her arms around my neck for good measure.

"It's time for bed, Chase."

"It is," she agreed with a yawn and fell backwards onto the rumpled covers. I was relieved and disappointed all at once.

"I'll bring up some water and painkillers, something tells me you're gonna need them in the morning."

"Thanks, friend, you're the best." She paused, yawning again. "Do you have something I can wear to bed? This thing has comfort limitations."

I found my undershirt from earlier on the chair in the corner and tossed it to her. She pulled it on and started shimmying as she rid herself of the costume underneath.

"I'll go grab that water."

"K."

I lingered in the kitchen until I was confident she'd be asleep because Drunk Chase was giving me way too many ideas. And Sober Chase would not want me following them. Was I an idiot for wanting to pursue something with her? Was I an idiot for not doing anything about it until now? All I knew was that I wanted to go back upstairs and crawl into bed beside her, not sleep on the fucking couch.

Edging into the room I strained to hear sounds of her slow, even breathing. It would have been fine if I didn't stand by the bed a second longer than I should have, looking at her midnight hair fanned out across the pillow. But that was exactly what I did. I stood there a moment too long and she rolled over and caught my hand.

"You're my best friend." Her voice was little more than a whisper, but I heard it loud and clear. *Friend.*

"Yep, and you're mine."

"Where are you sleeping?"

"Couch."

"Don't do that."

"Why not?" I asked even though I knew I shouldn't. I should just leave. Right now. She mumbled something I didn't catch. "What?"

"Just don't, you won't sleep well." She scooted backwards, dropping my hand in the process and held the covers up. I caught a glimpse of bare legs. This was a bad idea. I should go, right now.

"Go to sleep, Chase, I'll see you in the morning."

"Just get in, Mack." It was a growly command and I was grateful she couldn't see my smile in the low light.

With a resigned, and somewhat pained, sigh I peeled off my tutu and waistcoat and slid under the covers. Even without touching her, Chase's warmth swallowed me whole, wrapped around me to the point of suffocation.

I would have slept better on the couch.

5

CHASE

WARM. So warm.

I nuzzled deeper into my cocoon of coziness. My head was pounding, my tongue had been replaced with a dehydrated scrap of sandpaper, and my stomach was a nauseous, roiling pit. But it was dark, I was warm, and… was someone stroking my hair? I leaned into it, happy to let it ease the throbbing in my temples. Why did it feel so damn good to have my hair played with? If I could purr, I would.

Wait.

My eyes snapped open and I took proper stock of where I was, and with who—whom?—was this one of those times when whom was appropriate? *Not important Chase.*

Who. Whom. Whoever the fuck. It didn't matter because I was in a strange, yet appallingly comfortable bed, curled around Mack like he was my own personal body pillow. And his hand was in my hair. Oh. God.

I tried to stay perfectly still, now painfully aware of every point of contact between my body and his. My cheek was tucked against the spot his shoulder met his chest. My arm was slung across his torso. Muscles. There were muscles. My right leg was thrown over his thigh and oh no, no, no, was that? No. I was not thinking about the fact that my leg was basically touching my best friend's dick. Big. Hard. Dick. No! Absolutely not.

Slowly, so as not to jostle my—hopefully sleeping—friend, I moved my leg out of the dick zone and eased backwards, out from under his arm. I missed the warmth of his skin immediately but I was not going to be here when he woke up, no fucking way.

My clothes were folded neatly and in a small pile next to Mack's. So, last night, when I'd asked him for something to sleep in he could have just tossed me my own shirt, yet he'd given me his instead. I darted a look at him, still breathing slow and even, the arm I'd been curled under was thrown wide, like maybe he was looking for me in his sleep. My eyes followed the line of that arm, roped with long, lean muscle, to his shoulder and across his strong chest.

No more ogling, Chase, get the hell out.

I whipped off his shirt, pulled mine on, no time for a bra, and stuffed my legs into my jeans before sliding out into the hall. The door closed with a click and I sagged against it.

Drunk Chase had taken some serious liberties last night. The selfish bitch. More annoying was the fact that I knew why she—*why I*—did it.

Pip stepped out onto the landing from the room next door. The room that was not her bedroom and yet it looked like she'd been sleeping in there.

"Morning," she said, winding her long, shiny hair into a knot, her eyes uncharacteristically guarded.

"Morning," I croaked.

She started down the stairs. "How are you feeling?"

"Like there's an ax embedded in my skull. And you?"

"More of an ice pick. Hungry?"

The mention of food had my stomach clenching uncomfortably, but I also knew that eating would speed up the process of getting through this hangover. Sleep would have been better but that, sadly, wouldn't be an option until later. "Yes and no."

"I know what you mean."

It was on the tip of my tongue to ask her about sleeping in a different room than Tim, but maybe I was wrong. Maybe she was just checking something in there. Did I even want to get into it? It sure as hell wasn't any of my business.

"What time did everything wrap up?" I asked instead.

"Patrick and Kat were the last to leave. They're always the last to leave. You basically have to kick them out. I've got no idea what time it was." She paused and slid a sideways glance at me. "You looked like you had a good night."

I ignored that look because it saw too much and, even if I wasn't so hungover, I still wouldn't be interested in talking. "It looked like everyone had a good night. It wouldn't be a Pip and Tim party otherwise."

Her responding smile was little more than a stretch of her lips.

Tim was standing over a skillet at the stove with a mug in one hand as we entered the kitchen. He glanced up and smiled, a strained, joyless thing, just like his wife's. There was definitely something going on. I reminded myself it wasn't actually any of my business. Thankfully, Savanna came barrelling into the room, oblivious to her parents' awkwardness.

"Aunty Cheese! The bouncy castle is still up! Come on! Come on!"

The mere thought of a bouncy castle was enough to make my headache double in fear, but it was better than standing in the kitchen pretending like there wasn't shit going down between Pip and Tim.

"Let's do it," I said as I grabbed a piece of bacon and an apple on the way out.

My mind stayed in the kitchen, even as I fought to keep down my singular piece of bacon and three bites of apple as Savanna jostled me on the inflatable death contraption.

Pip and Tim had been married for over twenty years and had always been disgustingly in love. It was disconcerting, but also comforting, to know that not all adult relationships had to be fucking disaster zones. They still fought but they loved and supported each other. Could that still happen when they weren't sleeping in the same room? I didn't know, I had no experience in this arena.

All I knew was if those two couldn't make it work, what hope was there for the rest of us?

"Thought you could do with a coffee?" Pip's voice startled me out of my muddy thoughts. I tripped over Savanna and bounced out onto the grass.

"Ow, fuck!" I wailed, pain shooting up from my elbow.

"Bad word!" Savanna said from behind me. "Pay up."

"What?"

"We have to pay a dollar for every curse," Pip said.

"A dollar!?"

"She's probably going to have enough for a car by the end of next year."

"Well, I don't live here, and thus do not live by your rules." I was hit with an impressive scowl considering the kid was only just four. "I also don't have any cash... can I owe you?"

"She'll remember that," Pip said and handed me my coffee. "Daddy's got pancakes ready, baby."

Savanna squealed and ran inside, but not before giving me

a hard look. I had a feeling I'd be paying my dollar with interest.

Pip sat and sipped her coffee and I tried to ignore the elephant between us.

"We're having problems," she blurted and I almost choked on my scalding mouthful.

"I—uh—"

"It's been a few months now."

"Months!?" I said with a little more volume than I intended to. "Sorry, sorry. It's just a surprise." I cleared my throat and took another smaller sip.

"I know, for us too."

I dropped into the chair beside her. "You two, you'll work it out, though, right?"

She shrugged. "I don't know. We just—maybe we've grown apart..."

"Pip, you are like the ultimate couple."

Her hollow laugh chilled me. I had no idea what to say here. I wasn't good at relationships. Literally every guy I'd ever dated had bailed just when things were starting to get serious. I was the absolute last person to be having this conversation. If it was anyone else, I'd say cut and run. But this was Pip and Tim. Their relationship was immune to all the bullshit the rest of us dealt with. Wasn't it?

"Sorry. I shouldn't have said anything."

Fuck. I was making it worse. "No, no, it's fine. I—I'm here if you want to talk."

"I don't even know what I want to say," she said with a heavy sigh. "We've been seeing a therapist."

"That's good. Everyone needs therapy sometimes." I'd considered going more than once. But always ended up too scared of all the old wounds that would get yanked open.

"I'm not sure it's working."

"Oh." I took another large gulp of coffee. *Say something comforting, for god's sake!*

"Can you..." She shifted, eyes darting to me then away. "Just don't say anything to Mack, please?"

My stomach pitched and rolled at the thought of keeping this from him, but it wasn't my secret to tell. "Of course."

"Thanks." Her shoulders curled forward.

"Pip, it's fine, honestly. And, hey, if you need to talk, or a night in the city, my couch is awful to sleep on, but it's yours."

Her laugh was short, but it had more life in it this time, at least. "Thanks, Chase."

"You don't need to thank me."

We sat for a moment in heavy silence. I just couldn't imagine how you ended a relationship like theirs. One with history and children. But, I guess it wasn't necessarily ending. They were going to therapy together, you didn't do that with someone you wanted to walk away from. I had to believe they'd work it out. If I didn't, my faith in relationships would hit an all time low.

MACK PULLED up in front of my building. I needed a shower and more sleep, pronto. But first—

"Is everything okay?" I asked, because the silence on the drive had been less of our usual companionable comfort and more of an awkward third passenger all the way from Jersey.

"Sure, of course, why wouldn't we be?" he said with an easy shrug. Was I imagining it? Maybe it was just me feeling all awkward because waking up wrapped around my best friend had felt more natural than I expected. More natural than it should have. It should have been strange, shouldn't it? Awkward. Not good. Not right.

"No reason!" I said with way too much cheer. *Dial it down,*

Chase, dial it down. "We're good. Great, we're great. I'm hungover."

"You and me both." He ran a hand over his face, I could hear the scratch of his stubble from across the car and my fingers twitched against my palms.

"I'll see you later?"

"No!" I all but barked at him. "No you will not. It's your night off."

"And yet you'll be coming in on Tuesday."

"Yes, because I had last night off."

"So did I." So argumentative. It would be frustrating if it didn't also make me want to kiss him. Whoa! No, no kissing. There would be no more kissing.

"Only one of us can be the workaholic, and that's me. Don't go messing with our well-tested formula."

"Heaven forbid." His lopsided smirk told me he knew that my heart was beating a little too fast, and I wasn't just talking about work.

I climbed out of his enormous car and waved as he pulled away from the curb.

I needed to get my head on straight. I couldn't be going around fantasizing about kissing Mack. That was a disaster waiting to happen. It didn't matter that the memory of it still made my insides all squirmy and hot. What mattered was crossing that line again was not a good idea. Once could be written off as an accident. A fluke. A never to be repeated incident. That was where it needed to stop. Like I'd said, we had a well-tested formula, and it did not need to be messed with.

"Heads up!" The call echoed down the stairs when I was halfway to the third floor landing. There was a thump from above and a moment later a stray couch cushion came bouncing past me. I could have stopped it. Instead, I watched it go. The rogue cushion was followed by footsteps and then there was a tall man on the stairs in front of me. Or maybe he looked tall because he was a couple of steps higher than I was.

"If you're after a cushion, it went that way." I pointed behind me.

"Thanks. At least it was soft furnishings, right? Not, like, a skillet."

"Or a really big dildo."

His shocked laugh made me realize what I'd said. Why the fuck did I say that? I blamed the hangover and the persistent thoughts of kissing Mack for making my brain a useless pile of mush. "Okay, well I'm just going to ..."

"Sure, sorry."

We both stepped the same way. Once. Twice. Three times.

"Stay," I said and he gave me a salute as I stepped around him and carried on up the stairs. When I got to the landing there was another guy sitting on a couch that I couldn't get past. He scrambled up as he saw me glaring from the shadows.

"Hi. Hey, sorry." The apartment door across from mine was open.

"Whatever." I climbed over the arm of the couch and went to my door, kicking it closed once inside and dropping my bag on the floor with a thud.

Weird. Fucking. Day.

Pip and Tim were sleeping in different rooms and I was having *feelings* for Mack. I told myself that some sleep would put things right.

I didn't believe it one bit.

MY NAP RAN OVER. Or, rather, I ignored my alarm and slept for a solid hour after it went off. As a result, I was late.

"Fuck," I groaned, stumbling into the bathroom to splash

some water on my face. No time for another shower. I brushed my teeth, pulled my hair into a knot, tied a red and white bandana around my head and put in a large pair of hoop earrings to distract from the luggage I was carrying under my eyes.

I was still tugging on my coat as I pulled my front door closed and started down the stairs two at a time until I collided with a chest. I yelped as I landed on my ass.

"Fuck, sorry, sorry!" The owner of the chest said and a pair of hands pulled me up to standing. It was my new tall neighbor, who didn't seem quite as tall now that I was a couple of steps above him.

"All good, but I gotta go." Again we stepped the same way and he smiled. Huh, he's cute. I took him by the shoulders and again said, "Stay."

He obeyed. "I'm Brady, by the way!"

I didn't bother responding, just bounded down to the street.

6

MACK

THERE WAS something about making pie crusts that I always found calming. Maybe it was the simplicity. Or the gratification of making something with my hands. Or maybe it was the fact that every year at Thanksgiving Chase ate a whole pie over the course of a couple of days and it made me so fucking proud my chest could burst. She loved that pie so much that she insisted I make one just for her, which naturally I did. She didn't even cut it up, just sat it in the fridge and ate it straight from the dish.

I wanted to be the one to feed her that pie. To stand there beside her, in front of the open fridge with a fork in my hand and her eyes on me. I'd make her a pie every fucking day of the week if it made her happy. God I was a sap. I wanted to take care of her. I wanted to be there when she went to sleep and still there when she woke up in the morning.

Enough.

Enough pie. Enough Chase. I needed to get the fuck out of the house. I needed to stop thinking about Chase. The former I could achieve. The latter was probably a lost cause at this point.

But it would be easier to ignore the constant thoughts if I stayed away from Rudi Blue, and wasn't making her favorite pie.

When I walked into Buck's, not quite an hour later, the brewery was buzzing with a boisterous Sunday afternoon crowd. It was similar to what I'd see at Rudi, but also different —not that I could quite put my finger on how. The whole place had an easy going, no nonsense vibe, helped along by the mismatched couches and low tables made of recycled pallets. The central bar was clad in old kitchen cabinet doors, in a muted and flaking rainbow of colors. It was run by a pair of brothers who Chase and I had liked as soon as we'd met them and, as a result, we'd been stocking their products since they opened a few years back.

I spotted Hunter, one of the brothers, behind the bar.

"Hey man," he said as I approached.

"Hunter." I slapped his outstretched hand.

"You got a night off? I'm surprised you could peel yourself away." Like any well practiced bartender, he talked while still pouring beers and making change, most of which was deposited into one of the tip jars dotted around the bar. I was pretty sure I saw a phone number being slid his way on a napkin, too. The woman, who had added a bubblegum pink kiss mark under her digits, waited for Hunter to notice her not so subtle gesture then turned in a huff when it went ignored.

"It's been out of control, but Chase would have kicked me out." I didn't bother mentioning that I needed to stay away for my own sanity, too.

"What can I get you?"

I ran an eye over the taps. "Whatever's good."

"Coming up."

I leaned on the bar, casting an eye over the crowd when a familiar head of dark curls appeared beside me. Was there no escaping this woman?

"Well, well, well…" she purred, hazel eyes roaming over me.

"And what are you doing here?" I asked as Harley grinned up at me.

"You think Rudi Blue is my only haunt?" She replied with a *tsk, tsk.*

"Considering two weeks ago I'd barely seen you, no."

"Smart man." She winked. "Hunter, can I have a cherry sour, please?"

"You got it Harls," he said while delivering my pint. Of course they knew one another. I had a feeling Harley was the kind of person who knew everyone, you wouldn't be able to walk a block without her saying hello to at least a handful of people.

"So…" She started as Hunter delivered her beer. They shared a fist bump and she took a sip before continuing. "How long have you been hung up on Chase?"

I choked on my mouthful and felt it burn up behind my nose. "Excuse me?"

"It's ok, Mackenzie, you don't have to pretend with me," she said with a reassuring, and kinda gropey, squeeze of my bicep.

"One: my name isn't Mackenzie. And two: I'm not hung up on Chase."

She rolled her eyes. "Look, there really is no point denying it. I'm trained to spot sexual tension at twenty paces."

What the actual fuck was she talking about?

"I spend my whole day observing people," she continued. "You think I wouldn't notice that my new friend is hung up on my other new friend?" We were friends now? She took another sip of her beer and watched me squirm with a delighted glint in her eye.

I was starting to regret coming here. I should have stayed home with my pie crusts.

"Harley, where's my beer?" A towering ginger asked. I should have taken her moment of distraction to escape. I was too slow.

"Oh! Sorry I got distracted. Mack, this is my brother Murphy. Murphy, this is Mack—he's one of the owners of Rudi Blue, that bar I was telling you about."

I shook the guy's hand and asked, "How's it being related to this one?"

"Pretty much how you'd expect," he said with a shrug and ruffled Harley's curls. The pair of them could not look more different. She was all dark hair and smokey eyes and he'd be more suited to the rolling hills of Ireland, or maybe Scotland.

"Get off me you oaf," she said in a smiling growl. "And don't even try and pretend that you don't love me. Hunter, I need one for Murphy, too!"

Hunter returned with a beer for Murphy and a second for me. Despite holding a conversation with her brother, I could still feel Harley's attention on me. It was unsettling. Almost as much as the fact that she had somehow guessed at my feelings for Chase. I shot her a sidelong look. Maybe she didn't know. Maybe she was just trying to weasel out some information. It didn't actually matter either way. I was not about to confide in Harley when the chances of that information being on the cover of the New York Times the following day seemed like they were pretty much a given. She wasn't subtle, nor did she look like she could keep any information to herself. So, no, this was not a conversation I was going to be having with her.

"So, what are you doing about it?" She asked a half hour later, her amused yet assessing gaze on me. I'd been naive enough to think she'd drop the subject. More likely she was lulling me into a false sense of security.

"What's who doing about what?" Hunter asked, making himself comfortable on the other side of the bar. A couple of extra bartenders had arrived, leaving him free to join what I had to assume was going to be an invasive conversation, centered squarely on me. Fucking great.

Harley grinned and made herself more comfortable on her stool. "Mack here is in love with his business partner."

"In love?" I barked. What the hell happened to *hung up on?*

Hunter's eyebrows shot up to his hairline, not surprising seeing as he knew exactly who that business partner was. Thank you Harley. "Is that right?"

"I said what I said." Her arched eyebrow dared me to argue.

"She's usually right," Hunter said and I wanted to slap him like a soap star.

Harley nodded, smug satisfaction rolling off her in waves. "I was right about Peter and Cameron, and Jemma and Nash."

"I don't know who Peter and Cameron are, but Jemma and Nash didn't exactly end well."

She shrugged, unconcerned. "They'll work it out."

"How can you be so sure? He's gone back to L.A."

"I'm aware of that, thank you, Mackenzie."

"Still not my name."

As if I hadn't spoken, she continued, "They'll work it out because that's the only way. I know these things. Don't argue."

"Honestly, man, it's easier to just go with it," Hunter confirmed and Murphy nodded behind his sister.

"How do you two know each other?" I asked in a last ditch effort to change the direction of this conversation. Harley smiled, well aware of what I was trying to do but happy to humor me for the moment, probably because she'd be roasting me again soon enough.

"Hunter and I have been friends forever and ever, not unlike you and your lady love."

"Jesus Christ, really?"

She smiled. "Mack. Just go with it. How long?"

I scratched my cheek, took a long swig of beer. "Not long, or maybe since I've known her, I don't fucking know," I answered eventually.

She nodded, like she expected this answer. "So what are you doing about it?"

Despite not really wanting to have this conversation, the possibility that Harley might be able to provide some kind of insight kept me on my barstool.

And the short answer to her question was—"Nothing."

Pip's plan, as it turned out, was little more than the ravings of a drunk woman who was also high on the sound of her own voice. The top line idea was that I needed to get Chase to see me as a *man*, not just a friend. Although there was no actual instruction on how to make that happen. I vaguely remembered pointing out that dressing me as a fairy probably hadn't helped. And she might have said something about Savanna making up for it by saying how big my dick was. I was sure I strongly disagreed with that point.

My plan, if I could even call it that, was to somehow convince Chase to go on one date with me. Just one. And hope like hell that one date would lead to a second, and maybe a third. How I was going to do that, I had no idea.

"Nothing," Harley repeated with a small huff. "Well, we need to do something about that."

"Do we?"

"Yes, we do. Okay, are you ready for the plan?" She didn't wait for me to say yes. "You just need to kiss the hell out of her."

"That's not a plan." I looked to both Hunter and Murphy, but neither seemed inclined to argue with the curly-haired devil.

"She's the woman. Why are you looking at us?"

"Because—that is not a plan. What am I going to do? Walk into Rudi Blue tomorrow and go *'hey Chase, how's your day?'* and then just grab her face? She'd punch me." Or would she? Technically, she'd been the one to kiss me last week. But now, as far as she was concerned, it didn't happen. I was pretty confident that another kiss wasn't going to change anything between us.

Harley expelled a long suffering breath. "Mackenzie." I didn't bother correcting her a third time. "Are you being intentionally obtuse?"

"Not intentionally, no. But I can't just walk up to her and kiss her."

"I'm not saying you just walk up to her, in your place of business, and force yourself on her." She emptied her beer in a long sip and motioned for another from Hunter. "You need to show her that you want more than friendship."

"And kissing her is the way to do that, in your opinion?" Did I need to tell Harley that the plan was already dead in the water? That kissing Chase would change literally nothing between us. If anything, it was going to make things worse, push her further away.

"I'd start with talking to her, but shortly after, yes, you need to *seriously* kiss her."

"Question," Murphy piped up and all attention fell on him.

"Go ahead," Harley said.

"What constitutes a 'serious kiss'?"

"The fact you have to ask concerns me..." She patted her brother's shoulder. "It's a conversation for another day, Murphy Thomas." She turned to me. "Please tell me you know what I mean when I say you need to *seriously* kiss her?"

I was confident that our kiss last week would fit her serious kiss criteria. "Yes, Harley." But it didn't change the fact that I needed to do more than just kiss her. How the hell was I going to do this? A lead weight settled on my chest, making my breathing feel thin and useless. What if she said no? What if she maintained that we needed to stay like this? It was a distinct possibility—not one I could let myself entertain.

"Nope! You need to stop thinking whatever you're thinking," Harley said and shoved at my shoulder, hard.

"I wasn't thinking anything."

"Lies! You're thinking she's going to reject you, that's bullshit and you need to stop."

Was this woman a mind reader or something?

"I don't need to be a mind reader. You literally have every emotion plastered across that gorgeous face of yours. Now, what are you going to say?"

I had no fucking idea. How did you tell the person who knew you better than anyone, who you knew better than anyone, the person you usually told everything, that you wanted more?

7

CHASE

SHIT. Shit. Shit.

I was officially that person. The one mumbling to herself as she dodged the human traffic clogging the sidewalk, and slugging the occasional person with my bag as it swung wildly on my shoulder.

It wasn't my fault. I had set my alarm and gone to bed on time-ish. How was I supposed to know that the stupid thing was going to install an update and then randomly turn itself off? Sometimes, I really did loathe technology.

I skidded to a stop at the studio door but, just as I reached a hand towards it, my mother's ringtone came wailing out of my bag. I should leave it, I should leave it and call her back after my class.

"Hi Mom, can I call you back?" I hitched my bag higher on my shoulder and eyed the studio door. I needed to get my butt inside.

"I won't be long, I just need to know what you're bringing on Thursday?"

"Thursday?" I was confident we didn't have plans on

Thursday because Thursday was Thanksgiving and we hadn't spent a Thanksgiving together in two, maybe three years.

"Yes, darling." The tone had a slice of irritation that hit me somewhere between my ribs and belly button. "It's our first Thanksgiving as a new family."

"I have Thanksgiving at Rudi, Mom, just like I have done for the last five years, you know this."

"Yes, I do know that, but this year is different. Derrick and I want to establish some new traditions and that starts with having all of our children together."

The sharp response burned its way up my throat. They got married a week ago, after being together maybe six months, and now we're all expected to play happy families? I'd only met Derrick a few times and had heard next to nothing about his kids.

"And here I was thinking that would have started at your wedding. But the children weren't required there." I only just resisted adding that these people were *not* my family, nor did I want them to be.

Her answering silence was thick. I barely recognised her voice when she eventually said, "Chase, this is important to me."

But I was too far gone. I wasn't bowing to new traditions of a family I didn't ask for. "We can be together at Christmas, I can't do Thanksgiving. I've gotta go, I'll call you later." I hung up without waiting for a response. *It's our first Thanksgiving as a new family.* I didn't have any issues with the one I already had, small though it may be.

I hustled into the studio, tugging at the laces of my boots. Once, just once, I would like to arrive at this class on time. And yet, even after coming for over a year, every week I stumbled in, ended up shoved in the back and had to use the shitty weights because I was last to arrive. Every. Single. Time.

I blamed the fact it was Monday morning. No one was on time for anything on Monday mornings, right? Well, maybe sociopaths, of which Janine with the pixie cut was clearly one. She was front and center, like she always was, today in a pair of bubblegum pink booty shorts so tiny I could hear Aunt Peggy telling me she could *see that girl's religion*. The familiar sadness that came with thinking of Peggy rose up like a wave. It would be twenty years next year that she'd been gone. The world lost some of its color the day she left it.

I shook the thoughts off as best I could, my eyes drawn back to Janine's ass. I had to give it to her, she had an incredible ass. And thighs, stomach, shoulders, and arms. She was a package of finely tuned precision. I was convinced she was a former ballet dancer, lording her poise and grace over the rest of us uncoordinated mortals. No one had posture like that unless they spent an inordinate amount of time staring at themselves in a mirror.

"Sorry, excuse me, hi Katherine." My smile was all teeth as I weaved through the other women, took the last set of weights and settled into my dark corner of the studio. Well, as dark as a corner in a barre studio could get, anyway, which—with all the overhead lights—was close to the surface of the sun. So, I guess it was more of a metaphorical dark corner.

"You are cutting it fine, girl," Jeremy said with an amused slant to his mouth.

"I'm here, aren't I?" I replied, peeling off the last of my outer layers before I sweated through them.

"By the skin of your teeth."

"What are you doing back here?"

He, like pixie cut Janine in the booty shorts, was long and lean and a suspected former ballet dancer (he had so far refused to confirm). We'd had a brief dalliance years ago and I'd assumed we'd never cross paths again. Then I walked into his barre class and we'd been friends ever since. He taught at a few studios but First Position was his favorite. I liked to think it was because I was his favorite student, but it probably paid the best.

His dark hair was perfectly quaffed, despite being in an exercise class, his eyes were the color of a freshly brewed cup of coffee and his full lips were always tilted in a secret smirk. He was beautiful, there was no getting around it.

"New instructor. They wanted to test her out with an experienced group," he said, and I must have looked panicked because he added, "God you are such a creature of habit, you know that change can be a good thing sometimes, right?"

I shot him my plastic smile. The comment stung a little more than it usually would thanks to the call with Mom. Changing barre instructors was one thing. Changing my favorite Thanksgiving plans was quite another. Was it so bad to like things as they were? Was that a fucking crime?

Before I could fall too far down that rabbit hole, my attention was drawn to the front of the room as a woman walked in. She was tall and slim and graceful, and she didn't so much walk as *glide*. Her honey blonde hair was secured in a loose bun, with a few well placed wisps escaping at her temples. Her lithe frame was wrapped in lavender lycra and a loose fitting white shirt that was knotted at the back. Did everyone have to rub it in my face how together they were this morning? Granted, no one else was really aware of my inner turmoil. They weren't to know I had a downright pornographic dream about my best friend last night. Damn that fairy costume.

"Good morning, everyone, I'm Lindsay." Even her voice was graceful. How was that possible? "Before we get started, I wanted to say thank you to Jeremy for letting me take over his class today." He bowed with a dramatic swing of his arm, as a ripple of chatter went through the room.

"I guess we'll get started then."

Not quite forty minutes later I was convinced that Lindsay was Satan in lavender lycra. She was all smiles and encouraging words while making my limbs feel like they were going to drop clean off my body because all my muscles were about to collectively give up. Poof. Just gone. Even Jeremy had a sheen of sweat on his usually clear brow.

"You're doing great, Chase, just keep this elbow up a little higher." Lindsay's finger lifted my left elbow ever-so-slightly as my shoulders screamed. I smiled, at least I thought I smiled, but it was likely more the gritting of teeth as I silently cursed her to the bowels of hell.

"We're going to be pulsing for the last ten seconds." *Fuck you, wench!* "And pulse, ten, nine, eight, seven, six, five, four, three, two, one. Weights down! Great work everyone."

I dropped my weights in a rush, only just missing my toes, and let my arms hang at my sides like the limp, overcooked noodles they were.

"She. Is. Good," Jeremy said, dabbing his brow with a towel. I marveled at the fact he could still lift his arms that high. He was right, though, Lindsay was very good. Just when I was tempted to give up she'd appear at my side with her kind, encouraging words while making tiny adjustments that made me want to cry. The woman had a gift.

She was also absolutely stunning, with the kind of poise you just didn't see on people in the twenty-first century. It was like someone had plucked her out of *Bridgerton* or *Pride and Prejudice*, threw her in some expensive yoga pants, and dropped her in Brooklyn. Her smile made it really difficult to hate her, even though I desperately wanted to.

My desire to hate her only intensified as we moved through the abs portion of the class. And, yet, she'd come and she'd smile and I'd try to smile back while tears were collecting in the corners of my eyes. She was just so pretty and so nice and I really hoped I didn't vomit so she'd want to be my friend.

When the class finally ended I was sure I'd never been so relieved in all my life. I collapsed on my mat and tried to stretch my exhausted muscles before they seized up altogether as the rest of the class filed out around me.

And then Lindsay was there, smiling and serene and making me feel like an old potato.

"Jeremy, I cannot thank you enough for letting me stand in this morning. I really appreciate it." She was bouncing on her toes, her skin even more dewey up close. I made a mental note to make change my moisturizer.

He ran a hand over his hair, neatening up a few unruly strands that had escaped. "You're welcome, you did great."

"Really!?" Her smile was so wide I was momentarily blinded by the wattage. She seemed to genuinely want Jeremy's approval, which, for some reason, made her a lot more approachable than she would have been otherwise.

"Do you want to join us for a coffee?" I asked and Jeremy shot me a gaping look. *That's right! Who says I can't be spontaneous? Look at me breaking my creature of habit mold!*

"That would be great, I don't want to crash though." Her blue eyes were wide and sincere.

"Don't be ridiculous, we'd love to have you," Jeremy said with a reassuring smile.

"Then I'd love to, thank you. I'll just grab my bag."

"No rush, I'm still waiting for my legs to recover," I said with a smile and she laughed, like I was being hilarious. I wasn't joking.

"What are you doing?" Jeremy asked once Lindsay had sashayed out of the room.

I pointed to my own chest, looked over both shoulders. "Me? Nothing."

"Next you'll tell me we're not going to Huckleberry." He was looking at me like I'd sprang a second head.

He continued to eye me but I just smiled and got to work spraying down my mat and getting the rest of my things together.

Ten minutes later—after a much needed rinse in the shower for me—we met Lindsay out front.

"Where to?" She asked.

"We always go to Huckleberry," Jeremy replied.

And because I was feeling both a little vindictive and adventurous, I shot him a smug look and said, "Actually, if you don't mind, J, I've got a new place I'd like to try." Was I going to be missing my halloumi bagel all week because of this decision? Probably, but I was committed to be this person who tried new things and didn't care about routine. *Look at me!* Next thing I'd be telling Mack we should start sleeping together just to keep things interesting. Ha! No, that wasn't happening. That was a truly terrible idea.

I hitched my bag higher on my shoulder as Jeremy, Lindsay, and I approached Cream and Sugar. The thing that I had not taken into account was the Dallas effect. Like Rudi Blue, it seemed the association with Dallas and Duke's wedding had sent Cream and Sugar into overdrive.

There was a line snaking its way down the block and a crowd drinking coffee out front. Well, this may have been poorly thought through on my part. But I would not admit defeat.

"Give me a second, I'll see what I can do."

"Do you have a connection I don't know about?" Jeremy asked with one perfect eyebrow arched. I ignored him and walked up the line. There was a guy standing at the door. What the hell was I going to do? Say hi, can I have a table even though there is an enormous line—

"Chase!" My head snapped in the direction of my name and I found Harley hanging out the to-go window. "What are you doing here?"

"Harley, hey! Hoping to get a coffee and some breakfast. But you seem to be a tad in demand."

"Yeah, it's been out of control. Is it just you?"

"No, two more. It's fine if you're swamped."

"Give me a second. Strong latte and a double espresso!"

I should not have doubted Harley, a few minutes later the three of us were tucked into a corner table. The whole place smelled amazing. Coffee, cinnamon, and buttery pastry all swirled together, making my mouth water, and the menu was simple but all sounded delicious. Maybe Jeremy was right, change wasn't so bad after all.

MACK WAS SITTING on the bar staring at his phone when I arrived at Rudi a two hours later. He looked up as I approached, his face splitting into a wide grin, making my heart take off at a gallop against my ribs. He was just gorgeous. Cobalt blue eyes crinkling as he smiled, perfectly straight teeth framed by rosy pink lips and that not-quite-straight nose. He really should write Troy Parker a thank you note for breaking it in senior year. He deserved the drunken punch, he didn't have to go into that closet with Troy's girlfriend and he didn't need to do anything. But he was Mack, so he did go into the closet, and he did things, and Troy broke his nose. But, considering it only served to make him look even more rough and ready, Troy had done him a favor.

His hair was a little more unruly than usual today, which meant he'd probably been surfing this morning. How he could do that, in New York, in November, was beyond me but it sure did look good on him. And I already knew how he'd smell, like the ocean and sunshine and... him.

"What?" he said, running a hand through his hair, the curls flopping here and there.

"What?" I echoed, heat rising in my cheeks.

He narrowed his eyes. "You're looking at me weird."

"No I'm not," I scoffed, because I had totally been checking him out. I'd been checking my best friend out, and that was weird. "You had something on your face." I pointed at my own chin and he wiped his.

"Did I get it?" He asked, jumping down from the bar and dropping a kiss onto the top of my head.

"Uh-huh, yep, you got it."

He hummed a response as he handed me another coffee. I definitely didn't need it, I was high enough on the strong Americano I'd had at Cream and Sugar, but I accepted the cup all the same and took a long, scalding sip. The bitter black coffee was tinged with sweetness. I never got my coffee with sugar, but Mack did because he knew I liked it better that way.

"And a donut for the lady?" He proffered a bag in my direction. I peeked inside and grinned. One blueberry cake and one original glaze, because I could never decide. It was almost embarrassing how well he knew me.

"Do you know my cycle too?"

He choked on his mouthful of coffee. "What?!"

"Nothing!" Why on earth did I just ask that? "Thank you, for the donuts, I feel like a shit for turning up empty handed."

"Your presence is present enough," he said with a wink and my insides did a backwards flip off the high dive. What was happening? I was not letting myself get a crush on him. No, sir. Maybe I needed to set him up with someone? Lindsay? She'd been sweet and easy going. Nope, not happening. Just the thought of the two of them together sent a wave of revulsion through me. That wasn't good. I should want to see him with someone like Lindsay. Shouldn't I?

My phone started wailing from my bag, a welcome distraction from the riot of whatever the hell in my chest. Not so much when I saw who it was, though. I had so far ignored a further two calls from my mother because I didn't want to have this conversation. I told her I'd call back. And I would, just as soon as I'd figured out a way to tell her in no uncertain terms that I would not be attending her Thanksgiving celebration. Could I make it to dinner? Maybe, but I wasn't going to say that because I didn't like that my traditions were suddenly no longer important in the face of her 'new family'. There was nothing wrong with our family before.

"You gonna get that?" Mack asked, peering over my shoulder.

"Nope." We both watched as my phone fell silent and I dropped it back into my bag.

"You've escalated to screening calls. That's not a good sign."

I shoved a large piece of donut in my mouth to delay the conversation. If I'd been hoping he'd let me off the hook by the time I finished chewing (which took close to a minute) I was left disappointed.

"Well," he prompted, stopping me from taking another bite.

"She's trying to get me to go to Derrick's place on Thanksgiving. She knows that we host, but that's not important in the face of our 'new family'." I paused, my mind snarling. "We don't have a new family. She has a new husband. There's a difference." I took another large bite of donut.

"Maybe not to her."

"Of course not to her!" Crumbs flew from both my mouth and the half eaten donut in my hand. "She's all loved up after her shotgun wedding that she didn't bother inviting her own daughter to! Who gets married like that anyway?"

"People who are crazy in love?" he said with a shrug, spectacularly missing the point. If he hadn't bought me donuts I'd walk out right now.

"Whose side are you on, Milton?"

"I didn't realize there were sides, Chastity."

"Well there are." I pouted. "There always are."

"Then I'm always on yours." He nudged my shoulder.

I huffed out a breath. "I don't need to spend the holiday with a guy I've met twice and his kids who I've never seen. I love our Thanksgiving."

"I do too. Your pie is already under construction, by the way."

"I might need two this year." I said around another sullen mouthful of donut.

"Noted." He paused, I could feel the weight of his attention on the side of my face before he spoke again. "It's probably just an excuse to see you."

"She doesn't need an excuse to see me. She needs an excuse to get me to Derrick's house, after announcing she was selling *our home*. Another decision I was not included in." At some point I was going to have to go and clear out whatever I'd left behind. There wasn't much, and most of it would probably get trashed, but I still wasn't looking forward to it.

He gave my shoulder a squeeze. "Just talk to her."

"I will. Later."

"Uh-huh."

"Anyway, we've got things to do. Let's get to it!"

8

MACK

"WELL?" My sister said by way of greeting when I answered her call. I'd considered screening her for a solid fifteen seconds before picking up.

"Well what?" I hit the speaker button, dropped my phone onto the counter, and continued to dice the apples in front of me.

"I need an update on the plan!" Pip's voice was shrill, with irritation or anticipation I wasn't sure. I resisted the urge to tell her that calling the drunken ramble she'd unloaded last weekend a plan was extremely generous. I tipped the apples into the bowl beside me, tossing them through the lemon juice and sugar.

"No update." And, honestly, I wasn't sure there was going to be. Over the last week I'd been having some serious reservations about the whole thing. Had my feelings changed? No, obviously not. But it wasn't a good time. Things at Rudi were busier than I had ever seen them. Chase was having a family crisis, of sorts. And I'd realized that I didn't know if she was even seeing anyone at the moment. I could probably just ask her, but then she'd want to know why I asked her—because I didn't make a habit of asking her generally—and I was not going to be having that conversation.

I picked up another apple and listened to the displeased growls rumbling down the line.

"How is that possible? It's been over a week. Are you telling me you've done nothing in the last nine days?"

"No, that's not at all what I'm telling you, I've done plenty in the last week."

"Your pies, yes, I'm sure they're keeping you very busy." The sarcasm dripped from her words. "What is the matter with you?"

"Nothing is the matter with me," I fired back, frustration climbing my spine.

"I beg to differ!" she wailed.

My eyes rolled to the vaulted ceiling of my loft and I only just resisted hanging up on her. "Look, Pip, I've had some second thoughts—"

"Oh no, no, no. No, Mack! Now is not the time for second thoughts. Now is the time for action!" I could imagine her thrusting her fist into the air as she said it. Not that it changed anything. She didn't know Chase like I did. And it just ... it wasn't a good idea, not now. Maybe not ever. That wasn't what Pip wanted to hear, though.

I ignored my sister and her unwanted pep talk as I made short work of the last of the apples. I wasn't in the mood to have this conversation. Not when a cold lump of self doubt sat heavy on my chest. The only person whose pep talk could shift it was the one person I couldn't speak to about this particular issue. It was inconvenient.

"I've gotta go, I'll call you when there's an update." Which there wouldn't be. I hung up on her screeched protests.

It wasn't any one thing that had thrown me into this spiral

of self doubt and second thoughts. It was everything. My past, and hers. Our relationship now—which I wasn't willing to risk any more than she was. The fact that the longest 'romantic' relationship I'd ever had ended in a raging fight and me being told I was a child who'd never be able to commit to anything. In my defense, I was twenty-four at the time. In Tamsyn's defense, she wasn't entirely wrong.

We'd met while traveling through Australia and I followed her home to New Zealand, which might just be the most beautiful country on the planet. We'd been living in each other's pockets for months before we officially moved in together, so I assumed it would be great, but that was where it all started going wrong. She was settling back into 'real life' and accused me of still being in vacation mode which, admittedly, I was. Being anywhere other than New York felt like a vacation. I was far away from my mother's expectations and my father's disappointment. I was my own person, pulling beers and sleeping late and not giving a shit what the following day would bring.

But Tamsyn wanted more than a bartending backpacker. So she kicked me out, and apparently got back together with her ex. Last time I checked they were married with a few kids.

Eight years later, I was still essentially the same. Yes, I'd upgraded to owning the bar rather than just working in it, but that didn't feel like the monumental change I'd always thought it would.

My relationships since had been of the casual variety, and not just at my insistence. Every woman I'd been with since Tamsyn had, at some point, mentioned that I was the perfect rebound, or one night, or whatever else they called it—one had said revenge fuck and then snapped a selfie with my dick before I could work out what was happening.

The bottom line, I wasn't relationship material. Perfect for a good time, not a long time. I laughed it off, always pretended it was how I wanted it. It *was* how I wanted it.

But not now, not with Chase.

The problem, the one I didn't want to tell my sister, or Harley, or anyone else, was that I was scared out of my fucking brain. Because what if what all those women said was true? And what if, after one night with me, Chase figured it out too?

WHAT THE HELL was I thinking, attempting a new recipe for the first time on Thanksgiving? It was a rookie mistake. One I rarely made, I'd like to say. But for whatever reason I had become obsessed with the combination of apple and cheddar cheese and was now convinced that this pie was going to be a disaster. Were there bigger issues in the world? Certainly. Did I care right now, as I sat on the floor in the Rudi Blue kitchen in front of the oven—cradling my third (or was it fourth?) cup of coffee since six a.m.—after maybe three hours sleep and watched pies baking? Not one bit.

I had even tried to call Nash for some food related reassurance but it just ended in a garbled and borderline hysterical voicemail that had not resulted in a call back.

I wasn't sure why I needed this year's pies to be perfect, but I did. It felt important, imperative even, and I wasn't interested in analyzing the motivation behind it.

The timer went off and I startled, sloshing coffee down the front of my shirt and flour dusted apron, but I didn't care because it was the moment of truth. I pulled the two pies out of the oven and slid in a pair of bourbon pecan ones in turn. That recipe I'd perfected at least three years ago. These were the kind of pies I should be serving at Thanksgiving, not this untested, potentially disastrous creation.

I set the timer for twenty minutes and turned my attention

to the counter. At first glance, they looked okay. Golden. Well cooked. The mingled scents of apple, butter and the barest hint of cheese met my nose. So far so good. But I wouldn't know if they were up to scratch until this afternoon. Anxiety bubbled alongside all the coffee in my stomach. Food would probably help, but I didn't have anything within reach that wasn't pie.

The only thing currently calming my nerves was the fact that the unproven apple cheddar wasn't the only pie on the menu. In fact, this year I'd really stepped it up a notch. In addition to the last minute apple, there was Chase's sweet potato (naturally), bourbon pecan, salted honey, chocolate espresso and a pear and cranberry crumble. I'd also been perfecting a buttermilk ice cream for the better part of two months. There was an excellent chance I was overdoing it, it was a lot of pie for our guest list, but that was just how I rolled. The more pie, the merrier.

I didn't know much of what Chase had planned for the rest of the catered meal, but I did know that dessert was going to be epic.

It was our fifth Rudi Blue Thanksgiving, we had a few new attendees this year along with staff who had been with us since the beginning.

There had been questions over the years about why Chase and I didn't spend the holiday with our respective families, seeing as they were both so close by, but I'd take pretty much any excuse not to see my dad—who always attended the feast at Pip's place—and Chase's mom had come to a couple of our things. I guess that was why Chase was being so stubborn about Heather's invitation this year. Not that she'd mentioned it at all since I caught her screening her mom's call last week.

At any rate, this meal, this day, spent with our own little Rudi Blue family, was one of my favorites of the year. And it would be even better if my apple pies tasted as good as they smelled.

Once the bourbon pecans were out of the oven, smelling like a fucking dream I might add, it was time to head home and shower because I could smell my unwashed, over-caffeinated self under all the butter and sugar. I considered eating, too, but knowing that Chase would have over-catered for lunch—as she always did—I decided against it.

After a much needed nap, I showered and threw on a shirt and jeans then caught sight of my reflection. Did I need to change? Put on a better shirt? I rummaged through my wardrobe and put on a white button down. I looked like I was going to a fucking job interview. I pulled it off and switched it for a black one. Now I looked like I was headed to a funeral.

"For fuck's sake." I closed my eyes, reached out and grabbed a shirt. I didn't look until it was buttoned up. White with blue stripes. Not what I would have chosen if I was looking, but it didn't matter. I needed to get moving.

As I made the short walk back to Rudi, I considered how the day was going to go. For the most part I felt pretty good about it. And then there was Harley, who had confirmed her attendance earlier in the week. There was an excellent chance she would lock Chase and I in the store room or something equally ridiculous. I wouldn't put it past her to start up a game of spin the bottle or seven minutes in heaven. It didn't matter that none of us had any right playing those fucking games, she'd do it. Just the thought had a cold sweat breaking out on the back of my neck and across my brow, despite the fact it was barely forty out.

"There you are!" Chase said with a wide smile as I stepped through the door. She was looking at me weird.

"What? Do I have something on my face? Is it my hair?"

She shook her head, messy black bun bouncing. "No, you—nothing. Your hair is fine. You look—um."

"It's the shirt isn't it? The shirt's bad." I smoothed a hand down my chest.

"No. No, it's not bad. It's—you look good." She cleared her throat. "What do you think?" She threw an arm out and gestured around us, I'd been so focused on her I hadn't even noticed the atmosphere.

Rudi Blue was a Thanksgiving wonderland.

"Is it too much?" Chase worried her lower lip with her teeth as she watched me take in her work. The place was almost unrecognizable from when I'd left this morning.

"You haven't taken Adderall today have you?"

She leveled me with a deadpan stare, the bun flopping to the left as she planted her hands on her hips. "Your faith in me is astounding, truly. I've not taken Adderall since—"

"Not quite three weeks ago, right?"

"It was extenuating circumstances." A tempting slice of her stomach was revealed as she threw her hands up. "And it really did help me to focus and put together that cocktail menu."

"Of course it did." I pulled her into a half hug, not letting myself linger there with her tucked into my side. I also gave myself some major points for not smelling her hair, despite the fresh scent of her shampoo tickling my nose. "Anyway, everything looks incredible."

"You think so?" Her eyes were wide and questioning, the flecks of caramel and gold particularly bright today. I could have stared at her for hours, instead I turned my attention to the room.

The large table that had been barren when I left was now covered in an orange and grey plaid tablecloth, a collection of small white and gold pumpkins, and greenery scattered down the center. None of the plates, silverware, or glasses matched but it all worked. The theme was carried across the bar, which was also adorned with the same plaid and more of the painted pumpkins—and what looked like whole branches hung from the beams on the ceiling. How the hell did she manage that?

It was difficult to imagine anyone not liking what she'd done.

"Absolutely. Did you really do it all yourself?"

"Mostly."

"Liar." Jeremy's voice entered the room before he did, strolling in a beat later from the back. His dark eyes swept from my feet to my face and he smiled; it was only the slightest bit predatory. I was struck with the thought that he and Harley would probably get along really well. He was a good guy, but there was always this look on his face that made me think he knew something I didn't. It was particularly strong today and the hairs on the back of my neck prickled in response.

"You hung one garland and then complained that you'd pulled a tricep," Chase said with a roll of her eyes.

"I said my calves were tight and you shoved me aside like a used Kleenex. Do you listen to me at all?"

"No." She turned back to me. "Anyway, you sure you like it?"

"Yes, Chase, I'm sure."

A radiant smile broke across her face and my heart kicked hard against my ribs. Every time I told myself that pursuing something with her was a bad idea she'd do something as simple as smile at me like that and I knew I was fucked.

We stood there staring at each other, locked in this tiny world of just the two of us until Jeremy cleared his throat.

"Right!" Chase squeaked and jumped back from me. "I'm going—I need to get changed." She all but sprinted away. It took me a second to notice the knock.

"I'll get that then, shall I?" Jeremy drawled, the knowing smirk tipping his mouth up.

"All good," I said, wanting an excuse to leave this awkwardness. "I got it."

He muttered something under his breath as I walked away and I had a feeling I was going to have to keep an eye on him.

I pulled the door open and found a dude I'd never seen before standing there. "Hey man, sorry we're closed today."

"Oh, yeah, I'm, ah, I'm here for lunch? Chase invited me. It's Brady." He held out a hand and I stood there staring at it for what felt like five minutes. What the hell was going on? Why did she invite him? Why did she invite him and not tell me?

"Good to meet you. I'm Mack." I shook the outstretched hand and invited him in. He had an inch or two on me. I stood a little taller. "How do you know Chase?"

He looked around and I narrowed my eyes at his back. "I just moved in across the hall from her. We've run into each other a couple of times and then yesterday she just asked if I had plans today. I didn't, so here I am."

"Here you are," I said, trying and failing not to sound like an asshole. "Drink?"

"Sounds good, thanks, Mack."

I handed him a bottle of Pittsburg Pale and started on my Thanksgiving sangria. It was another of the traditions that Chase insisted on. She was a sucker for my Thanksgiving sangria.

Brady didn't move from the bar, just turned and leaned back on both elbows like he'd been here a million times before. Who the fuck was this guy?

The sound of heels on the polished concrete floors drew my attention and, a second later, Chase appeared. And, fuck, she looked incredible. Her black dress was loose fitting—to allow for maximum food consumption no doubt—but hit just above mid thigh, exposing the toned length of her fishnet-covered legs. Fuck me. She'd pulled her hair into a loose braid that hung over one shoulder and her lips were stained red. I swallowed as spontaneous emotion clogged my throat.

She stuttered a step as she saw Brady at the bar.

"Brady—hey, hi—you're early."

"Always, I hope that's not a problem, you look amazing," he said, abandoning the bar and pressing a kiss to her cheek, one hand finding its way to the small of her back. I had been trying to convince myself that it couldn't be true, but it was time to face facts.

Chase brought a date. Chase brought a date to Thanksgiving.

What. The. Fuck.

9

CHASE

I MAY HAVE TAKEN my *change-is-a-good-thing* kick a step too far. Brady seemed like a nice guy from our brief stair encounters over the last week. He was also hot in that broad, preppy, all-American kind of way, which meant I didn't think he was a serial killer. There was probably a lesson in that, but it wasn't one I was going to examine right at the moment.

When I saw him yesterday and spontaneously asked if he had Thanksgiving plans, I honestly thought he'd say yes. Most people had plans when it was the day before Thanksgiving. But he'd gone and said no because his family was in Ohio and, with his recent move and starting a new job, he couldn't get back. So, naturally the next words out of Change-Is-Good-Chase's mouth had been, "*why don't you come to ours?*" Of course, he'd gone and said yes.

I forced my smile a little wider and side stepped out of Brady's grip. "I'm so glad you made it." Had I said that already? What the hell was the matter with me? My brain was a hornets' nest. It wasn't so much Brady as it was Mack and the unreadable expression on his face. I had pretty much written the dictionary on all of his facial expressions and yet this one had me stumped.

I'd practically tripped over my own tongue when he walked in. He was sex on a stick, yes, but it was more than that, the way he looked at me did something to my chest. As did the way his jeans hugged his butt. It was all quite disconcerting.

"Of course I made it." My attention snapped back to Brady. "This place is great, I can't believe I've not been before."

"Chase's brainchild," Mack said, his face still weird, but the note of pride in his voice made my whole body warm.

"Our brainchild," I corrected, because as much as he tried to downplay his role in getting Rudi off the ground, I knew that there was no way it would be anything without him.

"Can I get the grand tour?" Brady asked with an easy smile.

"Oh yes, absolutely. Let me just—"

"I can facilitate a tour," Jeremy purred as he appeared from nowhere, eyes glued to Brady.

"Brady this is Jeremy, Jeremy, Brady." The two men shook hands and, with barely a second glance at me, Jeremy escorted Brady away. I watched them go, feeling intensely grateful for Jeremy.

"You brought a date. To Thanksgiving," Mack said, yanking me out of my perusal. It took me a second to recognise what he said.

"No." I gaped at him. "No, I did not." This was not a date. Brady and I were not on a date. Who has a first date on Thanksgiving? That was absurd.

"You sure about that?"

I narrowed my eyes. "Yes, I'm sure about that—he's my neighbor. I barely know him." And I was happy for it to stay that way.

"Isn't that the whole point of dating? To get to know the other person?"

"It's not a date," I snapped and fidgeted with the skirt of my dress.

He raised his hands in surrender, which only annoyed me more. Did he want me to be on a date with Brady? His questions didn't seem to come from a place of jealousy, he seemed genuinely curious. Did I want him to be jealous? It would be messed up if the answer was yes, and yet ... No. No, I didn't want him to be jealous. Why would I want Mack to be jealous of Brady? I needed a distraction.

As if my thoughts had summoned her, the door swung open and Harley exploded inside. "Happy Thanksgiving, beautiful people!"

For a solid fifteen seconds I wondered what on Earth I was looking at. Her breasts were barely contained in a black corset, which was actually more of a bra. Her skirt was cinched tight at her waist and went from black at the top, to brown, then orange and finally white at the hem. And it looked like—

"Are you a turkey?" Mack asked with a chuckle.

Harley beamed. "A *sexy* turkey, yes I am, Mackenzie." She turned and wiggled her feathered butt at us and I couldn't have stopped my bark of laughter if I tried. Of *course* Harley had turned up to Thanksgiving dressed as a sexy turkey. Of course she had.

"You look amazing." To set off the whole look her dark curls had smoothed up the sides of her head and were allowed to explode free in a mohawk of sorts. I didn't think turkeys had a crest but she was making it work nonetheless.

Harley's whiskey-colored eyes darted between Mack and I, a flicker of secret knowledge burning behind them. "Hmmm... I might have to start a round of spin the bottle later on. The air in here is sizzling"—she fanned herself, her gaze landing on Mack as he groaned—"don't think I won't, Mackenzie."

"I underestimate you at my own peril, Harley," he shot back and she grinned.

"Damn right you do. Where can I put this?" The question was directed at me as she held a large dress bag aloft.

"In the office."

She hooked an arm through mine and squeezed me into her side. "Well then lead the way!"

I was sure I felt Mack's attention on us until we disappeared into the short hall.

"Do you always bring a costume change?" I asked as I opened the office door and showed Harley inside.

"Not always, no. But, as much as I like being a sexy turkey"—she gave a small shimmy before hanging the bag off the shelves—"this corset is not conducive to the food baby I plan on having later. A change of costume was required today."

"What could possibly top this?" I nodded at her. "Sexy... pilgrim?"

"There's nothing sexy about genocide."

"Good point."

"So..." she purred, returning her hand to the crook of my elbow. "Who do we have our eyes on tonight?"

An awkward laugh slipped out as I said, "No one."

"Oh man, you've got it bad, come on, you might as well tell me who it is now. It'll save me the trouble of figuring it out for myself, which you know I will."

I didn't doubt her. Only there was nothing for her to figure out, because I didn't have my eye on anyone. Obviously.

"Honestly, Harley, there's no one. I'm not—I don't—I am quite happily single."

"Me too, girl, all the more reason to have a hot naked man in your bed by the end of the night. You can tell me, I'm basically a vault, is it Mack? You two would be—"

"No!" I spluttered. "No, absolutely not. Mack and I are

friends. That would be terrible, a really bad, terrible idea. It would probably be like kissing my brother." *Lies. Lies. Lies.* "Not that I've got one, but if I did..." I needed to stop talking, immediately.

"I do have a brother, and I have a friend like that... but I've not got that vibe from you two, that hundred percent platonic thing. Huh, maybe I got it wrong..." She unlinked her arm from mine.

"Got what wrong?" I asked as she stepped out into the hall.

"Hmm? Oh, nothing. Man, I need a drink!" Then she was gone in a flurry of feathers.

I LOVED THANKSGIVING. For the last five years, it had been my favorite holiday because I'd been able to do it on my terms. Mack and I planned the whole thing together, exactly how we wanted it. It was one of those things that made me feel like I was properly adulting, whatever the fuck that meant anymore. I wasn't married, I didn't own my own home, or have any children, but I could plan the hell out of Thanksgiving. That was satisfying.

Despite that, and the fact that this year's event was the biggest success we'd hosted, I was in a bad mood.

I really shouldn't be. I should be in a wonderful mood. I had a belly full of delicious food (including my favorite sweet potato pie). I was surrounded by friends who felt like family. I was warm and suitably buzzed on Mack's Thanksgiving sangria. On paper, things were downright perfect. I was even managing to compartmentalize my guilt over the argument with Mom earlier in the week—the sangria was helping in that department.

And, yet, I was in a bad mood.

"Chase!" Lindsay beamed at me, an almost empty glass in

one hand. Even well on the way to drunk, the woman was graceful. A ballerina, through and through. "Thank you so much for today. I'm sorry again for just turning up unannounced. I really did think Jeremy told you I was coming."

"Lindsay, for the fortieth time, it's fine, we've loved having you here." Some of us more than others. Mack had been paying Lindsay impressive amounts of attention throughout the afternoon. Not surprising, really. As far as I could tell, the woman was perfect. She was in a pair of emerald, wide-legged pants that emphasized the length of her legs and a silk blouse the color of fresh cream. I had secretly wished for her to spill pinot down the front of her perfect blouse more than once. If I had somehow developed the power of telekinesis, our lunch table would have been a scene from Carrie, with cranberry sauce or Pinot standing in for pig's blood. It didn't happen. And, honestly, I was confident if it had she probably would have made that look graceful, too.

I might as well have been covered in sticky, cloying cranberry sauce. It was an accurate metaphor for the feelings that were coating my insides.

Bad. Fucking. Mood.

Lindsay upended her glass, catching the last few drops of Pinot. I did the same with my almost full one.

"Okay..." she started, with a determined and somewhat sheepish look on her face. I noted that, despite at least three glasses of red wine, her teeth were still white. Did she have stain repelling teeth or something? "Is Mack seeing anyone at the moment?"

My vision was doused in red for a beat.

"Not that I am aware of," I said with what was probably a red wine smile after only one glass.

"Really!?" She made a high pitched noise, then looked me dead in the eye. "Would you—I mean, we don't know each other well or anything—and he's your best friend and everything—but would you set me up with him?"

My full body reaction was swift and visceral. Hair prickling. Stomach souring. Toes curling. No. Fucking. Way.

Mine. He's mine.

It was a cold bucket of water and the fires of hell all at once.

And it wasn't fair. I opened my mouth to say God only knew what, because I was little more than a snarling beast, but I was interrupted.

"What are you two conspiring about?" Brady asked, sliding into the conversation and the chair beside me. Close enough that I feared he was under the same misconception Mack had been earlier. He thought this was a date. With my beast a little too lively, that reaction was also: No. Fucking. Way. And, again, it was probably unfair.

Lindsay leaned in closer, her eyes glazed but twinkling. "I was just asking Chase if she'd consider setting me up with Mack," she said and nibbled her lip. I got the feeling that she needed me to do this because she wanted my blessing or something. We weren't the mob. Mack could date whoever he wanted. I ignored the raging in my chest because it was true. He was the best of people and he deserved the best. I couldn't tell him that I didn't want to date him and also stop him from dating someone like Lindsay.

I would never hold my friend back, or try to keep for myself something that wasn't truly mine.

"That's a great idea," Brady said. He was so close I could feel the heat of him and, yet, I wasn't the least bit tempted to turn into him and bury my face in his neck like I had wanted to do to Mack all day.

"It is," I agreed.

Lindsay's face split open in the most dazzling smile. "Are you serious? Oh my god! I've been trying to talk to him all day but I keep tripping over my words and—" She blew out a breath. "He's so gorgeous it makes me nervous."

"You'll need to do something about that before your date," Brady quipped. Their date. Because I was setting them up on a date.

"Why don't we all go on one together!" Lindsay said, clapping. "That way, I won't be so nervous because you'll be there too, Chase, *please*."

"Yes! A double date is a great idea!" Brady said, his hand grazing my hip. What the actual fuck was happening right now?

"We could go bowling!" Lord help me, she was on a roll, beaming as she poured another glass of wine.

"I fucking love bowling," he agreed.

They were both looking at me like I was somehow the final vote in this ridiculous plan. I hated bowling. I didn't like wearing other people's shoes. It was gross. I repressed a full body shudder and plastered a smile on my face.

"Let me talk to Mack."

"Yes! Ohmygod! Thank you! Thankyouthankyouthankyou." She pulled me into an awkward hug which, thanks to her height, meant I was basically motorboating her.

"Don't thank me yet," I warned, because this was very far from a done deal, but Lindsay just kept on beaming and Brady's hand was now rubbing circles on my back.

The two of them shoved me in Mack's direction when I had another overly large glass of sangria in my hand. Was I really doing this?

"Go, Chase. Go!" Lindsay whispered and I was glad she couldn't see my face because my eyes were rolling back so far I could almost see the inside of my skull.

I didn't know what the hell I was thinking, going along with this. There were numerous things wrong with the entire situation:

One, I didn't want to go on a date with Brady. Yes he was hot and seemed like a decent enough guy but there was next to no chemistry. I'd been staring at him periodically, wondering if it would spontaneously smack me in the face, but it was yet to happen. And what was the point of going on a date if there were no sparks?

Two, I didn't want to go on a double date with *anyone*, and I was confident Mack wouldn't either. He wasn't much of a dater, period. I couldn't see him agreeing to go on a double date. Or was I just hoping he'd say no?

Three, being there in person to witness Mack on a date was about the last thing I wanted to do, ever, but especially with Lindsay-the-perfect-ballerina, who was all sorts of delightful. I was not that much of a masochist, thank you very much.

There were probably more, but the sangria was making me fuzzy and Mack was giving me a quizzical look as I weaved my way towards him.

"What's up, Cheese?" he asked, slinging an arm around my neck. Electricity zinged the length of my spine. *Ignore it.* Ironic that the guy I should have sparks with felt like a dead fish, and the one I was trying to be normal around made me feel like my insides had turned to molten lava.

I took a long gulp of sangria in the hopes of dousing the heat. The mere thought of saying we should go on a double date was making me twitchy. Or maybe it was the fact I was suggesting *he* go on a date. A date with Lindsay.

No, Lindsay was adorable and sweet and intelligent and Mack deserved someone like that. Someone like her. And I was not going to be a terrible friend and stand in the way of that.

"So, um ... this is—I'm just gonna say it." I blew out a breath. "Do you want to go on a date with Lindsay?"

He laughed. "What?"

"Don't laugh! Are they watching?" I swatted at his chest. Too late, I realized it was with the same hand holding my drink and a wave of the crimson liquid slapped against his chest. "Oh fuck!"

"It's fine."

"It's not fine. It's going to stain, come on." I dragged him across the bar and into the bathroom. "Quick, off, off!"

"What the hell has gotten into you?" He asked, peeling off the shirt and I immediately noted my mistake. I was now alone, in a bathroom, with my half-naked best friend. My eyes tried to dart everywhere except his exposed chest but it was like trying not to look at a car accident, or the sun. My eyes were naturally drawn there, even knowing it would probably hurt.

"Nothing, I'm great." I snatched the shirt from him and got to work on the stain to keep my eyes and hands busy.

"Uh-huh..." He leaned on the sink beside me, watching me in the mirror. "You asked if *they* were watching just before you threw your drink on me, were you talking about Lindsay and your date?"

"He's not my date," I growled, although the fact he wanted us to go on a double date with Lindsay and Mack was going to seriously weaken that argument.

"Chase." My name was a chuckle. "What the fuck is going on?"

I slapped the now sodden—and probably ruined because I was not what anyone would call a housewife—shirt into the basin and turned to face him. "What is going on is that you, my friend, are too hot! If you could just tone down all of this"—I gestured at his face and exposed torso, which was frankly offensive and disturbingly lickable—"then Lindsay would be able to actually speak to you and I would not be passing notes like we're in junior high."

"Just going back to your earlier point—he is definitely your date. The guy has been touching your lower back like it's his fucking job. And two, I have no idea what you're talking about."

Brady had been touching my back a lot. It was getting annoying. But that was not the point of this conversation.

"Lindsay wants us to go on a double date," I said, abandoning Mack's shirt altogether and taking another large sip of my drink.

"Us? Us who? Oh, wait, are you talking about me, you, Lindsay and Brady?"

I did not appreciate the way he put us together. We were not the ones on the date. "I am talking about you and Lindsay, and me"—I cleared my throat—"and Brady."

"I'm sorry, what? I missed that last bit..." He leaned closer, his spicy, sunshiney scent invading my nose.

"Me... and Brady," I mumbled into my glass.

"Nope, I think—I think I still missed it. Just a little louder." The smile in his voice was utterly infuriating and did not make me want to kiss him one bit.

"Brady! You and Lindsay. Me and Brady. And this is all your fault—" I poked a finger into his broad, naked chest. "Because Lindsay is so blinded and tongue-tied by your hotness that she needs moral support on a date with you! So now, your stupid, handsome, perfect fucking face means I have to go bowling with Brady."

10

MACK

AT SOME POINT between the excessive amount of pie and right now, I had unknowingly stepped into the twilight zone. How else could I explain the conversation I was having with Chase? There was a lot going on, most of which I was having trouble processing. I glanced down into my beer, wondering if maybe Greyson had spiked it with one of his extras and I was hallucinating. I took an experimental sniff... normal enough. A sip... tasted normal, too. So then—

"You think my face is perfect?" Perfect. Not good. Not great. *Perfect*. No one had ever said that before.

Chase stiffened, swallowed hard, and studiously avoided eye contact. "Objectively."

What the hell did that mean? "You think my face is objectively perfect?"

"I don't—well, I do, but that's the thing about objectivity isn't it? It's not an opinion, it just is."

I couldn't stop my grin. "My face *just is* perfect?"

"Correct," she confirmed and, if I had to guess, I'd say she was nibbling the inside of her cheek to keep from smiling. "And because of that I have to go bowling. So I hope you're happy with yourself."

I was exceedingly happy with myself. Chase thought my face was perfect. But also—"You hate bowling." A more gross understatement had never been spoken.

She pursed her lips and blinked slowly. It was the *I'm a hot second away from slapping you* look. I knew it well.

"Yes, thank you, I'm well aware of that."

Now I was laughing. "Did you, Chase Linden, seriously agree to go bowling? Bowling."

"No." She let out a little growl. "Maybe, kind of. I was coerced. And I never actually agreed."

"Wow." I honestly never thought I would see the day. Not again. We'd all been bowling a few times in high school, but Chase would always pitch such a fit about wearing the shoes that she didn't actually bowl, she'd just sit there heckling the rest of us and drinking watered down beer thanks to a truly terrible fake ID. Maggie Titsmith, if I recall correctly.

"Shut up," she said and poked at my shirt in the basin beside us. "We should get you something else to wear."

"I can't go out like this?" I wagged my eyebrows at her and received a deadpan stare in return.

"Not unless you want Lindsay to either faint or throw herself at you. We've still got those promo ones in the office, don't we?" She blinked, the look on her face changing and electricity crackled across my skin. Then she was marching out and I wondered if I'd imagined it, or maybe it was one-sided. But, then, I didn't think I'd imagined the way she'd stared after instructing me to strip. There was something here between us, I knew there was. I could feel it. I just needed her to stop fighting it.

I followed down the short hall to our sardine can of an office, and found Chase rummaging in a pile of boxes in the corner. My eyes tracked up the back of her legs along the fucking seam that ran from her ankle and disappeared under the hem of her dress. I'd been mesmerized by those seams all afternoon. I wasn't the only one. Brady had been looking his fill as well, which had me tempted to slap him upside the head more than once. He was an okay dude but I would rather eat glass than have to watch Chase on a date with him. The double date was both a blessing and a curse.

"I can't believe you said yes to going bowling. You! I don't even know what to say."

She turned and tossed a long-sleeved, black shirt at me. "Just say yes so we can get your stupid first date over and done with. Lindsay will realize that you are much more than your face"—her eyes darted below my chin—"and everything else. And I won't have to see Brady again, aside from awkward stairwell encounters until one of us either dies or moves out." She slumped against the desk and gulped down her remaining sangria.

I shrugged into the shirt and came to perch beside her.

We sat there in silence for a few long moments, pressed together from shoulder to knee. I'd say it was because the desk was so small, but it wasn't. There was room enough for us not to be sandwiched together. My mind was circling the idea of going on a date with someone I wasn't at all interested in; as gorgeous and nice as Lindsay was, I could admit to myself that, right now, my heart was beating for only one woman. Who would also be on this date. The fact I would, indirectly, be on a date with Chase was about the only reason I wasn't saying no. That and the remote—seriously remote—possibility I'd get to see her in bowling shoes.

"Have you heard from Nash?" she asked, taking a sharp left turn away from the double date conversation.

"Radio silence." For over a week now. There had been

whole months when we hadn't spoken in the past, but this felt different, the silence heavier.

"I'm worried about him."

I slung an arm around her and her head dropped onto my shoulder like it was the most natural thing in the world. "I know, me too, but he'll be okay," I said with more conviction than I felt. Maybe I needed to plan a trip out to LA.

"How do you know?" It was little more than a whisper and she sounded like she was a second away from crying. Drunk Chase was a mixed up ball of emotions tonight. I squeezed her a little tighter.

"I don't know for sure, but I need to believe it."

She let out a heavy breath and I knew what she was thinking, because I was thinking it too: *what if he's back with Nadia?*

Despite what everyone saw from the outside, Chase and I knew that Nash wasn't himself in that relationship. He never had been. Not that I ever said that to him. How do you tell your friend that he's a shadow of himself when his wife's around? You don't. You keep that shit to yourself until you either explode, or nature takes its course.

Then, there was Jemma. I had to believe that whatever there was between them was something different, something intense that burned so bright and fierce he couldn't go back to what he'd had before. She lit him up like I'd never seen—he wasn't just himself, he was more, better. Plus, Harley said they'd work it out and, for some bizarre reason—maybe it was her unshakable confidence—I trusted her opinion on the subject.

Alarmingly, I realized I trusted her opinion on more than just that.

"Yes," I said, not needing to clarify what I was referring to.

Chase leaned away, her eyes jumping up and clashing with

mine, a mix of emotions playing out behind them. Relief. Confusion. And something else I couldn't quite put my finger on. "Excuse me?"

"You said: *just say yes*. So, yes." I shrugged like it wasn't a big deal. Like my heartbeat hadn't just sped up uncomfortably fast, and my palms weren't spontaneously sweaty. Like I wasn't already thinking about how to make Chase feel like she was the one I was on a date with.

"Great, that's great. I'm sure Lindsay will be beside herself with excitement." She shifted away so our legs were no longer touching.

"Brady, too, I'd say."

I received another flat stare, but the corners of her lips were twitching with the effort to keep her smile in check. "Har."

"I guess we should get back out there..." I said, although I had no real desire to leave this little bubble of ours.

"I guess so," she agreed, looking about as enthusiastic to rejoin the party as I was.

Her eyes strayed over my face and the air started to feel warm and thick, the same way it had just before our kiss after the wedding. Would it happen again? Her tongue slid out along her lower lip, her teeth followed, trapping the soft plump pillow between them. My fingers twitched against my jeans, hyper aware of each strand of cotton, wanting desperately to pull her lip free and then dive into the silken strands of her hair. I was losing my fucking mind. All I was aware of was the sound of our breaths as we sat there, separated by inches.

Until she abruptly stood and ripped me free from the moment. I shook my head in a vain attempt to clear the fog that had settled over my senses. It wasn't much use, my entire head was full of her. The jasmine and lime scent, with the slightest hint of sangria, the sound of her shallow breaths. The bow of her top lip. The curve of the bottom one.

The sound of a whistle broke through the haze and I realized that Chase must have heard someone approaching the office—that was what stopped her. All I needed to do was close the door and shut the rest of the world out and I might have been kissing her now.

But I could wait.

Chase marched down the hall ahead of me and I watched as, the step before she re-entered the party, she pulled herself together, shoulders back, chin high. She was just as affected by me as I was by her. I knew it. But she wasn't letting herself feel it, or she was hiding behind these fucking walls she'd thrown up since our kiss.

No, they weren't walls, they were doors; all I had to do was find the right keys.

THE WORST THING about Thanksgiving was dragging your thoroughly hungover ass into work on Black Friday. At no point in the last five years had I ever had the forethought to consider taking it easy to help make my Black Friday go a little more smoothly. No, every year I ate and drank with abandon and little concern for Future Mack and his problems.

Well, whiskey-swilling, pie-eating Mack could go fuck himself because I felt like death and there was a chance a small rodent had crawled into my mouth and died overnight.

I was not one of those people who routinely woke up after a big night and declared they were never drinking again. I owned a bar, for fuck's sake. If everyone who said that actually followed through, we wouldn't have any customers. So, no, I was sure that I'd pick up another drink. Just maybe not today. Today I would do my best to drink copious amounts of water in an effort to flush out all the residual alcohol, turkey, and pie. So. Much. Pie.

After my pie-induced almost-breakdown yesterday morning, the apple-cheddar had been one of the stars of the show. I was told by numerous guests that it went particularly well with the buttermilk ice cream, which I had been exceedingly happy with. Chase even requested a pint or two as her Christmas present. Naturally, I was already thinking of tweaks to improve it further.

I'm going on a date with Chase.

The thought slammed into me as more of yesterday's memories sharpened through the combined haze of sleep and hangover. I was going on a double date, with Chase ... and two other people. She was going on a date with Brady and I was going on a date with Lindsay. But at least we were together.

We had nearly kissed in the office. I could see her in my head, the way she'd looked at me. The way the air between us came alive. A couple more seconds and I would have been able to taste the sangria on her tongue. How the hell was I going to get any sort of work done today with those thoughts rolling around in my head?

I sat up, needing to move as a restless sort of energy started to build in my chest. She'd be at Rudi later—probably bleary-eyed and hungover grumpy, but I didn't give a shit.

When we first started Rudi, I thought that being excited to go to work meant I'd finally found the right place. Now I was wondering if it wasn't so much the right *place* as the right person. Being back with her after so many years away was like being able to take full breaths again. It wasn't that I'd been unhappy while I was away, quite the opposite, but being back in her orbit ... it was different. I was different. Better. Chase was my person, she always had been. I think I'd always known it, but I'd never let myself hope for more.

With unhurried steps I shuffled into the bathroom, shoved my toothbrush into my mouth and started up the shower. Yes, I was hungover—and my stomach was still working its way through yesterday's food—but there was a spark of hope under it all that was making my chest feel light. And, as much as I detested the Black Friday sales, I remembered I had some shopping to do.

11

CHASE

I NEARLY KISSED *Mack again last night.*

It was the first thought that popped into my head upon waking up and it came back to me over and over throughout the day. Each time it made an appearance, I would follow it with a resounding: *and it will not happen again.* I wanted to believe it, I really did. But there was this little voice in the back of my head that kept calling bullshit ... and it sounded an awful lot like Harley.

She had been the life of the party last night. Taking up residence behind the bar and dolling out drinks like it was her job, which I suppose it was, but the kind she usually dispensed were non-alcoholic. I didn't think it was possible for Harley to be anything other than the life of the party, she was just that person, smiling and chatty and unable to keep a single thought in her head to herself. She turned up as a sexy turkey, for God's sake. And the costume change saw her become a sexy pumpkin, which shouldn't have worked, and yet did.

As soon as Mack and I had rejoined the party after the almost-kiss, she took me by the elbow (again) and sat me down for a chat. Most of which had been about her and the fact that she had decided Jeremy was probably going to be the hot naked male in her bed by the end of the night. Considering I saw them in a dark corner not thirty minutes later I had to assume she was right.

The whole night, aside from the almost-kiss and me somehow agreeing to go fucking bowling, and telling my best friend he had a perfect face (what the actual fuck had I been thinking?), had been our most successful Thanksgiving to date.

Now the only thing souring my high was the slimy, residual guilt about Mom. I'd been psyching myself up to call her all day, but every time I picked up the phone I found something else more important to do. Like deep-conditioning my hair while scrubbing the grout in my shower. Or cleaning the oven. I even vacuumed under my couch.

Eventually I decided that I couldn't call because I wanted to see her, not have some passive-aggressive phone conversation. So I left my deep cleaned apartment with my particularly shiny hair and walked to the subway.

As had been the theme of the day, I dragged my feet getting out of the house, which meant it was going to have to be a quick visit or I wouldn't be able to make it to Rudi on time later. Would Mack care if I was over an hour late? No, but that was not the point. I was trying to go into this with positivity, while also being realistic. I had no real idea what to expect.

A tall guy with messy brown hair and over the top cologne sat down next to me on the subway and I fought off a wave of nausea, breathing through my mouth as best I could.

The fresh air of 71st Street was a welcome relief when I finally made it above ground. I had a feeling my hangover was making my nose extra sensitive today. Just what I needed.

I plugged Derrick's address into my phone and started

walking. I could have hopped an Uber to get here but I needed more time to think than a car ride would give me.

The house came up sooner than I was expecting and I didn't want to admit that I could absolutely see my mother living here but, I really could. It was almost annoyingly charming in a way our house had never been. I loved our house, it was the first place I'd really felt like I was home aside from Aunt Peggy's, it wasn't, however, what anyone would call *cute*.

This place, though, was downright adorable. And despite her not being here for long I could already see Mom's touches; on the short staircase that led to the porch, on the door with its pine cone wreath. Our wreath, I realized, as a sticky, uncomfortable feeling bloomed in the pit of my stomach.

I knocked and heard the sounds of Stevie Nicks coming from inside the house—Mom's music. I wasn't sure why it made my nose burn with impending tears, and yet as the door swung open I was blinking frantically to stop them from falling.

"Chase," Derrick faltered, but made a swift recovery. "Come in," he said with a smile, stepping aside to show me in. He was maybe five-ten, still had a full head of hair that was salt and pepper, which always made a man look distinguished and a woman told she needed to invest in a good colorist. He was the kind of guy you could tell had probably been hot back in the day. A real heartbreaker. The thought had my hands curling into fists, because as smiley as he was now, that was going to end. It always did. I just hoped Mom was the one to walk away. She always recovered better when she was the one to end it.

"Hey Derrick, happy Thanksgiving." I shrugged out of my coat, which he took and hung on the overstuffed hooks by the door. Family coat hooks. I didn't know why but looking at them made me itchy.

I followed down the hall, death gripping the pie dish. Why the hell did I think that coming here was a good idea? I should have opted for the passive aggressive phone call. Thinking an in-person confrontation was going to be better was delusional. I blamed my hangover.

Derrick entered the large open concept room at the back of the house just ahead of me, and I caught a glimpse of Mom and a younger woman seated together at the large kitchen island. I didn't like the burn of jealousy in my chest at seeing them together.

"Chase?" Mom was surprised, but still guarded. "I didn't know you were coming over?"

It took me a second to force words out through my tight throat. "H–Hi Mom, I hope it's okay that I dropped by."

"Of course it is," she said, slipping off her stool. "This is Derrick's Aubrey—Aubrey, this is my daughter, Chase."

"It's great to meet you," Aubrey beamed.

"You too, Aubrey." I didn't want to hate her because she looked vaguely like my mother.

"Happy Thanksgiving. We missed you yesterday."

"Happy Thanksgiving. I brought pie." My pie. The pie I should have been eating alone in my apartment. Instead I brought it here. It was my guilt pie.

"Thanks, sweetheart, it looks amazing."

"It's one of Mack's." Now that I wasn't holding the pie I didn't know what to do with my hands.

"How about I give you a tour?" Mom asked.

"Sure, that would be great," I said rather than run from the house like I was desperate to.

Mom showed me through the house, from the small, light-filled entry to the four bedrooms upstairs. Everything was neat and welcoming—I could see her touches everywhere. We ended back where we started. The large kitchen, living and dining room was light and airy and it was clear that Mom loved it. I could admit that it was a lovely home, but I had a crawling sensation under my skin and tension rolling along my spine nonetheless.

Mom paused for a beat and looked at me intently. I wanted to apologize, but the words lodged themselves in my throat because what was I apologizing for? I didn't think I'd actually done anything wrong in this scenario, and I'd still come and brought pie. And now that I was here I didn't want to talk about anything. I wanted to pretend that nothing happened and everything was fine. Easier said than done, considering we were standing on Aunt Peggy's hall runner in Derrick's house.

"Chase—"

"How about we get into that pie?" I interrupted, shooting Aubrey a plastic smile.

Her eyes darted between me and Mom before she asked, "Tea or coffee?"

I WAS DIALING before I made it to the end of the block. It had been weeks since I'd heard from Nash. I knew he probably had bigger things to deal with than my mother getting married and starting a new family, but I wanted to speak to him all the same. It had been so long since we lived in the same city but, after that month he was here for the wedding, his absence now felt heavier. I fucking missed him.

"Hey Chase," he answered on the third ring and I was already sniffing.

"Hey."

"You okay there?" I could hear the smile in his voice, and I hated that he was back on the other side of the country.

"Uh-huh."

"You sure?"

"Mom got married and I'm pretty sure she's replaced me

with a blonde. Well, blonde-ish." I stepped around a young couple and their dawdling toddler.

"What?" He could have laughed at the statement but, like Mack, he understood. I explained the whole sorry situation, including her insistence that I be at Thanksgiving even though I wasn't required at the wedding.

"She's not replacing you, Chase, you are utterly irreplaceable for pretty much anyone who meets you."

"What about Tommy?" Two days after we broke up he was making out with Sarah in the middle of the cafeteria.

"Tommy was an idiot and only dated Sarah because she looked like you."

I sagged. Mom might not actually be replacing me but that didn't change the fact I didn't fit with their new family. I hadn't even met the other two yet and I was confident it was true.

"How are you doing?" I asked.

The long pause was not the most encouraging thing in the world. "I'm okay, sorting myself out. Nadia and I are officially over, we can't file for divorce—yet—but we've seen a therapist together for some closure and things are amicable. I fucking hate that word, but it fits."

"I'm glad you're okay, and that things are not terrible. Does this mean you're coming home?"

"I will be, but not just yet, I'm trying to do all this right, and rushing ... it won't help." I had a feeling he meant Jemma, but didn't want to push. So long as he was planning on coming back eventually, I could live with that.

"What will you do for Christmas?"

"Hang with Keiran, his new place is incredible. I've been helping out here and there, finding my feet again. It feels good."

"I'm glad. I wish I could give you a hug. I miss you, Nash."

"I miss you, too, Chase."

We hung up with a promise to be better about speaking to

one another. I knew why I hadn't called him before now. I'd been scared out of my brain when he went back to LA, scared that he'd get back together with Nadia, scared that he'd never come home. But none of that had happened. The relief was real.

WITH AN AWKWARD SHOVE, the door to Rudi swung open and I stumbled inside with my overstuffed grocery bags. After the conversation with Nash and the trip back from Queens, I should have calmed down. And I had, a little, but the anger was still simmering way too close to the surface. I hadn't expected to feel so betrayed by seeing Mom make herself comfortable somewhere else. But seeing our things in that place had left me all sorts of mixed up. Maybe I had managed to trick myself into thinking that it wasn't that serious. I was wrong. It was serious. Not just because they were married, either, but because Mom was *in it*. That house wasn't just his, she put her stamp on it in numerous ways. That should have made me happy for her. It didn't. I was the only one not drinking the Kool Aid. The only one who was concerned about the speed at which all of this was happening.

Aubrey, from what I'd seen, had accepted Mom with open arms. Better than being an asshole, sure, which was probably how I came across whether I wanted to admit it or not. Even the way Aubrey said Mom's name made me feel like I was intruding. Like they were already this perfect family—Mom, Dad and the perfect blonde-ish daughter—and then there was me.

When Mom started talking about the Secret Santa I hit my limit. I did not know these people. Why the fuck would I want to buy a gift for one of them? Have one of them buy one for me? No thank you. But, of course, saying that out loud wasn't an option because I didn't want to be the grinch along with being the odd one out of our new family. So, I kept my mouth shut and kept on smiling my wooden smile as I shoved another mouthful of pie into my face and sipped my lukewarm tea.

Then I cried on the subway, which I didn't think I would ever do but it did have the positive side effect of stopping anyone from wanting to sit next to me, so there was that.

I just didn't understand what was so wrong with our family that Mom felt like she needed to go and get herself a new one?

I was not going to keep thinking about this. Not while I was trying to keep my shit together in front of Mack and my staff. And I would keep my shit together. All I needed was a little distraction. Hence the groceries.

Mack was talking before I could see him.

"So Greyson called and he's been throwing up since this morning, trying to blame my fucking pie but it was obviously the three day old curry he ate for breakfast yesterday." He paused, eyes taking in the various items now littering the previously clean bar. I'd managed to contain it to a corner at least. "Whatcha doin'?"

"Nothing, just thought I'd, you know, tweak the cocktail menu." My cheeks were already hurting with the effort of maintaining this smile. I fished the microplane out of the utensil jar for the ginger and lemon and scooped some ice into a shaker.

"And when you say *tweak*, you mean..."

"Overhaul," I finished for him.

"Uh huh..." The two syllables were thick with an understanding that I did not appreciate one bit. This was the problem with someone knowing you as well as Mack and I knew each other. He was well aware that this was classic Chase avoidance and would not be shy about calling me on it. But I plowed on nonetheless.

"I realized that with all the wedding stuff, and then how busy we've been since, I hadn't given a winter menu any kind of thought." This was at least true.

"And you thought today was the right day to do that?"

"Yep." I popped the *p*. "I'm thinking a riff on that mulled wine we did last year, maybe an apple cobbler martini, something fresh but warming, like the ginger fizz from the wedding but maybe with... pear, or tangerine. We just need to mix things up." I added a healthy pour of vodka over the ice in the shaker.

He nodded. "Sure, yeah, that all sounds incredible."

"Thank you."

"And all of this has nothing to do with your m—"

"It has nothing to do with anything aside from our tired cocktail menu." I said, not keen to have him finish that question. I peeled a tangerine, squeezed some juice in with the vodka and followed it with some ginger and lemon.

Mack stood watching me in silence and I shook the concoction, adjusted the flavor with a little more tangerine and then poured it into a glass for him, waiting for the verdict.

He sipped torturously slowly and my eyes focused squarely on his mouth as a spontaneous heat started to warm my blood.

"It's delicious."

"Good. You can think of a name."

"You know that if you need to go home—"

"Why would I need to go home? Besides, you just said Greyson isn't coming in. You can't be down a second person. Where are those cloves..."

"Chase." His tone was all soft and knowing and it was so tempting to unload everything on him in one long word vomit. I knew he'd never judge me, but something kept the words where they were for the moment.

"Mack, please stop looking at me like that."

"I'm not looking at you like anything."

"You are, now quit it."

"We are going to talk about this."

"Of course we are. Oh, I spoke to Nash." That was enough to distract him, at least for the moment and I smiled genuinely for the first time today as I relayed the conversation and pulled out the juicer from under the bar.

12

MACK

LINDSAY WAS AN ENTHUSIASTIC TEXTER.

I had all but forgotten we'd exchanged numbers on Thanksgiving, and then, a couple of days later, the first text came in. Quickly followed by the second, and the third. There was a very good chance I was going to have received her full life story via one line texts before we made it to the date tomorrow.

The date was tomorrow.

I would have preferred to be at Rudi today because at least it'd be a distraction. My recent purchase was under the sink—the last place I figured Chase would look—and, even though I couldn't see it, I could still hear the mocking whispers. *What were you thinking with this? She's going to think you've lost it.*

Anxiety was a hot knife in my gut. I'd never felt nervous about going on a date, but I'd never been on a date with Chase before, either. Yes, granted, I wasn't technically on the date with Chase but that was also part of the problem. I was going to have to watch her on a date with Brady. My lip curled as I sunk deeper into the couch cushions.

Fucking Brady.

The only reason I wasn't completely crawling out of my skin was because I knew Chase didn't actually want to be going on the date with Brady. She was doing all this for Lindsay and me. She was doing it for Lindsay and me when I had no intention of going on another date with her. Did that make me a dick? Maybe. Probably. If I'd been a better man I would have said no to the whole thing. I would have said thank you, but no thank you to Lindsay, owned my shit and gone after Chase.

I wasn't a better man though, I'd agreed to the date knowing I wasn't going to see Lindsay again. And I'd agreed only because Chase was the one to ask. I was an asshole. More so because, rather than thinking about Lindsay, and feeling guilty about my actions, my mind kept straying to Chase and the gift that was still mocking me from between my recycling and the eucalyptus counter spray. Would my gift mean she might actually enjoy herself? Only time would tell.

Forcing my brain away from the impending date, and my already too strong feelings about it, I went to the kitchen and took out my latest ice cream experiment. It was shaping up well, there was a good balance between the buttermilk and the maple syrup but it was still missing something that I couldn't quite put my finger on.

I pulled out cream, eggs, and sugar ready to make another custard for ice cream attempt number four... or was it five?

EVEN IF MY feelings for Chase hadn't come raging to the surface thanks to our kiss, I would have had serious concerns about my compatibility with Lindsay based on the fact that bowling had been her idea. Granted, there was nothing inherently wrong with bowling, it was fine, but it was an odd choice. And, judging by the texts I was still receiving, one Lindsay was extremely happy with. The only real explanation I could come up with was that she was an outstanding bowler and wanted to showcase those skills in a date setting. Honestly, I would be pretty impressed if she was a great bowler in addition to a professional ballet dancer.

"Mack, hi, so good to see you again," Lindsay said as she opened the door, her cheeks were pink and she nearly tripped over her own feet as she ushered me inside. "My roommate's out for the night," she added with a small laugh and I nodded, a tight smile stretched across my face.

Why did this feel so awkward? Was it me? Was it her? Was it us together? Was this some sign from the universe that I should cut and run?

We hadn't actually spoken that much on Thanksgiving and this date had been largely (read: entirely) engineered by Chase. And, for whatever reason, all of my usual small talk and—dare I say it—charm, had spontaneously abandoned me.

Lindsay's blue eyes darted to the box under my arm, expectation lighting them up, and I realized I'd made a miscalculation agreeing to pick her up while holding a gift for someone else. Of course she thought it was for her. But it was too late to do anything about that now, so I just smiled, again, and made out like I was admiring her sparsely furnished apartment. It was little more than a large armchair, a couple of beanbags, and what looked like a camping table.

"Nice place," I lied. It wasn't that bad, but it also wasn't what I'd been expecting.

"No it's not," she said with a small laugh. "I mean, it's fine, it was better. We had a third roommate, but he moved out and took most of the furniture with him, even the stuff that wasn't his. Anyway, can I get you a drink?"

Being still wasn't a good option for me right now. The nerves were making my skin pull tight over my bones, restless energy buzzing with the need to move, to do. "How about we grab one there?"

"Sounds good. I'll just get my coat."

I went back to the door while she collected her things and I ignored the churning in my gut. I should not have agreed to this date. I didn't date. I had mutually beneficial physical encounters, which, overall, I was perfectly happy with. Or I had been.

I didn't want that with Chase, I wanted a whole lot more than that with Chase. But there was probably a better way of going about it than a double date with a woman I wasn't interested in. There was that slight twinge of guilt again, because I was pretty sure that I was using Lindsay. It certainly wasn't my intention, but the result was the same nonetheless. I'd be lying if I said there would be another date with just the two of us.

"All ready?" I asked as Lindsay appeared and I offered my elbow—because I wasn't a complete dick and acting like a gentleman, even when you weren't, never hurt.

She smiled, slipping her arm through mine. "Let's do it."

Bronco Bowl was less a bowling alley and more a bar and venue that happened to have some bowling lanes in it. Once upon a time it had been a full bowling alley but, after a fire over ten years ago, it was abandoned until Bronco Bowl opened and breathed new life into the old building. They'd done a good job, too, maintaining all the vintage charm of the original bowling alley then adding a full bar and kitchen, a small arcade at one end, and a stage for live music at the other. And, yes, as the name suggested, there was also a bucking bronco.

The sounds of bowling pins being toppled greeted us as we walked in and a wave of nostalgic familiarity washed over me. It wasn't necessarily pleasant, but I remembered the first time I'd been taken bowling. Carmel, my nanny when I was around eight or nine, had brought me along to a family birthday party because my mother had refused to give her the day off. It was a peek inside another family and I liked it, but it also made me pine for brothers and sisters closer to my own age.

The unpleasant loneliness from that day wrapped itself around me now and the hairs at the base of my neck prickled through a spontaneous cold sweat.

But then I saw Chase seated at the bar and the tension in my muscles drained away as a smile tugged at my lips. It didn't matter how I was feeling, seeing her had the power to make it better. It had always been that way, since that first day of freshman year she walked into the girls' bathroom. She was a light. A sometimes grumpy, foul-mouthed light, but a light nonetheless.

Brady, who was facing the door, waved as he saw us approach and I had the urge to smack him over the head with one of the bowling pins. I didn't blame him for so obviously wanting Chase, she was incredible after all, but it didn't mean I wanted to sit back and watch him paw at her either. If he tried to pull some 'let me show you how to bowl' bullshit I might make good with one of those pins. Or, more likely, Chase would. Unless she'd changed her mind about him? The thought had my stomach bottoming out like I'd just gone over the crest of a roller coaster. It wasn't an option.

My palms started to sweat as we drew closer, the box under my arm now a dead weight, nerves swirling with nausea. If I'd ever felt this way before, I couldn't remember it.

"There you guys are!" Chase said, hopping down off her stool. Her smile was comical, her eyes wide, it was her bat signal and I had to cover my laugh with a cough, but it didn't help to distract from the way my pulse had also sped up.

She was in a short skirt, the same color as the filling of her favorite pie, and it showed off the toned length of her legs. Her usual black, shit-kicker boots were on her feet and a black leather jacket hung over the back of her stool. Then there was her shirt. Her sheer shirt. I didn't claim to know every item of Chase's closest—I wasn't a fucking creep—but when you see a person six, and sometimes seven, days out of seven you learned what was in their wardrobe. And that shirt ... I had never seen that shirt before. It was black and sheer with the exception of the little black spots all over it which were doing nothing to obscure my view of the two black triangles that covered her breasts. Jesus Christ, how was I going to keep my mind on bowling? Or my own date, for that matter?

There was a round of hellos and kisses before Lindsay said, "Are we all ready to bowl?" She sounded like a game show host. Chase shot me another look, but this one said *don't fucking laugh at your date.* And yes, the *fucking* was very much communicated in the glint of her eyes and slight crease of her nose. I winked and she glared a little harder.

"Let's do it!" Brady said with an equal amount of enthusiasm, and the color drained from Chase's face because it was time. She needed to part with her beloved boots and put on a pair of shoes that had probably seen more action than an eighties porn star.

Her panicked look had me swallowing another laugh and I handed her the box. She took it and her look morphed into one of curiosity and mild suspicion as she gave it an experimental shake.

"Just open it, Cheese. We'll see you over at the desk." I pressed a hand to Lindsay's lower back and steered her away. I was retreating as fast and as far as I could without fleeing the actual building in an effort to look casual, just one friend giving another friend a gift. *No big deal. We do this all the time. Totally natural.* I didn't want to walk away. I wanted to stand there and watch her face as she lifted the lid.

"You brought Chase a gift?" Lindsay asked as I dropped my elbows onto the blond timber desk. She was trying to sound casual, but there was an edge to her tone that betrayed her.

"It was either that or we'd lose our competition," I said with an easy smile. When her brow pinched in confusion I nodded at all the shoes in front of us and added, "Chase has a thing about the shoes. Flat out refuses to wear them. We tried to go bowling in high school and she got all of us kicked out after getting drunk and then trying to bowl barefoot."

"Oh my god." Lindsay laughed, her eyes clearing. "What's wrong with the shoes?"

"They're disgusting," Chase answered as she stepped up beside me. "And I wasn't barefoot, I had socks on."

"The result was the same."

"It was," she conceded, her eyes swinging up to meet mine. "Thank you for the shoes."

I nodded and tried not to look like my heart was going to beat out of my chest. "You're welcome, will you actually be bowling today?"

She glanced down into the box, then back up at me. I was in danger of pitching head first into the endless depths of her eyes.

"It looks like I will be, yes." Fucked. I was fucked.

"Alright then."

"Does this mean you've never bowled Chase?" Lindsay asked, edging a little closer into my side and reminding me who I was actually on a date with.

"Not with any real success, no, but it cannot possibly be that difficult. Plus, I'm a quick study." Chase smiled, she was only barely restraining herself from dropping to the floor and trying on her new shoes. The fact I knew that was inordinately satisfying.

"Well, if you need any pointers, I'd be happy to give you a

personal lesson," Brady all but purred at her and I nearly gave myself an aneurysm with the effort it took not to throat punch him. He hadn't been this much of a dick at Thanksgiving had he? I really hoped not, or I was going to be concerned for Chase and her decision making in agreeing to this date.

She shot him a too-sweet smile. "I think I'll manage, thanks, Brady."

The conversation ended as a kid with a star tattoo under his left eye finally appeared behind the desk and asked what size shoe we all needed.

Once everyone had shoes, Chase only gloated a little that hers were better than everyone else's, and—to her credit—Lindsay took it well. Now, it was time to choose balls. This was not something that I thought required that much thought, but Chase and Lindsay disagreed for quite different reasons.

"That one doesn't even have any glitter," Chase said as Brady suggested a ball.

"I don't think glitter is a prerequisite for a bowling ball."

"Well maybe it should be ... ooh look at this one!" She skipped to the next rack.

"She's going to be terrible, isn't she?" Lindsay asked, standing close.

"Absolutely awful," I confirmed as she picked up and then discarded the fifth ball. "Looking for your golden slipper?"

"Do you mean glass slipper?"

"Probably, but I'd take a gold slipper over a glass one, who wants glass shoes?"

"Sure, they'd be completely impractical."

"Exactly, and what if one broke? Messy."

She laughed. "Excellent point. Okay, then yes, I am looking for my golden slipper. Your ball can make or break your game, you know." She launched into a bowling ball related monologue that I was only half listening to as I watched Chase and Brady head back to our lane cradling their own balls.

"Everything okay?" Lindsay asked with a nudge to my elbow.

"Yes, great, let's do this." I grabbed a ball and she narrowed her eyes.

"Um, that one's probably too light for you." There was a good chance she was right but I was holding it now and didn't want it to look like the panic choice it was.

"Oh, no, this is just how I roll." Did I really just say a bowling pun? Lord help me, if Chase heard that she'd never let me forget it. Lindsay however, being the bowling enthusiast she was, laughed as we went to join Chase and Brady.

"I don't think we're going to have to do much to beat them anyway," she whispered as we approached.

"No, I think you're probably right there." Not that I gave a shit who won.

"Then let's go wipe the floor with them, partner."

"Yes ma'am," I said and she beamed. Maybe my charm hadn't abandoned me after all.

13

CHASE

BOWLING WAS weird and I was still terrible at it. But, despite my substandard skill level, it was also more enjoyable than I expected it to be—it might have had something to do with the fact I was pleasantly buzzed. Bowling at thirty-one was a different beast to bowling (or watching bowling) at sixteen or seventeen. For one, the drinks were much better. There were also my new shoes, which I could not stop staring at. The shoes that Mack had bought me, so I wouldn't have to wear those disgusting specimens they provided you with. *He bought me shoes.*

It wasn't the first time Mack had bought me a present, nor was it the first time he'd sprung one on me so unexpectedly. However, he was on a date with another woman, for god's sake. He shouldn't be getting me a gift, and yet he did, because that was just him. He knew that I would either sit out the bowling or be intensely uncomfortable for the entire night. So, he fixed it for me. Classic Mack.

To her credit, Lindsay took the whole thing pretty well. It was clear that she thought it was a bit strange but I got the feeling that Mack had managed to put her mind at ease. Halfway through our first game she had already bought a matching pair (overnight shipped) for our next bowling date, which I really hoped wasn't tomorrow—though I wouldn't be surprised. The woman really did love to bowl.

Brady, on the other hand, despite also being a very enthusiastic bowler, had been like a child who was being forced to share his favorite toy and I was a hot minute away from slapping him.

It didn't matter how many times I said the shoes were not a big deal. I believed they weren't—Mack hadn't even stayed to watch me open the box, he'd just handed it over and then left me to it while he and his date went to the shoe desk. If he had cared about my response, he would have waited around to see it. Yet Brady was behaving like I had a ring on my fucking finger rather than a pair of perfect black and white bowling shoes on my feet.

"Anyone need another drink?" he asked, emptying the last of his beer. I held up my mostly full glass in response, not that he was really asking me, he was looking directly at Lindsay, who was gazing at Mack like he'd invented bowling.

"Guess it's just me then," Brady grumbled like a petulant toddler and I only just resisted an eye roll so deep it would have detached a nerve.

"Actually! Can I get another?" I said with a wide smile as Mack howled in triumph behind me. Another strike then. He was wiping the floor with all of us. That was probably part of the reason Brady was all pouty too.

"Yeah, sure," he replied, like a little ray of sunshine. It was fine if he was having a shit time (plenty of people went on shit dates), but he could at least try to act like he wanted to be here, rather anywhere else. I, for example, would much prefer to be at home, snuggled up with curly fries, maybe some chicken nuggets, and a movie rather than having to look at his surly face. Yet I was here, still smiling. Again, this may have been the cocktails.

I took another sip of my drink as Mack strutted his way back to our seats. Lindsay beamed at him from their side of the booth. I wasn't sure how, or why, it had happened but as soon as we'd sat down one side of the little podium had become Lindsay and Mack's territory and the other mine and Brady's. Invisible battle lines were drawn and, so far, had been strictly abided by. It was either a bowling thing or a date thing; whichever the reason, it was weird. But I wasn't going to cross that invisible line because it seemed like Lindsay and Mack were having a good time together. And I wasn't going to get in the way of that.

She high-fived him and handed over his drink like the perfect housewife after a long day. I wondered idly if I could learn a thing or two from Lindsay, and not just in the posture department. She was charming and sweet and didn't mind if her date bought another woman a gift. Those were all excellent qualities. Then there was the fact you could bounce a quarter off not only her ass, but pretty much everywhere else, too. I pulled myself out of my slouched position and straightened my shoulders.

"You're up, Cheese," Mack said and I bumped his offered fist—while staying on my side of the line—before making my way to the ball thing. I had taken great care in choosing my ball. It was black, and pink, and glittery. And, yes, I was tempted to try and smuggle it out of here. It had not, however, helped me to hit more than a few pins at a time. With only a couple more frames left before the end of our second game, it was time to accept that maybe I just wasn't a bowler. But I still had the shoes.

I sent my ball sailing down the lane and once again it ended up in the gutter. It started off okay—mostly straight and heading in the right direction—but almost every time about half way down the lane it veered off to one side.

When I turned, Mack was alone in the booth. In the middle of the booth.

"Where did Lindsay go?"

He took a sip of beer before answering. "Bathroom." His eyes made a slow perusal from my feet up to my face and my pulse started the drum. "Maybe I shouldn't have bought you those shoes?"

"What?" I gaped, planting my hands on my hips. If he wanted these shoes back he was going to have to wrestle them off my goddamn feet.

"You are truly terrible at this."

"That has nothing to do with the shoes," I said, gesturing down at them as I did a small jig. These cocktails really were something.

He chuckled, taking another slow sip of beer and I was mesmerized by the action, by the bob of his Adam's apple as he swallowed. One arm was draped over the back of the booth, his knees spread wide. He was in a pair of jeans and a blue plaid button down that was making his eyes look bluer than I had ever seen them. And, even though they were gross, he somehow managed to make even the bowling shoes look good, which was ridiculous. Had he always been this sexy and I just hadn't noticed? It was confronting, knowing I had been next to him all these years and largely oblivious. Well, maybe not oblivious so much as in denial.

A movie started to play out in my head. I could see myself walking over there, straddling his lap and—

"Brady's gone," Lindsay said, breaking me out of the spontaneous, and highly inappropriate, fantasy in my head.

"He what?" Mack and I said together.

"Gone," she repeated, eyes wide. My mind was having trouble processing so soon after thinking about having Mack's tongue in my mouth.

"Maybe he went to the bathroom?" I suggested but she shook her head, blonde curls swaying over her shoulders. How did she get her hair to do that? Not important right now.

"No, that's what I thought, too, but the bartender said he just walked out."

I opened my mouth to provide another alternative, then closed it again when nothing came to mind. I honestly wasn't that surprised. Pissed, yes I was definitely pissed, but not that surprised. He couldn't have at least told me he was leaving? Feigned a headache or an upset stomach? *Something?* He was going to hear about this next time I saw him on the stairs.

As much as I hadn't actually wanted to be here with him (once he turned all grumpy and sour), I was even less interested in being a third wheel on Mack and Lindsay's date.

"You don't need to leave, Chase," Mack said, reading my mind.

"It's fine. As you said, I suck at this, so I'll just leave the two of you to it. You'll have more fun without me, anyway."

"That's not true," Lindsay said without any real feeling, not that I could blame her. She had initially wanted a buffer but now that we were here it was clear that what she actually wanted was Mack all to herself. Once again, I couldn't blame her. Not that I wanted to be the one on the date with him. I didn't. I still didn't want to date him. I couldn't want to date him. I needed to get out of their way.

"It's fine, really." I drained my drink, shrugged on my jacket and picked up my bag. "I'll see you guys later." I scurried off before Mack could argue any more. But, of course, he caught me before I made it three steps out the door.

"Cheese, hey, wait up." His voice was like warm honey down my spine. What the hell was wrong with me? He was my friend, my best friend. It didn't, it *couldn't* go further than that. Damn that stupid fucking kiss for making things so complicated. Things had never been complicated between us. I hated that it was changing. My eyes fell down to my shoes, the shoes I had not arrived in.

"Forget something?" He waved my boots at me and I snatched them off him.

"Thank you, you can go back inside now."

"You might not have forgotten them if you didn't run off like your pants were on fire."

"I'm not wearing pants."

His eyes dropped down to my legs, I felt his gaze like a touch. When did this happen? When did he go from being my friend, to this person who made my heart race and my stomach tie itself in knots? Had it happened even before the kiss? *Get it together, he is on a date with someone else.*

"And I didn't run off. I said goodbye, and then I left so that I wasn't a third wheel on your date."

"You weren't a third wheel."

I let out a snort. "I was about to be. And it's fine. You and Lindsay are having fun, I don't want to break that up just because Brady is a bag of dicks. I'm tempted to get Franco to fuck up his hot water or something ..."

"Chase, you don't have to leave, why not just finish the game off?"

"Mack, will you stop, I'm terrible, as you noted. It's fine. I'm fine. Go and enjoy the rest of your date. I'll speak to you tomorrow."

"I don't–I—" He ran a restless hand through his hair. "Text me when you get home, please."

"Yes, Dad," I said with a roll of my eyes and shoved him

back towards the door, feeling spontaneous tears collecting behind my eyes.

I WAS SPREAD out on my couch in a pair of sad, old sweatpants and an oversized hoodie, with a bowl of piping hot curly fries on my chest and my finger hovering over play on *The Great British Bake Off* when there was a knock at the door. I lay perfectly still, hoping that whoever it was would leave me to my fried potato and feel-good television. Instead I heard a key in the lock and a moment later Mack was in my apartment.

"What are you doing here? Where's Lindsay?" I glanced behind him like I expected her to be there too.

"At her place, where I left her." He said it casually enough but he looked tense, antsy. Gorgeous still, obviously, but not quite himself.

"And you are here because?"

He opened his mouth. Closed it. Opened it again. I shifted the bowl to the coffee table and sat up.

"What's going on, Mack? Is everything okay? Are you okay?" I stood up, feeling the need to close the space between us but unsure if that was what he wanted. He was freaking me out. Mack didn't do tense or anxious. Mack did cool, calm, and collected almost perpetually.

"Yes—no, it's not. Everything is not okay."

"Oh-kay, you wanna stop pacing, you're making me woozy." He didn't stop, in fact he just got faster.

"Brady is an asshole who doesn't deserve you."

I tried and failed to reign in my smile. "Agreed. Is that all?" It would be so like him to come barging in here and give me a pep talk about the fact Brady's actions had nothing to do with me personally.

"No."

"Okay."

"I didn't—I didn't like watching you on a date with him."

"I didn't particularly enjoy being on the date with him. I guess it's lucky he bailed then, right? And it will not be happening again. Is this what's got you all..." I gestured at him. "Worked up?"

He paced some more and I wasn't sure he was going to answer when he finally said, "You were the reason I agreed to go tonight." Oh no, no, no, he was not doing what I thought he was doing. *Play dumb.*

"Yes, because I was the one who asked. And it wasn't so bad, right? You and Lindsay actually looked like you were having a good time. I'm happy for you."

He stopped pacing and looked at me, really looked at me, his eyes moving up from my socked feet the same way they had at the bowling alley, a slow perusal that made my breathing quick and shallow, and bad decisions seem like good ones.

"I agreed because you were the one asking, but not just because of that. I agreed because you were going to be there."

Stay strong, for the love of god, stay strong. "You were there with Lindsay."

"And yet I bought you the shoes."

"You wouldn't have known her size."

He took a step towards me and I had nowhere to go. "Chase." My name was little more than a whisper; it threatened to scramble my brain. Well, I was not going to let it. I pushed up my chin and met his eyes. They were bright and fierce. He wasn't backing down here. But I couldn't afford to either.

"Please don't do this."

"I'm not doing anything." He shrugged and moved a hair closer. His smell invaded my nose and the sound of his stubbled cheek as he scratched it was almost enough to undo me.

"You are. I don't want us to change."

"We already have, Chase. There's a charge in the air whenever we're together, I know you can feel it, too. You felt it earlier. Why are you fighting this?"

"Because I don't—"

"Don't lie to me..." he warned, his voice low and so, so seductive.

"I don't want us to change," I said again, because everything else was fleeing in the face of him like this. Wanting. Persuasive. Determined. My body wanted so desperately to be plastered across his, every nerve was straining tight in his direction. But my mind was stopping me. I couldn't lose him. Not him. Anyone but him.

"You won't lose me, Chase, not ever, you have to know that."

I shook my head. "Not if things change... I know that now, but if—"

"Do you really think I could go anywhere? That I would ever want to?"

"I don't know, Mack, I want to say no, but I don't know." My eyes pleaded with him to leave it alone.

"One date."

"One date what?"

"Go on one date with me and, if you still don't want things to go further, then we won't. I'll never mention it again. I swear. But let me take you out once first." We were so close, and still not touching. The heat of him had me tugging at the neck of my hoodie as warmth crawled up from my collar bones.

"We just went on a date." My voice was embarrassingly shaky, and the left corner of his mouth twitched upwards.

"That doesn't count. One date. Just you and me."

I planted my hands on my hips in an effort to regain some

composure, it wasn't terribly effective. "And how will that be different to every other time we hang out?"

"Because I'll be kissing you at the end of it."

I sucked in a sharp breath as lust shot through me in a hot bolt. I remembered all too well the feel of his lips on mine. It was not a reminder I needed right at the moment.

"Don't give me an answer now, sleep on it. We'll talk tomorrow." And, with that, he was gone. The door closed with a click behind him.

I couldn't do it, could I? Considering I had been tempted by him tonight, when we weren't even on an actual date the chances of me surviving a real one were slim. Yet, if I listened to my body, my heart, rather than my head, everything was whispering *yes*. But I wouldn't decide now. I'd sleep on it and hopefully feel more level headed in the morning.

Or I wouldn't, and I'd be agreeing to a date with my best friend.

14

MACK

I'D GONE IN TOO hard. I'd gone in too hard and scared her off and she was going to tell me to go fuck myself. I didn't even know what I'd been thinking—going to her place last night. All I knew was that after walking Lindsay to her door and saying good night, I needed to see Chase. Immediately. I needed her to understand. I'd nearly told her when she was leaving Bronco Bowl, but I didn't want to do that to Lindsay. I wasn't a complete asshole, unlike Brady. He'd be lucky if I didn't pop him in the nose next time I ran into him. What kind of person just leaves a date like that? Without a fucking word?

That was part of the reason I wanted to see Chase—to make sure she really was okay—but there was also the fact that I wanted her. Only her. I was done pretending otherwise. It was scary as shit but it needed to happen.

When I'd told her how the date would be different, that I'd be kissing her when it was over, I'd only just managed to keep my hands to myself. The temptation to touch her, to pull her into my chest, had been immense. But I resisted. Because I wanted that tension, that crackling electricity that snapped in the air between us now. I was confident she felt it, too. If I let it intensify for long enough I was also confident she wouldn't be able to resist giving in to it.

At least, that's what I was telling myself.

The alternative was that she'd come in today—even though it was her day off—and tell me that no, she would not be accepting my date proposal and that things would not be changing, now or ever. I couldn't discount her saying no, but fuck I really hoped she'd say yes.

After a mostly sleepless night, I was lethargic and cloudy. I decided to go for a run in an effort to boost my mood and distract myself from the constant circle of thoughts. It worked for the most part, until I found myself running past Chase's building without actually intending to. So much for trying to keep her off my mind. It was a lost cause at this point, clearly. But it was hours before I needed to be at Rudi, and I wasn't ready to go home and pace a hole in my polished-concrete floors. My stomach gave a weak kind of rumble.

I knew just where to go.

Harley spotted me as I came across the street and waved me inside before I'd even managed to say hello, ahead of the sizable line that curled down the block.

"Mackenzie!" She beamed, barely pausing the movement of her hands. "What are you doing here on this fine morning?" How was she this chipper before midday? I'd put it down to early nights but I'd seen her at Rudi until close more than once. I had a feeling this was just Harley all the time. Her hair was tamed into a pair of braids today, giving her a deceptively innocent look.

"How was the date last night?"

"How did you know about that?"

"I know everything," she said with a half shrug. "Also, I was there, you know, on Thanksgiving at your bar—I have not stopped dreaming about that apple pie since, I might add. Anyway, how was the lovely Lindsay?" She was omnipresent. There was no other explanation for it. Despite feeling somewhat violated by just how much she seemed to know, it was also comforting in a strange way, like she cared enough to pay attention. I hated to admit it, but Harley was really growing on me. I would absolutely never admit that to her face.

I pulled myself onto the only available stool at the coffee bar. "It was surprisingly enjoyable. Lindsay was, as you say, lovely and Chase actually bowled because I bought her a pair of shoes. Brady, however, is a fuckhead who bailed without a word and I will bury him the next time I see him. Can I get an Americano, strong, and the baked eggs."

"Darc, can I get a baked eggs here," Harley called and I spotted Darcy, the red-headed owner of Cream and Sugar, as she came out of the saloon doors from the kitchen. She just nodded and carried on with whatever she'd been doing.

"So..." Harley said, after dispensing a number of coffees including mine. "Did I hear you correctly when you said you bought Chase a pair of shoes?"

"That's correct."

"Uh huh, you were on a date with Lindsay and yet you bought *Chase* a pair of shoes." She paused and gave me a long look. "You didn't give them to her in front of Lindsay did you?"

I took a scalding sip of coffee. "I did."

She shook her head. "Are you kidding me?"

"I am not."

"Wait. You look... kinda peaky Did you finally get your shit together and tell Chase that you luurve her? Oh, did you seriously kiss her!? Please tell me that wasn't in front of Lindsay." She really was frighteningly observant. Did I want to discuss this with Harley? The fact I had come here knowing that she'd be here suggested that maybe I did want to talk about it. I was a friend down, with Nash in LA sorting himself out, and I couldn't exactly talk to Chase about this, Harley was about my only option.

"There was no kissing," I started, before explaining the conversation at Chase's apartment last night. Harley lapped up every word and was then silent for a full minute. It might have been the longest she hadn't spoken since we'd met.

"Yes, Mackenzie, yes. I love this for you." She delivered a collection of coffees to the to-go window. "And, honestly, I think there is very little chance she'll say no." Her eyes snapped to me then back to her work.

"And you know that, how?"

She shrugged, giving me no real answer. Yet just the fact she thought Chase would say yes was comforting enough. Because, deep down, I agreed. One date. She only had to agree to one date. Then, hopefully, there would be a second, a third, a fourth. Date after date until you stopped counting because you were no longer dating, you were just together. But it all started with one, *just one*.

"It really is adorable how much you love her," Harley said, snapping me out of my daze.

"Harley—"

"Re-lax, Mackenzie, I'm not telling anyone." She swatted my concerns away with one hand as the other steamed milk.

"Anyone else you mean, because I'm pretty sure you told Hunter and your brother that I was in love with her when we were at Bucks."

She giggled. "I did do that, didn't I? Well It's not going to matter soon because you'll be all loved up together. Then you'll be thanking me for all of my incredible advice. I take payment in compliments and espresso martinis, oh and from you, orgasm-inducing pie."

I nearly spit out my mouthful of coffee. "Orgasm-inducing pie?"

"I said what I said."

I had no response for that, so I just shook my head and sipped my coffee as she took a few orders from the to-go window. A text from Lindsay lit up my phone. It didn't matter that part of me had been expecting this all day, my stomach still dropped through the floor. I had every intention of telling her the truth, but how exactly did I say: *sorry there won't be another date because I'm interested in someone else, who also happened to be there last night.* How did one phrase that tactfully?

After wiping my spontaneously sweaty palms on my shirt I opened the text.

Lindsay: *Hey Mack, I wanted to say thanks for last night, it was a lot of fun. You're a great guy, but I think we can both agree that there's someone else you'd rather be dating, isn't there...*

I didn't know what the fuck to say to that. I thought I'd done well keeping my shit together around Chase. Yes, I bought her shoes but Lindsay and I had been a solid team in the bowling. We talked, we laughed ... as she said, we had a good time. But she still knew. Relief swept over me in a rush and I sagged on my stool.

Me: *That was not what I expected you to say. But I'm not going to be an even bigger asshole and disagree. I'm really sorry, I probably should have said no to the date from the beginning.*

Lindsay: *No, I'm glad we did it. Like I said, I had fun but I know when someone's not really into me. Wanting the outcome to be different doesn't make it that way. I'm sure I'll see you around x*

I read the exchange three times, trying to think of something to say, but she hadn't left a great deal of room for further conversation.

"That doesn't look like a texting the love of my life face ..." Harley said, her attention once again on me. "You wanna talk about it?"

"There is nothing to talk about." And there wasn't. I still felt like a dick for leading Lindsay on the way I did but she didn't seem to be a grudge-holder.

Harley studied me for a long moment, her whiskey eyes scanning, then promptly started talking about the guy she was with last night. He was hung like a horse (good for him) but sadly, didn't know how to use it, or anything else by the sound of it.

"I mean," she continued, "if your face is literally in a pussy, how is it so difficult to locate a clitoris? You know? I bet you know where it is, don't you?"

"Yes Harley, I'm aware of the location of a clitoris."

"Praise be. It's not that hard, is it?"

"Not if you're paying attention."

"Exactly! He told me he wasn't a virgin, but I'm not sure I believe him."

If she was in virgin territory, I was tempted to ask how old the guy was, but thought better of it because I didn't actually want to know the answer.

Thankfully, my food arrived and Harley was distracted by the arrival of a new guy at the bar so I was left to eat in peace. Well, relative peace, I almost choked on a piece of toast when she asked him if he knew where the clitoris was.

BY THE TIME I made it to Rudi that afternoon, the anxious energy that had kept me up most of the night had well and truly evaporated and an easy kind of contentment was warming my chest. Harley, outrageous as she was, had a lot to do with it. Her quiet, or not so quiet as it were, confidence in Chase, in me and Chase, was encouraging.

The fact I had not heard from the woman in question was of some concern but, whatever her answer, I didn't think it would come via text. Because I already knew the answer wouldn't be a simple yes or no. Brevity had never been a particular strength of Chase's and, if it was a yes (as I hoped it would be), there would be caveats.

I hung up my coat and bag in the office, taking a deep hit of Chase's scent that always permeated the small space. I considered tidying the desk, which was strewn with papers but had a feeling I'd disrupt some system I wasn't aware of. She existed in a perpetually state of barely organised chaos

Quiet and empty, Rudi Blue was one of my favorite places. I couldn't put my finger on what it was exactly. A sense of home, maybe, or pride in being part of creating this place from the ground up. Despite that feeling, deep down I'd always considered Rudi Chase's baby and not mine, not really. I knew she'd disagree with me, but that didn't change the fact that, as much as I loved Rudi, it wasn't my *thing*.

Sometimes I was convincedI'd never find my thing and, if that was the case, I'd be okay. I'd still die a happy man because I really did love my life.

Only maybe I had found it. If I had the balls to actually claim it. Pies. I fucking loved making pies. Orgasm-inducing pies, if Harley was to be believed. But there was a big difference between enjoying making pies in the privacy of my own home and actually doing it full-time. What the hell would I do? Open a pie shop? I snorted out a laugh. How the hell would I do that? I wasn't a chef, not like Nash, and I wasn't a business brain either, that was Chase's department. I was the one who went along for the ride. I guess I needed to decide if I was happy doing that forever

The thoughts continued to swim around my head as I went through the routine of setup and headed into the store room for more bottles. I should talk to Chase about it, except then it would be out there in the world and I knew she'd tell me to do it. That scared me more than anything, of not living up to what she thought of me.

I stopped short, weighed down with a crate, because there she was. She stopped on the opposite side of the bar, her eyes going wide. I took her in, boots, black jeans and her cherry red peacoat, dark hair wild from the wind outside. She was perfect, as always.

"Okay," she said, stuffing her hands deep into the pockets of her coat.

"Okay?"

A nod. "Okay. One date." And just like that, pies were the very last thing on my mind. "Don't smile yet," she continued. "I'm only agreeing to one date and I have stipulations."

I smiled wider. "Of course you do."

"You're still smiling." She arched an eyebrow.

"Because you've just said you'll go on a date with me." She said yes. I was going to be smiling until fucking Easter at this rate. I could tell she was nibbling the inside of her cheek to keep from smiling herself.

"I've said I'll go on a date with you *if*. If. Maybe you won't like the ifs." She crossed her arms, tipped her head to one side. I was really going to enjoy kissing that almost smirk clean off her face.

"Give me your ifs, Chastity."

She poked out her tongue. "First: it's only one date." *To begin with.* I gestured for her to continue. "Second: after our *one* date we go back to this." She waved a hand between us. "And third: friends, we are friends first, always."

I pretend to think for all of one second. "Done."

"Just like that?"

I set down the crate and started to close the space between us. "Just like that."

She backed up a step. "I've got one more."

"What's that?" I said with a laugh. I was still advancing and she was still retreating.

"I get to choose what we do." Her voice lacked the conviction it had before.

"Are you trying to get out of this?"

"No." She meant it.

"Well, I'm afraid I can't agree to that last one, sorry." I wasn't sorry, not in the slightest.

"Why not?"

"Because I have plans." It was a lie. I had no plans. I would though. And, more to the point, I wanted to be the one to plan this. Our first fucking date.

"Fine, you can have your plans." A pause as her eyes darted over my face and a smile tugged at her lips. "What are we going to do?"

"And ruin the surprise? No ma'am." I grinned. My mind started to sift through options, each one discarded as quickly as it popped up because none were good enough. How was I going to plan the kind of date that Chase deserved?

She opened her mouth, then closed it again and twisted her lips to the side. "You should probably get back to work."

"And you should probably go home. Day off and all."

" I have emails to respond to, lots and lots of emails. We're in demand, in case you didn't notice." Smartass.

"I did notice that, yes, but I'm pretty sure you can reply to emails at home, no?"

"I have paperwork, too."

"You always have paperwork."

"That's because you never do any of it."

We stood there, a couple of feet apart, grinning at each other for a long minute. I didn't know about her, but my mind was spinning. We were going on a date. An actual date. If someone had told me a month ago that Chase and I would be going on a date with one another I would have laughed in their face. Now, here we were. Going on a date that I now needed to plan. Since making the declaration last night, I hadn't let myself think about what we'd do just in case she said no. But she hadn't said no, she'd said yes.

"Weren't you going to do paperwork?" I asked as that crackling tension built around us.

Chase blinked, bringing an end to whatever movie had been playing in her head, and cleared her throat. "Yes, yep," she stuttered. "That's why I'm here." Then she was striding past me without a backwards glance. Maybe I needed to be planning more than one date, just in case.

15

CHASE

I HAD LONG AGO ACCEPTED that I was what some people would call a control freak. I'd never really considered this a bad thing because it had served me well most of my life. Right now, however, as I scratched a nonexistent itch on my thigh I was willing to admit it might not always be beneficial to need to be holding the reins in every situation.

Not only did I not have the reins for the date with Mack (the fact that was even a sentence I was saying was still mad), but he was giving me absolutely no clue as to what he had planned. This could be because he didn't yet have any plans, which would not surprise me in the slightest, or he was trying to torture me. It was difficult to know which was more likely. I had to believe he had something in mind. He'd told me to keep Monday open, but had given nothing else away. Time had genuinely crawled to date day. Yesterday I'd been convinced that I'd wake up today and it would be Sunday again, forever stuck in this hell of waiting. I had well and truly lost count of the number of times I'd imagined kissing him.

I'd already been awake for close to an hour by the time my

alarm went off. My mind rolling around and around. The only thing I had been told was that I needed to be home, ready for him to pick me up, at four. Four pm. A whole eight hours from now. Barre and brunch would take up a solid three of those, if I stretched it out with an extra mimosa or two. That still left five hours. I couldn't even go to Rudi because I would be refused entry thanks to Mack also organizing for Greyson and Micky to do this week's stock count. The man had thought of everything, apparently.

Except what I was going to do with a spare five hours. At least I'd make it to barre on time for once.

I DID NOT MAKE it to barre on time.

I was starting to think that maybe it was physically impossible for it to happen. I'd had over an hour to get myself together yet, between thinking about kissing Mack (again) and wandering aimlessly around my apartment in a daze, I lost track of time. As usual, I skidded into the studio and took up my place at the back of the class, Jeremy once again beside me as Lindsay stood in front ready to torture us all in the name of fitness.

It was a good thing she was so damn nice because otherwise I would consider procuring a voodoo doll and doing my worst because, holy Hell, the woman was a devil when she was in charge.

I slumped on my mat as the class finished. I'd been coming for over a year, shouldn't it be getting easier? Shouldn't I feel more in control of my gelatinous limbs by now? Maybe one class a week wasn't enough, maybe if I wanted to have an ass like Lindsay I'd need to come daily (and have different genetics)?

"Come on, Princess," Jeremy nudged me with his toe.

"Do not touch me with your feet, that's disgusting." The statement lacked the required venom. He did it again. "Dooooon't."

"I'm just going to keep doing it until you get your sorry ass up off the floor," he said, smiling like an angel as he prodded my ribs with his big toe. Swatting him away would require me to lift my arms, which was no longer possible.

"I live here now."

He laughed. "Do I need to drag you to brunch?"

"That would be great, thank you, I'm sure I can get a straw for my mimosa."

"Okay, come on … you can do this, up, get up." He slipped his arms under mine and hefted me to my feet. I only swayed for a second when he let me go. He dealt with my mat and weights like the gentleman he was as Lindsay appeared looking fresh as a fucking daisy.

"You did so well today, Chase!" she said, making me stand just a little straighter.

"Thank you," I said as Jeremy snorted out a laugh beside me.

"So, where are we headed? Huckleberry or Cream and Sugar?"

My first instinct was to say Cream and Sugar, I was becoming somewhat dependent on Harley's ice coffee. But I was also in the mood for haloumi, and would rather not sit under Harley's x-ray stare, so I said, "Huckleberry, let's go to Huckleberry. I'm craving the halloumi bagel." That was true, at least.

The three of us settled into a booth fifteen minutes later and I immediately ordered my halloumi bagel, a coffee, and a mimosa for good measure. I really needed the mimosa. Now that I was no longer distracted by my muscles liquifying, thoughts of Mack and our date had returned to the front of my mind and I was on the brink of hysteria. Part of me was desperate to talk about it, to ask for some advice, maybe, not that I knew what I'd ask. But that was out of the question. I was not going to start talking about one date. Because that's all it was going to be. One. Date. Singular. Uno. After tonight, I would tell Mack that I had fun (I assumed I was going to have fun, it was rare that I didn't have fun with him) but that we were better off as friends. Without question. I was absolutely not letting myself think about his promise for the end of the date. No way. Not if I wanted to keep my shit together.

As soon as my mimosa hit the table I downed it in one long gulp. Jeremy and Lindsay shared a look.

"Okay I have to ask..." Lindsay started, after a delicate sip of her own mimosa, and the hairs at the back of my neck prickled. "What's going on between you and Mack?"

"What!?" Too loud. I needed a second mimosa. I attempted to compose myself before asking, "Why would you ask that?"

She smiled. "Look, we had fun, he's a great guy, but it was pretty clear that his interest lies elsewhere."

"No, that's–I don't–it's not—" Oh, god, I was going to be sick. I didn't want to talk about me and Mack. I definitely didn't want to talk about me and Mack with Lindsay, who he'd been on a fucking date with a week ago. That was a dick move.

"Chase, it's okay." She reached across the table and gave my hand a squeeze. "It was hard to not see it. I mean, he bought you shoes."

"He did do that, yes," I conceded. "But that's just him. I bet he would have bought you shoes too, if he knew your size."

She smiled, it held only the slightest bit of pity, like I was woefully underestimating the situation. "Maybe, but I'm pretty sure it's not just him, it's him *with you*."

"It wasn't—it didn't mean anything. We're friends." It wasn't technically a lie, we were going on one date, and that wasn't going to change the fact we were friends. Neither Jeremy or Lindsay looked particularly convinced but they didn't push the point and I spent the next two hours all but mainlining mimosas and halloumi.

I was well and truly buzzed by the time I got home. After a shower, during which I washed my hair and did a full body scrub and moisturize, I glanced at the clock. Still almost three hours to go. When did time start going so maddeningly slow?

I paused in front of my closet, wondering what I should wear on a date when I had no idea what we were actually doing.

Me: *I need some information.*

Mack: *Good afternoon, Chastity. Information regarding what, exactly?*

I laughed, while also wanting to slap him.

Me: *The date, Milton. I need information regarding the date.*

Mack: *Such as?*

He was taking far too much pleasure in this. I could imagine the angelic and infuriating look on his face all too well.

Me: *Are we going to be indoors or outdoors? Sitting, or moving around. How am I supposed to get dressed if I don't know these things?*

Mack: *Does that mean you're naked right now? Are you naked texting?*

I rolled my eyes heavenward.

Me: *That's not a thing.*

Mack: *You could make it one.*

Me: *Not interested in being the founder of naked texting, but thank you for thinking of me.*

Mack: *I'm always thinking of you.*

My heart tripped over itself. How the hell was I going to go back to just friends if he kept saying things like that?

Mack: *And we're going to be outdoors. But you might work up a sweat ;) Is that enough information?*

Me: *It's pervy, but yes, it's enough.*

Mack: *See you in a couple of hours x*

I was smiling as I threw the phone onto my bed. This feeling warming my chest was not one date and then back to friends. This was more than that; much more, if I was being honest, and it scared the ever-loving shit out of me. I wasn't used to being invested like this. But how could I be anything else with him?

My eyes found the clock on the wall, again, and I wondered if it were possible for the thing to be moving backwards.

After staring into my closet for so long my eyes started to blur, I settled on a pair of black jeans, a long sleeved shirt and a woolen jumper because outdoors in December in New York required layers. I stuffed my feet into my favorite boots and went to the kitchen to scrub down the counter in a last ditch effort to distract myself from the fact I was going on a date with my best friend.

AT PRECISELY 3:57, my buzzer went off. I knew it was precisely 3:57 because I was staring at the clock. And as soon as the sound filled my apartment, my heart took off at a gallop. It didn't matter how many times I reminded myself that it was just Mack. The same guy I'd known since freshman year of high school. The same guy I'd seen yesterday, and the day before that, and the day before that. My body didn't care. My body had gone well and truly rogue. One sentence was swirling around my head, making a mockery of all that 'it's just Mack' business.

Because I'll be kissing you at the end of it.

Those words had been taunting me. All. Day. Long.

And now, here we were. It was go-time.

I grabbed my coat and bag, took one last semi-calming breath and pulled the door shut behind me. I was going on a date with Mack. This was actually happening.

He was propped against a pole as I stepped out into the brisk fall wind, and god-damn he looked good. It still baffled me that I had been looking at him all these years and not actually *seen* him. Granted, I had always known he was hot, it was one of those objective truths: waffles trump pancakes, whiskey is best served neat, Mack is hot. But that hotness had never set off the butterflies that were currently wrestling in my sternum. Never made my palms clammy with nerves. Never made me want to mark my territory. And here I was now, tempted to rub myself all over him like a cat. This did not bode well for my one-date-only stipulation.

My eyes drank him in; from the scuffed black Vans on his

feet, the straight cut—but not too tight—blue jeans, past his well-loved coat with the hood of his sweatshirt poking out the top, to the navy blue beanie on his head that was low enough to cover his ears but not to tuck away all of those stubborn, dirty blond curls.

Holy hell I was in trouble.

"Cheese." I barely heard him over the rushing of blood in my ears, and stood mesmerized as he pushed off the street sign and stalked towards me. His long legs ate up the space between us in three strides and then he was bending to drop a kiss on my cheek before his arms wrapped me in a hug.

I sank into his chest, letting the familiar scents of sunshine, the ocean, and whiskey settle my jangled nerves. Yes, we were going on a date. And yes, at the end of it he was going to kiss me. But we were still us.

"How you doin'?" The words were muffled against my hair and I shrugged in response. It was easier than trying to put these feelings into words.

"I know what you mean," he said after a beat and pulled back, but kept his arms locked around my back. "What do you say we do this thing?"

"Does that mean I get to know what we're doing?"

"Nope." He shifted, tucked me into his side with one arm draped over my shoulders. "You can stay in the dark a little longer."

"Because you enjoy torturing me?"

"Maybe ..."

I jabbed an elbow into his ribs and he yelped but didn't let me go.

It wasn't until we got off the subway at Rockefeller that I got an idea of what we might be doing.

"We're going full tourist, aren't we?" Excitement fizzed under my skin.

His eyes held the slightest hint of nerves. "Is that a good thing?"

I pursed my lips. "That depends."

"On what?" Now he looked more genuinely concerned and I focused very hard on not smiling.

"On whether or not there will be hot cocoa."

A grin split his face and I almost choked on my tongue. "There will definitely be hot cocoa."

"Then it's definitely a good thing," I managed to say, although it was a good deal breathier than I intended as Mack's smile turned seductive. I felt it all the way down to my toes, and also a couple of feet further north.

The rink came into view, skaters already spinning around the icy surface, the huge tree standing proudly behind them. New York did a lot of things well, but Christmas might just be the jewel in its crown.

I remembered the first Christmas Mom and I spent in New York, we'd not long lost Peggy and I hadn't settled into our new neighborhood. New York was big and loud and there were so many people everywhere. I loved our house but I would have preferred to be just about anywhere else.

Then Mom took me to see the tree at Rockefeller and everything else faded into the background. I could have stood there for days, counting the lights, wishing Peggy could be seeing it all, too.

I shook off the memory as we joined the short queue for skates, and Mack produced a thick pair of socks from one of his pockets.

"What else are you hiding?"

"Not a pair of skates, unfortunately ..."

"But socks?"

"I thought they could provide some extra padding between you and the foreign footwear."

I laughed. "Thank you."

"Anything for you, Chastity."

"So, ice skating and hot cocoa huh? Very PG of you."

"Nothing like some wholesome entertainment."

"Are you going to walk me home, too?"

"I'm a gentleman, aren't I?"

"I suppose time will tell." Right now, I was sincerely hoping that he was not too much of a gentleman. We were only having the one date, so we might as well make it a good one, right? I stopped the train of thought, because there was no way I was going to get through the ice skating, let alone the hot cocoa, if I let my mind wander to what happened after that.

16

MACK

CHASE WAS WATCHING ME, a smile playing around the corners of her lips. Those perfect fucking lips. They were stained red, the same shade as a ripe cherry, making me want to bite and suck. I wanted to swallow the noises she'd make. Wanted to feel her breath on me. The fact I had not kissed her yet was a show of some serious restraint on my behalf.

"What are you doing?" she asked, now all out grinning and my heart gave an unsteady thump. "Earth to Mack? Are you coming?"

I coughed. Not coming, but definitely talking down a situation.

Her eyes narrowed like she suspected the direction of my thoughts. "You do know how to skate, right?"

"Of course," I said with a scoff, like I wasn't lying through my teeth.

"Then get your ass over here."

Why the hell did I think this was a good idea? I'd had visions of Chase holding onto me as we wobbled around the rink. The two of us tumbling, her falling on top of me, her nose brushing mine. And now I was thinking about kissing her again. It was basically a movie playing on a loop in my head.

What I hadn't considered was that Chase would know what she was doing. Judging by the way she laced up her skates and walked with even, balanced strides toward the ice, it wasn't going to be Chase who needed holding up.

She stepped out onto the ice and pushed off, wobbling a little before she found her feet. It looked easy when she was doing it, gliding smoothly before turning on a dime and coming back to the rink's edge. Her smile was wide and eyes bright. She knew what she was doing, and I was about to look like a complete idiot.

I shuffled towards the edge, Chase's eyes following my movement. She held out a hand as I took a tentative step onto the ice and immediately felt my weight shift unsteadily. My feet splayed underneath me as I tried and failed to get my balance. I lunged for the wall.

"You can't skate," she said. It was no longer a question. "Why would you suggest coming skating on our date if you can't actually do it?"

"I'm fine." It couldn't be that hard. With one hand anchored to the wall I tried to make my feet move forward. And ended up on my ass. I managed to contain my yelp at the cold biting through my jeans.

She slapped a hand over her mouth, only just covering the laugh. "Oh my god. You are terrible. Like, worse than me bowling."

"I wouldn't go that far." She'd barely managed to hit ten pins during almost two games. There was no way I was that bad. She was now attempting to skate backward a little. Of course she was.

"How are you so bad at this?" she asked.

"I'm not that bad," I said, pulling myself back up only to wobble again. It would get easier, it had to get easier, didn't it?

"You're like a baby giraffe."

I did not appreciate the comparison, no matter how accurate it might be. "Thank you for that confidence boost."

"Sorry, I'm sorry." She came to my side, the picture of grace and balance. "I just–you have good balance. I've seen it. You surf. You skateboard."

"That's true, but neither of those things require me to have knives strapped to my feet."

She smiled, with the slightest slice of pity. "Fair point. You want me to give you some pointers?"

"My own private lesson?" It might have sounded seductive... had I not once again landed on my ass after attempting to move an inch away from the wall.

"You could certainly use it."

For the next forty minutes, Chase walked me through the basics of skating. She was so good I just found myself watching her glide around. She could turn and spin and skate backwards with deceiving ease. By the end of my private lesson I was at least fifty percent better than when I started. Although, granted, the bar had been extremely low to begin with.

"Is it time for cocoa?" I asked as we completed a slow lap of the rink. Chase would skate ahead then double back and circle me.

"Yes! With the giant marshmallows?"

"Would it be a legitimate hot cocoa without one?"

She beamed at me. She'd done away with her coat and sweater and was in a red and white long-sleeved shirt that hugged the lines of her body, like a hot as hell *Where's Waldo*. God, she was beautiful, radiant. If I wasn't in danger of taking us both down I would have grabbed her and kissed her right now.

Chase offered to get the cocoas, being steadier on her skates than I was, and I watched as numerous heads turned in her direction as she walked away.

In the last week I had tried not to think too much about how it would actually feel to be on a date with her. Part of me was still having trouble believing that it was even happening. Then she'd take my hand or smile at me—a new kind of smile— and it hit me in the center of my chest. It was happening. We were here. I already had an idea for date number two.

"Hot cocoa for the gentleman." She dropped down beside me and handed over one of the enormous cups with an equally large marshmallow balanced on top.

"If I was really a gentleman, I probably should have been the one to get the cocoas."

She let out a very unladylike snort. "And have you spill them, or drop my marshmallow, on account of your baby giraffe legs? No, thank you."

I laughed as she took a sip. The low groan that followed had my muscles locking up.

"So, how exactly did you get so good at this?" I asked to keep my mind off how else I could get her to make those noises.

She chewed thoughtfully on a bite of marshmallow before answering. "Glen, no, Graham, one of Mom's boyfriends. His daughter, Amber, was a figure skater."

"Seriously?"

"Uh-huh." She took another sip. "I was ten, maybe, she was a couple of years older, and I was just in awe of her. We were at the same school so Graham would pick us up and take us to the rink most afternoons. I don't even know if Amber was that good, but at the time I certainly thought she was, and she had the coolest skates. They were metallic pink and gold leopard print, with gold laces. I had to use the hire skates, they smelled weird and never fit right—that might be where my aversion to bowling shoes started." She paused, took another bite of marshmallow, and I sat transfixed. How did I not know any of this?

"Anyway, I dreamed of Amber's skates, of any skates that were just mine really. I begged Mom for a pair of my own but she always shot me down and then she and Graham broke up. So we packed up and moved like we always did. I never saw Amber again and I don't know if I've been back to a rink since. Maybe a couple of times in middle school."

"You haven't skated since middle school and you're still this good?"

She gave a small, shy smile. "Muscle memory, I guess. And I'm rusty."

"You do not look rusty."

"I was tagging along to the rink four days a week for almost a year. I picked it up. I even got into a summer intensive program, but the break up happened before the summer and Mom sent me to some god awful sleep away camp instead."

"You were robbed," I said and she nodded.

"Totally robbed. I didn't speak to her for over a month. I was so pissed."

"And that was it? You just never went again?"

She shrugged. "I was busy, I don't know if you remember this about me, Mack, but I was kind of a nerd."

"Funnily enough, I do remember that." Chase was probably the reason I didn't fail my classes. She always managed to make studying seem fun, or maybe it was just being around her that made Calculus and English Lit seem more interesting than they actually were.

Everything was better when I was with her. Even falling on my ass on ice over and over again.

I took another sip of my drink and noticed a smudge of marshmallow dust on the tip of her nose.

"You've got a little something..."

"What?" She said around a mouthful of marshmallow and wiped both her cheeks.

"No, it's—here." My hand came up to her cheek sending a shot of electricity down my arm and my thumb swiped over her nose. "All done." I dropped my hand but Chase was now staring at me. The gold flecks in her irises bright and shining. My pulse drummed hard in my throat as her attention dropped down to my mouth. Then she was leaning forward, one hand landed on my cheek a second before her lips brushed over mine. It was the barest of touches but it was everything. The marshmallow and chocolate were so much sweeter for being on her lips. I wasn't sure I'd drink hot cocoa again and not think of this moment. Her fingers curled into the hair at the nape of my neck sending goosebumps down my arms. She pressed in, bringing us as close as we could get while seated side by side. I wanted desperately to pull her over my lap, feel the heat of her even through our layers of clothing. But we were still in public, surrounded by tourists and families.

She broke away, only a fraction, and smiled. I could feel it rather than see it, as her forehead rested against mine.

"I thought I was supposed to be the one kissing you at the end of the night."

A puff of chocolate-scented laughter escaped. "I guess I couldn't wait that long. You were being too much of a gentleman."

"I didn't know there was such a thing."

"Oh, there definitely is."

"I'll keep that in mind." But it wasn't going to change the way the night was ending.

We both straightened away from each other and I noticed a pink stain across her high cheekbones as she tipped her cup to her lips. If it was up to me, I'd sit here and kiss her for the rest of the night, studying the shape of her lips with my own, but we were still in public and I had a feeling Chase wasn't going to call it quits on the skating early.

Once our cocoas were empty and marshmallows eaten we headed back onto the ice. I lasted all of one lap before I bowed out, took off the death skates and settled at the side of the rink to watch Chase. With each lap she gained more confidence, her turns became sharper and flowed seamlessly into skating backwards. I could have watched her all fucking night, even with soggy jeans and numb toes. It was like seeing a secret side of her, one that had been hiding just below the surface all these years. It made me wonder what else was under there, waiting to be discovered.

She skated over and kicked up some ice as she stopped with the edges of her skates.

"Show off."

"I nearly took out a kid," she said with a laugh.

"They probably deserved it."

"Probably." She grinned, winding her hair up into a knot. A few flyaways were stuck to her temples.

"I told you you'd work up a sweat."

"That you did."

I reached for her and she slid into the circle of my arms without hesitation, tipping her head just enough for our lips to meet. Every time was like the first and I found myself torn between wanting to savor and devour.

"We're scandalizing children," she whispered.

"It's their own fault for not being at home already," I mumbled against her mouth and she laughed.

"Come on, a sweat wasn't the only thing I worked up, I'm starving."

Regrettably, I let her go and, with the usual Chase

efficiency, she was out of her skates and back in her shoes within minutes.

"Where to?" she asked, fitting herself under my arm like a piece of myself I hadn't known I'd been missing.

AT SOME POINT, between my teens and twenties, kissing had become a means to an end, rather than an end in and of itself. As I pressed Chase against her front door, my hands in her hair and our lips fused together, I couldn't help but think that was a damn shame. But, then, I couldn't remember the last person who I'd wanted to kiss quite as much as I wanted to kiss Chase. She panted against my mouth, her arms hooking over my shoulders to bring herself higher as one leg wrapped around my waist.

We were dry humping against her door like a pair of teenagers and it was the hottest thing I'd done in maybe a decade.

Her fingers tunneled up into my hair as my hands drifted down over her ass and squeezed. She said something that was more moan than actual words, and then—

"Inside," she growled.

"Not tonight." I shifted and pinned her tighter to the door with one leg between her thighs. Nimble fingers found their way under the edge of my shirt and I groaned as they explored. But it didn't matter how good all of this felt, it wasn't going any further tonight.

Her eyes fluttered open, pupils blown out with lust. It made me weak. "Wait—you—you're not coming inside?"

"Not on the first date," I said with as much strength as I could manage.

She blinked twice. I could practically hear her wheels turning. "But—but there was only supposed to be one date?"

I ducked my head into the crook of her neck and dragged my lips over the skin behind her ear. It smelled just as good as I always thought it would. Her head dropped to the side allowing me better access. Would it be out of line to give her a hickey? Did people still give hickeys? "Mmm ... so you said." I whispered, tasting her. "Are you still sticking to that, then?"

"It's probably a good idea." Her voice shook as her fingers bit into my shoulders. "Not to—ah—complicate things."

I met her eyes, cupped her face in my hands. "This isn't complicated, Chase. It's just you and me."

She leaned into my touch, kissed my palm. "So, if I agree to another date, you'll come inside?" God, if she had any idea the amount of restraint it was taking to not walk her through that door right now.

"Nope, no sex until date five." I was only regretting the decision a little.

"Are you serious?" She was looking at me like I'd lost my mind, and maybe I had, but that didn't change the fact that I'd made this decision and I was sticking to it. For better or worse. I was pretty sure it was going to be for better, though.

"Uh-huh," I murmured and she melted against me as I resumed kissing a slow path along her neck. Her thighs clenched around mine, but not even the heat of her was going to make me crack.

"B—but why?" she whined and I chuckled against her neck. She sounded like she was about to cry. I made a slow trip back up to her mouth, tasting, savoring, I'd never kissed anyone who tasted like Chase did. It was some distinct flavor that I wasn't sure I'd ever pin down. Her tongue teased then pushed forward and I groaned, letting my hands slide back into her hair. I would happily kiss her until the end of time. We broke apart, panting.

"Why?" she said again, voice pleading, eyes wide and her

hands tangled in the front of my shirt. I felt her desperation acutely, but it still wasn't going to change my mind.

I dragged my thumb along the plush pillow of her lower lip and before I could pull away she sucked the tip of it into her mouth. My eyes rolled back in my head.

"Because you're worth waiting for," I managed to choke out as her tongue swirled. I was released with a wet pop and refused to think about how that tongue would feel elsewhere.

"We've been friends since we were fourteen, I'd say that's enough waiting, wouldn't you?" She reached up and dragged her teeth down my earlobe. I shuddered and pressed her tighter to the door. I really didn't want to lose control of this situation, but she wasn't making it easy to keep my shit together.

"And you've wanted to have sex with me that whole time?" I asked, reasonably confident the answer was no.

Her hips pressed forward. "If I say yes, will it get me into your pants tonight?"

She was clearly intent on killing me, but I would not be broken. "It might, if I didn't know it was a lie."

She tugged on my hair, bringing my face in line with her. "Mack, come on. You can't be serious. We're adults, we do not need to abide by some expired dating convention. If you're worried about me respecting myself in the morning, I promise I will. I might even respect myself more because we'd be naked." She wiggled her eyebrows, and some of the heat rolling beneath my skin cooled. I kissed the tip of her nose.

"And what if I don't?"

A crease appeared between her brows. "What if you don't what?"

My eyes roamed her face as my stomach gave a nauseous roll. "What if I want to be able to respect myself?"

She opened her mouth. Closed it again. "You—you haven't

been on two dates with anyone, let alone five, for at least three years."

A prickling sensation crawled over my skin. "It's closer to five, actually, and that is kind of the point." I tried to pull away but she wouldn't let me, she just held me there, at the mercy of those piercing eyes.

"Well, when you put it like that..." She paused. "Do you not trust me? You think I'm going to leave in the middle of the night or something?" The look on her face promised violence, but I didn't think it was aimed at me.

I smiled and smoothed a thumb over the pinch between her brows. "I trust you more than anyone. It's about me, Chase, not you." I kissed her again and she once again melted against my chest. I would happily live in this moment with my hands on her ass and her tongue in my mouth until I died. But I needed to go, I needed to put a little bit of space between us so I didn't go doing something I told myself I wouldn't.

I broke our kiss, untangled her arms from my neck and took three steps backwards, opening a wide wedge of space between us. I wanted to close it again immediately, but I wouldn't. Not yet. "I'll see you tomorrow."

"Mmm, yep, tomorrow," she mumbled, eyes glazed and leaning heavily against the door at her back.

"Sweet dreams, Chase."

17

CHASE

SWEET DREAMS.

Sweet.

Fucking.

Dreams.

I was so wound up, I'd be lucky to take the edge off even with my favorite toy. And there was something about self-servicing while thinking of your best friend that was a step over some invisible line. There was no coming back from that, was there? He'd probably know it the minute I saw him, seeing as how he was so adept at reading me by this point. I wouldn't have been surprised if he correctly deciphered my *I brought myself to orgasm while imagining your head between my legs* face.

No, there would be no sweet dreams tonight. They were going to be downright filthy.

I guzzled down a large glass of water that did very little to temper the heat still bubbling in my blood. Date five. No sex until date five. It didn't mean we couldn't do other things instead. But already I wanted to feel him. Feel us, like that. I had to wait until date fucking five? There wasn't even supposed to be a date two. And honestly, at this rate I'd be in love with him by date five. Which would make the inevitable end that much harder to bear. But he promised we'd be friends first. Friends always. We could still do that, right? Yes, it would be strange at first, already I knew that seeing him tomorrow and not immediately kissing his face off was going to be a challenge, but we'd manage. We'd make it work.

I smiled. He took me skating. My feet already had a long forgotten ache in them as I kicked off my boots. I'd be lucky to walk without a limp tomorrow after waking up all those muscles that hadn't been used for over twenty years. I hadn't even realized how much I missed skating until we were there and that giddy excitement rose up in my chest. I could have stayed there all night. I was already itching to go again.

I collapsed backwards onto my bed, grinning at the ceiling, as one hand coming up to brush over my mouth. The feel of Mack's kisses lingered. The scratch of his stubble. The slide of his fingers through my hair. I could so easily lose myself in him. In us. I knew I would happily, enthusiastically, welcome the oblivion.

Of course, he had left the ball squarely in my court. If I said we needed to stop here, at dry humping that was better than a lot of the actual sex I'd had, I knew he'd respect the decision, even if he didn't like it. But did I want to stop now? Could I? The pulse between my thighs said no. That pulse wanted to feel more than just his thigh grinding through layers of denim.

The problem was his five date rule. If that hadn't been laid down I could have asked for one more date and lured him into bed. I could still try it, but I didn't want him to think this was just about sex for me. It wasn't, not by a long shot. But knowing how he kissed had given a very tantalizing indication of how everything else would be. And that was ... mind boggling.

Time for a cold shower.

I woke up the following morning with my hair plastered to my face and breath heaving like I'd just run a marathon. My dreams, as expected, had been of the naked variety and starring my best friend. If he was anything like he had been in my mind, he was going to be *incredible*.

Thanks to the filthy dreams, my sleep hadn't exactly been restful. As tempted as I was to stay in bed, the chance of it making me feel any more relaxed were slim while Mack was still on my mind. So I rolled out of bed and straight into a cold shower to douse any residual lustiness.

No amount of cold water was going to stop me thinking about the date, though. And the kisses. And the way Mack looked at me. The whole thing felt like a dream, and not the lusty kind—the perfect kind. The kind that made me think maybe this thing between us wasn't destined to end. Maybe we could make it work. Was that too much to hope for after only one date? Possibly. Probably. God, I didn't even know.

The thought of an actual long-term relationship usually made me break out in hives. But this wasn't a relationship with just anyone, this was a relationship with Mack. He knew all of my crazy already because he'd had a front row seat to most of it. I couldn't quite fathom why he'd still want me after seeing all that. Yet he hadn't been scared away. But sticking by a friend was different to wanting to be in an actual relationship with that person, right? Would he eventually decide that it was too much? That I was too much?

I slumped against the vanity, staring at my reflection as I brushed my teeth. What would it be like to stand beside someone else every morning and do this? Make coffee. Eat breakfast. Do nothing in particular. Would all those mundane life moments start to feel different with another person to share them with?

I was getting ahead of myself. I'd never even let another person in my shower (I'd broken up with more than one for the mere suggestion) and now I was thinking about us living together? It was time to get a hold of myself. One date. We'd been on one date. And yes, it was good—the best date I'd ever been on, if I was being honest—but it was still only one date. I hadn't decided if there was going to be another.

Liar.

A second date was a risk for more than one reason. First, it would be difficult to top yesterday's date. He really had set the bar high. Second, another date would make my feelings even more tangled than they already were. As I'd said to Mack last night, it would increase complications. But maybe he was right, maybe it wasn't that complicated, because it was just us. Me and him. Him and me.

Could it really be that simple?

If I'd thought the temptation to talk about the date was bad yesterday, before it had even happened, it was at a whole other level now. Like yesterday, I wasn't entirely sure what I wanted to say, or to whom. I'd never been one of those people who had a lot of friends. It hadn't really bothered me before, but right now it would have been nice to talk all this out with a girlfriend, just to see what they'd say. A little advice, maybe? But it was fine, I didn't actually need it, I was just feeling weird.

A distraction, that was what I actually needed, not advice, because what could anyone say? Nothing. Nothing helpful, anyway, so I just needed to take my mind off everything.

It wasn't until I was standing in the middle of my living room in a pair of yoga pants and an oversized sweatshirt that it occurred to me my usual distraction was work.

"God, that's sad," I said to my empty apartment. I was sure that, at some point, I'd had hobbies, things I did for fun aside from study and work. Skating had been one of them, for a while at least, but I just stopped. It had made me so happy, and I just stopped. Granted, it would have been difficult when we moved, and I didn't know anyone. I didn't remember missing it, not really. But as soon as I stepped onto the ice yesterday, it was like some part of me that had been asleep woke up.

My nose burned. Was I about to cry right now? Over ice skating? I sniffed. It wasn't just about ice skating, though. I'd been working and working and working for years and I hadn't stopped long enough to see that maybe there was something missing. Maybe I was a little bit unhappy, lonely. It was easy to convince myself otherwise, I saw my best friend everyday, my life felt full, but maybe it wasn't as full as I liked to think?

I brushed the rogue tears off my cheeks and shook out my shoulders. All this thinking on an empty stomach and not enough sleep was making my head hurt. I needed food. And coffee.

After a brief exploration of my kitchen cabinets, it was clear that the food and the coffee would need to come from somewhere that was not my apartment. I would just have to go foraging in the wilds of Williamsburg.

I pulled open the door, ready to devour the first food I came across, and found Mack standing there, one hand raised to knock and the other balancing a coffee tray and a large paper bag. My heart stuttered in my chest the same way it did when I saw him yesterday because he was just so fucking beautiful it made me want to cry, and I could have stared at him all day long. I also wanted to kiss him, very, very badly.

"Hi."

"Hey," he said, eyes darting down to my mouth then coming back up. "Are you okay? Have you been crying?"

"Not crying, I'm fine, great, I'm great. Why–uh–what are you doing here?"

He dropped a kiss on my cheek that sent a warm tingle down my spine and walked inside like everything was completely normal, like he hadn't pinned me to this exact door last night and almost kissed me into next year. "Thought you might be hungry."

I stared after him, then closed the door and followed into the kitchen. "And you just happened to be in the neighborhood?" Our apartments weren't actually that far from one another, but I still hadn't expected the house call—not that I wasn't appreciative of it.

"Nope, went to Cream and Sugar, have you tasted their cinnamon buns? They're out of control. I got a couple of bagels, too."

"And coffee?"

"What is breakfast without coffee?" Indeed. "Iced for you." He handed over the large to-go cup. "I still don't understand how you can drink that in December."

I took a long sip, perching on a stool to watch as he unloaded the contents of the bag across my small kitchen island. I almost asked if I'd forgotten a meeting but I held my tongue because I didn't want to burst this bubble where Mack spontaneously brought me breakfast in my most desperate hour of need. I wasn't sure what I'd done to deserved him. He was too good for me.

"What?" The word shoved me out of the growing fantasy in my head.

"What. Nothing."

"You were just staring into space with a dopey smile on your face."

"No I wasn't." I was staring at his chest, willing his shirt to magically disappear. Heat rose in my cheeks and he smiled. "I was thinking that I need to add coffee to my grocery list so I don't need to go all the way to Cream and Sugar for this." I wiggled the cup, enjoying the rattle of ice despite the aforementioned incompatible weather outside.

"You are an artist with cocktails, my friend, but let's not pretend you could make a coffee like that in this kitchen." He gestured around the cramped space.

"And what exactly is wrong with my kitchen?"

"It doesn't have Harley in it. Seriously, that woman does something with coffee that no one else can."

"Maybe she sprinkles a little heroine on top, keeps you coming back."

"Maybe," he agreed and took a large bite of bagel.

I picked up one of the pieces, oozing egg yolk and crispy bacon peeking out from between the perfectly toasted, golden brown halves, and my mouth watered.

"So..." Mack started as he swallowed his mouthful and I tensed. Was he going to say that yesterday was fun but he'd had some time to think overnight and maybe it would be better for things to not go any further? It was too complicated, I knew it, I'd said as much, and he'd realized it too after he'd slept on the idea.

"Our new staff members have worked out better than I expected, especially Samson—I seriously thought that guy was going to quit on day one—but we still need at least two more."

I gaped at him, my mouth still mostly full of chewed bagel.

"What? I figured seeing as we missed our weekly meeting yesterday I'd save you the trip to Rudi later, don't even try and deny you weren't going to come in."

"You got me," I mumbled and was rewarded with his triumphant smile, which shifted into something more wolfish the longer he watched me.

"What else would I be here to talk about?" He rounded the counter, coffee and bagels forgotten as his attention locked onto my mouth.

"Nothing. That, Rudi. About staff. More people, we need..." The garbled sentence trailed off to nothing as he stood over me, eyes dark like the deepest parts of the ocean. I would happily drown in all that hunger and want.

"Did you think..." he whispered, hands coming up to my face, one thumb grazing my lip. "I was here for a different kind of meal?" Oh God. His voice was low and husky and I was light headed with lust. Our mouths hovered a breath apart for a long moment. I closed the distance when I couldn't take it any more, and we met in a duet of moaned appreciation. Why on earth had we not been doing this all along? Why had I been fighting this? There was a reasonable answer somewhere in the back of my head but right now it was barely a whisper, much too quiet in comparison to the roar of my need for him. My arms wound around his neck pulling our chests flush and he lifted me onto the counter. I needed his mouth. His hands. All of him.

One arm snaked around my back as his lips explored across my cheek, then jaw, and down my neck. Teeth teased then sunk into soft flesh, any sting quickly soothed by the sweep of his tongue.

My fingers found skin under the edge of his shirt, discovering the smooth muscle that spanned his back as my thighs squeezed at his waist in a vain effort to relieve the growing pressure at my core. Did this count as date two? Could I have him naked in a matter of days if every meal counted as a new date?

His mouth climbed back to mine, tongue sinking inside, and I was lost. To him. With him. All I could do was hold on and hope I came out the other side.

"I've been thinking about that all morning," he whispered as our kiss broke, his forehead resting against mine. I licked my lips, breath short, chest heaving. I knew what he meant, I'd been thinking about it too, even before I was conscious of it.

"Miranda."

"Mir–what? Who's Miranda?" I asked as he stepped back, leaving me slumped on the counter.

"And Henry. They were the two from our interviews who just missed out right?" He was straight back to business and my brain was still squarely focused on getting him naked. I rubbed a hand over my face and straightened up.

"Yes, Henry and Miranda."

"I'll call them today, see if they still need work."

"Great, perfect." I picked up my coffee and took an icy slurp.

18

MACK

I SHOULDN'T HAVE COME to Chase's. I should have waited for her to come to Rudi Blue, which she inevitably would have at some point today. Because, now that I was here, I didn't want to leave. Now that I was here, all I wanted to do was touch her, kiss her, until neither of us remembered our own names. But I couldn't, because I needed to take this slow. Well, as slow as possible without us both losing our minds. Or maybe that was the point? To leave us both so mindless with need that it was the only thing left.

Leaving last night had been an act of restraint I hadn't been sure I was capable of. But I did it. I wanted to sink into her and go to that place where there was nothing but the two of us, but I left. I left because, if I was being honest, I was scared. I was still scared. Of her seeing me the way others had. Deep down I knew she wouldn't, hoped like hell she wouldn't, but old wounds felt raw in the face of this feeling that was already growing in my chest.

Then there was the fact that I didn't want to scare *her* off. Granted, she didn't seem like she'd run right now. No, right now she looked more likely to jump me, which made focusing on work all the more difficult. I didn't know when, or if, that might change, though. So, we were focusing on work because if I kept kissing her there was no way we were going to make it to date five—and I had every intention of doing that.

"I want to plan the next date," she said, still swirling the icy slurry of coffee in her cup. Was this why people drank iced coffee? Purely to shake the ice around? I tempered my smile at the fact she wanted to organize a date. Not that I could let her have number two.

"No can do, Cheese, I already have plans." This time it was true. If I was smart I'd drag it out, wait until Monday when we both had the whole day off so I could enjoy her, and our time together. Unfortunately, I was impatient. Waiting a full week was not an option. "What are you doing Thursday?"

"Working, same as you," she said with a shrug.

"And before that?" I tore off some cinnamon scroll and dropped it into my mouth—butter, sugar, and cinnamon exploding across my tongue.

Her eyes followed the movement, she pursed her lips. "I could be available for the right offer."

"Is that right?"

"Mmm-hmm ..." She hummed, full, red lips wrapped around her straw.

"Then I suppose I'll have to provide the right offer."

We were quiet for a long moment, watching one another before she said, "And will I be given adequate detail beforehand?"

"I think that can be arranged."

She was only just holding onto her smile. "Good to know. I want to be in charge of the next one, then."

My eyebrows shot up, excitement making my heart beat

faster. "You want to lock in date three before we've even been on number two?"

She shrugged. "There doesn't seem to be much point in pretending we won't get to five, now, does there?"

"I suppose not." I tried to sound cool, but probably failed. "You can have three but I've got four. And five." I received an indignant look.

"How do I only end up being able to plan one date in this scenario?"

"Are you saying we're just going to stop at five?" I asked, relieved my voice didn't betray the nerves behind the question.

Her lips curled into a slow smile as she looked at me through her lashes and said, "Stop counting maybe ..." If I hadn't already been in love with her, now it was official. My heart had clearly missed the *we're taking it slow* memo.

Not quite two hours later, I left Chase's apartment with a wide grin plastered across my face. Once again it had been difficult, dragging myself away, but it needed to happen or I'd be there all day. I was never going to get sick of kissing that woman, I was sure of it. I couldn't remember the last time I had just kissed anyone without the expectation of it going further. Deep, unhurried kisses that made my head spin and my stomach dip. I was drunk and high on her. It had not just been kisses though, we had also managed to get through a decent amount of work. All of Chase's outstanding to-dos had been dealt with, or at least assigned, mostly to her because she was an unapologetic control freak. And because I wanted to keep kissing her, until the end of time, preferably, I didn't fight it.

I started walking towards the courts to meet Hunter, my mind throwing up pictures of her straddling my lap on the couch. Two days. I had two days to plan our next date. The ideas were there but they required refinement and execution. Excitement tingled through my chest. It had never been like this, not that I was really surprised, because it had never been with Chase. She changed everything.

A familiar silhouette in a passing car had me doing a double take and nearly tripping over a dog. I pulled out my phone and Pip answered on the second ring.

"Hey little brother, what's up?" She sounded weird, distracted.

"Nothin'. What are you up to? I thought I just saw you on Kingsland, near Chase's apartment."

"That would be difficult, considering I'm in the office." A driver laying on the horn echoed down the street and through the phone. I looked in the direction of the car but it had disappeared into traffic. Was Pip lying? But what reason could she possibly have to lie about that?

"Sorry Mack, I'm about to walk into a meeting, can I call you back later?"

"I'll be at Rudi from two-ish."

"Tomorrow then? I need an update." She was forcing it, I could tell.

"Tomorrow it is."

We hung up, but I couldn't shake the suspicion. It was like a moving thing, crawling through my head. I hated that the first place my mind went was Pip having an affair. She and Tim had been together forever. They were the relationship that gave me hope. But it was usually true that no one really knew what went on behind closed doors.

I tried to think back to Savanna's birthday, to remember if anything seemed odd, awkward or strained, and I came up empty. I had been seriously drunk by the end of the night and disgustingly hungover the next morning, but surely I would have noticed if my sister was unhappy? Wouldn't I? Had I been that distracted by Chase that I didn't notice? I already knew the answer to that.

. . .

HUNTER HOWLED from beside the ring as the ball left my hand and sailed in a smooth arc. It sank into the basket with a satisfying rattle of chain.

"What the fuck is going on? You are killing me today. Where's the Mack who misses more than half his shots?" he asked as I slapped his offered hand. He wasn't wrong, as much as I enjoyed basketball I was far from a skilled shooter. Yet, today it appeared I couldn't miss. It was Chase. It had to be. How could I not be in a good mood when I kissed her for a solid couple of hours this morning and would be doing it again in two days? Nothing was going to bring me down right now. Certainly not a little trash talk.

"Just feelin' good, I guess."

He didn't look the least bit convinced, but didn't push me on it, either. I'd been expecting some comment for at least a half hour, seeing as the last time we saw one another Harley went and announced I was in love with Chase. I would be eternally grateful if that comment never came, because as much as I was enjoying whatever was going on between us, I wasn't sure I was ready to talk about it. Part of me wanted to, sure, but I was still in that uncertain place. We'd been on a date, we were going on another one, but what the fuck did any of that actually mean?

"You know anyone who'd want to buy a food truck?" Hunter asked as he drove through me on his way to the ring.

"I—what?" I caught the ball and took it to half court as he lingered around the top of the key. That had been about the last thing I expected him to say. I glanced around just in case he was talking to someone else, but the overnight drop in temperature meant the court was all ours today.

"One of our bartenders bought this food truck a few

months back, planned to start selling specialty hot dogs. He made them for us a few times—they were really fucking good. The thing is decked out, mostly, he's put a lot into it. Thought you might know someone who'd be interested."

"And he can't keep it?"

He shook his head. "He wanted to, but his girlfriend got pregnant and now he's freaking out because he needs to support his family. He's a great bartender, so I'm relieved I don't need to replace him but I'm also kinda bummed for him, you know? He's been talking about hot dogs for a fucking year, more, and now he's just giving it up." He shook his head. "Anyway, you know anyone?"

I flicked the ball from one hand to the other. "Not off the top of my head, but I can ask around."

"Thanks man, let me know if you hear anything."

We went back to the game and, for the first time, I came close to beating him—not that either of us ever really kept score. But, if we did, I was sure the margin would be a whole lot closer today. My brain kept circling back to the food truck. I didn't think there was room in my brain for anything aside from Chase today, but the food truck would not leave me the fuck alone. Why? It wasn't like I was going to start selling pies out of a truck. That was ridiculous. That was not a good idea. I didn't want to do that. I was quite happy making pies for friends and family with no pressure whatsoever, thank you very much. So why couldn't I stop thinking about it?

THE NEXT MORNING, I pulled open the door ready to greet the UPS driver who was bringing supplies for tomorrow's date, only to find Chase with two coffees and a large bag that smelled like cinnamon.

"Hey, wh—what are you doin' here?"

Her eyes narrowed. "Good to see you too." She pushed past me.

"It's always good to see you Chase." I hooked her around the waist and swallowed her squeak of surprise as our mouths met. As much as I had to do today, I was more than happy to put plans on hold for the time being. My fingers slid through the dark silken strands of her hair as she pressed against me from chest to toe.

"That was more like it," she said, her lips grazing mine.

"I wasn't expecting to see you until later."

Color bloomed across her cheeks. "I guess I couldn't wait that long. And I wanted to return the favor for yesterday."

"That wasn't necessary, but I love your impatience."

"That's good news because I'm hungry and I really want these cinnamon rolls."

Ten minutes later Chase was perched on one of my kitchen stools cradling her coffee. "I feel like I'm getting a peek behind some previously off limits curtain..." she said, wagging her eyebrows as I retrieved a disc of chilled dough from the refrigerator.

"What are you talking about?"

"You're making pie." She gestured at me like a gameshow host. "In front of me."

"And?" I laughed, dusting the counter with flour. I thoroughly enjoyed the way her eyes followed me when I moved.

"And you have literally never let me watch you make pie. You're wearing an apron, it's a good look. What are those?"

"Baking beans. Yes I'm wearing an apron, and I have let you watch me make pie. Why does that sound like a euphemism?"

She giggled. "No idea, but it totally does. And no, you haven't."

I opened my mouth to argue, because surely she'd watched me make pie before, only I couldn't think of when. I could remember plenty of times that I had delivered and eaten pie with her, but I guess the making had always been a quiet, solitary affair.

Initially it was probably because I was embarrassed, or unsure of myself at the very least. I wasn't a bad cook, but then, when one of your best friends is one of the country's best young chefs, you've got a different benchmark. There was something about pie though. And, naturally, pie went with ice cream, which had become my newest obsession.

"Until this very moment, I thought my favorite pie was store-bought pastry and canned filling."

I gasped, actually, genuinely, gasped, flattening a flour covered hand against my chest. "You did not."

"No." She winced and shook her head. "Maybe. Yes, okay, I totally did. Or it was at least an option. You don't really talk all that much about this, Mack. But look at you, you're a pie chef. Is that a thing? Pie chef? Maybe not. Oh! You're the pie guy!"

"I don't know if I'd go that far. I do have something for you to test though." Ordinarily, there was usually an undercurrent of nerves whenever I had her taste things. Today, though, I felt pretty confident.

"My tastebuds are at your disposal."

"So generous."

"I do have exceedingly generous tastebuds."

I pulled the pint of ice cream from the freezer and slid it over to her, followed by a spoon. "Taste."

"Yes, sir," she said with a slightly glazed look, like maybe she enjoyed being ordered around. I tucked that snippet of information away for another time.

"It's buttermilk and maple, thinking it could go well with the apple cheddar." Which I'd be making again for Christmas after its rousing success at Thanksgiving. "What do you think?" I busied myself with rolling out the dough so I wouldn't become entranced by the way the spoon disappeared between her lips. Too late. She pulled it out clean, her face a mask of concentration as she moved the ice cream around her mouth. My jeans started to feel uncomfortably tight as I imagined her cold, ice cream covered tongue sinking into my mouth.

"What's the other flavor in there...?" she asked, licking her lips.

I blinked, clearing the fantasy out of my head. "Nutmeg."

"Yes, that's it!" She beamed. "Mack, this is in–fucking–credible. I thought that one from Thanksgiving was good but this is even better." She dug in for another spoonful, and a warm satisfaction spread through my chest. It had always been this way, wanting her seal of approval.

"You're really good at this, you know."

I ignored the prickling sensation at the base of my skull. "Is that a hint of surprise?"

"Not in the slightest," she assured me. "Would you consider ... doing more with them? Selling them?"

"The pies?"

She nodded and licked the spoon clean. "Yeah, and the ice cream, too. Seriously, Mack, they're so good. You're sitting on a money maker here."

I appreciated her confidence in me, but it didn't change the fact that actually pursuing it scared the ever living shit out of me.

"One of Hunter's guys is selling a food truck." I wasn't sure why I said it, but since he mentioned it, the truck had been circling my head more than I cared to admit. I still had no idea how I'd do it, or even if I wanted to, but I couldn't stop thinking about it all the same.

"Oh really? I do remember getting stuck talking to Dean

about hot dogs for like an hour once, I'm sure he mentioned a food truck at some point during his monologue. Wait! Are you saying—you mean for you? You want to start a pie truck!? That would be amazing! I volunteer as your official taste tester, obviously. You could cook them at Rudi, seeing as we have a kick-ass kitchen now that is sadly underutilized, and then you load up for all the markets and—"

"Whoa there. Just—just hold up. No, I'm not—I wasn't— How would I even do that? No. Besides, I have a job already." It came out sharper than I intended, but her enthusiasm was like a spotlight for my panic. Even if I did buy the truck and bake the pies and schlep them out to every market in Brooklyn, there was no guarantee that anyone would actually want them. Pies were a hobby, not a career.

"Yes, I'm aware of that," she said, rolling her eyes. "But you should see yourself right now. You're glowing."

"Like a pregnant woman?"

She nodded. "Yup, exactly like a pregnant woman, only with washboard abs instead of the belly. But you are all dewy complexion and twinkly eyes."

"Thank you, I think." It didn't change my thoughts on the subject, though.

"You're welcome."

"And thank you for your feedback, but I have enough on my plate with Rudi, I don't need to sell my pies. I don't even know if I want to sell my pies."

"Okay." She shrugged. "I was just asking. I'm finishing this."

"Be my guest," I said, grateful to have the subject dropped, for the moment at least. Thinking about all of this was one thing, mentioning it to Chase had been another, and actually pursuing it? That was a step too far. Starting Rudi Blue with the two of us had been hard enough, starting something alone, on top of another business, just the idea of it was overwhelming.

No, I was comfortable where I was. Rudi was busier than we had ever been. Chase and I were finally getting our shit together. All of that was enough for me.

19

CHASE

DESPITE BEING TOLD I would have adequate detail regarding our second date, I had only heard two things from Mack.

Last night: *Dress warm.*

This morning: *Dress less warm.*

On what planet was this anywhere near enough information? Naturally, my first thought had been, how warm? Followed this morning by how less warm? I glanced out the window for the hundredth time. It was still snowing. He didn't actually intend for us to be out in this, did he? Granted, we were still a long way off full-blown blizzard status, but it was definitely more than a gentle flurry.

I wasn't opposed to a date in the snow, but I really would like to know a little more of what he had planned. My guess was whatever he intended was outdoors and the weather meant we would now be indoors. But these were merely assumptions I was being forced to make in the face of zero actual detail.

There wasn't too much more time for me to obsess because he was going to be here to pick me up in under an hour. Should

I have been dressed before now? Maybe. Did it change the fact I wasn't? No.

I stood in my underwear in front of my open closet, considering the options, one foot tapping against the floor. This wasn't a big deal. It was Mack. Just Mack. I had never taken this long to get dressed to see him—ever. Yet my bed was still littered with discarded clothing options and I was no closer to coming to a decision.

I'd made it as far as a pair of woolen tights when a knock echoed through my apartment.

"Fuck." I grabbed a red plaid skirt and a black turtleneck sweater, threw them both on and stuffed my feet into a pair of boots that would hold up against the snow before racing to the door.

Mack stood in the hall, hands deep in his pockets, looking hotter than anyone had any right to. Would I get over this feeling of seeing him anew? Right now, it seemed doubtful. Those stubborn curls poked out around the edges of his beanie and my fingers longed to play in them. I'd never given much thought to men's hair before. Now, though, this hair that I had seen so many times before was suddenly irresistible. I busied myself by stuffing my arms into my coat to keep from reaching out and twisting one of those curls around a finger.

For all my staring, Mack didn't seem to notice as his eyes made a leisurely perusal from my feet up to my face. A grin tilted his lips in the most devastating way and I was sorely tempted to just drag him inside and lock the door. Date two. This was only date two and, despite the look on his face right now, there would be no ravaging until date five. The reminder was enough to pull me out of the lust hole. Mostly.

"A picture'll last longer," I said with a playful scowl in an effort to diffuse the tension. A useless attempt. He had been right when he said it was always there now, hot and crackling.

Making my skin tingle and my stomach dip. At times, I wasn't sure I'd survive it, but I also knew I was already an addict.

I couldn't stop staring at his face and imagining sucking on his lower lip, would be taste like mint? The click of his phone camera went off, snapping me out of my daydream.

"I don't know how you have any sounds coming from your phone. Do I get to see it?" I held out a hand.

He turned the screen to face me and there I was. Caught between a scowl and a smirk, pupils blown and cheeks stained pink. Seeing myself like that was a gut punch and I had to focus very hard on breathing even—and swallowing against the rising panic. How was I supposed to maintain my denial of feelings if that was how I looked at him?

"How is a camera click offensive?" he asked.

"Every sound that comes from a phone is offensive."

"What about when it rings?"

I gaped at him. "*Especially* then."

"This is why you never answer your phone, it's literally always on silent." He reached out and slipped an arm around my back and my hands shot up, landing on his chest just before his mouth came down on mine and I lost all conscious thought. He really was an incredible kisser. Firm and commanding, yet, at the same time, slow, tender, explorative. Our tongues tangled and as I guessed there was mint with the slightest hint of coffee. I didn't know why the thought of him brushing his teeth before he saw me made me kiss him harder, but it did.

I was well and truly light-headed by the time he pulled away. I licked my lips, blinked my eyes open. "What were we talking about?"

"The fact you never answer your phone because it's always on silent."

"I never answer my phone because I hate talking on it, for the most part." There were a couple of exceptions.

"How do you expect to communicate with anyone?"

"There's this new fandangled thing called texting, Mack. It means I do not have to speak to anyone, pretty much ever. Magic."

"You are such a grump sometimes," he said with a chuckle and tucked me under his arm. Most of the time when someone called me a grump, or a bitch, or anything else, it went along with: You'll never find a husband with that attitude. You'd be pretty if you smiled. Blah, blah, blah. But, when Mack said it, it didn't feel like something that needed changing. It was just another thing about me—brown eyes, black hair, grumpy disposition. It was just me, and he accepted it. A girl could get drunk on that kind of unconditional acceptance.

"So, what are we doing?" I asked as we made it out onto the street. The snow had finally stopped and, although the air was still icy, I was happy to walk, our footsteps softly crunching across the white sidewalk. This was the point when the snow was still magic, before it turned to gray sludge piled up in the gutters, or ice that threatened to make you lose your footing and break something.

"Well, the weather meant I had to make some last minute changes, but I think the vibe is still there." Well, that told me absolutely nothing. It was like he was intent on keeping me firmly in the dark.

"The vibe?"

"The vibe," he confirmed, still telling me nothing.

"And what exactly is 'the vibe'?"

He grinned down at me. "You'll just have to wait and see."

"You are enjoying this way too much. I'm going to make you wear a blindfold."

"Excuse me?" His eyebrows disappeared under his beanie.

"When we go on my date. You will be wearing a blindfold and I will tell you nothing. *Nothing.*"

"Rude."

"Necessary. It'll teach you a lesson for all this secrecy."

"Ah, but you're so damn hot when you're pissed at me."

I elbowed him in the ribs, but he just laughed and kissed the top of my head. I wanted to be genuinely pissed at him, but I wasn't, not really. I actually liked that he was keeping so much a secret to surprise me, but I would never admit it. I didn't need to, he probably already knew.

"Maybe we can use the blindfold elsewhere..." The low rumble of his voice had me stumbling a step as a picture of him tied to a bed with half his face hidden behind a blindfold popped into my head. Fuck, I did not need that particular visual when I was going to have to keep my hands to myself.

I swallowed against my dry throat and it was a good thing Mack was all but holding me up because my knees had lost all their strength. "Oh really?" I squeaked, then cleared my throat.

"You're getting ideas too, right? I'll tell you mine." It was a low, seductive whisper that tickled all the way down my spine and curled my toes, even as I walked (or attempted to).

"Nope. No, I don't–I'm not having ideas. No ideas here."

"Liar."

I shoved him. "You were the one that insisted on the five date rule."

"Oh, the five date rule stands. But there is so much that we can do before then." Was he trying to drive me out of my goddamn mind? Was he trying to kill me? He was lucky I hadn't turned into a puddle of lust at his feet.

"You okay there? You look a little pink."

"Fine, I'm fine."

"Uh-huh." I ignored the teasing edge to his voice and focused on putting one foot in front of the other, and not dragging him into the closest semi-secluded spot.

We turned onto Jackson and I stopped short, pulling him to

a halt with me. "You are not taking me to your apartment." Not after all that *there is so much we can do before date five business*. I needed to be somewhere public. Somewhere I wouldn't be tempted to rip his clothes clean off. I mean, I'd still be tempted—I was tempted right now—but I didn't want him naked in front of half of Brooklyn. Just me. And now I was thinking about him naked. Fuck.

"I told you, there was a change of plans."

"Yes, right." I nodded, willing the warmth in my cheeks to subside. "And where would we have been if it hadn't dumped eight inches overnight?" He scratched his ear. "We were still going to be here weren't we?!"

"No."

"You are a terrible liar." I laughed as he towed me towards the front of his place. The squat converted warehouse sat between two considerably larger buildings, giving it shelter from most of the weather on two sides, but with a south-facing facade it always managed to catch the sun.

"Sort of."

"Clarify."

"We were always going to be at this general location, we've just moved from the outdoors to indoors. How about I show you?"

"Lead the way."

Mack's home was one of those places that belonged on the pages of *Architectural Digest*. Like Rudi Blue, it had been some kind of factory in a previous life, then left alone for years before being given a new identity as an apartment. You probably could have fit four or five in the building, instead it was just Mack and an inappropriately large garage given the location, which housed his also inappropriately large car along with two motorcycles and a vintage, cherry-red Vespa, which I was always threatening to steal. I had no idea how to ride the thing, but it could just sit in my living room and I'd stare at it because it was so shiny and gorgeous.

We entered through the garage and I blew a kiss at Ms Vespa.

"You know I could teach you how to ride it."

"No, thank you, that would only ruin the mystique. I just want to look at her." I cast a glance over my shoulder before we stepped inside the loft apartment.

And I promptly stopped dead.

Mack's place was open, light, and airy and, despite how much I loved my own apartment, his made it feel like a dark and dingy hobbit hole in comparison. Today, though, it was something else altogether. Huge swathes of sheer white fabric hung from the beams that ran the length of the ceiling. They all pooled at the floor around a tent that looked like a perfect upside down waffle cone.

I glanced up at Mack who was watching me take it all in with a soft smile on his face. I wanted to say something, but I wasn't sure I had words.

The front of the tent was open wide. Inside it was a pile of coziness, the likes of which I had never seen; there were blankets, pillows, and cushions arranged in a half circle around a large picnic basket, all lit by the soft light diffused by the draping fabric. My eyes prickled and my nose burned, but I refused to cry. Even though this was the most effort anyone had ever gone to for me on a date. Or ever, really.

I cleared my throat and stepped closer to the front of the tent, wanting nothing more than to dive in, headfirst, and snuggle down for the rest of the day and night. Leaving to go to Rudi later was going to be a serious struggle.

"It was supposed to be up on the roof," Mack started, coming up beside me. "I nearly still went for it, but if it kept on snowing the way it was..." A shrug. "Plus, I wasn't sure if this thing was actually weatherproof—I'm guessing not—and putting any kind of decent heating device inside a canvas tent didn't seem like the best idea. So, I improvised."

I swallowed against the emotions climbing my throat and croaked out, "It's perfect."

"Really?" His nerves settled mine.

"Are you kidding me? Yes, it's fucking perfect! Look at it! You made us a nest!"

He laughed. "I hadn't thought about it that way, but yeah, I guess I did."

I turned, grabbed his neck and pulled his face down to mine. "I love it," I said against his mouth before kissing him hard. I only meant it to be brief, I had pillows to collapse onto, but he clearly had other ideas. One hand cupped the back of my head as his tongue swept into my mouth. My heart beat hard behind my ribs as my fingers pushed off his beanie and tangled themselves in his hair. He stood straight, arms now locked around my back, my feet dangling above the floor and walked the couple of steps into the tent of cozy, depositing me inside.

"Stay," he said, like I had any intention of moving ever. He was going to have to drag me out of this place kicking and screaming. I would leave only to use the bathroom, and then I would come right back. I lived here now.

After a couple of minutes he reappeared at the mouth of the tent (my new home) with a large mug in each hand. Crouching to come inside, he handed me one.

"Do we have a hot cocoa theme happening?"

A sly smile curved his lips. "This is not your ordinary, innocent hot cocoa." As soon as he said it, a waft of whiskey hit my nose and I took a sip, warmth tracking down my throat and into my stomach. Oh yes.

"That's really fucking good."

"Not too heavy handed on the whiskey?"

"Is there such a thing as too heavy handed with whiskey?"

"Not in this tent, I guess," he said, as we watched one another over the rims of our mugs.

This was both completely natural and utterly surreal. Usually, on a date you were getting to know the other person. Where they grew up. Their favorite restaurant. Whether they accepted pineapple on their pizza. Did they think Lebron had eclipsed Jordan as the best basketball player of all time (no, obviously. The original *Space Jam* was superior, too). But I knew all that, and more, about Mack. And he about me.

"You remember Tatiana Marcus?" he asked, breaking the silence. Despite not having any idea where this was going, I nodded.

"How could I not?" Tatiana Marcus had quietly made my life a living hell for a solid year at Carrington Collins Prep. She was an egotistical bitch with a serious superiority complex and I had unintentionally stolen her favorite toy. She and Mack had apparently been off and on for most of eighth grade and had broken up in a blaze of glory after being caught naked in the Egyptian exhibit of the Natural History Museum just before I joined their class in ninth. She blamed his friendship with me for their permanent off status. Even after being broken up for a year, they still had the most talked about sex life in our grade.

"I never slept with her."

I choked on my mouthful of dirty hot cocoa. "What are you talking about? You were sleeping with her until two weeks before we met."

He shook his head. "Never even got to second base."

"Are you joking?" This was astounding. It was on par with learning the moon landing had been a fake.

"Nope."

"But the Natural History Museum—"

"Was a lie, mostly."

I opened my mouth. Closed it again. How did I not know this? How had he managed to keep this to himself all this time? I wasn't sure whether to be impressed or horrified.

"Does Nash know?" Surely I couldn't be the first person to get this juicy, albeit fifteen year-old, gossip.

"Nope, just me, Tatiana, and now you."

I gaped then took another large slurp of cocoa. "Why?"

"Why lie? Or why am I telling you?"

"Both."

He leaned back on one elbow and tipped his mug to his lips. He looked like something out of a winter porn, all wrapped in plaid and sipping his hot cocoa amongst a nest of faux fur. But my mind was so engrossed in the whole Mack and Tatiana being a lie that I wasn't solely focused on the view. I did manage to catch a glimpse of lower abdomen as he scratched his head though.

"She didn't have a great relationship with her dad, I figured it was all about attention. She always told me she was saving herself for *the one*." The answer didn't surprise me, half our school had similar issues, but the way he phrased it made my spidey senses tingle (I was pretty sure it wasn't the whiskey).

"And what the hell did she consider you then?" If Mack wasn't 'the one' material I didn't know who the hell was. Certainly no one at Carrington.

"Not that, evidently." The response was uncharacteristically flat.

"Okay, so she was a moron with A-grade daddy issues, not surprising. Although I would like to be able to slap her retroactively."

"As much as I would have liked to see that, there is no need to slap her on my account."

"Oh there is, but we'll move on. Why did you go along with it?"

"I understood how it was to have a shitty relationship with your dad. Plus, I got to feel her boobs, and that was a pretty good pay off at the time," he said with a shrug and I laughed.

"Charming."

"I'd known her since we were five or six and she wanted to change her rep. Until we started dating she was the good girl, for the most part, and she hated it."

"But you guys were together for a year, more."

"And she was cool for a lot of that time. But by the end of it her plans were getting crazy and Nash was telling me it was time to break up permanently. He didn't need to tell me, I already knew. So, when she pulled my dick out behind a fucking mummy, or whatever it was, in the Natural Histroy Museum I knew I'd had enough. Right after I got done for indecent exposure, that is."

I didn't quite manage to catch my giggled snort before it escaped.

"Oh, you think this is funny, do you?" he asked, setting aside his mug and rising onto his knees, stalking toward me as best he could through the sea of blankets and overstuffed cushions between us.

I shook my head holding my mug out like a sad little shield. "Nuh-uh. Don't look at me like that, I am not spilling hot cocoa in here."

He took the mug and set it down with his, just outside the door of the tent. I tried to wiggle away in the limited space but he grabbed my calf and pulled me flat, amusement lighting his eyes.

"I definitely do not think you having your dick out in the Egyptian wing is funny," I assured him, but the fact I was almost crying with the effort of not laughing seriously undermined the statement.

"I'm not sure I believe you."

"Please, don't tickle me."

His hands trailed up from my calves and over my knees. The amusement of the situation shifted to something else entirely as I realized the edge of my skirt had ridden up high, leaving most of my wool wrapped legs exposed. I swallowed hard as heat engulfed me, watching Mack as he watched the slow progress of his hand, up, up, up.

One knee landed between mine and his words swarmed in my head: *there are so many other things we can do.*

He was moving so slow I wanted to scream and squirm, but I didn't. I held still, pulse thundering in my ears and breathing shallow as the light drag of his fingertips on my tights sent shiver after shiver across my skin. If it was possible to die of anticipation, then this was it for me.

I was done for.

20

MACK

WHAT THE FUCK was I doing?

I knew that moving things inside was going to be trouble—necessary, given the state of the weather when I woke up, but trouble. And now here I was with my hand high on Chase's thigh not fifteen minutes into our date. This would not have happened if we were on the fucking roof. Or maybe it would have.

It probably would have.

But it wasn't going any further just yet.

Even so, I couldn't stop staring at my hand. It was halfway between her knee and hip, my fingers splayed, skin stark against the black wool of her tights. I had all but memorized the lines of Chase's legs over the years, but having them under my hand was something else altogether. I could feel the muscle shift, the slight tremble as she fought to keep still.

"And why tell me now?" It was little more than a shaky whisper and it was comforting to know that she was as affected by everything between us as I was. My eyes jumped up to hers, dark and hungry, but with the light of curiosity. Of course she was curious. I'd dropped a goddamn bomb. It probably wasn't the best idea, to talk about an ex while on a date. The look on Chase's face, though, both horrified and thrilled all at once, set my mind at ease. She might try to deny it, but Chase loved some gossip.

My attention dropped back to my hand, still on her thigh. I couldn't quite believe I was here with her and part of me was cursing my decision to bring up Tatiana, but I did have a point.

I dropped down beside her, my hand migrating up over the curve of her hip. "Well, first of all, I didn't want you to think I would get intentionally naked in the Natural History Museum." She laughed. "And I guess it was a secret for a secret?" At her look of confusion, I added, "I thought I knew pretty much everything there was to know about you ... and yet you surprised me with your stories of being a childhood skating prodigy."

Another laugh, this one large enough to have her head tipping back, exposing the long elegant line of her throat.

"Childhood prodigy might be a stretch, but I see your point. And your equivalent is admitting that it was not, in fact, Tatiana Marcus who popped your cherry?"

It was my turn to laugh. That had been another part of the reason I'd been happy to go along with Tat's messed up plan.

"Cassie DeMarco?"

"What?"

"Was it Cassie DeMarco?" she clarified, and I was suddenly not so sure about this topic of conversation.

"It was not," I said, my fingers running a lazy track across Chase's waist as she scooted ever so slightly closer.

"Wait," she breathed. "There was someone before Tatiana? How old were you? Like fourteen?"

"Thirteen, actually."

"No!" She sat upright, eyes and mouth wide in shock. "You're kidding. *Thirteen!?* Who was it?"

My hand had fallen into the cushions beside her and I drew circles in the fake fur.

"Mack," she said when I didn't answer immediately. "Who was it? You weren't—" She swallowed. "It wasn't—"

"It was very much consensual, if that's where your mind is going."

A relieved breath left her in a rush. "Okay, you had me worried there for a second. Why the hesitation? Was it a *teacher?*" She wasn't even trying not to be horrified. Even though if I said yes, I knew she wouldn't judge. Not out loud anyway. And she was closer than she realized.

"Not a teacher no ..."

"But," she nudged.

"But what?"

"You said that like there was a but. So what is it?"

"She was my tutor."

She let out a delighted giggle. "Oh my god, scandalous! What did she tutor you in?" I should not have been surprised that this was her follow up question.

"Math and Spanish."

"Oh man, the poor girl didn't even know what she was getting herself into, did she?"

"She was a neighbor's daughter who my father organized to tutor me." She was also almost five years older than me, which at the time made her seem like a worldly adult, who blew my tiny thirteen year-old mind.

"Uh huh, bet he regretted that decision." Chase paused, far off in thought for a moment. "I can't believe I never knew this about you."

My hand had once again made its way to her leg, I was incapable of not touching her now that I knew I could. "It happened before we met. Not everyone likes to give an extreme amount of detail about their sex life. Unlike you after your first time with Tommy Hawson. I did not need to know all that."

She shook her head and shuddered. "That boy did not know what to do with a vagina." But she'd still gone there with him less than a month after our first kiss, which she never mentioned again and yet talked about him almost non stop. I hadn't realized how much it still bothered me.

"I did it to prove I wasn't into you," she said, so quickly I almost missed it.

"What?" I gaped at her.

"After ... our kiss"—she shook her head, cleared her throat, her eyes everywhere but on my face—"I thought you were either so drunk you didn't remember, or that I was such a bad kisser you did remember but would rather not."

"Chase."

"I didn't want to lose your friendship, and I knew that if I did you would totally get Nash in the divorce and I couldn't stomach losing you, let alone both of you, so I just pretended it never happened." Her eyes came up to mine. "And I thought that would be it. Until Tatiana asked if we were dating now, in that smug, sarcastic way she did. She knew we obviously were not dating. And I—I didn't think anyone saw us, but they must have. And I freaked out. Tommy had always flirted with me and he was hot—dumb as a pile of bricks, but hot—so at the next party I flirted back. I didn't actually intend to sleep with him that night. I had too much tequila trying to work up the courage to speak to him and then things probably went too far because I was drunk. And then I told you all about it partly in the hopes that it would make you jealous, but also to prove I didn't care that you didn't want to kiss me." She pressed her lips together, looking like she regretted the whole speech but it was out there now.

I just stared at her, with absolutely no idea what to say. My mind was tripping over itself. Thoughts piling on top of one another each louder than the last but nothing really making any actual sense. The only thing I could decipher amongst the din was *kissherkissherkissher*.

"You're going to need to say something, or I'm going to need a lot more whiskey. Maybe I'll just take the bottle." She shifted towards the door of the tent but I blocked her way, my heart beating so quickly it was almost painful. Had we really both felt the same way all this time and never knew it? Had we both been so stubborn and scared to lose the other that we didn't do anything about it?

"I always wanted to kiss you. Probably since you walked into that bathroom like some pint-sized knight defending my stoned ass."

She froze. "But you—"

"I was a dumb kid, Chase. I was a dumb kid, and you were my best friend, and right after kissing me you downed so many jell-o shots you nearly had to get your stomach pumped. I thought—I don't know what I thought, honestly. Then you never mentioned it, and—"

"You never mentioned it, either!"

"Because I was fucking scared. Because—because it was *you*."

We sat there staring at one another, the weight of these spontaneous confessions hanging in the air.

"Chase I—" I had no idea where the rest of the sentence was going, not that it mattered because I didn't get to finish it. Chase's hand hooked around the back of my neck and pulled me in, pausing for one long, agonizing moment, her eyes bouncing between mine. I didn't dare move. I didn't dare breathe. She closed the last of the distance, brushing her lips over mine and, just like every other time we kissed, there was this sense of home that threatened to crack me wide open.

Then, everything shifted, the kiss turning deep and needy, and suddenly we couldn't get close enough, hands and mouths greedy. She straddled my lap, pressing us together as her fingers tangled in my hair, nails dragging over my scalp, sending heat barrelling through me.

I needed to slow this down or there was no way we'd be making it to date five, but I wasn't sure I could. Not with Chase in my lap like this. Not when my hands were on her ass. Not when we'd both wanted this for longer than either of us had wanted to admit.

"Date five," she panted, our noses bumping. The rise and fall of her chest pressing her breasts against me. I was light headed.

"Date five?"

"Are you—are you really set on date five?" Her voice was pained. I knew the feeling.

"I'm having some second thoughts right now ..." I admitted, giving her a squeeze. "But yes, I am really set on date five."

She nodded and leaned back a fraction so her face came into focus, cheeks flushed, hair messy. "Okay, that's—we should probably stop then, or slow down at least. I don't want things to go further than you're comfortable with."

"You're right," I agreed but neither of us moved. Then her mouth was on me again, still deep, but slower, more intentional, like she was memorizing the shape of my lips with hers. And it was all going to drive me out of my fucking mind. Her hips rocked and I momentarily forgot my own name. How the hell was just kissing this woman still the hottest thing I'd ever experienced? Was it all the build up? Was it because I'd wanted her, consciously or not, since I was fifteen?

I nipped at her lower lip then sucked, swallowing her

answering moan.

"Shirt off," she said.

"Chase ..." I said, a weak warning as her fingers dipped under the edge of my shirt and pushed it up.

"I'll be good, I promise." If only she knew how much I did not want her to be good. Her fingers tugged at the buttons and then my shirt was gone and her hands were everywhere. Nails dragging over my nipples, fingers tracing muscles. I was so hard I was pretty sure I was going to pass out.

I really needed to take control of this situation, and I needed to do it now. I lay back and she followed, a beat later I was hovering over her and fuck if she was not the most beautiful thing I had ever seen in my fucking life. I kissed her cheek, over her jaw and she tilted her head to give me better access to her neck. I groaned against her skin as one leg curled over my hip. Her breathing hitched as the back of my hand skimmed over her breast, and I could feel her taut, straining nipple. I wanted my tongue there. I wanted to taste every inch of her, and I would, in time. *There's no rush.*

Chase pulled her sweater up and over her head and, at my obviously glazed look, she said, "You can't be the only one with the goods on display. Plus, it's hot in this tent of yours."

Yes, it was. More so now that I could see the two black triangles of lace that covered her breasts. My god, she was perfect.

We were kissing again, I wasn't sure how it happened, I must have blacked out staring at her. Not that I minded, because I would happily kiss her until the end of time.

My hands, which I noted were a little shaky, started a tentative exploration as our tongues tangled, fingers grazing skin that I had never let myself dream of actually touching. She was so soft, so warm. One finger trailed along the line of her collar bone from her shoulder to the hollow of her throat then down along the scalloped edge of lace. I broke our kiss, letting my lips travel the path my fingers had just taken and Chase shuddered, her breathing shaky as my tongue met the soft skin on her chest.

I kissed across the lace, covering her nipple and sucking, she arched up, moaned, and I had to remind myself why I wanted to wait until date five. Why I needed to be sure, why I needed her to be sure. Her fingers found their way into my hair as I continued to tease her nipple through the fabric of her bra.

"More," she whispered. "If—only if you want to ... I don't want to pressure you or any—"

"I want to," I said against wet lace, my voice low and rough. She took my hand and guided it down over her stomach, under the edge of her skirt as I continued to worship her breasts.

"Please, Mack, please. I need ..." The sentence trailed off as I pushed inside her tights and underwear. I groaned as I met slick skin and her hips rocked, chasing my hand.

I drew lazy circles, willing myself not to rush even as Chase's breathing turned shallow. She wiggled her tights down, then pulled my face to meet her and kissed me, hard and desperate. One finger dipped into her heat and she moaned in my mouth. A second and she gripped me.

"Yes, god, Mack, yes. I—" She threw her head back, one hand at my throat. I was mesmerized, lost to her sounds and the feel of her. I could make her come apart, but I knew I was the one who would be truly altered here. Her hips rolled, I pressed the heel of my hand against her clit and returned my mouth to her nipple.

"I—I'm com—" She cried out as her muscles contracted and pulsed around my fingers. My eyes rolled back in my head at the feel of her. Wet, hot, perfection.

Long moments passed as I listened to the sound of her breathing slow and even out.

"That was ..." she started, bringing her mouth back to mine in a tender kiss. "Was." Another Kiss. "Incredible." And a third.

"Should I be offended that you sound surprised?"

"Not surprised," she assured me as she rolled onto her side and I regrettably withdrew my fingers, immediately missing her heat. Then they were in her mouth and I was a hot second away from coming in my pants as she sucked and her tongue swirled. She released them with a pop and a dazed smile and I really wished we did not have to go into work tonight. I would quite happily stay here with her like this until I could no longer keep my eyes open.

"You're beautiful," I said. It wasn't enough, not nearly, but it was all my addled brain could currently come up with. Did I even know the right words to adequately describe her? I doubted it. She was ... everything and more. And I was so far from deserving her.

Her answer was a kiss that threatened to render me unconscious as the taste of her met my tongue. One hand edged its way down my chest but I stopped her as she made it to the top of my jeans.

"Wait."

"Mack."

"Chase." I pulled her hand up to my mouth and kissed her knuckles. "You don't need to do that."

"I know I don't need to do that. I want to. Now quit being a gentleman."

"But I so enjoy being a gentleman."

She shimmied her tights back up and righted her skirt but didn't put the sweater back on, which was a problem because when she sat up I was eye to breast. The fabric was still wet and glistening from where I had been sucking it.

"Is this about you respecting yourself in the morning?" she

asked, head tipped to one side, considering me.

It wasn't, at least, I didn't think it was. I wanted today to be about her, but I knew she'd hate it if I said that. "And if it is?"

"I would never want you to feel anything other than utterly respected," she said, eyes serious yet bright. "Can I at least keep kissing you?"

The question had me grinning as I glanced at my watch. "For another forty-five minutes, yes you can."

She groaned, pushing me onto my back and straddling me. "I really wish we didn't have to go to work."

"Me too..." My hands anchored on her hips and she leaned down, her hair falling around us. Our lips met, the desperation from earlier had cooled, leaving behind lazy satisfaction. No rush, just this, until we had to make ourselves look like respectable business owners again. Her wet-lace covered nipples grazed over my bare chest as her body stretched over me.

"You should have started this date at nine," she purred, lips moving along my jaw.

I laughed. "I'll keep that in mind for next time."

"Next time? Oh no, sir, the next one is mine, remember?"

"How could I forget?" I sucked in a breath as she made it to my nipple and bit down, the sting immediately soothed as she licked. My cock throbbed in my jeans. "And what are we doing? Do I–do I get a clue?"

She chuckled, kissing her way across my chest and then back up. "Absolutely not."

"None? Not even a little one?"

"Not a single one," she said with a grin that I felt and heard more than saw.

"Teaching me a lesson.'

"Indeed."

It was one I would happily take over and over again.

21

CHASE

KISSING MACK WAS OFFICIALLY my favorite thing.

It wasn't a surprise—I had kissed him as a teenager, after all, and he had been good then, alarmingly so. It was probably why I got blackout drunk immediately after. Now, though, I wasn't even sure how to properly formulate words about the way he commanded my mouth. And my nipples, even through my bra. He really did have the most perfect mouth I'd ever had the pleasure of tasting. Perfect lips. Perfect tongue. Just the thought of what he was going to do with it between my legs had me momentarily breathless ... and uncomfortably warm.

Would I have liked for both of us to be completely naked while we kissed? Yes, undoubtedly. However, I was surprised at how much I was enjoying the "let's take it slow" thing. Okay, enjoying it wasn't exactly a hardship—it would be difficult to not enjoy kissing Mack. Naked or otherwise. There was also something to be said for building the anticipation. It was a constant struggle to not kiss him.

Which was why it had taken us three times as long as it usually would to walk to Rudi. Every few minutes I was overcome with the need to crush my mouth against his, so I'd stop, pull him down by the lapels of his coat, and kiss the hell out of him because I was incapable of doing anything else. The whole thing was more than a little alarming. And surely temporary. I couldn't keep feeling this way, could I? Skin tingling and just so aware of his presence? The fact I was high on two orgasms in as many hours was probably helping to make me feel particularly unhinged. The man had turned me into a writhing, panting, incoherent mess, and I was almost fully clothed. What the hell was going to happen when we were totally naked?

This was a problem. It was one thing to kiss his face off in the privacy of our own tent—I still could not quite believe that he had put up a fucking tent in his apartment—but it was quite another to want to lay him out on the bar in our place of business and lick his chest like an ice cream. I'd like to be able to say I wasn't in danger of doing that, but I was. I would quite happily lay him out like my own personal buffet. However, we both had work to do, Greyson was going to be here in a couple of minutes and, despite my raging hormones, I didn't actually know how to feel about everything.

I was happy, obviously, but there was still an undercurrent of nerves, like I was waiting for the rug to be pulled out from under me, out from under us. It was a difficult feeling to ignore, but I was doing my best. It was easier when my mind was occupied with everything we did earlier. And everything that was ahead of us.

"Yo, Chase, you okay? You look kinda pink." I hadn't even heard Greyson come in, distracted as I was with the fantasy in my head.

"Yes," I snapped. "I'm fine, great, you've got glasses to polish."

"Yes boss," he said without missing a beat. I didn't miss the smirk as he walked past.

"What?" I growled.

"What?" he shot back with a butter-wouldn't-melt look on his face. A cold sweat broke out on the back of my neck and across my upper lip. Oh god, did he know something? Not that there was much to know right now. But the look on his face said *something*. It said, *I know all of Chase's secrets and I'm not afraid to spill them.* I tugged at the neck of my sweater, regretting not putting a lighter shirt underneath.

I could not go through the entire night like this. I needed to compartmentalize. Now. And a lot. When we were here we were not two people who had been kissing for half the afternoon and wanted to continue doing that. Here we were two business partners. That was it. Platonic. Business. Partners.

I marched into the office and kicked the door shut, relishing the silence as I took a few deep breaths. Why the hell was it so hot in here when it would be lucky to be forty-five outside? I pulled off my sweater and rummaged in one of the boxes in the corner. I couldn't let this thing with Mack interfere with our business. I was not going to let that happen. I could keep my shit together here and not let everything else bleed into this place. I could do it. I would do it.

Just as I was feeling slightly more in control, but still without a shirt, Mack came into the office and had me on top of the desk, his hands on my ass and his tongue in my mouth, and my god he was just the most incredible kisser. I sunk into it, melting against him, my legs curling around his hips. Swallowing his groans, which were without a doubt the sexiest sounds I'd ever heard—

No! What the hell were we doing? We couldn't do this. Not when Greyson was already looking at me with some secret fucking smile. I didn't even have a shirt on.

I shoved at Mack's chest and our mouths broke apart.

"Sorry," he said, breathing ragged and voice rough. "Not sure how I'm going to get through the night without doing that every thirty minutes at least." I knew the feeling, but I was no longer giving into it here. I pushed him upright, and fidgeted with my skirt, pulling it down over my thighs as best I could. Although my skirt was the least of my problems, I crossed one arm over my chest and grabbed at the box for a shirt. This would be a lot easier if he wasn't so fucking hot and I didn't want to keep kissing him until the end of time. But I did, I really did.

I slipped off the desk, pulled on the first shirt my hand found and put some space between us. It did little to clear the fog, he was too big for the small space, his scent filling up everything and making me weak.

"We can't do any of this here," I said, squaring my shoulders to give an illusion of conviction I didn't quite have.

"Any of what?" he asked, cocking an eyebrow and taking a half a step closer to me.

"No, no, no. Any of that. Any of this." I waved an agitated hand between us and studiously avoided looking at the obvious and tantalizing bulge in his jeans. I regretted not making him come earlier but he was determined to be the gentleman. I could not think about that now.

"We can't do this here. In fact, I think it would be a good idea if we keep it all to ourselves." Yes, that was definitely a good idea. I did not need everyone up in my business any more than they usually were. It wasn't for anyone else. It was just for us, and I liked it that way. If I wanted to keep it that way I should probably stop making out with him on the street though.

"Keep what to ourselves exactly?"

"All of this, us." I cleared my throat. "There's not really—

um anything—anything much to tell, say, whatever, right now, anyway, so I think keeping it to ourselves would be best."

The light in his eyes extinguished, his features turning hard. "There's not really anything to say? Are you kidding? How about the fact we're dating?"

I blew out a breath, refusing to acknowledge the 'we're dating' statement. "Mack, you know what I mean."

"No, Chase, I don't think I do."

"Come on, there is no need to get all pissed at me. I just mean that seeing as all of this is still very new—less than a week new—and we don't know what we are exactly or where it's going, so maybe it would be better to not tell anyone."

"Better for who?" He asked, crossing his arms over his chest. It was the 'Mack is ready for a fight' pose. I didn't want to fight about this. It wasn't even something that required a fight. It was a simple, *you're right Chase, let's keep it between us for the time being*. And besides, wasn't that hotter, anyway? Sneaking around like teenagers after curfew. Not that either of us really had a curfew. Maybe we needed one. Then and now.

"What do you mean?"

"Keeping us a secret," he all but growled. "Who is keeping us a secret better for?"

I still didn't understand what he meant, it wasn't better for anyone, it was just a better idea than putting all our shit out on the street. Greyson was already looking at me funny and I didn't need more of that, thank you very much. Why was he being so unreasonable?

"Why are you making this a big deal? This is not a big deal."

"You—are you serious?"

"Mack."

"Fine, you got it, I won't tell anyone. We're a big fat secret. Happy?"

"Thrilled. I love it when you're pissed at me."

"Sure seems that way."

"That's not fair."

"I've got work to do." He turned on a dime and was gone in less than a second. What. The. Fuck? What the hell was his problem? I wasn't saying we needed to keep it a secret forever. I was just saying that until we knew where it was all going that it would be prudent to keep it to ourselves. Was that such a bad thing? I really didn't think so. But he was acting like I'd taken his fucking virginity and never called again.

He'd get over it. Give it an hour, maybe two, and he'd realize that he was overreacting and that I was right.

By the time we locked up, Mack had not come to his senses and I wanted to slap him. He hadn't spoken a single word to me since storming out of the office and had been scowling at pretty much every single person all night long, staff and customers alike. Which meant I had to be the smiley one. It didn't suit me. At least three people asked if they could have some of whatever I'd taken.

"See you tomorrow!" I called with sarcastic cheer as Mack walked off in the direction of his apartment without a word, not that I'd been expecting one.

"Can't wait," he said, not bothering to turn around and look at me. Dick. I narrowed my eyes at his retreating back. If he really wanted to play the silent treatment game, then he better buckle the fuck up because he was not getting a goddamn peep out of me until I got an apology. A good one. Maybe some groveling. Definitely a donut.

THERE WAS NO DONUT, apology or otherwise, upon my arrival at Rudi on Friday. And if Mack thought I would have slept on our conversation—our argument—and woken up ready to be the one who apologized, well, he would be left disappointed. I was not apologizing.

If anything, I was more annoyed today because I'd woken up hot and bothered after constant dreams of the two of us in various states of undress. Hands. Lips. Skin. Tongue. He was almost as good in my head as he was in real life. Almost. The fact he wasn't as good in my head was another source of annoyance. As was the fact that as soon as I saw him a bolt of heat shot through me and my nipples went hard. Great. Just fucking great.

Despite my nipples straining hard at him through my bra and shirt, I marched past Mack and went directly to the office with my nose in the air. I would not cave. Not even when I wanted to—nope, I was not even letting myself think about it. He did not exist to me right now. I had plenty to do, a lot of which would happen in the office today. I was not taking the laptop out to the bar like I usually would because my nipples would get ideas they shouldn't. The nipples had gone rogue and I would not encourage them.

There were numerous issues with working in the office; it was small, there was no natural light, it smelled like Mack, and every minute or so I was reminded of the way he'd kissed me on top of the desk last night. Not a reminder I needed right at this moment—I was trying to respond to countless emails about event requests.

I snapped the laptop shut. Why was I the one being punished? Locked away in the tiny, windowless, Mack-smelling office? I didn't deserve to be in here. I deserved to be out front like I usually was. And that was what I was going to do.

He was behind the bar when I marched out. I gave him only the briefest of glances but I felt his eyes moving over the side of my face and down my neck. I ignored it, which was not without difficulty because it was like a featherlight touch. For all his staring he didn't say a word.

Still a silent standoff, then. Fine by me. I really hoped he was prepared to lose.

I pulled up a stool, perched myself on top of it and opened the laptop. Unaffected. I was unaffected. And very busy. Lots to do. Definitely no time to watch Mack in my peripheral vision to catch glimpses of his abs when he reached for a high bottle. Nope, no time for any of that.

I was busy. Busy. Busy. Busy.

"Why are you two acting weird?" Micky asked, one hand planted on a popped hip. Her pixie cut hair was a vibrant, cherry red today.

I flattened a hand against my chest and glanced over both shoulders. *Who, me?*

"Yeah, you," she said at my overly confused look, then pointed at Mack. "And him. What's up with you?"

I shrugged. "No idea what you're talking about, Micky. I'm working. He's working. Seems pretty normal to me."

"Normal?" She snorted. "I usually can't shut the two of you up, but neither of you have said a word to one another in over an hour?"

I shrugged, still steadfastly avoiding looking in Mack's direction. "Maybe we just don't feel like talking today."

Her eyes narrowed into slits but she didn't say anything else. It took all of my self-restraint to not look over at Mack to see his reaction. I wasn't looking because I didn't care. Not. One. Bit. When he was ready to apologize, we'd talk. Until then. Silence for all.

The Friday night crowd arrived all at once. Or at least that was how it felt. One minute there were only a few people milling around and the next we were slammed. I wasn't complaining because it provided a substantial distraction and put an end to my overthinking, for the most part. Was I still watching Mack out of the corner of my eye? Yes, occasionally, but there wasn't time to dwell on the fact he was leaning on the bar and smiling his most flirtatious smile at a particularly cute girl with platinum blonde french braids and a nose ring.

Something hot and ugly bubbled in my stomach the longer I watched them and I realized with alarm that I knew this feeling. Jealousy. I was jealous. I wanted him to be smiling at *me* like that. Instead, he had barely looked at me all day.

I forced myself to look away and focused my attention on the long line of customers waiting for their Friday night fix. But my mind continued to wander as I pulled pints of IPA and mixed countless Negronis—the evening's drink of choice, it would appear. He wasn't speaking to me but flirting his fucking face off with platinum french braids. What the hell was that all about? I ran over yesterday's argument in my head. Had it really been that offensive for me to suggest that we keep things to ourselves for the moment? Unless, did he think I was embarrassed? Of him? No, why the hell would he think that. You cannot be friends with someone for almost twenty years if you're embarrassed of them. That couldn't be it. It had to be something else getting his boxer-briefs in a bunch.

"Thirty-two-eighty," I said to the guy who had a serious Kurt Cobain thing happening. He dropped a couple of singles into the tip jar and left, and I could no longer see Mack or cute french braid girl.

"Yo, Chase," Greyson called from further down the bar. "We need napkins."

"Can it wait?"

"Nope, need 'em pronto."

I didn't bother arguing, just turned and headed for the office and Greyson's napkins. I weaved through the bodies between the bar and the hall. Everyone was in a particularly jovial mood, the holiday spirit alive and well at Rudi Blue. I wanted to choke them all with string lights and tinsel.

"What are you doing?" Mack asked as I entered the office. I hadn't been expecting to see him perched there on the desk. The sight of him only irritated me more.

"Greyson needed—hey!" I was shoved from behind and went sailing forward straight into Mack's chest as the door slammed closed. "What the fuck?" My hands were flattened against wide pecs and I was half sprawled across his thighs with his strong hands at my waist. I wanted to sink into him, bury my face in his neck and take a long, satisfying sniff. But I was still angry at him.

"I don't know what's going on with you two but you're not coming out until you sort it," Greyson yelled through the door. This was a joke. This had to be a joke.

I peeled myself off Mack and tried the door handle only for it to come off in my hand. "Greyson," I growled. "You had better open this fucking door. Right. Now."

"No can do, boss, you're both killing the vibe. Now kiss and make up." He rapped on the door and then footsteps retreated. I was going to kill him. But first I'd make him scrub the entire bar from top to bottom and clean every toilet with a fucking toothbrush.

"Can't you do something?" I said to Mack, throwing him the useless door handle.

He caught it only to put it on the desk. "Like what, Chase?"

Was he serious? "I don't know, Mack, maybe like open the fucking door."

"You say that like it's my fault we're in here."

"That's because it is your fault we're in here." I poked a finger into his chest. "Aside from the fact you were supposed to fix the door months ago, if you hadn't gone and had your hissy fit yesterday we would not be locked in our fucking office with a full bar of customers out there."

He stood, using his height as a weapon. I hated it when he did that but, right now, with my heart beating fast, it was difficult to tell if I was just mad at him, or something else as well.

"I still don't see what the big deal is." I said before he had a chance to open his mouth. "So, we don't tell anyone, so what?"

"So what?" he echoed.

"Yes." I backed up against the door as he came closer, willing my voice not to shake. "So. What? We've been on two dates. Two dates, Mack. And I didn't want to get carried away. I just wanted some time to get my head around everything."

"Why the hell didn't you just say that yesterday?" Was he serious?

"Because my brain has turned into a pile of mush! I see you and all I can think about is kissing you. It's a fucking problem. Also, you didn't exactly give me the chance to elaborate, you just jumped straight on the defensive and got all pissed at me without actually waiting for an explanation."

He opened and closed his mouth a couple of times, adorably (and frustratingly) speechless. "I—yeah, I guess I did. But I—I want to tell people. I want people to know you're my girlfriend."

I sucked in a startled, wheezy breath. Mack hadn't had a girlfriend in years. Why now? Why me? Did he miss the part about two dates? Two dates wasn't a relationship status. Two dates wasn't much more than we liked the way the other one looked. Or it would be if it was anyone other than Mack.

"I'm not fucking around here, Chase, I'm not doing this for shits and giggles. I'm doing it because I want you. Just you." My brain was scrambling to keep up with his confession.

Girlfriend. He wanted me to be his girlfriend. He wanted to tell people I was his girlfriend.

"What about platinum braids?"

His brow pinched. "What?"

"The girl with the platinum French braids and the nose ring. You were lookin' awful cozy while you were talking to her earlier."

"I have no idea who you're talking about. I've talked to a lot of people tonight, Chase."

"A lot of people who aren't me," I grumbled, watching the toe of my boot scuff the floor. "I'm scared." The words tripped out before I had a chance to stop them.

"Of what? Of me?"

My eyes shot up to his. "No, not you. Well, sort of." I fidgeted with the knot in my shirt. "This is all moving kinda fast and I'm scared because it doesn't feel fast enough. I'm scared because I don't do well with change—as you know—and this is about the biggest change I've dealt with ... maybe ever, and that's coming from a kid who moved a couple times a year. I'm scared because the thought of losing you as a friend is one thing but losing these new parts too ..." I shook my head.

There was more. I was scared he'd wake up one day and realize we shouldn't have crossed this line. I was scared that he'd meet someone else, someone better, someone who deserved him and what the hell would I do then? I was scared he'd leave. Because growing up that was all I saw men do.

But I knew if I said that he'd tell me he wouldn't leave and I couldn't stand to hear him say it only for it to happen later. Telling people now, letting their opinions in, I didn't know if I could do it.

"Chase ..." His hands slid over my hips, pulling me into him. "I'm scared too."

"You are?"

He dropped his head back and laughed. "Of course I fucking am! Feels like we've got a lot on the line here, you know?"

I slapped his chest. "Yes, I know. That's why I wanted some time to get my head around things, before we tell people, you dunce."

"I thought you were ashamed."

"Ashamed!? Of what? Ashamed of you?" He nodded. "Milton Alfred Carmichael, you are the best person I know."

He snorted. "Don't go saying things you'll want to take back, Chastity."

"That is one thing I will never want to take back," I assured him, fingers twisting into his shirt. He really was the best person I knew, and I didn't see that changing, which was why all of this scared me even more.

We stood there, staring at one another. The tension seeped out of his features, softening the lines of his face, bringing light back to his eyes.

"Well, I guess that means there's only one thing left to do..." he purred.

"What's that?"

He leaned in, a wicked glint in his eyes and I anticipated the words just before he said them. "Kiss and make up."

I started to laugh but it cut off in a gasp as he lifted me up, spun us around and laid me out on the desk before his mouth descended over mine. Electricity erupted across my skin as my legs curled around his hips, hands exploring, tongues tangling. I was dimly aware that we should not be doing this here. Not when Greyson held the keys to our cell and could walk in at any moment. But I didn't care, not when Mack tasted like heaven and his fingers were biting into my ass and all I wanted was to stay here until we were both limp and satisfied.

He groaned into my mouth as I explored the muscles of his

back, my thighs squeezing in an effort to relieve the growing ache in my core. We should stop. We should stop this now, before things went further than they should. I knew it was the right thing to stop and yet my body was not listening to reason. It wanted skin. It wanted Mack mindless.

I pushed a hand past the waistband of his jeans, fingers finding hot, hard flesh and his forehead came down on my shoulder.

"Fuck, Chase."

22

MACK

"IS THIS—ARE YOU OKAY?" she asked, her breath ruffling my hair.

"Are you serious?" I panted. "Your hand is on my cock. I'm more than okay." I was going to black out from sheer sensory overload. The smell of her. The feel of her. The taste of her. The sound of her. The fact she was just as scared as I was, but we were still fucking doing this thing, because the only way was forward. We were in it—together.

I leaned into her, planting one hand on the desk behind her as she popped the button on my jeans to give herself a little more room to move. Fucking hell, her hand felt good, warm and firm without being constricting. She'd barely even done anything yet and I already felt embarrassingly close to coming.

Then she was moving, and all I could do was grip the desk with one hand and her thigh with the other and will myself to remain upright. Her hand moved in even strokes with just enough pressure to make me go cross eyed.

Sweat beaded on my forehead as I focused on not coming like a fucking teenager. I collected my wits enough, through

the fog of feeling, to realize that I wanted to be making her come, too. I fumbled with the edge of her skirt, pushing it out of the way as best I could as she sat on the desk and continued to jack me off in the hottest fucking handjob I'd ever experienced.

Greyson would be back, probably sooner rather than later, because there were a lot of people out front and they were two staff members down, but I needed another five minutes. Ten if I wanted to do things right, but I could work with five.

Chase's legs eased open and, as much as I wanted to be buried inside her, over the clothes was going to have to do. Her moan as soon as I made contact with her clit through her tights sent a shot of heat down my spine, tightening my balls.

Our mouths came together in a messy, desperate kiss as our hands worked each other to the point of madness. The small space was filled with the sounds of us, panting, moaning, needy. I had never wanted to come so badly in my life, while also wanting it to last forever.

"Yes, Mack, there—oh God, there."

"Here?" I managed to choke out as I circled the spot and her grip tightened.

"*Yes.*"

"So close, Chase."

"Me too. Don't stop," she panted.

"Fuck."

"Mack."

In a moment of clarity I grabbed for the box of promo shirts and managed to cover Chase's skirt just before I came with a long, tortured groan.

"Don't stop," she begged, one hand still on my cock while the other twisted in my hair. "I'm—"

I swallowed her cry as she came, thighs pinning my hand between them, moisture meeting my skin through her

underwear and tights. God, I wanted to lose myself in her entirely.

We sat there for a long moment, breath slowing, just staring at one another. I had this feeling that my entire world had shrunk down to this office, to this woman. This was all that existed. I wanted to say something, but had no idea what. Nothing was enough.

Her eyes went wide and darted to the door. Part of me recognized that she was trying to silently communicate something but I was still too out of it to decipher it.

"If you still don't fucking get it, Mack," she screeched and I stumbled backward. "Then I don't know what to do for you! I can't explain it again!"

"Wh—"

"They're still at it, give 'em another five," Greyson said beyond the door and I stared at Chase. She gestured at my cock, still half hanging out of my jeans. I stuffed it back in as my brain started to regain full function.

"Fine, fine, you're right," I said, overly loud, and she grinned. Even in a fake fight Chase loved to hear she was right. I really wanted to kiss her again but figured that might start an actual fight. Although, considering how we resolved the last one, I might start picking fights a couple of times a week. Not speaking to her for nearly a day had almost killed me, though.

She slid off the desk, hands coming to my waist. "So glad you've finally come to your senses. Now where *the fuck* is Greyson. If he doesn't come back and let us out of here I am going to get seriously creative with punishments."

"Like you don't have one in mind already ..." I whispered and she winked. She was going to make him wish he was dead.

There was some rattling on the other side of the door and a second later it swung open, Greyson and Micky standing in the hall.

"It was his idea," she said immediately and he swallowed as Chase came to stand in front of me. I didn't have to see her to know the glare she was delivering. The look on Greyson's face said it all.

"You were bringing down the vibe, I stand by it," he said, with an audible gulp. "Am I fired?"

"No," Chase said, her tone deceptively cheery. "But you might wish you were. Get back to work, both of you."

They each mumbled some form of 'yes boss' and bolted. Chase turned to me with wide, how the hell did we not just get busted, eyes.

"They never call me boss."

"You nearly got caught with your cock out in our office," she whisper-hissed. Hearing her say the word cock made it twitch in my pants.

"Lucky you have hearing like a meerkat and are always ready to berate me at a moment's notice."

She smiled, took a quick peek back out the door and then pulled me down for a kiss. "No more fooling around here. That was way too close."

"Agreed. I prefer to really feel it when you come."

She choked on her response and retied her ponytail. When it was done, she was back to business-mode Chase. I followed her out front, enjoying the extra sway in her hips as she went.

The rest of the night passed without incident. And, despite saying there would be no more fooling around, Chase had pulled me into the office twice to make out. I was not complaining.

We locked up and I walked Chase home so that I could have the pleasure of once again pinning her to the door. Her fingers curled into the top of my waistband as she sucked on my lower lip.

"Well," she started, taking a second to breathe. "I should probably go inside."

I nodded, hands still roaming over her hips and butt. "And I should probably leave."

"You should do that, yes." A grin. "Oh, and you won't be working Tuesday."

"I won't?"

"No, we have a date." Her smile stretched into a grin.

"Is that right?"

"Yup."

"You're not telling me anything about it, are you?"

"Absolutely not." She tapped my cheek before shoving me backwards and disappearing inside with a wink and wave. Tuesday could not come soon enough. Not that I wasn't going to see her pretty much everyday between now and then anyway.

IT SHOULD NOT HAVE COME as a surprise that Chase had followed through on her threat to blindfold me going into our date. She wasn't usually one to back down once a challenge had been set. She was, however, a little late.

"There's no need for this now, is there?" I asked, as she waved what looked like an oversized sleep mask in my direction. "I don't know if you noticed but the date started over an hour ago." And I was stuffed to the gills with wings and jalapeno poppers as a result. The woman knew me well.

She shot me an indulgent smile, and I was momentarily mesmerized by the cherry red curve of her full lower lip. "In fact, Milton." My eyes snapped to hers. "That was merely the warm up, now the actual date begins."

"Is that so?"

"Oh yes." The amusement in her eyes stuttered for a beat.

"I hope I haven't oversold it, actually. What if it's not all that exciting? Maybe I should just tell you ... the pressure of delivering an outstanding date after you put a fucking tent in your apartment is kind of hectic. I don't know why I even insisted I wanted to plan it. Well, that was before the tent, wasn't it? Okay, so we're—"

"No!" I clamped a hand over her mouth, the other arm curling around her back to keep her from tipping backwards onto her ass. "We have not come this far for you to spill the beans now. Tell Maureen to shut the fuck up."

"But what if you hate it?" she mumbled.

"Do you really think I'll hate it?"

She kissed my palm and heat shot down my spine. "No, I don't think you'll hate it, but what if you're bored, or underwhelmed. Do I need to mention the tent again?"

"You do not need to mention the tent again, and if you planned the date then I'm sure it's going to be great. I have endless faith in you."

"Mm-hm. Blind faith."

I kissed the tip of her nose. "You could not plan something underwhelming if you tried."

"I suppose we'll see. Come on, put this on." She slipped the mask over my head and pulled it down to completely obscure my vision. Blind faith indeed.

Ten minutes later we were in an uber heading uptown. Or at least I assumed we were heading uptown. Part of me would have preferred to be on the subway, yes I would have looked like a crackpot, but at least I'd have some idea of where we were going. It was surprisingly difficult to get your bearings when you couldn't see a thing.

"Stop fidgeting with it." Chase slapped my hand away from my face before I could adjust the mask. For something that looked plush it was really fucking itchy. Lucky for me the car slowed and it was plucked from my head as we pulled up.

I took in our surroundings. The Garden. "It has been far too long since we've gone to a game."

"That's what I thought," she said with an uncharacteristically shy smile. Still worried that I wouldn't like it—please, she could take me pretty much anywhere and I'd be happy to be there so long as I was next to her.

"Let's get in there." I dragged her out of the car and into the swarm of people flowing inside.

I fucking loved The Garden. I still remembered the first time I'd gone. I was maybe six or seven, the sound had been completely overwhelming, and I could barely see a thing unless my middle brother Marcus was holding me up, but I loved every minute of it. I made a mental note to ask Pip about bringing the twins.

Chase and I swung past the refreshments stand before heading to our seats and, despite just eating dinner, she still bought a large popcorn and a hot dog along with our four beers. As a general rule, I didn't drink watered down, lukewarm beer but basketball beer was the exception. I didn't care that it tasted like beer-flavored Kool Aid, it was all part of the charm.

"You know you didn't have to worry, right?" I said once we were in our seats. She'd peeled off her jacket, revealing an old Knicks jersey knotted at her navel. She looked seriously fucking cute.

"It's not ice skating or a super romantic tent in my apartment though, is it?" she said after swallowing her mouthful of popcorn and washing it down with a gulp of beer. "Who would have thought you'd be such a date overachiever."

"I can't say that I have been in the past." I'd never put any kind of thought into dating in the past. There was drinks, maybe dinner, and then sex. That about covered it. It wasn't anything against the women I'd dated, I just didn't feel invested, not like I did now. Not like I did with Chase.

"I bring out your overachiever, do I?"

"You certainly inspire it."

She tipped her head back and I dropped a brief kiss on her smiling mouth.

The next two-ish hours were spent yelling ourselves hoarse as the Knicks lost by two points to the Timberwolves. Chase and I had been featured on the kiss-cam twice, and I took great pleasure in pulling her in and kissing the hell out of her in front of all those people. I happily finished at least five (maybe six) warm, watered-down beers, and I couldn't stop fucking smiling.

It wasn't the first time that we had been to a game at The Garden. It wasn't even the first time we'd been on the kiss-cam —although the last time it happened she palmed my face and pushed me into the aisle (which got a lot of cheers). It would be easy to say that tonight was different because we were different, but it was the same, too. We still teased and Chase still stole the last of my popcorn and tried to get me to get her a diet coke in the last minute of the game (I only fell for it the one time). We were still us. There was something comforting in that.

23

CHASE

I WAS STARTING to think I might have been wrong about Mack and I being able to go back to friends. It might have been possible after our first date. Now, though, after date number three (and, if I was being honest, it was true after date number two), after he walked me home again and kissed me like he was starving and I was food. The line had been crossed.

For whatever reason, I had told myself, had unwaveringly believed, that line was in the bedroom. There was this movie moment in my head, of him and I together and it was that *'this is it'* moment. I figured so long as we didn't get to that moment we'd be okay. Before we went *all the way* it would be simple enough to pull up the reins and bring this baby to a stop. I was mixing metaphors. It was a sure sign of discombobulation.

I growled under my breath and the woman beside me shot a look from behind her book. And now I was scaring fellow commuters. *Great work, Chase, really great work.*

In short, I was fucked.

Because there wasn't one moment that changed everything. It was more pieces falling into place, a growing realization, a slow dawning, and the sky was already well and truly pinkish over here. But I refused to accept the truth of the situation. Accepting that meant I had far too much to lose and I just couldn't do it.

I suppose, then, I should be grateful for today's activities and the distraction they would provide.

It was a short walk home from the subway and, despite not living here for a solid ten years, it was still home. I didn't know how it could be anything else. The narrow row house was white with salmon-colored shutters and a small porch I had lived on in the summer. It was the first place since Aunt Peggy's that had actually felt like home because it was just ours. Unlike every other weird-smelling, drafty place we'd lived in from Idaho to Tennessee. I had never understood Mom's need to pack up and leave as soon as she went through another break up.

Now, though, I was starting to get it.

"I didn't think I'd see you today," Mom said, giving only the barest glance over her shoulder as I walked into the empty kitchen. She was in business mode; no makeup, no earrings, her ashy hair secured in a large clip up and out of the way. She was getting shit done today. And she was beautiful, even when I was mad at her. Even when I knew she was mad at me.

"I told you I'd be here, didn't I?" I was well aware of how childish I sounded but I couldn't stop it. Selling this house, it wasn't just the house, it was Peggy too. She was the only reason we could afford it in the first place, the only reason I could go to Carrington, the only reason I wasn't buried under student loans after college. The woman was like a grandmother and a guardian angel and it just didn't feel right to be letting it go.

"I miss her, too." The words were so low I almost missed them. Mom turned and bumped a hip against the kitchen counter. "She was the only one who accepted me, after everything."

"You mean when you got pregnant with me." It was sometimes difficult to feel great about your existence when both your father and grandparents didn't want you. When you were considered a mistake.

"Even before. I was different from the rest of my family, so was Peggy. I think it's why she was always my favorite. She blazed her own path and that made other people uncomfortable. But there are better ways to honor her memory than to keep a house that neither of us are living in."

The temptation to say that she might live in it again when things didn't work out with Derrick was strong. I held the words back, not keen to make the tensions running between us worse than they already were.

"She would have been proud of you."

"Thanks, Mom." I swallowed against the spontaneous tightness in my throat. I didn't often let myself think of Peggy. It hurt too much, and the memories of her were faded now, so much so I wasn't sure what was real and what I'd made up from looking at photos. I'd only been three or four when we left the stability of Peggy's home. I'd go and visit over the summers but Mom and I didn't go back for any real length of time until she was sick. And because she hadn't told us until there wasn't anything left to be done we only had a few months before she was gone. Stubborn old thing. Mom was right, she did blaze her own path and wouldn't be told by anyone. Her raspy voice floated through my head, *I miss you like I love you, baby girl—madly*. Twenty years last July and her loss still hurt like hell.

"I'm proud of you too, you know." The words were wobbly, Mom wasn't good at fighting. She wasn't a grudge holder like I was.

"I know, Mom." I let myself be wrapped in her hug and

sunk into it. She had smelled the same for as long as I could remember. Roses and fresh laundry and something else that was just her. Probably some perfume that had long been discontinued but she somehow had a black market supply of the stuff. Peggy had been the same, her scent a specific and comforting combination that was forever imprinted in my brain. Tobacco, jasmine and cedar. I'd tried to have it replicated over the years but could never get it quite right.

"We never needed a place to be home, we had each other. We'll always have each other, Chase. You'll always have me, you have to know that."

"I do know that, Mom." I squeezed her tighter, once again not willing to spill the words that sat hot on the tip of my tongue. It was selfish of me to be mad for having to share her. I was an adult, and she deserved a life of her own. At least we had today, just she and I, soaking in memories of how our lives had once looked. I was genuinely scared for what I was going to find in my old closet.

"Ah, Chase! You're here. I wasn't sure we were going to see you today!" Derrick said and just like that all those warm and fuzzy feelings evaporated. I worked really hard to school my features that so desperately wanted to settle into a deep sneer. Mom's hand twitched ever so slightly on my waist.

"Derrick, hey, I didn't realize I'd be seeing *you* today." I stepped out of Mom's grip and shot her a bland smile that I hoped didn't communicate too much of what was going on in my head. "I'll be upstairs."

"I'll bring up some boxes and trash bags!" she called after me.

I knew I needed to be okay with this relationship, and I was, for the most part. But that didn't mean I was okay with him being here today. We were dismantling our old lives so she could move forward with her new one, so she could move forward with him. Did he really need to be present while we picked through the carcass? Did he not have a fucking job? It was ten on Thursday morning, that was usually when people were at their desks in their offices, right?

Oh god, he wasn't going to get half of this place when we sold, was he? Was that why he was so enthusiastic about moving us out, because he was set to gain? I pushed the thought aside. Mom might be dopey in love with the guy but she wasn't going to let him take half of what was ours.

After a brief pause on the landing I pushed open the door to my old room. The space was a time capsule of young Chase. Everything I'd wanted when I moved out came with me and the rest had stayed behind to gather dust and remind me of simpler, more cringe-worthy times.

The mirror was still ringed with photos from school, showing the numerous phases I passed through before I knew who I was. Although, admittedly, I still wasn't entirely sure who that was a lot of the time.

The braces phase. The acne phase. The blunt bangs emo phase. The pizza rolls every night of the week until I started to resemble a pizza roll phase. The I don't care about how I look (except I really, really do care about how I look) phase.

And through all of them, good or bad—mostly bad—Nash and Mack were beside me, smiling like goofballs. I should really put some of these in our group chat.

From the moment we met in the girls' bathroom, we'd been pretty much inseparable. Not on my account. I was perfectly happy to go through high school without any actual friends, it had worked up until that point, after all. You get used to being alone when you move schools as often as I did. Alone was easy. Alone worked for me. It meant I could focus on my school work and get into college and make Aunt Peggy proud. But the two of them had other plans. They didn't leave me alone. They saved me seats at lunch. They somehow managed to rearrange class schedules so the three of us were together in every period. They dragged me along to every godforsaken party no matter the night of the week. The three of us were a unit. They were the first people that didn't have to be friends with me because we were neighbors or because our parents were dating. Those were less friendships than they were truces, agreements to get along until we never saw each other again. And, as grotesquely cheesy as it was to admit, they made me feel like just being me was enough. That I was worthy of friendship just because of who I was.

"Okay!" Mom said, pulling me out of my head. I hadn't expected to feel quite so emotional. But then everything with Mack was not helping my mental state right at the moment so I guess it was to be expected. I wondered if I should tell Mom. Ask for advice. But the words lodged themselves in my throat and refused to move.

Oblivious to my internal meltdown, Mom kept talking, "You've got three choices. Keep. Donate. Trash. Keep can go into this box. Donate this one and trash in the bag. You want me to help?"

"I got it, Mom, thanks." I turned back to the room, to young Chase. Mom hadn't left, I could sense her hovering just inside the door.

"He offered to help. It felt strange to say no."

I hated that I'd made her feel like she needed to explain. But of course she felt like she had to. I had never been an easy person.

"You don't need to justify why your husband is here." The word husband only sounded slightly sarcastic.

"Chase, will you look at me please."

I turned to face her.

"I understand that this has all been hard for you. Things

happened quickly with Derrick, I certainly didn't anticipate the two of us being married and living together before Christmas. And, yet, here we are."

"Here we are," I echoed.

"But I'm happy and I want you to be happy for me." God that made me feel like a terrible daughter, and it should, because I hadn't been acting like I was happy for her. I'd been too busy moping and thinking of myself.

"I am, of course I am."

"Are we going to talk about Thanksgiving?"

"Do you think right now is the best time to do that?"

"I don't think there is a best time for it, sweetheart, but considering Christmas is a little over a week away, I think it needs to happen. I want you to be part of this family."

Just when I thought the knife in my chest was gone it twisted again. She wanted me to be part of the new family. Because our little family was gone now. It would never be just the two of us again. Or, more likely, it would, when things with Derrick went sideways and she was alone again. The same way she had been over and over. Why was she putting so much into this one? What made Derrick different? He was nice, sure, but that didn't mean it was going to last any longer than the rest. Could she really not see the ending?

"We're having dinner on Christmas Eve, at home, it won't be the same without you there."

Home. They were having Christmas dinner at *home*. I wanted to scream and run as fast and as far from here as I could. But I didn't. Instead I just nodded and picked up the trash bag.

"Of course, I'll be there." Maybe I'd even bring some of Mack's new ice cream. Maybe I could bring Mack. That felt like both the best and worst idea all at once. Would he come with me? Did I want him to? I didn't particularly like the person I was with Mom and Derrick and their new family, I wasn't sure I wanted Mack to see that and yet I couldn't deny the fact that him being there would make me feel like I had someone on my side.

"Thank you."

"You don't need to thank me for that."

She came up behind me and wrapped her arms around my middle, her chin resting on my shoulder. "You're my whole heart walking around outside my body, I hope you know that, baby."

I squeezed her hands. "I better get started if I want to make it to work on time."

"Of course, let me know if you need any help."

"I will, thanks."

After one last squeeze she let me go and left the room and I stood there staring at posters of the Jonas Brothers and Kings of Leon with no real idea where to start.

24

MACK

I ROUNDED the corner onto Grand and heard my name ring out. Once. Twice. I wondered if it could be another Mack, I certainly wasn't the only one, but then—

"Mackenzie! Are you ignoring me!?" Harley called and I spotted her, curls contained under a bright yellow beanie and wrapped up from knee to neck in a black and white houndstooth jacket. I jogged across the street at her wildly beckoning hand.

"Not ignoring, Harley," I assured her, bumping my knuckles against her fist.

"I should hope not," she quipped, pointing to the bubblegum-pink haired woman beside her. "This is Odette, Jemma's assistant." We shook hands.

"Hey, good to meet you."

"O, this is Mackenzie."

"Just Mack, actually," I corrected. Harley shook her head like I was a child she often humored and I wondered where the hell that kind of unflappable confidence came from. Perhaps it went along with her presence that took up space and drew you in until you found yourself in her orbit without quite meaning to be there.

"Nice to meet you," Odette said, her smile crinkling the corners of her steely eyes.

"How's everything?" I cleared my throat. "How's Jemma?" I didn't get to know her all that well before the wedding and things turned to shit between her and Nash, but what I did know of her I liked. And I was still hoping Harley was right about them working things out.

"Good, busy."

"What are you doing?" Harley asked, diffusing the ripple of awkwardness. "We're about to meet Hunter for lunch at Dodos, you want to join?"

"That's cool, I don't want to crash."

"You're not crashing, I just invited you, also I have something important to discuss."

"What's that?"

"Well, you'll just have to come to lunch and find out, won't you." She hooked her arms through mine and Odette's. "Come on."

We walked a couple of blocks, with Harley chatting away about nothing in particular, before we came to a hole in the wall place that smelled incredible. Hunter jogged around the corner a second later, his face split in a grin.

'Hey man, didn't know you'd be here, too." We clasped hands and bumped shoulders before he pulled Harley into a hug.

"You remember Odette?"

"Sure do, hey."

"We picked Mack up along the way. Come on, I am craving kimchi and barbeque pork," Harley said, leading the way inside. The rest of us were given no choice but to follow.

Halfway through lunch I made a mental note to bring

Chase back here because it was outstanding. There was barely enough room for the ten tables inside and you couldn't move your chair without bumping into someone—but the food and the service were incredible.

"So," Harley started as she finished her mouthful. "I need a pie."

"Oh-kay," I said, taking a sip of water and waiting for more information.

"I need one of *your* pies," she clarified and I waited for the rest of the question but that appeared to be it.

"Did you have one in mind?"

"I'm glad you asked, because yes, preferably the chocolate espresso. Although, honestly, I'll take whatever you are willing to give me. Obviously I'll pay you both for the pie and your silence."

"My silence?"

"I need to pass it off as my own."

Hunter laughed. Harley didn't look the least bit repentant.

"You cannot judge," she said while pointing her fork at me across the table. "You have not eaten this man's pie. I took some of your pie home after Thanksgiving and Murphy found it in my fridge. He said it was the best pie he'd ever tasted, so, naturally, I told him I made it. He thought I was lying because he's not a complete idiot, but now I need to back up my lie by taking an equally impressive pie to Christmas."

"And you can't cook one?"

"Well, yes, but I am a caffeine dealer, that is my strong suit, not pie. Only yours will do. And maybe some ice cream because that stuff was good enough to get me a little wet."

Hunter choked on his mouthful and Odette squawked out a laugh. Harley once again looked entirely unphased.

"Don't. Judge," she said, spearing a piece of pork. "You can't, not until you've eaten it for yourselves. I thought Nash was good when he gave us a sneaky peek tasting of the wedding menu—it was blow your fucking socks off good—but phew, I tell you what, man, you have a gift with pastry."

"Thank you, Harley," I said, wishing this conversation would come to a swift end, even as my cheeks went warm at the praise.

"You're welcome." She beamed. "So, how much?"

"You don't need to pay me, I'll make you the pie and keep my mouth shut."

"No. Way. That is your art, Mack, you can't just give it away! It deserves remuneration for your time and skill. I would be robbing you otherwise."

"I don't want your money. My pie. My rules," I said and couldn't help but wonder if maybe Chase had spoken to her. Either way I was happy for Harley to take a pie and call it her own.

I WAS ROUSED from sleep on Saturday morning by a knock at the door. It couldn't be Chase, she would have just invited herself in, but I couldn't think of anyone else I knew that would be dropping by this early on a Saturday morning.

I was sorely tempted to ignore whoever it was, but then my phone started up and I threw out a hand, feeling blindly on the nightstand before bringing it to my ear.

"Is someone dead or dying?" I asked without bothering to look at the caller ID.

"Get your butt out of bed and let me in or I'll start shouting about how you've got crabs," my sister said, then promptly hung up. Someone was in a mood this morning. Not that she had any right to be when she was the one waking me up after roughly four hours sleep. Sometimes I wished I worked a nine to five, then I considered how soul destroying it would be for me to sit in an office all day and my hours at Rudi didn't seem so bad after all.

With a groan I pulled myself to standing and shuffled through my apartment. Pip was standing on the doorstep with two large coffees and a bag full of something that made my mouth water. A wise choice.

"What the hell are you doing here?" I asked, running a hand over my face, as she pushed past me. The scents of coffee and cinnamon had me following in her wake.

"I was doing some shopping and thought I'd stop by."

"You were doing some shopping in my neighborhood?" Never had a lie been easier to shoot holes through, and that wasn't even taking into account the fact it was barely eight in the morning. She must have left her place close to six.

"Well no, I haven't done the shopping yet."

"Right."

"I wanted to talk to you about the Christmas menu."

"The Christmas menu? You needed to talk to me about the Christmas menu, right now?"

"You'd rather I come back?"

I took a slow sip of coffee, hoping the bitter, caffeine-charged liquid would help to fire up the extra brain cells that I was in need of to make sense of this conversation. "I'd rather you just tell me what's going on?"

"Why would anything be going on?"

"Oh, I don't know, maybe the fact that you've turned up on my doorstep at eight a.m. on a Saturday is ringing a couple of alarm bells, is all."

"Mack, we cannot all sleep until noon." She whipped a notebook out of her enormous shoulder bag, flipped it open and sat, pen poised. "Now, how many pies will you be making and will Chase be coming along?"

"Considering Chase has been for the last four years, yes, I think that it's fair to say she'll be there."

"Excellent, and has there been any progress between the two of you since we last spoke?"

"Why the fuck are you talking like a robot?"

"I'm not."

"You are, it's weird." I took another gulp of coffee, letting it burn its way down. I knew I had confided in Pip about all of the Chase stuff but now that things were actually happening, and Chase was less than enthusiastic about people knowing, I wasn't sure if updating Pip was really the right thing to do. Even assuming I swore her to secrecy, which would be necessary, there was still an excellent chance she'd have one too many mulled wines at Christmas and tell anyone who'd listen. No, it wasn't worth the risk. Did it annoy me that I needed to keep this a secret from my sister? Yes, a little. But the long term pay off making a relationship work with Chase was worth the temporary annoyance.

Could Pip provide some insight, though? Maybe some advice on what might make Chase more comfortable and less likely to get skittish and freak out? I had no fucking idea what I was actually doing in the whole relationship arena. I figured that you just had to treat the person with respect, start from a base of mutual trust and friendship and you were good, right? In theory it made sense to me. Chase and I had all those things along with the kind of chemistry that threatened to set my hair on fire, but was that really all there was to it? Was I missing something?

"Can I assume that means you've not talked to her then?" Pip said, taking a sip from her own cup.

"No updates." The lie slipped out easily and she looked suitably disappointed enough to show me she believed it. I didn't like the idea that we were both keeping things to ourselves, when Pip had always been the one that I could confide in. Soon, I reminded myself, soon I'd be able to tell her everything, assuming Chase and I got past date five and she didn't pull the pin. I couldn't let myself think that her changing her mind was an option.

IN THE SUMMER between junior and senior year, Chase, Nash, and I spent an inordinate amount of time out at The Rockaways. And almost every day Chase managed to complain about how the water was too cold. This memory came back to me as I got into the car on Monday morning and I wondered if I'd perhaps made a mistake with today's date. If she thought the water was cold in the middle of July, what the hell was she going to think about it the week before Christmas? In my defense, I'd been watching the swell forecast all week and today was the pick of the days. It was now or never and, considering I hadn't been in the water in a couple of weeks, I was taking now.

"She'll be okay," I said, the words filling the empty car and laughing at me. I could even go so far as to say she might have fun, but that might be a stretch. It was too late to back out now though. We were doing this thing—and I felt moderately confident that she'd be happy with it... once it was over.

I started the car, pulled out onto the street and headed in the direction of Chase's apartment. In keeping with our previous three dates, I had given her very little information about what we were actually doing. The only thing I had said in the text yesterday was: *pack a bag*. Naturally, she'd had a laundry list of questions, all of which I managed to answer with as little detail as possible to drive her mad. I wouldn't be at all surprised if she slapped me as soon as she saw me today.

Was it a good idea to be planning an overnight trip when

this was only date four? No, it was probably the worst and most torturous thing I could have done to the both of us. I had gone back and forth on whether or not to actually do it. But, in the end, the idea of being curled up with her in front of a fire had won out over any blue-ball related issues. I also had a bottle of whiskey with our names on it, and I was not going to be one of those people who'd drink and drive.

Nerves were making my palms clammy as I pulled onto Chase's street. I hadn't intended to keep this a secret from her, I just figured I'd show her once everything was done. But, as with all remodeling, it took longer than I anticipated and other things got in the way.

Chase was already on the sidewalk as I pulled up to the curb. She looked ready for a snow trek, rugged up from head to toe. Snow boots, black jeans—that I could almost guarantee had thermals under them—and a black coat that hit her at mid thigh.

I got out to put her bag in the trunk but she threw it in the backseat, while balancing two coffees in her other hand, before I could even get around the car.

"What are you doing?" she asked with a startled little squeak as I pinned her to the passenger door. God, she was beautiful.

"I was trying to be a gentleman," I said, mouth hovering over hers as the electricity crackled between us.

"Well, a gentleman has got to be quicker than that, sir." The golden flecks in her dark eyes twinkled with amusement. "What's this new obsession with being a gentleman anyway?" She pressed up ever-so-slightly to bring our lips together but I retreated.

"Making a lady wait isn't terribly gentlemanly," she added with a pout, arching further up.

"Oh, but it is fun..." I closed the distance with a low growl and was rewarded with a breathy moan and the slide of her tongue past my lips. I could happily kiss her right where we were for the rest of the day, but I had plans.

I took the coffees, gave her one last kiss and opened the door. "In—we've got places to be."

"Oh, do we, now?"

"Yup." I handed her back the tray once she was situated then rounded the hood and climbed into the driver's seat.

"And where, exactly, are we going?" she asked, handing me a cup.

"Surfing."

Her own cup paused an inch from her mouth then came down slowly as her eyes went wide. "I'm sorry, I just hallucinated. I could have sworn I heard you say that we're going surfing, but that cannot possibly be correct."

"And, yet, it is. You didn't hallucinate. That's what we're doing. Surfing."

She blinked a few times, her mouth opening and closing like a fish struggling for air. "It's December."

"Yes," I confirmed.

"It's forty degrees out."

"Maybe even less."

"I can't surf." She was starting to look genuinely freaked out now and it shouldn't make me want to laugh but it did, just a little.

"You can't surf, *yet*," I corrected and received a withering glare in response.

"Mack, please tell me you're joking. This is a joke. Not a funny one, but a joke all the same."

"At least it isn't snowing."

The look on her face told me she thought I'd lost my mind. And hey, maybe I had. But we were still surfing today.

I pulled into traffic, enjoying the feel of her eyes on the side of my face, even if they were leveled in a glare.

"The water will probably be warmer than the air temp," I said, darting a look at her.

Her eyes narrowed further. "Is that supposed to be comforting?"

"Just stating a fact." I shot her a grin and wondered if she was about to throw her coffee on me. If she didn't need it to stay awake, the answer would definitely be yes.

"Look, Cheese, I get why you're freaking out, I do, but you'll be fine, I promise. I'll be right there with you. And you know I'd never let anything bad happen to you." I reached across the space between us, caught her hand and kissed the back of it.

She hummed. "That's not terribly comforting, either, to be honest, we'll just freeze to death together. How romantic." She sipped her coffee and slid the hand I'd been holding behind my neck, toying with the ends of my hair. Electricity zinged down my spine.

"Better than one of us freezing and one not. Would you make room on the door for me?" I asked and, to her credit, she almost kept a straight face. But the smile lifted the corners of her lips all the same.

"You are not joking your way out of this," she said with as much severity as she could manage, while clearly on the brink of a laughing fit.

"Wouldn't dream of it," I shot back.

"I don't even have a wetsuit." She was clutching at straws now. "And if you think I am going to wear some hire-wetsuit that other people have peed in! Oh my god, I can't even think about it, I think I just threw up in my mouth a little."

The arguing was not surprising, I'd expected her resistance, and I was not backing down now. "Please, can you give me a little credit. Do you really think that I would try and get you in some well-used wetsuit when you won't even put on a pair of shoes that someone else has worn?"

She pursed her lips. "Well I can't go in the water in a bathing suit. I didn't even bring a bathing suit."

"Will you relax please, I have everything you are going to need."

"Really?"

"Really, really."

"You bought me a wetsuit?"

"That's correct."

"And a bathing suit."

"Also correct." And I'd given it way too much thought. I'd also been tempted to buy a few just to see her in them.

"How do you know they'll be the right size?"

I shot her a sidelong look, which I hoped conveyed my offense. "Give me a little credit here, you don't think I'd be able to accurately guess your size?"

She shrugged. "I don't know. Maybe you're not as clever as you think you are, Milton ..."

I barked out a laugh. This was going to be fun, whether she knew it or not. "Just drink your coffee, put on some music, and enjoy the ride, Chastity."

25

CHASE

MACK WAS LOOKING INFURIATINGLY SMUG, and I wanted to be mad at him for springing surfing on me in the middle of fucking December, but it was difficult to stay mad at a face like that. Also, there were worse things to be doing on a Monday morning (even this early) than sitting in a car with your best friend, drinking coffee, and listening to good music—I was an exceptional DJ.

I was not at all sure about the idea of going surfing—because it was fucking ridiculous to be considering going in the ocean in the middle of winter—but I found myself curious about it all the same.

I peeled off my coat and threw it into the back seat. "So, where are you going surfing?"

"We. Where are *we* going surfing?" He corrected with a wink. I threw a balled up napkin at him.

"That remains to be seen. I make no promises."

"The Rockaways."

"No shit, really?!" We had spent a heap of time down there just before we started senior year. It was one of my favorite beaches because of the memories from that summer. This date was absolutely my fault, I shouldn't have posted all those photos I found in the clean up to our group chat.

"It's not too far, and it's a nice break, good for someone just starting out,. Plus, I've got another surprise up my sleeve."

"Another one? You're going to run out of room up there if you're not careful."

"Nah, I've got big sleeves."

I clapped a hand over my mouth to stop the coffee from spraying out all over his fancy, leather upholstery, but I felt the liquid burning up behind my nose as I tried and failed to stop laughing. I managed to swallow most of it, only the smallest of dribbles escaping, before I descended into a coughing/laughing fit. It really hurt, but I couldn't stop. Mack was laughing too, though I wasn't sure if it was at me or with me.

"You are such a perv," he said eventually, wiping a tear from his eye.

"Me!? You were the one talking about *big sleeves*." I tried to keep it together but it was no use.

Not quite two hours later—thank you New York traffic—we pulled into the short drive of a small, gray-shingled shack one block back from the beachfront. It was the cutest thing I had ever seen and, without even seeing inside, I already knew I wanted to stay here forever.

"Did you rent this place for the night? It's adorable."

"Not quite ..." He grabbed the bags, refusing to let me carry mine because he was still on his gentleman kick, and led the way inside. As soon as I was over the threshold I knew this wasn't a rental, it was his. It was impossible not to see it—the colors, the style, the art and photographs on the walls. Even if I hadn't recognised myself in some of them, it all screamed Mack.

"Wh–you bought a house down here? How–When did you

do this? Why didn't you tell me?" I was dangerously close to crying, what the hell was the matter with me?

"I didn't keep it a secret on purpose. It was a complete dump when I bought it and I was waiting until it was all finished but it took longer than I thought. I know about remodeling a kitchen and a bathroom now—it's a bastard—and then there was the wedding and things got busy and it just..." He shrugged. "Sorry I didn't tell you."

I laughed. That was not something he needed to apologize for and I told him so. I was in awe. He remodeled a house, maybe not all by himself, but still, he was incredible.

"You want the grand tour?"

"Of course, show me everything!" I threw my arms around his neck and jumped onto his waist, kissing him fiercely. Just when I thought I knew everything there was to know about him, he showed me something new.

"What was that for?" he asked, walking us towards the kitchen with his hands planted firmly on my ass. Couldn't we just do this, hang out in the adorable almost-beachfront cottage rather than get into the icy waters of the Atlantic.

"I just like kissing you," I said, peppering kisses across his cheeks and jaw to demonstrate.

He angled his head up and I moved down his neck, giving him a nip on the ear lobe on the way past. His fingers bit into my ass a little more firmly. Yes, let's just stay here doing this all day long. I doubt he'd need much convincing.

"That's lucky, because I really like kissing you, too, but do not think that you can kiss me and try to get out of your surfing lesson."

Busted.

He deposited me on the speckled charcoal counter of the small kitchen island, one hand trailing up my side to cradle my jaw and tip my head back. "This is the kitchen," he said against my throat.

"It's very nice." It was more of a breathy groan than actual words. And, honestly, we could have been in a meth den for all the attention I was paying to the room now that his mouth was on me.

"Thank you, I'm glad you like it. I painted a lot of the cabinets." His lips were grazing along my neck, raising goosebumps down my arms. I glanced at the white-washed cabinets, he'd done a good job.

"They look great."

"I'm pretty proud of them."

"You should be."

He chuckled, his tongue darting out and tasting the skin along my jaw. I was never going to look at kitchen cabinets the same again. Gone were the days of watching HGTV. I'd be wet at the mere mention of paint swatches and shaker cabinets. I wasn't mad about it.

He straightened, hands still gripping my hips. "Shall we move on?"

I draped my arms around his neck. "I've gotta be honest, I've never had a house tour that was quite this hands on."

"You don't like it?" he purred, leaning forward to bump my nose with his.

"No, no, I do. I really do."

His head snapped up. "Well, we might need to postpone the rest of the tour until after your lesson."

I blew out a breath. He was such a tease, I wasn't sure if my poor vagina could take it much longer.

"Okay, fine, let's go surfing."

He whooped, kissing me hard before putting me back on my feet and leading the way back into the living room where we'd left our bags. I was pretty sure I was out of my mind, agreeing to go surfing in the middle of December. But I was also stubborn, and didn't like to shy away from a challenge, so I wanted to at least try and do it. Even if it ended with me shivering and sore and maybe in a bad mood. Not that any bad mood would last long with Mack around.

Unsurprisingly, the bathing suit—a practical, black two-piece—and wetsuit Mack had chosen fit like they'd been made for me. Before we went out in the blustery weather, I was given a mini intro-lesson in the warmth and comfort of the living room.

"You ready to go?" Mack asked when he was satisfied I grasped the very basics.

"No, but let's do it anyway."

"That's my girl."

Surfing was awful. Or rather, I was awful at it. However, I was pretty sure I had a skewed view of the sport having my first real experience of it in winter, when shortly after we entered the water I could barely feel my fingers or my toes even with booties and gloves on. And the first time I dove under a wave I got the most intense brain freeze of my life. I was convinced I was going to throw up. I had no idea what possessed people to do this on a regular basis.

We were far from the only ones out here. The rest of the considerable crowd all braved the conditions with a smile. Maybe all this time in the cold water had affected their brains. It seemed to be the only explanation.

Naturally, Mack was a great teacher—patient and helpful and endlessly encouraging. But there was only so much a wonderful teacher could do with a student who would rather gnaw off their own hand than stay in the water a minute longer.

"Come on, Bodhi, let's get you warmed up," he said and I could have cried. He scooped us both up onto the large board and paddled us into shore. His strength as he propelled us through the water was incredible, my own arms could barely get just me up and over a wave. How his teeth weren't chattering was also beyond me.

"I was terrible," I said, the words wobbly as I shivered and skipped across the sand beside him. If I did not get into the car right now I was going to freeze solid. I was about to be a Chase-shaped ice block.

"It was your first time. And it wasn't exactly ideal conditions."

I shoved his shoulder. "You said it was ideal conditions! That's why we're here. *Ideal conditions.*" My eyelashes were icy. This was it. This was the end.

"Well, yes, the conditions themselves were ideal, but maybe not the temperature."

"The temperature is a good fifty degrees south of ideal. Next time it needs to be over ninety. Maybe even a hundred." Why were we so far from the car? Had it really been this far down to the water?

"Next time? There is going to be a next time? I haven't ruined it for you entirely?"

"If I don't lose my finger between now and dinner, I'll consider it."

He grinned and I knew I'd say yes to just about anything if he kept looking at me like that. I might even go back in the water tomorrow. No, that was too far. We made it to the car—finally—and Mack instructed me to strip off my wetsuit and get in while he strapped the board to the roof. When we left, I'd asked why we couldn't just walk. I definitely got it now. My toes were already dangerously close to dropping off as it was.

I peeled the wetsuit off and couldn't stop my squawk as the icy wind buffeted against me. This was absolutely mad.

Once inside the car, I turned the heater up to 'high' and

wrapped myself in one of the large, fluffy towels we'd brought along. My fingers were stark white, there was no blood left in them.

Soon enough, Mack was in the driver's seat, wrapped in his own towel, and we drove the embarrassingly short distance to the house. I couldn't remember ever being so cold in my life.

"Ohmygodohmygodohmygod. I need whiskey. Or hot cocoa. Or whiskey in hot cocoa," I said as we raced inside, very grateful that we'd turned the heating on before we left.

"You need a hot shower," he said, rubbing my arms.

"Yes! Yes, I definitely need that. Maybe whiskey in the shower, too." My teeth were rattling against one another but just the idea of a warm shower was enough to make me feel a little better. I followed into the small but light-filled bathroom and immediately dropped my towel, only to realize I was now standing in the bathroom in a bathing suit, which covered about as much as underwear, with Mack. Who, under his towel, was also in a bathing suit—I assumed. I hadn't actually seen him take the wetsuit off. What if there was nothing under the wetsuit and, as a result, nothing under the towel?

I swallowed. For as much as we'd been fooling around since our second inside-picnic date, most of our clothes had always been on. This was as close to a naked Mack as I had been so far and we were still one date shy of his five date rule.

My heart took up a wild pace against my ribs as he watched me. "Shall I leave you to it?" he asked, leaning over to turn on the faucet. The room filled with the sound of running water, but it was nothing compared to the rush of blood in my ears. Had I been cold? I was no longer cold. I was burning the hell up.

"You–no–I mean, yes, you probably should, leave— shower alone. We should shower alone. This is only date four." Date four. Date four. Date four. I was not going to have sex with him right now even though he looked good enough to eat.

"You don't think we can control ourselves?" The question was so low and seductive I felt it in the backs of my knees and I had to reach out a hand to steady myself against the wall. I honestly didn't know if I could control myself. I'd had trouble controlling myself with him when we were both fully clothed, and in public. Now we were alone in a bathroom and a hot second away from naked. How was I supposed to keep it together when all that separated me from the whole package was a little more than a towel?

The towel in question dropped to the floor, leaving him in a pair of black boxer briefs that left nothing to the imagination. I'd felt his cock a few times in the last week, but seeing it like this, straining against the black fabric, made a whimper roll up my throat. Was shrinkage not a thing?

"You–you're taking the–the first shower then?" I stuttered, my eyes glued to the bulge. It twitched under my attention and I bit my lip.

"Unless you want to join me. Eyes are up here, by the way." I heard the smile in his voice.

"They are," I said, not looking up to meet them. "But your cock is down there."

He laughed. And then he hooked his thumbs into the waistband of those boxer briefs and pulled them clean down his legs.

"Fuck me." It was as eloquent as I could manage. Mack was naked. Mack was naked in front of me and my brain was short-circuiting. He was glorious. It wasn't the first time I'd seen his chest, but seeing it, along with everything else. Long, muscular legs, trim hips, abs, on abs, on abs, pecs that stretched out to his wide, strong shoulders. And the prize between his legs.

"You're staring."

"Yes." I was staring. I was going to be staring for days, weeks, months. He was just perfect. And he expected me to be able to control myself? I was lucky to still be upright.

Steam was swirling through the air as the shower continued to run beside us and I knew that I should leave now, before things got way out of hand. Granted, things were already kind of out of hand because Mack was naked. But then he took a step forward and was right in front of me. I leaned in, rubbing my nose over the center of his chest. He smelled like the ocean. My hand trailed up to his neck and pulled him down and we were kissing, tongues moving against one another, stroking, exploring. His hands slid down from my ribs, through the dip of my waist and the curve of my hips. Our bodies fit flush, each dip and rise coming together like two long-separated puzzle pieces.

"Get in, Chase," he said and I nodded, stepping into the near scalding spray without even taking my bathing suit off first. He followed, clearing the lip of the tub with more grace than I had managed. We stood there staring at each other for a long moment. Me still in the bathing suit. Him naked.

I pulled him under the water with me, his hands at the ties that held my bathing suit together. One tug. Another. And the top fell away. A syncronized third and fourth and the briefs went too.

We were both naked. Nothing separating us but air.

His forehead rested on mine as he looked down the line of my body. One hand smoothed down my middle, from my throat all the way past my belly button, as he looked at me with what I could only describe as reverence. I was happy with my body, but even still I'd had moments of self consciousness with other men. Not here, though, not now, not with him. He cupped my breasts and I arched into the touch, desperate for more but terrified of things going too far. As much as I wanted all of him, I wouldn't break his rule.

The smooth drag of skin on skin moved up over my collar bones until his hands slid into the soaked strands of my hair. My eyes fell closed as I absorbed the sensations of his touch. He spun me, then I could smell jasmine and lime and he was massaging my scalp as he washed my hair. It was the most tender, and yet wildly erotic, thing that I had ever experienced. I leaned into him, relishing the feel of his strong fingers. More. All I wanted was more.

When he was finished with my hair, rinsing it without letting a single soap bubble get in my eyes, he moved onto the rest of me. A slow and methodical exploration that left no inch of skin untouched. I was a boneless pile of woman by the time he was done.

"Let's get you dried off," he whispered, hands still roaming over me.

"But you—"

"I'm fine," he said without letting me finish.

"Still being a gentleman then?" I asked with a smile as he brushed his lips over mine.

"Trying to be." He lifted me out of the tub and wrapped me up in another towel that was gloriously warm. A second materialized and he secured it around his waist. I was once again warm—and so turned on I could barely see straight.

We both snapped at the same moment, reaching for one another, mouths coming together with twin groans. The press of skin on skin was heaven. My dreams had been filled with him for weeks and to have him like this now was almost too much for my mind to comprehend.

My towel fell to the floor as he lifted me onto the vanity and then dropped to his knees in front of me. My breath froze in my lungs. He took one foot and kissed his way north along the side of my calf, past my knee, up the length of my thigh. I was panting and, just when I thought he'd kiss me where I needed him most, he took up the same devotion to my other leg until I could barely sit still.

I was writhing and desperate by the time his lips ghosted over my sex. I gasped and shifted my hips, chasing his mouth. And then it was there, a gentle press that set all my nerve endings on fire. He started slow, an easy exploration as I gripped the counter and wondered if it were possible to die from pleasure. If so, I was not long for this world.

He sucked, licked, kissed, and teased until I was breathless and begging. My hands tangled in his hair as one finger circled my entrance, then a second; they pushed inside and a noise I cried out as my ecstasy crested.

"Ohgodohgodohgod, M–Mack." It was all too much. My thighs clamped his ears and he groaned against me.

"St–stop." I panted and he immediately pulled back.

"What's wrong? Are you okay?" he asked, concern lacing his tone.

"Fine, yes, great, I just need a second because I think I nearly passed out." I sagged against the mirror at my back, unsure if I was going to regain control of the muscles in my legs, which had started shaking.

"You need to eat something."

I nodded. "Yes, probably, but it wasn't because I'm hungry."

His concern morphed into proud satisfaction as he rose to stand. "You came too hard," he said with a disgustingly pleased smile before I pulled him in for a kiss. The tension that had momentarily broken shivered through the air again and I reached a hand between us, his cock eagerly fitting into my palm.

He groaned something I couldn't make out as I stroked him

and dragged my teeth over his ear. It didn't take long before he was panting, kissing me with bruising force that I not only took but gave back in equal measure. I had never been so utterly gone for another person as I was for him. It terrified me.

The wide head of his cock nudged against my stomach as he leaned into me, his kisses growing more messy and desperate the closer he was to coming. I reached my other hand between us, cupped his balls and squeezed.

"Oh *fuuuuuck*," he groaned a second before he pulsed in my hand and sticky warmth branded my skin. His head rested on the mirror, his breathing ragged. I kissed his shoulder.

"I came too hard," he said and I laughed.

He stood and we both looked down between our bodies. I'd never been quite so happy to be this messy.

"I think we need another shower." I said as his hands slipped under my thighs and lifted me onto his waist.

"I think you might be right."

26

MACK

I WAS HAVING the wildest sense of deja vu.

Chase was sitting cross legged on the floor in front of the fire, wrapped in a robe that was at least two sizes too big, with her hair piled in a messy heap on top of her head and cradling a mug of hot cocoa (with a healthy pour of whiskey, naturally). I knew that I'd never been here before, knew that this was not something I'd already experienced. But it was a scene I'd imagined so many times that seeing it come to life felt strangely familiar.

The surfing had been a disaster. Everything that came after it, however, had been sen-fucking-sational. We stayed in the shower until the water went from third degree burn–Chase's preference–to lukewarm. Then got out and dried off, which took longer than it probably should have, seeing as we stopped to kiss and touch one another every few seconds.

Eventually her growling stomach gave us a little more focus.

I flipped our grilled cheese sandwiches and watched as she sipped her drink while idly leafing through one of the surfing magazines on the coffee table. It was all so perfectly natural. And I was scared out of my fucking brain. Because I knew, all the way down to my bone marrow, that this woman was it for me, and I didn't know how to not fuck it up. I didn't know how to keep her. My desperate reaction was to hold on so tight she couldn't get away, even knowing that would only end badly. But how did I do it? How did I keep her close but not scare her away?

The connection we had was more than I had ever experienced. Not surprising, when we'd known one another for so long. It was more than that, though, more than just history. There was a synchronicity, an understanding, a deep, unwavering rightness. I couldn't lose it. Not now. I sure as hell couldn't go back to being just friends. I think I'd known that all along. It was the first real lie I'd ever told her. I wasn't proud of it, but we wouldn't be here right now if I hadn't said those words.

It was a lie I could live with and one that wouldn't matter soon enough. We weren't going back to the way we were before, too much had passed between us now.

I slid the sandwiches onto plates and cut them—triangles for me and straight down the middle for her. She looked up from the magazine as I approached and I nearly tripped and sent our food flying at the weight of emotion in her endless eyes.

"You need to eat something before you go looking at me like that." I tried to joke but my chest felt like it was being cleaved open, my heart exposed.

Her eyebrows wagged. "Don't get ahead of yourself, hot stuff, I'm looking at the sandwich." She accepted the plate and the kiss I dropped onto her lips. "Thank you. Maybe it's not just about the sandwich."

"I knew it wasn't just about the sandwich," I said as I

settled beside her. The chill from the ocean had long since subsided. It had probably happened about the same moment Chase dropped her towel in the bathroom. I'd seen her in bathing suits before, but not like that, not with the air charged with lust and anticipation. Not when I knew I was about to be standing in the shower with her—there was nothing that could have got me to leave that room once we were in it.

It all still seemed too much for my mind to really wrap itself around. We had kissed, yes, then she'd agreed to a date. At every point part of me had expected it all to go up in smoke, for me to wake up from this dream I'd found myself in. But I didn't wake up. Each step closer to everything was the one I was sure would be the last. Yet it wasn't, or it hadn't been so far. Because this was Chase. Because it was us.

I was tempted to lament the amount of time we'd wasted not being this way. All those years spent together, and yet not. If I was being honest, though, I knew that before now I hadn't been ready, I'd been happy to swim around on the surface of relationships, not letting myself get too swept away. Before now the depth of these feelings would have ruined us both. The fact they still could made my stomach roll.

I leaned over, wanting to pull her into my chest but settling for a kiss on her fuzzy shoulder.

"What was that for?" she asked, dusting crumbs from her hands. Her plate was empty.

"Jesus, you were really hungry. And I don't think I need a reason to kiss you."

"You don't. And, yes, I was." She smiled a slow, contented smile and my heart drummed. It wasn't one-sided, was it? She had to be feeling it too. "I think I could get used to hearing the ocean instead of traffic and fist fights."

"Is that right?" I set aside my plate and she crawled over my lap, her legs coming to rest on either side of mine.

"Uh-huh." she said, fingers sliding into my hair. "I always forget how much I love the ocean. And it's so close, really. I should make an effort to come out here more often."

"You should. At least now you know you have somewhere to stay." My hands roamed over her back.

"That's true!" She beamed. Kissed me once. Then again. "I still can't believe you managed to keep this place a secret."

"I wasn't trying to keep it a secret. I figured you'd see it at some point, once it was all done. I just wasn't sure when that was going to be. I'm not sure if you've noticed, but it's difficult to drag your butt away from Rudi, you're kind of a workaholic."

Her smile was shy and self-conscious as she ducked her head, the mess of her hair tickling my nose.

"It's not intentional. I guess I just don't have any hobbies. You surf—and I'm sure you're very good when not babysitting a newb like myself. You make pie, fucking incredible pie. You have these things that light you up that aren't Rudi, that aren't *work*." She fiddled with the tie of my robe. "I don't–I don't have that. I'm not sure I ever really have. When I was in middle school I studied hard so I could earn a spot at Carrington. Then I kept studying hard to get into college. When I was at college I needed to focus on getting the best job, one that would help me to get a better understanding of what it was like to run a business. There was always something else. The next thing. Now I work hard, partly because I want to and I love what we've created, but also ... I don't know what else to do. Work *is* what I do. It's different now, though, because it feels final somehow, like this is it until I die or something. And if I stop then things will fall apart and all these people rely on me now and I can't disappoint them. Can't let them down. So I work, and work, and work." Her eyes swung up to meet mine. "That's sad isn't it? I don't have a life outside of work. I'm a workaholic loser."

"You are not a workaholic loser." I laughed. "Just because you haven't found something you love outside of work, doesn't mean you never will. Maybe it will be surfing."

She barked out a laugh. "I will be, at best, a fair weather surfer. Strictly summer only, and only when it is close to one hundred out. I do not want to experience a brain freeze like that ever again, I honestly thought my eyeballs were going to freeze. It was awful. However, during the cooler months I will be more than happy to accompany you here and sit inside while consuming hot beverages. Drinking may not be much of a hobby but it's all I've got right now." There was something else she loved, too. I'd seen it, I just needed to bring it to her.

"I don't feel like I've ever really chosen anything." The words tumbled out before I realized they were there.

"What do you mean?"

"I've always just gone along with the flow, happy to follow other people."

Her brow creased. "Like me? Is that—do I boss you around? Have I made you—"

"No. No, no, that's not what I meant." I wrapped my arms around her back and squeezed, burying my face in her neck and taking a long breath. It was difficult to sort out the thoughts rolling around in my head. "My dad was always so set on me having a direction, a path. Like you and Nash, you had plans, goals. You study at school to get into college, you work hard at college to get the best job. There are steps. Boxes to tick. I knew I should want that but ... I just didn't. The expectations were always so high, the failure inevitable. It seemed easier not to try. It wasn't just because I wanted to piss my dad off, although that was a lot of it, I never knew what I wanted to do. I never had that goal waiting for me. I went to college because you were going to college, and what the hell else was I going to do? I could have gone to LA and surfed my days away while Nash busted his ass but I figured getting a degree was better than not getting a degree, even if I had no intention of ever doing anything with it. Traveling was great. And that became a goal, I guess—seeing as much of the world as I could—but it got lonely, too.

"It pains me to say this, but maybe Dad was right and I should have just picked something and done it. Should have *applied* myself." I shuddered. The most common refrain from report cards was that I could do so much if I just *applied myself*. Whatever the fuck that meant.

I didn't let myself think too much about all of this stuff. What was the point when I continued to come up without answers every time I strayed down this path? I'd never been unhappy with my life, I was well aware of how good I had it, so it was easy to go along smiling. But underneath there was this itch that was getting harder and harder to ignore.

Why couldn't I just be happy with this, with what I had right now? With a warm fire, a grilled cheese, and Chase in my lap.

"Sounds like you might have your own Maureen, maybe we can call them, Lionel."

"Lionel?" I laughed and she nodded.

"Lionel is feeding you a whole lot of bullshit. You. Are. Remarkable," she said, her gentle touch turning my face until we were eye to eye. "I'm sorry your dad made you feel like you weren't enough if you weren't striving for something. As someone who was striving and ticking the boxes, I'm not sure it's all that it's cracked up to be. And, for the record, you are enough. You don't have to do anything other than be yourself to be enough. Anyone who can't see that doesn't deserve you. You are my best friend, Milton Alfred Carmichael. I would not change a fucking thing about you." She paused, eyes fierce, and held my chin between her thumb and forefinger. I was a hot second away from crying like a fucking baby. "To me, you are perfect."

"Did you just quote *Love, Actually?*"

"Did you just correctly recognise a quote from *Love, Actually?*"

CHASE HAD MANY TALENTS: delegation, making cocktails, ice skating, inspiring staff members with both praise and inventive punishments, the list went on and on. But, for all her numerous skills, cooking was not among them. Even with her obsession with cooking shows, it just wasn't her thing. She mostly accepted this, defaulting to take out and anything that could be heated in the oven or microwave. Occasionally, though, she decided to test herself. Now, apparently, was one of those times.

I snuck out for a quick surf after she fell asleep on the couch. I didn't think I'd been gone that long but, when I returned, it was to find her standing in the kitchen in a pair of black yoga pants and one of my hoodies, with wooly socks stretching half way up her shins. There was flour everywhere, including on her cheeks and in her hair. It was one of the most perfect things I'd ever seen.

"Hey, what's going on in here?" I asked, momentarily distracted from my need to regain feeling in my toes.

She turned around like a kid who just got busted, eyes wide. "No! Shit! I was hoping to have cleaned up a bit before you got back." She waved her hands over the disaster in front of her then hustled me away from the counter, which was covered in yet more flour. Had she just been throwing it around? An image of her dancing and singing into a wooden spoon under flour confetti jumped into my head and I coughed to cover the laugh.

"Did you think I wasn't getting back until tomorrow?" I asked over my shoulder.

An adorable little growl rolled out of her. "I had things completely under control. The flour just got a little away from me is all. I'm making us pasta for dinner." She was still herding me in the direction of the bathroom.

"Pasta? You're making pasta? Like, from scratch?"

"Yes, pasta, and yes, from scratch. I consulted numerous recipes and YouTube videos, all of which made it look easy enough to put flour, salt and eggs together." The confidence in her tone was waning the more she spoke.

"Right, sure, sounds straightforward." I laughed, letting her push me along, her hands warm on my back.

"Your confidence in me is astounding. Don't you have fingers to thaw out?"

"Yes, I do, would you care to help?" I dropped my towel and spun to cage her against a wall, my still cold hands ducking up under the edge of the hoodie and finding warm, soft skin.

She yelped and squirmed. "Mack! Oh fuck, you're freezing!"

"And you're helping to warm me back up." I nuzzled into her neck.

"The kitchen is a mess," she said without any real conviction as her arms went over my shoulders.

"Yes, it is."

"You're naked."

"Yes, I am."

Her fingers started exploring across my back and shoulders as her hips rocked forward to meet mine.

"I really did want to have everything cleaned up before you got back." The words trailed off into a low moan as I nudged the hoodie aside and sucked at the juncture of her neck and shoulder.

"I don't care about the kitchen, Chase." Okay, so I did a little, but not enough to stop what I was doing right now.

"Me either." She pulled me up with a tug on the hair and the heat of her kiss threatened to buckle my knees. We stumbled sideways into the bathroom, Chase trying to wiggle out of her yoga pants and socks as I pulled the hoodie off. She wasn't wearing a bra. I'd seen her naked earlier today, but peeling off my hoodie to find her naked underneath it sent a rush of heat through me.

I would happily surf in arctic waters every fucking day if I got to warm back up like this afterward.

27

CHASE

MACK and I watched as the dough I'd made disintegrated almost as soon as it hit the rapidly bubbling water.

"I think we might need to scratch pasta making off your list of potential hobbies," he said. It hadn't happened in any of the YouTube videos I watched earlier. Granted, my dough didn't look like it was quite the same texture, but still, it shouldn't be doing that, should it?

"Maybe I could take a cooking class?" I dropped another noodle into the pot. The result was the same.

"You're not going to take a cooking class," he said with a smile in his voice.

"I'm not going to take a cooking class," I agreed. I'd probably burn the whole place down. I didn't understand why I was so bad at this. I made the dough just like they said, mostly, it shouldn't be floating around in chunks rather than the long strands I'd rolled out. How had I learned nothing from years of watching *Iron Chef* and the *Great British Bake Off?*

This wasn't my first kitchen failure. I'd lost count of the number of things I'd attempted only to have things flop, or burn, or just taste awful. Food just wasn't my thing. Maybe it was time to accept I was more suited to *Nailed It!*

Mack pulled me into his side. "You want me to order pizza?"

"Well it's not like we're going to be able to eat this now, is it?"

"I might have some noodles in the pantry..."

"Do you really trust my sauce when the noodles I made look like that?" We both peered into the pot.

"Pepperoni."

"And mushroom."

"You got it." He kissed my temple and went in search of his phone. I set about cleaning up my mess. I drained the water and dumped the soggy, yet somehow still raw, dough into the trash.

At some point I was going to have to get good at this, wasn't I? Even mediocre would be an improvement. Or maybe I could just leave all the cooking to Mack. A picture of him cooking for us in his kitchen back in Brooklyn flashed up behind my eyes. Not the strangest sight, he'd cooked for me plenty of times before, but this looked different. Felt different.

Everything was feeling different. It was hard for it not to when he continued to surprise me. This man who I was confident I knew everything about kept pulling things out of those big sleeves of his. It both scared and delighted me. And also made me realize that, even with him, even for as long as I'd known him, for the hours upon hours we'd spent together, I'd held him slightly away. Never risking my whole heart, even for our friendship. One foot was always on the threshold because, in my head, it was easier to leave than be left.

I couldn't go on like that. I didn't want to go on like that. I wanted to pull him close and hear all his secrets and tell him mine. I wanted to keep him forever. As much as the idea of that scared me, I knew he was worth it. But how did I go about trying to change something so deeply rooted in my psyche? Something that went all the way down to my wiring? Was it even possible?

He smiled at me from the living room, his hair sticking up at wild angles and his eyes bright, the blue so vivid I could imagine myself diving right in and drowning. My heart flipped over in my chest. I was in love with him. I was in love with him and we hadn't even had sex yet. Not that the sex really mattered, because I had a feeling I'd been in love with him since we kissed on the night of the wedding. Even before.

I was in love with him, and I was going to hurt him. I knew it already because I wasn't good at this. Because I didn't know how to be in a relationship without looking for the first crack.

Panic rose up like a wave in my chest, threatening to take me down whole and never let me up. I tried to breathe through it, to tell myself that it would be okay, but I was a terrible liar. It wasn't going to be okay. How could it? How could it be okay when I knew, with an unshakable certainty, that I was going to mess all this up and lose him forever?

"Hey, what's going on?" Mack asked, arms sliding around me, anchoring me back into my body. "Where'd you go?"

I shook my head, not trusting myself to keep it together if I opened my mouth.

"It's just pasta, Chase. And hey, if you're serious about the cooking class maybe we could go to one together?"

I choked on a sob. Of course he'd suggest we do it together, because he'd do anything I asked and more. He'd do things I didn't realize I even wanted.

"Or not, no cooking class. Maybe I could give you a private cooking class?" he said, eyebrows wagging and I let out a soggy laugh. "There she is ..." One finger slipped under my chin and tipped my face up. "You cannot be the queen of cocktails, a boss ice skater and cook killer noodles. It wouldn't be fair. What would be left for the rest of us?"

"You can make pie and ice cream, and you surf," I said with a sniff.

He shrugged. "I am a fucking pleb, grateful you let me stand in your shadow, Chastity Heather."

That got a laugh that was a little less soggy. "You're ridiculous."

"And I will continue to be if it means I get to see you smile."

I buried my face in his chest. Letting the panic subside for the moment. It was going to hurt like hell when I messed it up. But for right now, I was happy to live in denial, and pretend like maybe this could be forever.

SLEEP LIFTED SLOWLY, and as I blinked my eyes open it took me a second to remember where I was. The Rockaways. In Mack's bed. The previous day came back in pieces, each new one sending a swirl of warmth through my belly. I would not have been surprised to wake and find it had all been a dream.

Only it wasn't, I knew this because there was no way any dream of mine would include going into the ocean in the middle of December. Or failing to make pasta noodles correctly. All the rest of it though, dreamy.

I snuggled deeper into the warmest, fluffiest duvet I'd ever felt and realized that, despite being in Mack's bed, I was alone. Before I could drag myself up and go in search of him, he appeared in the doorway holding a large tray.

"Good morning." he said with a slow, seductive smile. He was in a pair of low-slung, plaid pajama pants and a long sleeve Henley pushed up to his elbows. I'd seen him naked yesterday. I'd been naked in the shower with him—twice. And yet, right now, the sight of those forearms was getting me hot like the flash of an ankle in Victorian England.

"Good morning," I said, wiggling myself up to sitting as he crossed the room and joined me on the bed. My mouth watered. The tray held two large mugs of coffee, a bowl of chopped fruit, croissants (both chocolate and plain) and donuts. Maybe I was still dreaming.

"Good. Morning." I repeated, not only for the food but because he looked good enough to eat himself. Messy hair, sexy sleepy eyes, and just enough scruff on his jaw to make my fingers twitch to touch it. He was rarely clean shaven, but he was usually neater than this. It was a shame.

I bypassed the food and coffee and went straight for him, straddling his lap, fingers running over the line of his jaw.

"Coffee first?" he asked, blue eyes roaming my face.

"You first." Morning breath be damned, I couldn't wait.

He smiled, hands moving over my lace-covered butt. I kissed him, slow and lazy, enjoying the drag of his stubble on my lips, cheeks and chin. Mint and coffee met my tongue and an appreciative sigh left me. Perfect. So fucking perfect. I would never get tired of his mouth. Not ever. A flicker of the panic I felt yesterday licked at my insides but I ignored it. I was too lost to the moment, to the man. I wanted to stay here forever. We'd escaped the real world and found a little bubble that was just for us.

I fumbled with his shirt, struggling to pull it over his head, but it was soon free and my chest met his, skin to skin. The feel of it sent lust racing through me. Lust and more. We needed to slow down, though. It was a miracle that we'd managed to behave last night. I didn't know if I'd be able to do it again this morning.

"Coffee now," I said, once I'd managed to pull away.

"Fuck the coffee," he growled, claiming my mouth with

unrestrained need. I met him, clinging to his shoulders as he stood. The breakfast tray was disposed of on the floor and then he was on top of me on the bed. The weight of him was everything. The press of his hip bones, the nudge of cock on my stomach.

"Wait," I mumbled against his lips. "Mack."

"Breakfast date," he said between the kisses he was raining down on my neck and chest.

"What?"

His head popped up. "Chase, would you like to have breakfast with me?"

"Of course but–"

He rolled off me, I missed his weight immediately, and handed me a croissant. "Eat."

"I–sure–what is happening right now?"

"If you eat then we can call this a breakfast date."

"Oh-kay, cool ... breakfast date." I took a bite of croissant and chewed trying to get my mind to catch up with whatever was going on. Then—"Breakfast *date*. Date five!"

"Date five," he said, and butterflies exploded under my ribs. I wasn't ready. No, that was ridiculous, I was absolutely ready but I figured I'd have more time to prepare, to, I didn't fucking know, get my head around it. I was about to have sex with Mack. Holyshitholyshitholyshit.

"Unless–we don't have to–if you'd rather–we don't–I can take you on an actual date five. I—"

I threw my croissant on the ground and tackled him. As nervous as I was, I didn't want to wait any longer. I couldn't wait any longer. And I certainly didn't care about an actual date. I just wanted him. But now that we were here, I also didn't want to rush my way through it. I wanted to savor him. I sat up, taking a slow, calming breath.

"I'm sorry. I just attacked you. I got a little carried away."

"Quite alright," he said with a grin, hands wandering my thighs.

"I don't want–I want us—"

"To take our time."

"Yes, thank you, your hands are distracting me."

"Your boobs are distracting me."

I glanced down at my chest and shrugged. "There's not all that much of them to provide a distraction."

"They're yours and they're fucking perfect." His hands trailed up my stomach, sending shivers over my skin. He cupped them, massaged, and rolled my nipples between his fingers. It sent heat through my core and my hips rocked in response.

"I have no intention of rushing this, Chase." He licked his lips.

"Good," I said, though it was more of a moan. He sat up, his fingers sinking into my hair as he kissed me, slow but purposeful, lips tender, yet firm and commanding. I let him lead, tipping my head so his tongue sunk deeper, swallowing my sounds as I took his.

I felt his nervous anticipation in the tremble of his fingers as they touched, explored. He'd learned every dip and curve of my body yesterday, today he was committing each to memory with thorough, devoted study.

His lips slipped off mine as he held himself above me, watching with eyes that burned. I'd barely noticed him flipping us, lost as I was in the feel of him. Then his lips and tongue took up the task his fingers had started, memorizing the lines of my body from my ear, across my collar bones, down through the shallow valley between my breasts. On and on. I was breathless and desperate.

My underwear was gone and his kisses turned hungry,

going from learning to devouring, making my insides coil hot and tight.

"Need. You," I panted, aching. "*Please.*"

He crawled up my body, languishing yet more kisses as he went. I rolled onto my side and reached for him, my hands greedy like his mouth. My name was a tortured groan on his lips.

I hooked a leg over his hip and rubbed his wide head against my clit, we both sucked in a sharp breath, noses bumping.

"Condom," he said.

"Clean, I'm clean." I sighed, relishing the slide of him over my soaked skin.

"Me too." He groaned as I shifted my hips and his cock nudged at my entrance. God help me, I was going to pass out.

"Mack," I whispered, still not quite believing we were here. That after all this time, all these years of never knowing, never admitting I wanted this, wanted him, we were here. "Is this ok?"

"More than okay." He cupped my face with one hand, my hip with the other, and thrust forward as he kissed me. Our sounds rang out in harmonious pleasure. I absorbed the feeling of stretching, filling, bliss as we lay there breathing each other's air. He slid back, tortuously slow, then forward again, his mouth never leaving mine. I curled my leg tighter around him as he came forward, our chests flush, our breathing shallow, our tongues tangling. He maintained the maddening rhythm, the slow drag, sending wave upon wave of pleasure tingling through.

"Ride me, Chase," he said, rolling me on top of him.

I straightened up and sank low. Too much, it was too much. "Oh my god, Mack."

"I got you," he purred, hands resting on my hips.

"It's—"

"Unbelievable. I know, I'm right here with you." It really was. I gave my hips an experimental rock and moaned, my eyes rolling back in my head.

"More," he growled.

I did it again.

"Fuck, Chase, *more.*"

I leaned back and planted my hands on his thighs, letting my head drop back as I found a rhythm. My heart was hammering hard and my breath was short and shallow. It wasn't supposed to feel this good the first time, was it? I knew we'd been doing other things but this, this feeling was going to render me unconscious.

"So perfect." Mack's hands moved up to my ribs then down again, as his hips met me thrust for thrust. "Beautiful. Fucking beautiful. I want to feel you come."

"Clit."

His thumb was there immediately, circling slow with just the right amount of pressure. "There?"

"*Yes.*"

He circled, pressed, circled again. And holy shit I was balancing on the ledge.

"You want to let go."

"Yes."

"Let go, Chase."

"*Mack.*"

He drove upwards while keeping the divine pressure on my clit and I toppled, my nails dug into his thighs as my toes curled. It went on and on, and then I was collapsing into a heap on his chest.

Holding me close he spun us over and hooked one of my legs over his shoulder. With slow circles of his hips I was once again close to coming, or maybe I was still coming. It wouldn't have surprised me either way. He leaned in and captured my mouth, his angle shifting, and I saw stars. His shoulders tensed and I knew he was close. I wanted to tell him to let go, too, but my voice had abandoned me, all I had left was nonsensical moans.

"Fuck, I'm—*Chase*." He came with a groan so low it rattled my bones and I arched into him letting my body say what my words couldn't.

We stayed there, wrapped in each other and breathing hard. The weight of him heavy and perfect on top of me. I was in no rush to move, except my hands, which were roaming over his back.

"What do we do now?" I asked, toying with the hair at his nape.

His head popped up an inch or two, just enough to meet my eye, a lazy grin on his face. "Eat breakfast and then do it again." Kiss. "And again." Kiss. "And again, until we need to go back home."

"We might need fresh coffee."

"And I should probably find that croissant you tossed so it doesn't attract rodents.

I laughed. "That was your fault."

"How was you throwing French pastries across the room my fault?"

I shrugged. "I was overcome. You'd dangled the sex card and I thought you were going to take it away. I had to act fast."

"I enjoyed it."

"Me too." I wiggled my hips.

"Oh, yes, I enjoyed that, but I was talking about your dramatic moment of throwing food around. It was incredibly sexy."

"I aim to please."

"You succeeded."

28

MACK

I HAD SPENT the majority of the day naked in bed with Chase and had decided that I didn't want to be anywhere else, possibly ever. We needed to find a way to leave our lives in Brooklyn behind and just live here, by the beach, making sweet, sweet love all day, everyday.

What a way to fucking live.

She was currently plastered across my chest, sweaty, despite the temperature outside, and panting. At the slight sway of her hips, and the corresponding twitch of her walls, my cock started to thicken again.

"You're kidding me," she said, voice muffled in the crook of my neck. "You cannot possibly be ready to go again?"

"Pretty sure I'm insatiable for you, Chastity," I replied, sifting my fingers through her dark hair. It was like silk, cool and smooth against my skin. I felt her smile.

"Insatiable or not, I need sustenance."

Cradling her perfect ass I swung my legs off the edge of the bed and stood. "Shower first," I said, dropping a kiss on her lips. "Then food."

Her arms went around my neck as her legs tensed against my hips. "We were in there for a while before, will there even be any hot water left?"

"Only one way to find out."

In fact, there was some hot water left. However, it started to run cold roughly two minutes after we turned it on. Chase wailed and threw herself out onto the mat as soon as it was no longer the temperature of lava. At least it was enough time to clean up. As I watched her stand there, drying off and wrapping a large towel around her hair, I wondered when this would stop feeling surreal. When I would stop waiting for the rug to be pulled out from under me, for the other shoe to drop, for the bubble to burst. I didn't love the feeling of impending doom that was starting to creep in but it was difficult to fight it.

This was where things usually stopped for me. One night, sometimes a re-run in the morning, and then that was it.

That wouldn't happen with Chase. That couldn't happen with Chase. Granted, we hadn't actually talked about how we'd work together, as a couple. Maybe we didn't need to talk. Maybe it would just work. Somehow I doubted it. But a guy could always dream.

"What's with the look?" she asked, smothering her face, neck and chest with moisturizer. It was clinical, something she clearly did every single day and, yet, seeing it was enough to get me hard again.

"What look?" I said, trying to talk down my cock.

"Well, not that one, I know that one. We've already covered the fact that I need to eat." She was trying to look stern but her eyes were lingering on the front of my towel. She cleared her throat. "And honestly, we should probably get going soon." The reminder that we couldn't stay in this bubble was necessary but still very much unwanted. "I don't want to leave, either. But the real world beckons whether we want it to or not." How badly I wished she wasn't right.

We came together like magnets, reaching for one another at the same moment, her hands at my waist and mine at her jaw. How had I managed to convince myself, for so many years, that she wasn't the only one I wanted? It seemed so utterly obvious now. But we needed to find our way together in our own time. I believed that, and I was just grateful we'd made it here.

"What are you doing tonight?"

"Sleeping," she said without missing a beat.

"Would you like to do that in my bed?" After everything we'd done this morning asking her to sleep over shouldn't feel like a big deal, and yet it did.

She pursed her lips, tipped her head to one side. "I suppose I could be persuaded on the merits of your bed over mine."

I kissed her, swallowing her sigh of satisfaction as my tongue swept into her mouth.

"Consider me persuaded," she said with a slow smile.

"You don't have to wait up."

"Oh, I won't be. Someone kept me up half the night with orgasm after orgasm." She rolled her eyes.

"How rude," I scoffed.

A nod. "Right? And then today, it's just been more of the same. I really need some rest." She exaggerated a yawn.

"Well, then, my bed is at your disposal." And the thought of her being there when I got home was more than I could put into words. The same as it had been to wake up this morning with her curled around me like a limpet.

"The couch, too?"

"Of course."

"And there's pie in your fridge," she said with a bounce of her brows and a twinkle in her eye.

"Always." I kissed the tip of her nose.

Her smile shifted to something less certain as her teeth worried at her lip. She nodded, pulled away. I let her go and followed to the bedroom. I had known Chase long enough to know when something was on her mind, when to push her to talk and when to leave her be. But it was harder now to let those thoughts stay in her head and not know what they were.

"Yesterday, last night, this morning, it's all been ... perfect. Beyond perfect. But I don't know how to do this, Mack, not really. I'm not good at it. I—" She broke off, fidgeting with the edge of her towel, then let it fall to the floor and reached for her shirt. I caught her before she'd managed to pull it on, sat on the bed and held her between my knees. I knew why she was freaking out, I was too, but I still believed in us.

"Take a breath." She did, her hands coming to rest on my shoulders. "It's us, Chase. Don't let Maureen tell you otherwise."

"Maureen has nothing to do with this." She shot a very pointed look down at her chest and then at me. "We're both naked and my boobs are basically in your face. That's not us."

"It wasn't us. It is now. And I, for one, am not mad about it." I ducked my head to take her nipple in my mouth and her fingers threaded into my hair. I was sure I'd had a point, but now I was having trouble focusing on it. I released her nipple with a wet pop and thoroughly enjoyed her small whimper of disappointment.

"I don't know how to be around you when we're not naked. What do we do now? How do we act? How do I not just kiss your face off every time I see you?"

I smoothed the crease in her brow with my thumb. "I would not be opposed to you kissing my face off whenever you felt the need."

She punched my shoulder. "I'm serious, Mack. We can't

just be making out in the office at Rudi." I opened my mouth to argue but she cut me off. "It would be unprofessional."

"You're right," I agreed. "So maybe we just need to lay down some ground rules?"

"Ground rules?" Her eyes lit with the prospect of a little structure. My girl loved a plan.

"Sure, number one, no fucking in the office. And I hope you understand the sacrifice I'm making there."

"You're a true saint." Her tone was comically deadpan.

"Thank you, I'm glad you see it too," I said, giving her ass a squeeze. "Look, I know it's going to be weird for a while. And I can't really tell you how long that'll last, either. My main concern is my cock."

"What?" she said with a laugh.

"Well, I'm hoping it's not constantly hard when you're around. That's great right now, sure, but as you point out, not so much when we're at work."

She winced. "Yeah, that could get awkward real fast."

"I'd be lucky to not be accused of sexual harrassment."

She smiled, the tension in her frame draining away. "Okay. We can do this."

"We can. We're a team."

"The best team," she added as her mouth descended over mine. The kiss started slow but quickly deepened and turned hungry. Then she was straddling my lap, taking my cock and bringing it to her entrance. My eyes rolled back in my head as she lowered herself slowly, inch by torturous inch, until there was nothing left between us. God, the feel of her was enough to scramble my fucking brain. Her pussy pulsed once, twice, a third time as she adjusted. I wasn't sure I'd ever get used to the wet, hot grip she had on me.

My hands rested on her ass, letting her take control of the pace, at least for the moment.

"Wait," I said, an idea coming to me.

"What's wrong?" Her eyes were already lust-blown and unfocused.

"Absolutely nothing, just hop up for a second."

She did, swaying slightly on her feet. "What are you—" The question ended abruptly as I got up and opened the wardrobe, revealing a full-length mirror on the inside of one door.

I sat back on the bed. "Come here, turn around." I helped her climb up, her back flush against my chest and watched in the mirror with my breath frozen in my lungs as she took my cock and slid it through her folds. It was the hottest thing I had ever seen in my fucking life.

Her legs were spread wide over my thighs, my arm holding her steady as she once again lowered herself onto my cock. I was riveted by the sight of it disappearing into her glistening pussy. She let her hand linger at the base, fingers stroking as she started to move. I couldn't look away.

"You're amazing," I said, though it wasn't enough.

"We're amazing. And we look really fucking hot." She groaned then added, "Feels so good. I love your cock." I just about came on the spot.

"You cannot say shit like that or I am not going to last."

"But it's true," she said on a sigh, her fingers trailing down to my balls.

"Fuck, Chase." Her movements were slow, like she was trying to drive me crazy.

"I want to come, Mack, can you make me come?"

"Yes."

"*Please.*"

I continued to watch us in the mirror, her riding me, stroking my balls, my thumb circling her clit. She moaned my name and I dropped my mouth to her neck, tasting the skin behind her ear.

I felt the wet pulse of her, a beat before she cried out, shuddering against me.

"I could watch you come all day," I said as my hips snapped up to meet her. She sank lower and heat rolled over me. My hands gripped her hips, taking control of our pace.

"God, yes Mack. Harder."

I wanted to last, I wanted to feel her come again but I was too close and she was squeezing my balls and it all felt too fucking good.

My teeth sunk into her shoulder as I came, so hard I thought I blacked out for a second. She cried out, grinding herself down on me. I could barely see straight. I kissed the mark on her shoulder then rested my forehead on the same spot.

She kissed my temple, tunneling her fingers through my hair. I couldn't move, could barely think, my entire world had just shifted, rearranged itself so I was no longer held on the earth by gravity, but by her.

Her stomach rumbled.

"I didn't feed you."

"No, we had sex, again."

"I would say I'm sorry, but I'm not."

"I can't say that I'm sorry about it, either," she said, her voice smiling.

I'D MADE the drive from The Rockaways to Brooklyn more times than I could count, and never had it been as quick as it was today. Or maybe it was the fact that I wished Chase and I could still be sitting by the fire or rolling around in bed. As soon as we got in the car it felt like our bubble had burst. She was right there beside me, but my own insecurity felt like another presence in the car, telling me that she was pulling away, that no matter what I did I wouldn't be able to keep her the way I wanted.

Too soon, I pulled up at the curb in front of her building. I wanted to drag her into my lap, kiss her, not let her go.

"I'll see you later?" she said.

"Yep, I expect you to be waiting for me when I get home, in bed and completely naked."

Her eyes sparkled. "Is that right? Well, if I'm asleep there is only one acceptable way to wake me." She slid out onto the sidewalk.

I rounded the back of the car to grab her bag. "And what's that?"

She shrugged a shoulder, an impish smirk lighting up her face as she leaned against the passenger door. "I'm sure you can figure it out." Her fingers curled into the front of my shirt and pulled me down, brushing a too swift kiss against my lips. "Have a good night."

I wasn't ready to let her go though, so I wrapped her up and buried my face in her neck, breathing her in. Her arms came around my neck, fingers straying into my hair.

"See ya, Cheese, don't miss me too much."

She stepped out of my grip and shouldered her bag. "I'll try my hardest, and if it does get too much ... I could always just take care of business. In your bed."

I hooked her around the waist with a groan. "You cannot leave me with that image right when I have to go to work." She laughed. The sound, along with the image of her in my bed, pleasuring herself in my bed, had my balls pulling tight.

"You could always take care of business, if you missed me too much ..."

"You're giving me the green light to jerk off at work?"

"No," she said immediately. "That's probably not a great idea. You'll just have to wait until you get home."

"To you."

"To me. But you need to actually leave first." She nudged me away. I went reluctantly, already counting down the minutes until I'd be able to crawl into bed beside her.

"See you soon."

"You will." She blew me a kiss before turning and walking up her stoop. "You're gonna be late if you keep on standing there staring at me, Milton."

I dropped into the driver's seat with a dopey grin on my face. Nothing was going to bring me down tonight.

I'D BEEN STARING at Chase's text for a full two minutes, trying to understand what could have happened in the time since I left her. I read it again.

Something's come up. I'll have to take care of business in my own bed tonight. But I'll see you tomorrow xx

What the hell could have 'come up'? That was a bullshit excuse, if ever I heard one. There was a reason, she wasn't telling me what it was. And I knew that she had mentioned taking care of business to distract me, which only made it more fucking suspicious. It was difficult to stop the swift downward spiral of my thoughts. To quiet the voice that told me this was it, the way it always went.

It wasn't going that way now though. It couldn't. Because this was Chase. Because this was me and Chase. She was different, *we* were different. If she said that something had come up, then maybe it had. And I'd see her tomorrow and she'd explain and I'd be able to fucking relax.

Everything would make sense tomorrow.

29

CHASE

THIS WAS NOT how I saw my night going.

The plan had been simple enough. Shower. Day dream about all the sex I'd had this morning. Eat. More thinking about all the sex, specifically watching us in the mirror—holy hell that had been seriously fucking hot. Then I was going to take myself off to Mack's place and curl up in his bed, huffing his pillow while drifting in and out of sleep and maybe masturbating a little (or a lot) as I waited for him to finish up at Rudi and come home.

Simple. The plan was simple.

Instead, Pip was on my couch, cradling a mug of tea and sobbing like a baby. I'd not been able to get much out of her since she turned up on my doorstep a couple of hours after Mack dropped me off. What I had managed to put together was that she and Tim were done. Officially done. *Done-done.*

There probably wasn't a great time for your marriage to break down, but the week before Christmas did seem like particularly shitty timing. Not that I was about to say that to her, obviously.

I collected the pizza from the door and handed over a tip to the pimpled teenager who barely looked old enough to drive. He stuttered out a thank you before all but sprinting down the stairs.

The smell of pepperoni and mushroom wafted up from the box and I realized, with a dull pang in my chest, that I missed Mack already. It had been a couple of measly hours and I missed him. I wanted to sit at Rudi and watch him work. I wanted to be in his bed breathing in the scent of him. I would have settled for watching him fold laundry. What the hell was the matter with me?

Maybe it wasn't such a bad thing that I couldn't see him tonight, maybe a little space was good, healthy. It might help to stop me from going full blown goo-goo over him. Although, admittedly, I had gone and fallen in love with him already, and that was before we had mind boggling sex so many times I lost count. Goo-goo was probably a forgone conclusion at this point whether I saw him tonight or not.

And just when I thought that maybe relationships were okay, that they were possibly not all on a ticking clock to failure, Pip turned up on my doorstep to prove that even the strongest ones could fall apart.

I was not the woman to help you deal with an existential crisis. Not by a long shot. Not unless you were happy to be given a lot of alcohol and very little food in the process, which, apparently, she was.

I collected a bottle of whiskey and dropped down on the couch next to Pip as she set her mug on the coffee table.

"You wanna talk about it?" I asked because that was what you asked in these situations, even when your insides felt like they were crawling and you didn't actually want to know. Because the knowing couldn't be erased. The knowing stayed with you long after the conversation ended.

She sniffed and accepted a swig of whiskey and a slice of pizza then slouched into my lumpy cushions. There was no way I could let her sleep on this thing tonight if that really was her plan.

"I thought we were working through it, you know? Our counselor was really good, making us stop and think about things. But maybe it was just too far gone. Maybe it broke too long ago and now it's set badly and there's no fixing it." She took a bite of pizza.

I hadn't admitted it to myself until this moment but part of me had secretly been hoping that maybe there was some cheating involved. I didn't know what it was about that situation that softened the blow of a collapsing relationship. Did it seem less messy, in my inexperienced relationship-brain? Less messy than falling out of love or growing apart, because how do you fix those things? Yes, cheating was easier, cleaner, you cheated, you won't do it again. Problem solved. The ridiculousness of my brain terrified me sometimes.

"Did something happen?"

"Nothing at all, and too many little things to even count." She sighed.

"Do you still love him?"

"I always will." It was a sad, almost resigned confession. "But I don't know if it's enough. Not anymore. It might have been when it was just the two of us. When we didn't have the kids and the house and all the other bullshit. When it was just us everything was simpler, but now ... it's like I blinked and lost all this time and I don't know who I am anymore. I don't know who we are anymore."

I sat in stunned silence. How was being in love not enough? I thought that was the whole point? Once you were in love, you could do anything, right? Whatever came your way you handled it, together.

God, I was so naive. Being in love didn't change anything. It wasn't this magic pill that fixed everything. It made things worse. It made it harder because there was so much more to lose. It took you all the way up to the roof and sat you on the edge and then told you not to fall off. But the fall was inevitable. It always had been. I'd just been trying to convince myself otherwise, because I wanted to keep Mack. But if this had taught me anything, it was that I couldn't. Not like this.

Yes, I was in love with him, but ending it now would surely be easier than six months, a year, two years from now. Wouldn't it? My stomach twisted as a war of emotions played out.

I was being a selfish bitch. I shouldn't be sitting here wallowing about my own situation. I should be comforting Pip in her time of need, like a good friend.

"I'm sorry," I said, though it was a woefully undercooked response given what she had just confessed.

She took a swig of whiskey. "God, I'm going to be a divorcee. And I know there's not actually anything wrong with that, but after the shit my parents went through—after the shit they put us through—I swore I wouldn't do it, not to myself, not to my kids ... But here I am."

"Can I play the role of devil's advocate, for a moment?"

"Go ahead." She shrugged, still cradling the bottle.

What on earth did I think I could say to turn this situation around? "Could all of this be a test or something?"

"A test?"

"Yeah, like, the universe only gives you what it knows you can handle or whatever, right? So maybe this is a test for your relationship."

"If it is a test, we're failing."

"Pip, I feel confident in saying that I don't think you've ever failed anything in your life, it's not in you."

She smiled at her own lap at that.

"What I mean is..." I had no idea what I meant but I'd started this train and had to see it through. I couldn't accept that their relationship was just over. "That maybe, even though this feels like the end, it's not, maybe it's just another chapter, and once you get to the end of this one another new one will start. Does that make sense, or am I just deliriously tired?"

"It does make sense, and I agree that this is a chapter, and there will be many more, but I don't think they're going to look the way they do in your head." It wasn't pity in her eyes, but it was close. "Why are you so tired? Big night?"

"Didn't sleep well."

"Uh huh ... any particular reason why?"

The hairs up the back of my neck tingled. She knew something, or at least she thought she did. Had Mack talked to her? It wouldn't have been all that surprising if he did, but knowing she knew something made me desperate to ask. Even though I absolutely shouldn't. Especially not when I was considering putting a stop to everything. Or pumping the brakes at the very least, although what good would that do at this point? Just delay the inevitable.

"Nothing in particular," I said, doing my best to look aloof and like I wasn't having my own crisis. "Just didn't sleep well, you know?"

"Right now, yes, I do. You know, if there's anything you wanted to talk about, I'm happy to listen."

"Thank you, I appreciate that, but I'm good. Nothing exciting happening in my world." I was over playing it, I could see the suspicion firing in her eyes. "I think it's just everything at work. Things have been so chaotic since Dallas and Duke's wedding ... I figured it was just a phase, that it would settle down but that's not happening. We were doing pretty well before, but there used to be slow nights where it was just me, Mack, and the regulars—those nights are well and truly gone and I guess I kind of miss them. Which I know sounds ridiculous, more customers are better than less customers. I just —it's been an adjustment." I bit into my slice of pizza. I hadn't realized all that was floating around in my head. I'd been shoving it aside, convincing myself I was okay, but every time I went to work there was this anxious pang in my chest that the Rudi I loved was gone, and I still didn't know if I could handle this new one.

She nodded. "Change can be daunting. It's hard to know if we like it at first. Hard to know if it's the right kind of change or the wrong kind. But it's also inevitable, and you know that you and Mack will make it all work, whatever happens."

I nodded as my voice failed me. She was right, I had always known that Mack and I could figure anything and everything out together. Mack was my constant. My rock. But we'd gone and messed with it now. Thrown out the well established balance of our friendship and I had no idea how to go back. Worse, part of me wasn't sure I wanted to go back. Unease rippled through me. I wanted to believe that what we were doing was the right kind of change, but how could I ever be sure?

I WOKE up with a splitting headache and a nauseous feeling in the pit of my stomach. After sitting and talking to Pip until after midnight, I'd gone to bed and quietly cried myself to sleep because I didn't know what the fuck to do. I was so mad at myself for that first kiss. If it hadn't been for that, then none of this would have happened. But then, if it weren't for that kiss, I wouldn't have seen all these secret sides of Mack. The secret romantic. The secret house remodeller. The secret magician at making me come. How had I known him so long and not known these things? I certainly couldn't unknow them now, and I didn't want to. Well, maybe I did kind of want to unlearn just how devoted he was to my orgasm, because that was making what came next all the more difficult.

Pip had talked a little more about Tim, and I'd done my best to not interrupt and beg her to tell me that they'd work it out. The more she talked, the more clear it became that they probably wouldn't and my heart broke a little more with each word.

I knew that it was ridiculous of me to put all of my relationship faith in just two people. But when all you've seen is things never working out, when all you've seen is the roller coaster of love and then crushing loss, the first time you see something that wasn't that, it makes an impression. It shows you there is a different way. Now, though, I guess it just showed me how much worse it can be. Maybe Pip and Tim's situation should make me grateful for all the times I didn't get attached to Mom's boyfriends, for all the times it was easy to hold the pity party and tell her she was better off without them. She was always better off without them, in my opinion.

But Pip, was she better off without Tim? I knew she'd get through it, she was one of the strongest women I knew, but they'd always seemed like such an incredible team, such a force of nature, how could you be better off without that? I didn't know the answer, nor was I going to. And, right now, I had myself to think about.

I reached out blindly for the Tylenol I kept on the nightstand and threw two back to deal with the piercing pain in my skull, then dragged myself out of bed. My apartment was silent and empty, the only sign that Pip had ever been there was a note on the kitchen counter, sitting beside an empty bottle of whiskey. I didn't remember it being empty when I went to bed.

Chase, thank you for being my Brooklyn hideaway, I appreciate it more than you know. Tim and I haven't decided how best to break the news to the family yet, so if you could keep it to yourself a little longer, I'd really appreciate it.

Take care, P x

I reread the note three or four times, willing the words to change so I didn't have to lie to Mack about this. Even if I hadn't decided what needed to happen between us, lying to him was one of my least favorite things. Sending him that bullshit text last night had been hard enough. Actually backing up that nonchalant lie in person was going to be near impossible. I already knew he wasn't going to let it go easily. I guess I just had to pray he'd be so thrilled to see me, he'd choose to look past the fact I was supposed to be sleeping next to him last night and instead sent him a blow off text that I couldn't explain.

Today was going to suck.

30

MACK

I COULDN'T REMEMBER the last time I slept so badly. I'd been awake half the night, staring at the ceiling, with my stomach churning and my heart in my throat.

It wasn't about Rudi, but it sure as shit didn't help that it had been one of those nights where nothing went right. Too many customers were amped up and aggressive, one of our new bartenders nearly lost a finger on a shard of wayward glass, and I came very close to firing a security guard who failed to stop a fight because he was making out with someone in the fucking office. It was a straight up shitshow.

None of it ever seemed to happen when Chase was there. Okay, so I was sure it did, but maybe she handled it better than me. Who was I kidding, of course she handled it better than me. Every time something else went wrong, I could only think: *fuck I wish she was here.* Not because I needed her to deal with the madness, although that would have been nice, but because we were better together. We always had been. A team. *The best team.*

She hadn't been there, though. She'd been at home, hers,

not mine. Because *something came up*. Those words had been running through my head on a loop since I finally collapsed into bed. I was no closer to believing it, no closer to understanding why she'd bailed. It didn't matter how many times I tried to convince myself that everything was fine, the sneaking, sinking feeling of dread wouldn't leave me.

History told me this was the way things went. It had happened enough times for me to recognise the pattern. I hadn't always minded, some things weren't meant to last more than a night, more than a few hours.

Chase and I, however, we *were* meant to last. I knew it, felt it, believed it all the way to my core. It had always been the two of us. It would always be the two of us. And I had zero fucking intention of letting her go now we were finally here.

I ambled into the bathroom and straight under the frigid spray of the shower. I needed to decide if I sought her out, or waited to see her later on at Rudi. My gut reaction was to go to her and ask what happened after I left. Would it push her further away? Even so I just didn't know if I could wait.

Fuck it.

I shut off the shower, dried off and threw myself into the first clothes I found that didn't smell like stale beer. I needed to see her, and I needed to do it now.

Apparently I wasn't alone, because as I opened the door Chase was there—with two coffees and a large brown bag. She'd been to Cream and Sugar, I'd know those cups anywhere. The sight of her sent my pulse pounding, but I refused to crush her into my chest and bury my face in her hair. Even though I desperately wanted to.

"Hey," I said, leaning on the door-jamb, hoping for a look of casual aloofness.

She shuffled from one foot to the other, boots scuffing the polished concrete, eyes darting around before they landed on me. Tired. Nervous. "Hey." She held up the bag. "I come bearing coffee and cinnamon buns."

"I see that, why?" The aloofness was sliding into asshole territory.

"Because I know you like coffee and cinnamon buns?" I didn't think she meant for it to come out as a question, but it did all the same. God I wanted to wrap her up, pull her inside and let the coffees go cold making up for the night we'd spent apart, but I was trying really hard to play it fucking cool. "I even went to Cream and Sugar," she added. "Harley coffee ..."

"I figured I'd just see you at Rudi later." A lie. But she didn't need to know I was charging out to see her when I pulled open the door and found her standing there.

"I—" She cleared her throat, took a step closer to me, jasmine and lime mixing with the cinnamon and coffee. "I guess I couldn't wait that long to see you. Not when I should have been waking up next to you." They were the exact words I wanted to hear, and I hated that I didn't immediately trust them.

"What came up?"

The pause was long enough that I knew whatever she was about to say was going to be a lie, and because Chase was an awful liar it wasn't going to be a good one. "Just things. But it's all fine now." She wasn't even trying to make me believe it.

"Just things. *Just. Things.* Are you serious? Chase, you're going to have to do better than that. You can tell me what's going on, whatever it is." I gripped my arms tighter to keep from reaching for her. She had to know she could tell me anything. When did she start keeping secrets? Was it hypocritical for me to be pissed at her for keeping secrets when I was keeping one from her, too?

"Nothing's going on," she said, her voice strained. It was her *please let this conversation be over* voice. But I couldn't drop it so easily, not when the uncertainty was still eating me alive.

"Chase."

Her shoulders sagged. "Can I at least come inside?" I stepped back, giving her enough room to pass, but not so much that she could do it without touching me. She went to the kitchen, dropped the bag on the counter then fished out an enormous cinnamon bun. I snatched it off her before she could take a mouthful that would render her mute for a good two minutes.

"Start talking."

She waved me off as she shrugged off her red coat, revealing one of my old hoodies underneath. "There's nothing to talk about, honestly, everything is fine."

"You are the worst liar." I put down the gooey, sweet-smelling bun and rounded the island. She took a step back and came up against the opposite counter, trapped. "Chase."

She looked everywhere but at me as I leaned in and caged her with my arms. I wasn't going to let her run away from this, run away from me.

"Chase ..."

"I freaked out," she said to her hands, which she was wringing in the sleeves of my hoodie. Her voice was low and shaky, and my heart just about broke.

"Why?" I asked, though I already had an idea of why.

Her hands flew up so quickly she almost hit me in the face. "Because–because this is all moving so fast!"

"It took three weeks from when you first agreed to go on a date with me for us to see each other naked and you're saying that's fast?"

"You know what I mean." She was speaking to my chest.

"Do I?"

After a small growl and another agitated breath she said,

"Yes, you do. My ... *feelings* are moving too fast." Her eyes met mine, deep and sincere and that look punched me square in the chest. "And it's scary," she continued. "Because I don't think you understand how fucking bad I am at all of this."

"I don't think you're giving yourself enough credit."

She jabbed my shoulder. "I don't think you're taking me seriously."

"I am, I swear, but I think you're over-complicating, over-dramatizing." I recognized the irony of this statement when I'd been tripping my way down a dread spiral since receiving her text yesterday.

"Until two days ago, I had never showered with another person."

"And I am honored to have been your first." My arms curled around her back as her hands came to rest on my pecs. I ducked my head to look her in the eye. "I know this is going to take some work, some ... adjustment. But we can move as fast or as slow as we want. We're the ones that make the rules, Chase, no one else." I didn't want to take it slow. I wanted to barrel ahead and move her into my place and wake up next to her every morning but, in order to do those things at some point in the future, I needed to chill the fuck out now.

"How slow?" she asked, eyes narrowing.

"Glacial."

Her lips pursed. "That's pretty slow."

"It is."

"And you'd do that, for me?"

"Chastity Heather, I would do just about anything for you." I squeezed her a little tighter.

"Just about..." she mused, some lightness returning to the depths of her eyes. "Well, now I want to find the limit. Would you take a bullet for me?"

"In a heartbeat."

"I'd take one for you, too. Would you help me bury a body?"

"Yep."

"Me too."

"No question?"

"I mean, I'd have questions," she said with a roll of her eyes.

"Like, *why'd you kill this guy?*"

"Or girl."

"I'd never kill a woman."

"Never say never. Anyway, yes, I'd have questions, but I'd still do it." She smiled and suddenly everything was right in the world, and I could breathe easily again. Somewhere in the back of my head those nagging doubts were still there, just quieted for the moment because she was smiling at me and I was a hot second away from kissing her. I was also dimly aware that this probably wasn't all that healthy, her having this much power over me, but it was hard for me to shake it now.

She went to grab her coffee but I lifted her onto the counter and fit myself between her knees. "Next time"—because we both knew there was going to be a next time—"just talk to me, agreed?"

"Agreed."

"Now, I really need to kiss you."

"Then do it," she purred.

My hands came up to cup her face and I covered her mouth with mine. She sighed, her fingers curling into the front of my shirt as she pulled me closer. As much as I wanted to strip her right here and worship her until we had to work, I wanted to be mindful of her need to slow things down, which meant ending the kiss long before I would have liked to. Her lips chased mine for a second before she leaned away.

"Slow," she said.

"Glacial," I agreed and stepped back to let her slide off the counter.

We both took up our still warm coffee cups and sipped, watching one another. Despite her confessions, there was still an uncertain niggle in the pit of my stomach that told me something else was hiding behind my favorite pair of eyes. I knew that she'd tell me eventually, but the fact she was holding back still left me edgy.

Rather than dwell on it, because nothing good would come from that, I decided to regale her with a blow by blow of the disasters from last night. As expected, she looked horrified on all fronts, but mostly about Ray and his office groping.

"What did you say when you found them?" she asked around a mouthful of cinnamon bun.

"I didn't know what the hell to say! I just told her to get out and him to get back to work."

She snorted a laugh. "You really are terrible with confrontation."

"I guess that's another reason we make such a good team then. Confrontation is not my thing and you're always jonesing for a fight."

"I am not always jonesing for a fight!"

I raised a brow in challenge.

"I'm not! I am simply sure of myself and my own opinions."

I couldn't stop the barked laugh from escaping and she punched me.

"Shut up."

"One of us needs to be the bad cop."

"With the most inventive punishments."

"What are you going to give Ray? Cleaning the toilets with a toothbrush?"

"Possibly. I was going to give that to Greyson after his stunt locking us in the office but—"

"That didn't turn out so bad," I finished, closing the distance between us. She hummed a yes as she set her coffee aside and reached for me.

I lifted her back onto the counter, my hips once again fitting between her knees, hands gliding into her hair. I relished the cool silk of it between my fingers. Hers curled into the front of my shirt as our tongues met and caressed. I could lose hours, days—hell, *months*—with Chase's mouth on mine. We weren't just good, we were a perfect balance, harmony. We worked.

Did she feel it too? The synchronicity? Our chests came flush and her drumming heart matched mine. I had to believe she felt it, too, and that was what had scared her. I got it. I was scared out of my fucking brain as well, but I also knew that everything was better with her. Everything was better when we were together.

Her thighs squeezed me closer, but I was very aware that this was not glacial, not even when we were still fully clothed and all hands remained in PG zones. Not that I could make myself pull away.

Chase flattened her palms on my chest, the slightest push was enough for me to break our kiss and put a half step of space between us. .

"Not glacial," I said.

"No," she agreed.

"Sorry." I shot her a grin as I ducked my head, hoping I looked somewhat apologetic. She reached for her, likely now tepid, coffee and held the cup between us like a shield.

We needed a change of subject or I was going to throw that coffee in the trash and kiss her again. I had just the thing. "So... I know that it's still a few days until Christmas, but I have really outdone myself on your present this year and the waiting is killing me."

Some of the tension in her shoulders loosened as a smile lifted the corners of her lips. "Is that right?"

"Oh yeah ... you wanna see it?" I wagged my eyebrows and her smile grew a little wider.

"Yes, obviously." She scoffed. "But we can't exchange gifts if I don't have yours here."

"It's fine if you don't have anything."

She shoved at my chest. "Oh I have something alright. And you'll find that I have also outdone myself.'

"Really?"

"Really, really." So smug and sure of herself. I loved it.

Ten minutes later Chase was finally leaving to go and retrieve her gift for me and bring it right back. I'd considered going with her, the emotional hangover from last night was making me seriously clingy, but I managed to stay where I was as she disappeared onto the street and promised to be back in thirty minutes.

Twenty eight minutes.

31

CHASE

TIME PASSED DIFFERENTLY when Mack's mouth was on mine. Everything else—the world around me, my valid concerns about our relationship, all common sense—seemed to fade away until there was nothing left but the press of his lips and the sweep of his tongue. I was lost, adrift, with only the feel of him to ground me.

It was dangerous. Even more so when the only thought that looped through my head was that I wanted to do this forever. That I would die happy kissing him.

I wasn't entirely sure what I thought was going to happen when I turned up at his place with coffees and cinnamon buns. The fact I went all the way to Cream and Sugar had *serious apology* written all over it. Serious apology and *please don't hate me when I say we need to pump the brakes.*

But then he'd gone and opened the door and stood there, leaning against the door jamb with his arms crossed and looking all gruff and broody and, frankly, edible. No other man I'd met wore a pair of low slung jeans and a plaid shirt like this one. My brain stopped functioning properly and just threw up a tiny movie montage of me pulling that shirt off and tackling him to the floor. It was not in the least bit helpful.

Nor was it taking things slow.

Glacial. That's what Mack had said. Unfortunately, no amount of slowing things down would change the tick-tocking of our inevitable end. The fact he was oblivious to it was both maddening and a relief all at once.

I side-stepped a woman pushing a double-wide stroller as my thoughts continued to race. I couldn't shake the feeling that we were just delaying the inevitable, dragging out the heartbreak, and making it that much harder to go back to how we were before. The idea that it was already too far gone, that we wouldn't be the same, was not one I was letting myself consider. But it was there all the same, laughing at me, daring me to imagine being near him without touching and kissing.

That was the other problem with slowing down. There was a very large part of me that didn't actually want to. That part—including my vagina and, more concerningly, my heart—wanted Mack. All day. Every day. As mine, *really* mine.

I shoved the thoughts aside. All of them. Because right now I was going to focus on giving Mack his Christmas present. The thought came to me a couple of weeks ago and, despite worrying I wouldn't be able to pull it all together in time, the last item was sitting on my doorstep when I arrived home yesterday. Now, I just had to pray he liked it. I'd been so sure of it initially, but as soon as I said out loud that I'd outdone myself, too, the doubts immediately started to swarm in my head.

Mack leapt off the couch as I let myself in, a grin splitting his face in two. God, I loved him so much it physically hurt, like some kind of sharp object was embedded in the center of my chest. That couldn't be healthy, could it? The thought that our end might rip me in two, and it wouldn't be a clean wound, it would be ragged and messy, the kind that never quite heals right.

"Prepare to be outdone, Cheese," he said, rubbing his hands together; the muscles in his forearms twitched in response.

"I don't think so," I shot back with far more confidence than I felt. What little there was dropped another couple of pegs when I spotted the two brightly wrapped boxes sitting on the coffee table. Two! And they were big. What the hell was in them? My fingers tightened on the package I held as I stopped a couple of feet away. This was ridiculous, I'd never felt this nervous giving him a gift before. He was going to like it. He had to like it.

"So, how do you wanna do this?" he asked, eyes sweeping down to my feet then back up. Was he making it sound sexual on purpose, or was it just my brain making it that way?

"Same time?" I said as casually as possible, while my heart thumped hard against my ribs.

"Same time it is." He dropped down on the couch and waited, an expectant look on his gorgeous face, as I joined him.

With a steadying breath, I handed over his gift and he slid the two large boxes towards me.

I couldn't stop the smile that tugged. "What the hell have you done?"

"Open it and see." He said with a wink and I shook my head, pulling the boxes closer. Even as I tore at the wrapping, I watched him out of the corner of my eye, with my heart in my throat.

"What is this?" he asked, voice low and just a little shaky. I abandoned my own gifts and turned to him, needing to see his face, needing to know that I hadn't stepped over a line he wasn't comfortable with. I didn't think we had those anymore, but he was stubborn and scared, almost as much as I was.

"It's ... it's you, if you want it to be."

He held up the sample menu, the logo I'd had designed sitting proud at the top of the page. "You—" The sentence went no further and my stomach churned. Long moments passed as he stared, at the piece of paper in his hand and me in turn. If he didn't say something soon, I was going to need a drink, a big one.

"Chocolate espresso. Apple cheddar. Salted honey. Bourbon pecan. Chase's sweet potato."

I nodded, nibbling my lip. "There's ice cream on the back."

His eyes went glassy and he let out a soggy sort of laugh. "Are you fucking kidding me?"

"I know you're scared of doing it for real, but ... I guess I wanted to show you what it could be."

"That's a food truck," he said, holding the poorly photoshopped picture up. I nodded again, not trusting my voice. I had almost contacted Hunter about the one he mentioned a couple of weeks ago, but I'd resisted, just. It had felt like a step too far, even for me and my unwavering faith in the man in front of me.

"Chase, I—"

Unable to take even the small amount of distance between us, I nudged the rest of the items onto the couch beside him and climbed into his lap. I wrapped my arms around his neck, leaning in until our noses bumped. "I'm sorry if I overstepped, I just–I wanted you to see what I see. I don't want you to feel like you're not worthy of this, like you just have to go along with what other people want for you. You deserve to go after your dreams, even if they scare you, Mack. You are intelligent and capable, and fucking remarkable, exceptional—there aren't enough words for me to explain how much I admire and adore you." I almost told him I loved him, I'd said it before, more times than I could count, but saying it now, like this, it carried a different kind of weight. "And if you want to do this, really do it, I will be right there next to you, tasting every single thing and doubling the size of my ass, if need be."

His arms curled around my back and he buried his face in my neck, wet eyelashes brushing my skin. "I don't deserve you," he mumbled.

"You deserve the world, Mack, and I will give you as much of it as I can." I squeezed him tighter, letting my fingers comb through his hair.

I lost track of time as we sat like that, clinging to one another, and I counted his heart beats drumming against my chest.

"There's more, you know?" I said eventually and his head popped up, eyes ringed with red and eyelashes still stuck together in clumps.

"I don't know if I can take anymore."

I cupped his face and brushed a kiss across his lips. "You can, besides, the last bit is my favorite."

Curiosity glinted in the blue depths of his eyes. "Is that right?"

"Uh-huh." I nodded. "I've got plans for it ..."

"Okay, now I am curious."

I slid sideways, one leg still draped across his as he unwrapped another layer of tissue. The apron peaked out, the black stitched logo proud against the soft, faded denim, his name just under it on the pocket.

He swallowed, sniffed, cleared his throat. "Chase, I ..." It unrolled as he lifted it up.

"My plan was to see you wearing it."

"I can make that happen." His voice was still shaky but he stood and slipped the top loop over his head. It was perfect, just like I knew it would be.

I reigned in my smile. "It does look good like that ..." I said, with mock seriousness. "But I think it would look even better if it was the only thing you were wearing."

His eyes jumped to mine, the blue going dark and hungry. "As much as I'd like to follow that train of thought immediately, I want to see you open your present first." He sat, our thighs pressed together.

"You like it though? It's not–it's not too much?"

He pulled me back into his lap, fingers spreading over my hips. "Chase, it's perfect. It's fucking terrifying, but it's–I think it's exactly what I needed."

"A little nudge?"

His smile was slow and made a tendril of heat uncoil in my core. "I'd consider it more of a shove, but yes. Thank you."

"You're welcome." I leaned in and kissed him, bringing our chests flush and letting my body say what I wasn't brave enough to. He pulled away before I could get too carried away.

"Open your present, Chase."

"Presents," I corrected, sliding back onto the couch beside him and returning my attention to the half-ripped wrapping paper. I was laughing before I had it all the way off. "You did not." The pink box was covered in neon lightning bolts and palm trees and on the front was a pouting girl in a pair of pink inline skates. I tore into the box, and squealed.

Nestled inside were a pair of rainbow-pastel inline skates. Mint green. Lemon yellow. Pale purple. Pink.

"They're not exactly what I had in mind—"

I tackled him before he could finish the sentence. "I love them!"

"Really?"

"Yes!" I peppered kisses all over his face then turned back to the skates, pulling one from the box and admiring it.

"I almost got you ice skates, but figured you'd be able to use these anywhere."

I was going to cry. I'd been thinking about buying some skates since our date but other things, mainly work, kept getting in the way because that was just how I operated. How did he know just what I needed before I did?

"What's in the other box? Safety equipment?"

"No, I got that too, but it doesn't count as part of your gift. It's in my room."

"What? How does that not count?" I set the skates aside and reached for the second box. It was a similar size and shape to the first, but he wouldn't have bought me two pairs of skates, right? Why would he do that?

He did buy two pairs of skates. And the why became abundantly clear as I opened the box. The roller skates were metallic pink and gold leopard print with gold laces and clear wheels filled with gold glitter.

"I know you never mentioned roller skating–although I have no doubt you'd be able to do it–but I saw these and thought of the ones you told me about and couldn't not buy them. Plus, I figured you'd look sexy as fuck in them."

I laugh-cried as I once again threw myself at his chest. How he had managed to find a pair of skates like the ones I coveted as a kid I would never know, but I wasn't surprised he had. If anyone was capable of doing this, it was Mack.

"I hope that's a good cry."

"Yes," I said, the words muffled against his shirt. "Yes, it's a good cry."

His hand rubbed circles on my back until I sat up.

"Thank you," I said, though it didn't feel like enough.

"You're welcome. I can't wait to see you in them."

"If I break something, it'll be your fault."

"I will happily take full responsibility, and provide sponge baths." He wagged his eyebrows.

"You outdid yourself," I said, still marveling at the two pairs of skates sitting on the coffee table. I was itching to get into them, but that would require tearing myself away from Mack and I wasn't sure I was ready for that just yet.

He looked down at his chest, one finger tracing over the logo, including the little pie dotting the *i*. "I think you might have won this round, Chastity."

I shook my head. He didn't understand that he'd given me more than skates, he'd given me permission. Permission to do something that wasn't productive. Permission to play. Permission to turn my brain off. Permission to stop. "Let's call it even."

32

MACK

THIS. Fucking. Woman.

Chase had blown me away so thoroughly with her gift, I still wasn't sure I had the right words to thank her. They may never come. When I'd eased open the wrapping and seen the menu, my first reaction had been to fight it, to argue, to push back. Because that was what I did when anyone tried to talk about this and push me further than I was willing to go. But I couldn't, not this time. Not when Chase was looking at me with those eyes that went right to the heart of me, past all the bullshit and fear. She *saw* me. All of me. It was scary as shit but I knew I'd never change it, not for anything.

I looked back down to the logo stitched across the top of the apron. *The Pie Guy.* The name she'd jokingly given me as I stood in my kitchen a couple of weeks ago. I'd laughed it off at the time, even while thinking I quite liked the sound of it. And now here it was. On my chest, my name just below it on the apron's pocket. Scary. As. Shit. But, also, a small voice whispered, *right.*

"It really does look good on you," Chase said, drawing my

311

attention to her. She crawled into my lap, her thighs sliding over mine as one finger followed the black stitching.

"You think so?" I asked, pulling her closer, letting myself breathe in the floral and citrus scent of her.

"I do. Although part of me was terrified you wouldn't like it." She nibbled her full lower lip as her hips shifted forward and a low groan rolled up my throat. My hands explored her back, pressing our chests together.

"Worrying for nothing ... that doesn't sound like you."

A laugh burst out of her. "No, not like me at all."

She ran her nose along mine before closing the last of the space between us.

The glacial conversation from earlier was still there, hovering in the background, so, as much as I wanted to tear her clothes off and worship her until we had to go to work, I resisted, letting her set the pace. It wasn't exactly difficult when her tongue swept into my mouth with a sound somewhere between a sigh and a moan that had my brain melting. Her hips rolled over my already hard cock as she explored my mouth and I desperately tried to keep hold of my leash. I wanted her so badly I could barely think straight and I once again marveled at the fact we'd been able to hold all of this tension at bay all those years. It would be utterly impossible now.

Chase's fingers pressed between us, popping the button on my jeans. "Need you," she said, giving herself room to dive her hand into my boxers.

"You, too."

Our mouths came back together, the kiss messy and desperate. Then her lips cut a trail over my jaw and down my neck, and she was sliding off my lap, between my knees.

"Ch—oh *fuuuck*." I groaned as her tongue swirled around the head of my cock. I was going to pass out.

"Pants. Get your pants off." It was a difficult instruction to comply with, considering she was essentially in the way, but I did my best to at least get my pants halfway down my thighs and she ripped them the rest of the way down to my ankles. I would have made some kind of joke about it but then her mouth was on me again and I was no longer thinking, let alone capable of speech. All I could do was feel her, warm and wet as she sucked and licked and drove me fucking crazy. It wasn't enough though; I wanted us naked and feeling her skin against mine.

She moaned, the vibrations sending heat barreling down my spine.

"W–urgh, feels so good." I sucked in a sharp breath as she sunk lower and my cock hit the back of her throat, she swallowed. "Fuck, wait."

She released me and licked her swollen lips, eyes bouncing between me and my straining cock. "Problem?"

"Just that you're not naked."

She smiled slow as she stood, ripping off her hoodie—my hoodie—as she went, and, God help me, there was only a bra underneath. I tore off the apron and my shirt, then leaned forward to work on peeling off her jeans, the need pounding through my blood making my hands shake. It was on the tip of my tongue to tell her how much I wanted her, now and fucking forever, but I couldn't, not when it had the potential to send her running. I would do literally anything to keep her right here with me.

I helped her out of her jeans and then she was standing before me in nothing but a pair of black lace panties, she'd wasted no time in throwing her bra onto the couch beside me. Her nipples were tight buds calling out for my mouth.

"Fucking perfect," I said, reaching for her, licking over her left breast.

"You're not so bad yourself." She arched into me, her

fingers threading into my hair and tightening just enough to make my scalp prickle. Pleasure-pain raised goosebumps down my arms.

I kissed a trail down her stomach until I reached the sheer fabric of her underwear. Her hips rocked forward, a silent plea.

"Take them off," I ordered as I slid off the couch and sat on the floor at her feet. She kicked the scrap of lace off to the side.

I dropped my head back, hands gliding up the backs of her legs. "Sit."

She went to lower herself onto my cock. And as much as I wanted that, I had other plans first.

"Not there."

Her eyes widened, the dark irises swallowed by her lust-blown pupils. I shuffled to get more comfortable as she stepped over me, hands going to the back of the couch. I guided her down, fingers splayed wide over her ass until her pussy met my mouth and we both groaned.

She sucked in a breath, her legs shaking as I licked up her slit. I could lose myself eating her, the taste of her, the sounds she made.

"Oh, God, Mack."

I growled against her, unwilling to pull my mouth away from the honey on my tongue. I kept hold of her with one hand, the other kneading her ass before dipping between her legs and teasing her entrance. She moaned, hips rocking, and I sucked her clit.

"More."

I sucked harder, flicked my tongue and she cried out, pressing down with shaking legs. Her breathing turned into shallow pants as she raced towards her climax. I gazed up the line of her body, mesmerized by the movement of her breasts as she rocked against me.

"I–keep going–please—" The words descended into

nonsensical sounds as I continued to suck and lick, my own hips rocked, my cock aching to be inside her, but not until I'd made her come first. I slid two fingers into her pussy.

"Yes," she moaned. "Coming." Her walls squeezed as she panted through her orgasm.

"Need you," I said and nipped the inside of her thigh. She made a noise of agreement and half climbed-half fell backwards, then gripped my cock and lowered herself in one smooth, swift motion.

I buried my face in her neck, telling myself not to come immediately as I felt the wet heat of her pulsing around me.

"God, Chase."

"Feels so good." Her arms wrapped around me as her hips began to rock, taking me deeper. She pulled my face up and crushed her mouth to mine. I swallowed her desperate sounds, sucked her tongue as my hips thrust up. The kiss broke and she threw her hands back to my knees, pushing her breasts forward. I sucked one nipple into my mouth, relishing the answering squeeze on my cock.

Time stretched as we moved together, two halves of the same whole. Her nails bit into my knee and shoulder as she came again with a cry and I followed shortly after, both of us collapsing and panting.

"Wow," she said against my neck.

"How many more times do you think we can do it again before we have to be at work?" I asked, letting my hands roam over her bare back.

Her laugh pressed her breasts against my chest and rustled my hair. "There's only one way to find out."

. . .

THE ANSWER WAS THREE. Although two would have meant we might have made it to Rudi on time. Not that I regretted that particular decision at all.

The problem was, despite showering before we left, I could still taste Chase on my tongue, still feel the sting of her nails as she clawed my back, my shoulders, my knees. It was really fucking distracting. More so when she kept shooting me looks like she was thinking about her straddling my face, too. I was talking down my cock while also counting down the minutes until I had her naked and in my bed.

"Well, don't you look disgustingly happy." Harley said and my eyes snapped away from Chase at the other end of the bar, hoping I hadn't looked like I'd been trying to stare a hole through her shirt.

"Harley, lovely to see you as always. What can I get you?"

She whistled as she planted her elbows on the bar top, wild curls flying free and spilling forward over her shoulders as she yanked her beanie off. "Just how much sex have you had today?"

I ignored the question, biting the inside of my cheek to stop the shit eating grin that wanted to unfurl, and poured her a Buck's cherry sour.

"You remembered," she cooed, accepting the glass and taking a slow sip as she watched me over the rim. Those whiskey-colored eyes saw far too much. "Does this mean you took my advice?"

"And what advice would that be?"

She smiled. "You *seriously* kissed her."

"Kissed who?" It couldn't hurt to play dumb for a little while.

She laughed, the sound sweet and husky all at once. But before she could question me any further, Hunter appeared at her side. I was grateful for the distraction.

"Mack, how are you my man?" he asked and I bumped his offered fist.

"Doin' well, what about you?"

"Also doin' pretty well, but I'll be even better with a beer."

"Coming right up."

The twinkle in Harley's eye told me she knew exactly what I'd been doing all day, whether I wanted to admit it or not. It also promised we would be picking this conversation up later, which meant I would need to studiously avoid her for the rest of the night.

I sat Hunter's local IPA on a coaster as my mind swung swiftly away from Chase (for the first time today) and straight to pies. A ball of nerves sat heavy in my stomach. Was I ready for a food truck? No, absolutely not. I'd only just decided that I might actually do something with my pies today, but seeing Hunter meant all I could now think about was the food truck. And if I didn't at least ask him about it I was going to kick myself later.

I drummed my hands on the bar for a beat, then leaned in on my elbows like Harley had done not two minutes ago.

"You look like you got something on your mind," Hunter said after a sip of beer.

I nodded, stomach churning. "Yeah, just–ah–just wondering if your guy found a buyer for his food truck?" I really hoped I didn't sound as nervous as I felt.

Harley's face split into a huge grin. "Mackenzie!" she crowed, wrapping my hands in hers. "Please tell me you are going to start selling your pies! This is amazing. Our deal still stands for the chocolate espresso for me, right?"

"Yes, Harley, it'll be ready for you on Christmas Eve."

She nodded happily.

Hunter cut in before she could say any more. "You serious, bro? That's fucking cool. Last I heard, he'd had some luck with a guy but I can let him know you're keen if it falls through."

Disappointment made my stomach pitch, but I wasn't surprised. "That'd be great, thanks."

"No worries, I still need to try one of these pies of yours. Harley talks about them every chance she gets."

She swatted his shoulder. "You'll understand if I save you any at Christmas." Her eyes swung to me. "Is it too late to order two?"

"Two it is," I said and received a grin in response.

The conversation moved on as the bar filled with a festive Wednesday night crowd. But even as I served drinks and made conversation, my mind didn't stray far from what might be next. I had no idea how I'd even make a food truck work, it wasn't like I could bake in the truck, could I? No, more likely, as Chase had suggested, I'd bake at Rudi and then load them up into the truck. Could I really do it? I wasn't sure, but Chase's faith in me made me want to try.

33

CHASE

AS A GENERAL RULE, I didn't like sleeping next to other people. I never had. I would tell myself that I just couldn't do it, that sleeping next to another person made me restless and antsy no matter how tired I was. But maybe that had been about *who* was next to me. Because sleeping next to Mack was like taking some magical pill, making me sleep like the dead for a solid six hours.

Of course he would prove the exception to my long held rule. Was it just his presence? His warmth? It could be both of those things, or, more likely, it was the obscene amount of sex we were having that left me sated, boneless, and oh so sleepy.

Whatever the case, I woke up on Thursday morning refreshed and sore, in the best possible way. And, despite the hard length pressed against my hip, my mind was squarely focused on skating. Thanks to all of the aforementioned sex, I'd barely even managed to strap on one of my two (!) pairs yesterday. Mack tackled me before the laces were even done up and we'd had sex—again—on the floor. I had no regrets, obviously, but today I wanted to put them to good use.

Mack shifted, falling onto his back and I considered waking him up and having my way with him. He really did look delicious. My fingers twitched with the need to crawl along his chest, and follow his happy trail that disappeared under the edge of the duvet. No! Well, yes, but later.

With one last look at him, I slipped out of bed and tiptoed to the bathroom. He was going to wake up soon enough, when I started skating around his living room, but I would do my best to be quiet until then.

I rubbed some toothpaste over my teeth in an effort to deal with the morning breath and pulled on a pair of Mack's sweatpants and a shirt. The knee and wrist pads were easy enough to find in his closet and, once again, there were two sets: one pink and one black. Like he couldn't choose between the two.

"Such a goober," I said with a smile.

Now, I just had to decide which pair to test out first. The rational part of me said the inline skates. I'd be able to find my feet quicker on them rather than the quad skates. However, that pink and gold leopard print was calling to me. It couldn't be that hard—and Mack had promised sponge baths if I broke something, which wasn't a bad consolation prize.

There was still a small voice in the back of my head that told me slow wasn't going to be enough to save us, that we were still doomed whether we wanted to admit it or not. The prospect of losing him, properly losing him, made my stomach twist. I didn't want it to happen, but that didn't change the fact it would. It was the cycle, and it could only go one way. To its natural, inevitable conclusion. I would have to deal with it, sooner rather than later, but not today. I wanted to live in denial just a little longer.

No more thinking about this. Not now. Not when I had

skates to test out. I stuffed my feet into them, thoroughly enjoying the perfectly snug fit. I laced them up, put on my knee and wrist pads because, as much as I would enjoy a sponge bath from Mack, I didn't actually want to break anything on my first attempt.

"Oh, shit!" I squeaked as I pushed up to standing and wobbled. "I can do this, it's fine. This is fine." I pushed off my right foot, then left, finding a rhythm as I did a loop of the living room, then through his kitchen. Oh yes, I could definitely get used to this.

By the time Mack shuffled out of his bedroom a couple of hours later, in a pair of low slung gray sweatpants, I was attempting to spin after I managed to work out how to transition to backwards skating. It had not all been smooth, as the blooming bruise on my butt could attest, but it turned out it wasn't as different from ice skating as I thought it would be.

I was gifted with a wide, albeit sleepy, smile as I completed a backwards loop of the couch and squeaked to a stop in front of him. My cheeks were hurting from smiling so much.

"Have you been up all night?" he asked, arms curling around my back. I pressed up onto my stoppers and kissed him hard. He squeezed me closer, hands moving down over my ass.

"What was that for?"

"Just because." I shrugged. "Might have something to do with how fucking good you look in sweatpants. Also, I love my Christmas present." I wiggled a little for emphasis.

"And I'm not even done yet," he purred, nuzzling into my neck. I tipped my head to give him better access, melting against him as he nipped and kissed.

"What?" The word wobbled as he bit the junction of my neck and shoulder.

"There's one more surprise."

"Seriously?" What else could there possibly be? I tugged on his hair until he was facing me. "You're not going to tell me, are you?"

"Nope." He kissed my nose. "It's too much fun watching you squirm."

"Sadist," I said and he winked. "Well, as much as I'd like to stay here and squirm for you, I need to get some clothes."

"What's wrong with what you're wearing?" His eyebrows wagged. He liked me in his clothes. I liked being in his clothes, too, but I couldn't stay in them forever.

"Aside from the fact they're yours, and I don't have underwear on? No, no, don't look at me like that." I slapped his chest. "I need to go home. I can bring you coffee and bagels on the way back."

The heat in his eyes shifted to something very different and my pulse spiked. I could see the words sitting there, just waiting to be given life. *Maybe you should have some clothes here then.* He'd say it like a joke, like it wasn't a big deal. But it was a big deal. It was a really big fucking deal. Too much. Too soon. I said I wanted things to go slower and all we'd done since was have a whole lot of sex. Having all the sex wasn't a bad thing, admittedly, but moving in? That was too much.

I rolled away to perch on the arm of the couch and started unlacing my skates, words tumbling out of my mouth in a rush. It wasn't that I hadn't thought about living with him. I had. It had been sitting there in the back of my head since our first date. But thinking about it and actually doing something about it, even talking about it, that was different.

"I won't be too long," I said, now striding into the bedroom to find yesterday's clothes. "Maybe I can even swing past Cream and Sugar for some of those cinnamon buns." I was trying to distract him, he had to know it.

He leaned against the door-jamb, arms crossed over his wide, well-defined chest. I had no godly idea why that move was so hot but the door jamb lean, plus the low hanging gray sweatpants and no shirt, was making me feel more scrambled than I already was. He wasn't saying anything, though, just letting me dress and ramble. I'd moved onto work topics, they felt safer when my head and heart were this out of control.

"I'll be back before you know it." I stretched up to kiss him, the need for more was there, simmering under the surface but I pulled away. Space. I needed a little space.

"I'll be here."

I WAS STILL a messy jumble of warring emotions by the time I got to Cream and Sugar, toting my overnight bag. I'd packed it and unpacked it at least three times before leaving my apartment. In the end, practicality won out. If I wound up staying at Mack's again tonight, then I was going to need clothes tomorrow. I even brought my toothbrush, which would be coming straight back home with me, and not living in his bathroom. I couldn't even entertain the *not yet*, that tried to tack itself onto the end of that sentence.

Unlike every other time I'd been here, Harley was not at the coffee machine, which felt oddly jarring, or maybe that was just my mood. Despite not being able to see her, I could still hear her infectious laughter floating out from behind the double saloon doors that led to the kitchen. She appeared a second later balancing two plates on each arm.

"Chase!" she said, her face breaking into a wide smile. "How you doin', girl?"

Considering my current state of mind, I wasn't actually sure how to answer that. Thankfully, I didn't need to. Harley delivered the plates to a waiting table and slipped back behind the counter.

"You want it iced today?"

That was a simpler question to answer. I nodded, and added, "And a large Americano for Mack, two cinnamon buns, and ... a couple of bagels."

"Coming right up." She got to work, moving with smooth efficiency in the relatively narrow space.

"So..." Her eyes darted between me and the coffees in front of her. "You got big plans for Christmas?"

"Oh, ah, not big ones. Just the usual, seeing family." I shrugged, remembering I needed to buy a bottle of whiskey for Prescott as part of the family Secret Santa. Or was it Lachlan?

She nodded, an impish smile on her face. "Yes, of course, family plans, lovely, very wholesome. But what about other plans, with a certain business partner ... ?" At my blank look, she rolled her eyes and added, "Subtlety is not my strength. *Sexy* plans, Chase, I'm talking sexy plans. Don't make me drag it out of you."

Sexy plans? Sexy plans with a certain business partner? Did Harley know about Mack and I? Had he told her? How the hell else would she know?

"If you need anything in the costume department, I got you covered," she continued. "Sexy elf. Sexy snowman. Sexy reindeer. Sexy gift, that one's fun, it's got this bow that you pull and *voila*—you get the idea, right?" She giggled. "But I think my personal favorite is sexy Santa. You can't go wrong with the classics, you know?"

She knew. She had to. Why the hell else would she be giving me a full rundown of her sexy Christmas inventory. Oh, God, if she knew, who else did? Who else had he told? What if he'd told Pip? There was no way I could go to the Kent Christmas if they all knew. It was too much, too much pressure, too much expectation. Fuck! Why did he have to tell anyone? I didn't think I needed to spell out the fact that we were still keeping this to ourselves. That was part and parcel of going slow. But instead of respecting that, he'd gone and told Harley!

I accepted the two coffees tucked into their tray and the brown bag full of goodness that I no longer wanted to eat. My stomach was now a hollow churning pit of acid.

The trip back to Mack's apartment was both too long and too short. Part of me recognised that I might be overreacting but I couldn't stop it, not now. Not when I was a hot second away from breathing into the bagel bag to ward off hyperventilation.

His hair was still damp when I found him in the kitchen, the counter covered in a mess of pie paraphernalia. He glanced up from what he was doing, smile slipping as he registered whatever was on my face.

"You okay there?"

"You told Harley." I dropped the coffees and bag onto the counter.

"Told Harley what?"

"She knew Mack, Harley knew about us."

"And why is that a big deal?" He wiped off his hands and came around the counter. I took a step back.

"So, you did tell her?"

"I didn't say that, but you've clearly made up your mind."

"How else would she know?"

"Maybe she guessed!"

"Based on what!? I cannot fucking believe this." He went to talk but I kept going. "Slow, Mack, I asked for us to go slow. But you can't do it! You nearly asked me to move in with you earlier! Like we don't spend enough time together already. And before you try and deny it, don't bother, I know you were going to. I know you."

"And I know you! I know you're scared."

"Of course I am! I'm scared out of my fucking brain about losing you. Things were better when we were just friends. We shouldn't have stepped over that line, it's only made things complicated."

"You don't believe that."

"Don't tell me what I believe."

He blew out a breath. "Chase, one person knowing is not a big deal. And, yeah, maybe I was going to suggest that you leave some clothes here. It's a drawer, not a marriage proposal."

Yet. The word hung between us, as clear as if he'd said it. Because he would ask me to marry him, even knowing the disasters that both our parents had been in their relationships—and continued to—he still would. And if he thought we'd fare any better than they did, he was kidding himself. Not even Pip had been able to break that cycle.

"Why can't you see that you're just setting us up for failure?" The kisses. The sex. None of it changed anything.

"It's not that I don't see it, it's that I don't agree."

"Come on, Mack, how can we honestly work? Neither of us have ever seen a healthy fucking relationship. I told you from the start that this wasn't a good idea, and you didn't listen."

"I did listen, but you just needed time," he said with a slow shake of his head as my blood fizzed.

"Don't fucking patronize me. I'm trying to be realistic and save us both the hellscape of this ending six months or a year from now. Ending it now, before anything, before it goes too far, it's the right thing to do for both of us, and for our friendship."

"That's bullshit," he growled.

"It's not."

"It is, Chase."

"Look, I get that you thought we could live happily ever after. And the absolute last thing I wanted to do was hurt you. It was the reason I didn't want to start this in the first place, because I knew I'd fuck it up! There is a reason that none of my relationships have lasted longer than a couple of months."

"Yeah, there is, because you always push them away."

"What are you talking about?"

He shoved his hands through his hair, pulling at the ends. "Fucking hell, let's not pretend that you don't know this. As soon as shit starts getting serious, you push them away. You did it with Tommy in senior year. You did it with Ben. You did it with Simon."

"You never even met Simon!"

"I didn't need to. This is your MO, Chase. You start pushing, like it's some kind of test, and then when they leave it's a confirmation that it was never going to work out. Well, guess what? You can push as much as you fucking like, I'm not going anywhere."

He wasn't listening. Why wasn't he listening? They left because I'm not girlfriend material, I'm messy and stubborn and grumpy and not that nice to be around a lot of the time— and they all figured it out. Mack would, too, if we kept going like this.

"I am trying to stop us both from getting hurt. I'm not pushing or anything else. But you're too stubborn to accept that I'm right. I don't want to fight about this. I think we both need a second to think and cool off." I went for the door, suddenly desperate to get the hell out of here and away from him.

"What a surprise, shit is getting too real and you're bailing," he said, following.

I spun to face him and poked a finger into his chest. "What is your problem?"

"My problem is you lying!"

"I'm not lying!"

"Yeah, you are. You're lying and trying to run away before you've even given us a chance."

"Oh, now I'm running, not pushing? And I gave us a chance, Mack. Five dates worth."

His eyes hardened. "So that was it, huh? You were just waiting to see if I was a good fuck and now you're done?"

I sucked in a sharp breath. "That is not what I'm saying and you know it."

"Do I? Because it's pretty fucking clear from where I'm standing."

Anger and disappointment collided in my chest. "Fuck you, Mack! I'm trying to save our friendship, which clearly you don't give a shit about anymore." I regretted the words as soon as they were out but I wasn't going to take them back, not when he'd just accused me of using him for sex. I waited for him to disagree, and when he didn't I got the hell out of there before I started crying.

The clear, crisp morning had been overshadowed by a blanket of thick cloud that looked like it was moments away from dumping an icy shower on everything. It seemed fitting, given my mood.

I choked on the tears that tightened my throat. How could he accuse me of only staying until we had sex? He had to know that wasn't true. We'd been friends for years and I'd never cared about whether or not I had sex with him. Did he really think that would have changed? Granted, that was kind of how it looked with me ending things less than a day after we'd last been naked together. But still, he had to know that wasn't actually true.

He just needed some time to cool off, that was all. He'd cool off, take the day to think and realize that I was doing what was best for us. He might even apologize when I saw him later. Okay, so an apology was less likely. But I still had hope for him not hating me when we were both at Rudi later.

Already the thought of seeing him made my stomach

squirm and cramp. How did I let it get this far? I'd known it wasn't a good idea and yet I'd let myself get swept away with him—in him. And look where it had gotten me, gotten us. Fighting. Saying awful shit that we couldn't take back.

I had to believe that we could move past it, because the alternative was not an option.

34

MACK

FUCK.

I'd known Chase was teetering on the precipice of a freakout when she left earlier. It was why I didn't say anything after the almost-comment about leaving some clothes here. I figured she'd go home, grab coffees, and reset the crazy, like she usually did.

Only the crazy didn't reset, it amped the fuck up.

And she ended us, because she was fixated on things that weren't going to happen. I wasn't one of the douchebags she'd dated in the past. I wasn't going to throw up my hands and leave just because things got tough. Although I had done a decent douchebag impression when I accused her of only staying for the sex. That was low, and exceptionally douchey. My frustration, and anger, got the better of me and I fucking loved her and couldn't tell her because she'd run even faster than she already was. But I'd meant what I said, she could push as hard as she fucking liked, I wasn't going anywhere. I was going to prove to her that I wasn't like all the others and that we were better together than apart. I believed it. I believed it with everything I had. I needed her to believe it, too. I needed her to believe in *us*.

There were two possible courses of action.

The first: give Chase the space to think all of this through and hopefully come to the conclusion that I was right and a relationship was not the disaster she'd built up in her head. This required a large amount of faith. Faith I wasn't sure I had right at the moment.

The second: don't give her time and space to think. Find her and better articulate my point, without accusing her of using me for sex (maybe even apologize for that at some point), and tell her that I had no intention of backing down. This, though requiring less faith, required a lot more spine because it probably meant another fight, and I fucking hated fighting with her.

I had no idea what to do. Letting Chase work all her shit out was almost always the best way to go. But I wasn't sure I had the patience for it.

EXPECTATIONS WERE both sky high and hovering somewhere near the gutter as I pushed open the inky-blue door of Rudi Blue a little after three. Unlocked. So she was already here. I didn't know if that was a good sign or a bad one. Everything felt like it could go either way at the moment. The uncertainty of it all was making my skin feel uncomfortably tight.

And if I thought about it anymore I was going to drive myself crazy, so I either needed to throw myself into something distracting and work related, or go and seek her out.

I managed to not look for her immediately. Instead, I busied myself with prep and set up, which was usually made more entertaining because Chase was propped at the bar with her laptop, running through figures and paperwork, and we'd just talk. About nothing in particular, but I didn't care because the sound of her voice had always affected me.

God, I missed her. I missed her and it had only been a few hours, but there was more distance than just the physical. This distance was worse because I didn't know if I'd get to kiss her again and that was making it hard to breathe. Would she even want me to hug her again?

"Hey." That one syllable was like a bell in my head, even though her voice didn't hold its usual strength. My eyes found her the second I lifted my head and, just like she did almost every time I saw her recently, she took my fucking breath away. Even looking sad and kind of puffy. She'd been crying. It crushed me to know I was the cause of those tears.

"Hi," I croaked.

"Hey," she said again, looking small and more uncertain of herself than I'd ever seen her. Fucking hell this was awkward. We'd been a lot of things over the years, frustrated, infuriated, mad, sad, but never awkward. Was she right? Had we messed everything up?

No, I had to believe that this was a detour, a bump in the road. We would find our way back to the path and be stronger when we got there.

"I've been doing a lot of thinking," she started. "And I think—I–I just—I want to—" A slow breath. "I *need* to go back to how we were before." She swallowed heavily, fidgeting with the rolled hem of her shirt. I'd tried to convince myself that she wouldn't say it. That she'd think everything through and realize we couldn't go back, because what we had now meant too much. And yet, here we were. I tried not to be hurt, disappointed, thoroughly fucking gutted, and failed miserably. My insides might as well have been strung up with the rest of the Christmas finery along the bar.

"You want to—you want to be friends?" I could barely get the words out, they tasted like ash on my tongue. She nodded, but her eyes still wavered with uncertainty. Was there still a chance? Even a tiny one? I had to hope.

"I need us to be friends." *Need.* She needed us to be friends. God, she sounded so desperate, it was like a jagged knife to my chest. "I'm sorry. I shouldn't have—"

"I can't do it, Chase," I said, seeing no point in dancing around the issue.

She gaped. "What? Wh—why not?"

"Because I don't want to just be your friend, I can't, not anymore. I can't go backwards."

"It's not backwards. Friends first. You *promised me.*" Tears were already collecting at the corners of her eyes. Fuck, I didn't know how I was going to do this if I had to see her cry.

"I lied." It was the first and only time I'd ever intentionally lied to her, and it hurt like hell. Worse now, seeing the betrayal etched across her face. But I didn't think it would matter. I didn't think we'd need to go back. I'd been an idiot.

A single tear tracked down her cheek as her eyes went hard. "You had no intention of us going back to friends."

"No," I admitted, not willing to lie to her again.

"You just said it, so I'd agree to go on the date with you." Not a question, but I answered all the same.

"Yes."

She shook her head, the hurt making her eyes darker. "You said we would always be friends first, Mack."

I came around the bar. "And I meant that."

"Bullshit! That's bullshit." She backed up as I advanced towards her. "You tricked me, you lied to me, to get what you wanted."

"Because I thought it was what you wanted, too!"

"You assumed, you didn't know that! You should have told me the truth."

"And then you wouldn't have agreed to the date! And we wouldn't have—" I stopped short. "I am sorry I lied to you, but I'm not sorry about everything that came after it." How could I be sorry for that?

Her laugh was harsh. "That's not an apology. You took away my *choice*, Mack. But you're right, if I'd known I'd lose our friendship I wouldn't have agreed."

I sucked in a breath. "So, that's it?"

"You've said you won't go back."

"And you're not willing to move forward."

"Move forward to what? More fighting. More lies. I don't want that. I want our friendship." The tears were flowing freely now, sliding down her cheeks in glittering tracks.

"We can have that, and more."

"I don't want more, I don't need more. How do I even know anything you're saying is true?"

"I will never lie to you again."

"Unless you want something." She swiped at tears.

"Chase. I—" It wasn't the right time but I needed her to know. "I love you, I'm in love with you. Please don't do this."

She stared at me, mouth hanging open. "No, you can't, you —I can't do this."

"Can't do what, exactly?"

"This. Us" She waved a hand at my chest. "I can't."

"I tell you that I'm in love with you and you're telling me you can't do this? *I love you.*"

"That makes it worse, don't you get it!?"

"I think you feel the same."

"Don't tell me how I feel, Mack."

"So you don't love me?" I knew she did, could feel it when

she looked at me, when she touched me, but she needed to admit it to herself.

She shook her head. "Of course I do, but not like that."

"Bullshit."

A long moment passed as we watched one another, wondering if the other would soften and admit they were wrong. It didn't happen.

What the fuck was I supposed to do now? This couldn't be it, I couldn't let this be it. I told her I loved her, what the fuck else could I do? Before my brain could conjure something, anything, to say to try and salvage the situation, she left. Turned on her heel and, with a flick of black hair, she was gone.

MERRY FUCKING CHRISTMAS.

This was not how it was supposed to go. And, yet, here I was anyway. I plastered on a smile as I collected the mountain of gifts from the trunk of my car and turned towards my sister's house. Two days. It had only been two days. Despite seeing Chase, nothing had been said. Not a word. That wasn't strictly true. Plenty of words had been said, just none that made any difference. I was doing my best to wait her out but, as far as I could tell, she was pretending like nothing ever happened between us. It was driving me fucking crazy.

"Uncle Mack!" Savanna squealed as she met me at the door. Her tiny arms wrapped around my hips and squeezed. "Santa's coming tonight!" The words were muffled against my ugly Christmas sweater.

"Only if you've been good, though, right?"

"I have been good!" she assured me. "I'm *always* good." I smiled properly, knowing *always good* was probably a stretch. "Where's Aunty Cheese?"

I knew the question was coming, but it made my stomach lurch all the same. "She had to work, Sav, but she sent me with a gift just for you."

"Really!?" She jumped, trying to get her hands on the tower of boxes I was balancing. I held them higher and she pouted.

"Later," I promised her, leading the way into the large living room.

"No Chase?" Pip asked as I put all of the gifts by the tree. There wasn't any room under it.

"Aunty Cheese had to work," Savanna answered for me, planting herself in front of the tree, fingers creeping towards the gifts collected beneath it.

Pip gave me a quizzical look but I shrugged it off. I knew I'd tell her everything at some point tonight, seeing as Chase's embargo on people knowing about us wasn't relevant now we were over, but I didn't want to open with it.

Over. We were over. I told her I loved her and she still walked away.

I'd been trying to convince myself otherwise, because I needed to believe we would eventually figure everything out. But, in the meantime, I was going to be a sad sack of shit and wallow—as much as I could with a hyped up four year around, anyway. I would have liked to do my wallowing with a side of whiskey, however, that would have to wait until I was on the west coast. By some stroke of luck, I'd managed to move my flight to LA up to tonight. The fact I was going without Chase still fucking sucked, though.

An hour later, I was slouched in one of Pip's overstuffed armchairs nursing a virgin eggnog—it just wasn't the same without the rum.

My sister sat on the couch beside me with a fish-bowl sized

glass of red wine. "Come on, time to start talking," she said, nudging my knee with her foot.

There was no point putting her off. "Chase and I were dating."

"Were."

"Yep. *Were.* She put an end to it a couple of days ago." And she had yet to come to her senses and see that we were fucking perfect for each other.

Pip pursed her lips. "I'm going to need more information, Mack."

I dropped my head back against the cushion and stared at the ceiling as I spilled my guts. I didn't tell her *everything*-everything, she was still my sister after all and didn't need to know how much outstanding sex we'd been having, or how often I replayed Chase straddling my face (it was a lot).

"She's freaking out."

"Yes, I figured that much out myself, thank you."

Pip tucked her legs underneath her. "What are you going to do?"

Wasn't that just the million dollar question? One I was no closer to answering. "I don't know. But honestly, I'm not sure there's a lot I can do at the moment. I need to let her work it out."

"And if she doesn't?"

I rolled my head to face her. "Your faith is astounding."

"I am merely entertaining the possibility."

"I'd rather you didn't."

"We both know the kind of relationship role models she's had. Her dad left before she was even born, Mack." I knew this. Of course I knew this. But I thought that she'd be able to move past it. I thought I could help her move past it.

"It's not like our parents' relationship was any better."

"No," she conceded. "But at least they were around, mostly."

"Might have been better if they weren't."

Her answering smile was sad, and she was silent for a few long moments.

"Tim and I are getting divorced."

I gaped at her. Of all the things I thought she was going to say, I definitely had not been expecting that.

"Fuck, Pip, I'm sorry. Are you okay? When did this happen?"

"I'm okay, for the most part. We've been having problems for a while. We gave counseling a try but it just seemed to solidify the decision to separate. We made the official decision earlier this week, but won't tell the kids until after Christmas. I'll be relieved when it's all out in the open. It's been difficult keeping it all a secret."

"I'll bet."

"I feel like maybe it has something to do with Chase ending things between you two."

"How could it have anything to do with—wait, she knew?"

Pip nodded. "I told her we'd been having problems after Sav's birthday. I didn't mean to, it just came out. Then I turned up on her doorstep on Tuesday night like a sobbing mess because I didn't know where to go. I shouldn't have asked her to keep it to herself, but I wasn't ready for everyone to know yet, I was scared, I suppose. Still am."

Tuesday night. Pip was at Chase's on Tuesday night. That was the thing that came up. Pip, whose relationship had just ended. I wasn't about to put this all on Pip, but it definitely explained her sudden need to go slow. Not that this knowledge was going to help me change her mind, though.

"You asked her—"

"Not to tell anyone." Which was why she never explained

what 'came up'. "I'm sorry, Mack, I was still coming to terms with everything, and I wanted to tell you myself." She paused and took a large gulp of her wine. "Honestly, I half expected her to tell you."

"She didn't. She wouldn't do that," I said, trying to keep up with the crush of thoughts rolling through my head. I wanted to go to her and tell her I understood, I understood why she was so scared, I understood why she thought we wouldn't work. But also that she was *wrong*. I couldn't, though. Because I didn't want to have to convince her. I wanted her to figure it out herself.

"For what it's worth..." Pip covered my hand with hers and gave it a squeeze. "I do think she'll come around."

"Thanks."

"What's her alternative? She never speaks to you again? We both know she's not capable of that. And, even though she said she wanted to be friends, I don't know if that's what she really wants, either. I think she knew where she stood with you, and then you tipped it on its head. She needs time to adjust."

I nodded and sipped my substandard eggnog. I really fucking hoped she was right.

35

CHASE

I HAD NEVER in my life been so angry with one Milton Alfred Carmichael Kent.

Part of me was quite sure I was being unreasonable, but I didn't care. He told me he loved me, was *in love* with me. He said that he wouldn't leave. Swore that it didn't matter what I did, he'd be there. And then he fucking left! Flew across the country to get away from me.

I knew this, not because he told me but because when Micky turned up on Boxing Day she made an offhand comment about how she wished she could be sunning herself in LA, too, rather than trudging through the snow. I nearly took her head off. He went to LA without a word. Without *me*.

It had been days. Almost a fucking week. And I hadn't heard from him. Not one word. It was slowly killing me. But it was my own fault. I'd let my heart get all squishy even knowing it was going to hurt like hell (and it did). I'd let myself hope that we could be *more*.

What did hoping for more get you? A lot fucking less, as far as I could tell. Because not only had I lost his kisses and his

340

hands and his outstanding dedication to making me come, I'd lost the rest of him, too. The quiet comfort. The unwavering confidence. The goofy smiles. I'd lost my best friend. And I didn't know what to do about it.

No amount of apologizing was going to get him to change his mind, I already knew that, which meant I was having to come to terms with a life where Mack was *only* my business partner. Even that was optimistic. He didn't need his half of the bar, he might choose to sell and cut ties with me altogether. He might move to LA with Nash and the two of them could live out their days surfing and cooking.

My lip wobbled as I blinked at the ceiling. He was getting Nash in the divorce, I could already feel it. They'd been friends before I wandered into the girls bathroom. They had more history, more in common with their rich, snobby, shitty parents.

I pulled myself up before I went too far down the spiral. One loss at a time was all I could deal with at the moment. Besides, I might still be able to work on Nash.

IF ANYONE NOTICED that I was slowly caving in on myself, they didn't say so. Even Christmas as part of the Linden-Davis blended household wasn't as bad as I'd been expecting. I kept my shit together through the entire event. No one brought up my appalling Thanksgiving behavior. Prescott was thrilled with his whiskey and Lachlan got me a cocktail recipe book 'for fresh inspiration'. I thanked him with my wide, dead smile as I sipped my wine.

Then I got home and cried my face off while eating Mack's ice cream on the kitchen floor like a tragic cliche of a woman.

I'd done that most nights since I learned he went to LA. The fact he still wasn't back was lending more weight to my theory that he was going to abandon me and our bar for greener pastures where he could surf in the sun all year round. He'd probably love it there. I couldn't even begrudge him that, because surfing in New York in December had been awful. Until I got to warm up in the shower, that had made it all worthwhile, but I was not thinking about that right now. Or maybe ever again. Because it hurt. It hurt way too much.

Despite the hollow, gaping feeling in my chest, I still believed—hoped, fucking *prayed*—that I had made the right decision in ending things between us. But there was no point letting my mind race around the same thoughts and regrets. Nothing was going to change until I saw him again, assuming he spoke to me before he moved to Malibu permanently and married surfer Barbie (in my head her name was Brittany and she was stunning).

My buzzer went off and I stared accusingly at my front door. The only person I wanted to see right now would not be buzzing. But he wasn't here, he was in LA meeting Brittany the surfer Barbie.

Another buzz, this one in my mother's tell tale pattern. Buzz-buzz-buzzzzzz-buzz-buzzzzzz-buzz. I heaved myself off the couch and shuffled to the door, pressing the button without saying anything as I flicked the lock. I wasn't in the mood to talk, not right now, not when I had to work tonight and be all smiles and cheery fake conversation. I'd never disliked working at Rudi, it had always been fun even when I wasn't in the best mood, but it just wasn't the same without Mack there with me.

Mom let herself in, two brown grocery bags cradled against her chest. "Hey, baby." She didn't sound like herself, but I was too deep in my hole of self pity to do much about it.

"Hey, Mom," I said from my place on the couch, slumping deeper into the cushions as I scrolled the Netflix menu.

She ran her motherly eye over me, looking entirely

unsurprised at my current state. "I knew there was something wrong at Christmas."

Still not in the mood to talk, my only course of action was to deny. "I don't know what you're talking about. I'm fine." The fact I could see a ketchup stain on the front of my hoodie (Mack's hoodie), and I was surrounded by a sea of used tissues and takeout containers weakened the statement considerably.

"You're not fine, you're droopy."

"Droopy?" I almost laughed at that, almost.

"Yes, droopy." She wasn't wrong, droopy was a pretty apt descriptor of my general vibe right now.

"Thanks."

"Chase, look at me."

I shook my head, staring resolutely, albeit unseeing, at the television.

"Chase." The softness of her voice threatened to break me and I wasn't strong enough to fight it. I just wanted her to tell me it was all going to be okay, even if it was a lie. My eyes darted up to her face.

"Sweetheart, what's wrong?"

I shook my head again, blinking against the tears but it was no good, one leaked out, then another.

"Come on." She shifted the bags onto one arm, pulled me off the couch and towed me into the kitchen. I perched on a stool and watched as she unloaded the makings of grilled cheese and hot cocoa onto my small kitchen counter, both of which were now so tied up with memories of Mack I just cried harder.

It shouldn't hurt this much, should it? Not when I'd done the right thing. It was supposed to feel less scary now. It didn't. Instead, I was sure my world was caving in around me.

"Talk to me."

I shrugged, any words I might have said lodging themselves

in my throat. "There's not much to say." *I miss him. I want him. I think I made a mistake.*

"Don't bullshit me, baby girl, there's always something to say when someone looks as heartbroken as you do right now. It was obvious you weren't ready to talk about it at Christmas, but I figured you'd call when you were ready. You took too long."

A puff of laughter escaped. "I was an idiot."

"Doesn't sound like you. Start talking." She asked as she warmed milk in one of my two pots.

I let my head drop onto the counter. This was going to be easier if I didn't have to actually look at her. "Mack and I were kind of seeing each other, dating, whatever." It was so much more than that, but I didn't know how to put it into words.

"Past tense?"

"Past tense," I confirmed, rolling my forehead back and forth on the speckled granite, it was surprisingly comforting.

"So, what happened?"

"I ended it."

"That does sound pretty idiotic," she said with a snort I did not appreciate.

I straightened. "Ending it wasn't the idiotic part, Mom, starting it was."

"Why?"

I accepted the mug she handed me, ignoring the pang in my chest. "Because it just made things complicated. I told him it was a bad idea. That it was destined to end, that it was a one way ticket to hurt feelings, but he talked me into it anyway. He promised me we'd be okay, and surprise, surprise, we're not." I took an angry sip and swore as I burned my tongue.

"Okay... and why did you think it was destined to end?" Was she kidding?

"Because that's what happens. It's the nature of the beast. All relationships have expiry dates."

"Not all relationships."

"Yes, Mom, *all* relationships," I fired back. "I spent my entire childhood watching it happen, sometimes messy and loud, sometimes quiet, but they always ended and then we'd pick up and move somewhere new. I don't know why Mack thought we'd be any different. We're not."

"Oh, baby, of course you're different."

"No, we're not, we're over."

"I seriously doubt it. That boy has looked at you like you hung the moon since you were fifteen." She sipped her hot cocoa, looking vaguely smug, but she was wrong. Even if she wasn't, that look was gone now, and I wasn't getting it back.

"When we were friends, maybe, but that's gone up in smoke, too, because we crossed a line we shouldn't."

"Most lines are more like guides really, they're meant to be crossed."

"Mother."

"Chase." She paused, her eyes drifting off to the side. "Do you know why all of my relationships ended?"

My brow pinched. This was not the direction I'd expected our conversation to go, and I wasn't sure I wanted to hear all the reasons that things didn't work out the way you wanted them too. Even still, I said, "Enlighten me."

I felt her hesitation before she eventually spoke. "Because none of those men were your father."

I opened my mouth. Closed it again. "My father? Why on earth would you want them to be him? The man left as soon as you were pregnant. Why—" The look on her face pulled me up, regret, worry, and something else I couldn't place. "What?"

"He didn't leave," she said, the words shaky.

"He—what—what do you mean he didn't leave?"

"He didn't leave us, leave you." A pause. "He never knew you existed."

I didn't understand. All my life, she'd told me the same thing. That he didn't want her, want me, want us. That he left. And it paved the way for every other man to do the same thing. Even Mack. I was in free fall, plummeting through nothingness. "He—what?" I said, trying to wrap my head around this. "You told me—"

"I told you what I had to. It was easier."

"*Easier?*" I gaped. "Easier for who?"

"Me, Chase. It was easier for me. Easier to tell you that your father left us, because the truth, the truth was—the truth *is* —that your father might have been the love of my life and I walked away. *I* left."

"Y—you left? *You* left *him*? When you were pregnant, you left him? What did he do? Wh–why, what made you leave?" This made no sense.

"I didn't know I was pregnant." She blew out a breath. "Your father was amazing, Chase, I think I fell in love with him the second I saw him."

I had no words. I was vaguely aware that I should probably be mad at her for hiding all of this from me but I was too confused and curious for the truth right now. The anger would come later. "Then why? Why leave? Why never tell him? Why never tell *me*?" Did I not deserve to know the truth? I'd hated this man, this faceless, nameless man my entire life. Tarred him with a reputation he didn't deserve.

"I didn't tell you because I was ashamed. I took away your chance to know your father because I was young and scared. How did I tell you that?" She shook her head, eyes fixed on the mug in her hands. "My father, your grandfather took me to Korea, to Seoul, to see the Olympics. Your father was an athlete and we met, by accident, but not. I think I was supposed to meet him because he gave me you. We spent a week exploring Seoul together, then it was time we both went home. Him to

Japan, me here. I don't think I've ever cried so much as I did on that flight. A couple of weeks after I got home I realized I was pregnant. Your grandfather wasn't thrilled at the news and sent me off to live with Peggy."

Holy. Shit.

"Hold on. Just—I need to get my head around this." I slid off the stool and started pacing. "You only knew him for a week?"

"One single, perfect, week."

"And then you got on a plane? No phone numbers, no email address—was email even a thing yet? Probably not. But you got on a plane with no way to contact a man you had already fallen in love with!? You never told him about me? You couldn't tell him about me. You never—"

"Chase, when your grandfather discovered I was pregnant he was very vocal about his disappointment, about how ashamed he was. I knew I wanted to keep the baby, keep you, but lived with that shame for a long time. I let it keep me small and scared. The thought that I would go there and tell him and he wouldn't want me anymore, wouldn't want us, it was too much. My heart couldn't take it."

"You never tried to contact him again?"

"I tried. So many times. I kept track of him over the years, whenever another relationship ended I'd consider going—but it was too hard, you were small, I couldn't take you to Japan. A country where we didn't even know the language, let alone any people, on the chance he might want us."

I didn't know what to say to any of this. Not only did my father not leave before I'd even been born, he didn't even know he had a daughter. He didn't know I existed.

All my life, I'd believed that men would leave, because the one man who was supposed to stay hadn't. But none of it was true. And I could see now what Mom had been doing all those years. I thought she'd been running away from the hurt, but she'd been chasing the feeling she had with my father. But none of them were good enough, because they weren't him.

My heart started to beat uncomfortably fast. I'd been doing the same thing. Every relationship failed, not because they all did, but because they weren't right. No man was going to be good enough because they weren't Mack. Because they didn't make me feel the way he did, even when we were just friends. It had always been him. Only him. I'd been so convinced that I was right, that nothing would ever work. I was too stubborn and scared to see what was right in front of me.

Fuck.

Fuck. Fuck. Fuck.

"Mom, I've really messed things up."

She smiled. "He'll forgive you."

"How do you know?"

"Because he loves you, baby."

He loved me. He told me he did, and I'd thrown it back in his face. I needed to fix this. I needed to tell him. But how? I could fly to LA? But what if he was on the way back here? The thought that I'd missed my chance made my stomach threaten to send the hot cocoa back up. I could camp at his apartment until he got home. Plead my case. Tell him I was an idiot and I was wrong and I fucking loved him.

No, not like that. I didn't just want to tell him, I wanted to tell everyone. He didn't deserve to be treated like a dirty secret, which, whether I wanted to admit it or not, was exactly how I'd been behaving. Like I was ashamed.

"Looks like my work here is done," Mom said.

I rounded the island and pulled her into a hug. "I love you, Mom."

"I love you, too, Chase."

"And I know you're married to Derrick and all, but maybe you should take a chance and get on a plane to Japan."

She laughed, the sound made my chest warm. "You think so?"

"You're fifty years young, don't you think it's time you stopped settling?"

"And if he doesn't want me?"

"Then he's an idiot, and you can move on. But you're not going to know unless you put yourself out there." I squeezed her shoulders. "You deserve to be happy, Mom, properly, madly, happy."

"So do you."

"I know." I grinned. And I knew just how to get that happiness.

I walked Mom out and leaned back against the door. Step one. Find out when he was coming home, because he had to be coming home. New step one: whiskey. I gulped down two shots, relishing the warm tingle that spread outwards from my stomach once they'd landed. Step two. Text Mack. Where was my phone? I took another shot of whiskey and tore around my apartment in a mad search, nearly losing an eye on the corner of the coffee table after tripping over my bowling shoes. Seeing the shoes made a sob roll up my throat because I just missed him so fucking much and I didn't know what the hell I'd been thinking, trying to just be his friend when I'd gone and fallen in love with him.

He'd been right, of course, I was scared out of my head. Scared that he'd leave. Scared that he wouldn't. Scared that I genuinely didn't know how to be in a relationship without one foot out the door. Just fucking scared. But if there was one person I trusted with all my fears, and everything else, it was Mack.

I found my phone stuffed between couch cushions and

proceeded to write and delete five versions of the same text before settling on something almost rudely simple.

Me: *Are you home for New Year's Eve?*

After staring a hole through my phone for a solid three minutes, I tossed it aside and started getting ready to head into Rudi Blue. It was ridiculously early to be going in but I was going to need the distraction.

The reply didn't come for an hour and I nearly screamed with joy as I read it.

Mack: *Yes.*

It was a good thing he didn't ask why, because my lying skills sucked both in person and via text. But, now that I knew he would be back, it was time to put some plans in motion.

36

MACK

I WAS BEGINNING to see the appeal of Southern California.

It was a pleasantly mild sixty-five and sunny. I was walking back from my second surf of the day. And it was just fucking *nice*. There wasn't any trash. People were smiling. No one tried to run me down when I crossed the street. I knew this was not true of all of LA but, in Nash's pocket of Huntington Beach, it was nice. A much needed change of pace and scenery. I could see myself getting used to it real easy.

There was just one thing missing. A sometimes grumpy, sharp-tongued brunette with a penchant for black jeans and an unhealthy dependence on curly fries. She should have been here with me, seeing Nash and eating burritos and maybe even surfing, I think I could have tempted her into the water at least once. Fuck, I missed her.

I'd made the mistake of telling Nash that the two of us would be coming—I could only manage to keep a secret from one of them at a time. We were supposed to arrive at the reasonable time of four p.m. on the twenty-sixth. Instead, I turned up on his doorstep at three on Christmas morning. I let myself in with the key he left out and collapsed in his guest bedroom feeling really fucking sorry for myself.

Nash was in the kitchen when I surfaced somewhere around ten. "You look like shit," he said, sliding over a coffee.

"Merry Christmas to you, too."

"So, where is she?"

There was no point pretending I didn't know who he was talking about, but I slid onto a stool and swallowed a scorching sip of coffee before replying. "At home."

"What happened?"

I shrugged, casting an eye around the space. It wasn't huge but more than enough for one person. It was somehow both bright and cozy all at once. And a lot more *him* than the sparse, industrial chic place he and Nadia shared.

My attention landed on Nash, who looked a hell of a lot better than he had the last time I'd seen him. Slightly thinner but not dead behind the eyes like he had been.

When it became clear I wasn't going to answer his question, because I didn't know what the fuck to say, he abandoned whatever food he was preparing and came to stand in front of me, arms crossed over his chest.

"What did you do?"

"Why do you assume I did anything?" I tried to sound offended at the assumption, it was difficult when he was right.

He arched an eyebrow. "Things obviously went past your kiss." Not a question.

"A long way past it." I confirmed. And it was so fucking good. We were so fucking good. Good enough that I'd managed to convince myself she wouldn't run like she always did. That she'd want to stay. I still wanted to believe that we'd work it out, but my confidence was waning.

"So, then I'll ask again, what did you do?"

"I'm still offended that you think this is my fault."

With an eye roll he turned back to the large skillet and flicked in a knob of butter that immediately sizzled and my stomach growled. "There is no fucking way Chase pursued something between the two of you," he said, dredging some bread through what I assumed was a mix for french toast.

"And if you're wrong?"

"Then I'm wrong."

"You're not wrong," I said to my coffee. "I convinced her to go on a date."

He glanced back over his shoulder. "Just the one?"

"To begin with."

"How did you get her to agree to that?" He flipped the slice in the skillet while dredging a second.

"It wasn't that difficult actually." I gave him the condensed version of events. Had I been an idiot to think that she'd be different with me? I guess I'd always thought that she'd never been in a long term relationship because the guys weren't right for her, didn't deserve her. I didn't know if I deserved her, either, but I'd spend the rest of my fucking life trying to.

"You're in love with her?"

Had been half my life, if I was being honest. "Yup," I said with a nod. "And I'm pretty sure she is, too, but she's too stubborn, or scared, to admit it."

He nodded, moving smoothly around the kitchen. French toast here. Bacon there. Soon enough there were two loaded plates on the counter along with fresh coffee.

"Gotta be honest, I'm surprised she agreed to the date in the first place." He poured a healthy swig of maple syrup over his plate before taking a bite.

"I may have misled her."

His eyebrows told me to continue as he chewed.

"One of her stipulations to the date was that we could go

back to being friends. I said yes, knowing she wouldn't agree to it otherwise. And then when she wanted to go back to being friends—even though we'd been so good together—I couldn't fucking do it. How the hell do I go back to 'just friends' after everything we did?"

He held up a hand to stop me. "She's like my sister, please do not elaborate on that."

I shook my head. "Not elaborating."

We ate in silence for a few minutes. "I love you both, so I'm not going to take sides. Although, if I was, I might take hers because lying was kind of a dick move. However, I want you both to be happy, and I know you'd be good together. You love her, Mack, you need to fight for her."

"Like you fought for Jemma?"

For a second I wondered if he was going to punch me. "Low blow. But just because you don't see the fight doesn't mean it's not happening." He pinned me with a hard look. "You need to decide whether you bury your feelings and go back to friends, or you get her back for everything. They're your only two choices."

"I can't just be friends."

He nodded. "Then you go for broke."

We didn't speak about it again.

I PROPPED my borrowed board against the back of the house, peeled down my wetsuit and snatched one of the towels from the laundry to dry off. And, as I had been doing at various points, I wondered what Chase was doing. Was she at home? At Rudi? Did she miss me like I missed her?

There had been a lot of thinking over the last few days, and I was still no closer to knowing what to do. Half of me thought I should fight for Chase until the end of fucking time. She deserved to know I wouldn't give up on her, on us. But what if I was wrong, and she really didn't want that? Would I just be driving her further away?

I wanted to be happy with her friendship. If she never changed her mind I'd just have to learn to stop thinking about the way she felt curled up beside me, or the soft press of her lips. That sounded fucking impossible right at the moment, but I'd try, if it meant keeping her. I wasn't sure I believed in soul mates or anything like that, but I knew that she was my person. And I'd do whatever was necessary to keep her in my life.

"I've been thinking some more about your pies," Nash said as I stepped inside.

"Oh yeah?" Pies had been taking up quite a lot of conversation. I set up an Instagram account before coming to LA, which, despite only having a single post—of one of Chase's sweet potato pies from Thanksgiving—already had over five thousand followers. I had Harley to thank. Apparently, her ruse to pass off my pie as her own hadn't quite worked out and she'd tagged me in a reel of her eating said pie. I didn't know how viral was classed, but a lot of people saw it.

"I don't think you need to rely on the food truck."

"I'm listening." I'd been trying to understand how my day-to-day could look as *The Pie Guy*, but my mind was stuck on the idea of the food truck.

"The truck is perfect for markets and shit like that, but I don't think it needs to be your only sales avenue. You could wholesale them around Brooklyn. Cafes. Coffee shops. You could also sell them to order from wherever, Rudi would make the most sense, seeing as you have a fully functioning kitchen that you're not currently utilizing."

"How far in advance would people order?"

He scratched his cheek. "However far in advance you wanted them to. I'd give them a menu for each day. Tuesday is chocolate-espresso. Wednesday is salted honey. And so on. Then, you'd have a cut off for orders, say two or three days before. You could bake them the day before, give them time to set and develop flavors. Then people collect by whatever time you want."

"You've given this some thought."

"It's a great idea, and you're fucking talented. If you want to do this, you know that I will support you in whatever way I can. Right now, that's ideas."

"Thanks."

"You're welcome," he said with a tip of his head.

I chewed over the ideas as I showered and dressed, nervous anticipation bubbling. This could actually happen. It would be a shit load of work, but it was work I wanted to do, work I was excited to do. I picked up my phone to make some notes and noticed a text from Chase. My heart leapt into my throat.

Chase: *Are you home for New Year's Eve?*

The fact she didn't know, because I hadn't told her I was leaving, made my gut twist. I regretted the decision, especially after telling her that it didn't matter what she did, how hard she pushed, I wouldn't leave. Then I left. Not my brightest move. It was temporary, though. And it was necessary to give us both some space—me to feel sorry for myself and her to hopefully think things over and realize I was the love of her life.

I stared at the text. Seven words. No *hi,* or *hey,* or *how are you.* It was not the most encouraging first contact.

Me: *Yes.*

I hit send before I could think too much about it. She asked a question. I answered it. Did I ask her why she wanted to know? I was definitely curious and the temptation to do so was strong, but I resisted because it was probably just about staffing. We always worked New Year together, only right now everything was up in the air and there was no way for her to know I would be back without asking. I glanced at my bag, packed and ready to go. Nash was driving me to LAX in an hour or so. How I was going to see her and not immediately bury my face in her hair I didn't know. I'd need to develop some serious self restraint between now and tomorrow afternoon.

THE PLANE TOUCHED down in New York and, despite how good it had been to hang with Nash these last few days, my body still sighed with relief at being home. And so close to her.

I shouldn't go to Rudi Blue tonight. I should go home and do laundry and buy groceries. Give myself the pep-talk I needed to see her tomorrow and not fucking cry with relief, or maybe dread.

My apartment was cold and empty and I could still just make out Chase's scent mingled with mine. How the hell was it still here? I'd even stripped the sheets, after allowing myself to sleep with the pillow that smelled like her for one night. But it was still here. I wanted to think it was because she'd been sneaking in while I was gone, but I doubted it.

I went to the bedroom and fell onto the sheets that didn't smell like her. I had no interest in laundry or groceries. Even still, I forced myself to empty the contents of my duffle bag into the washer and turn it on.

Don't do it. My brain said. *Do not go and see her.*

I considered the merits of staying home, and away from Chase, until tomorrow and then promptly left my apartment and headed straight to Rudi.

The line was shorter than we'd seen it recently. The buzz from the wedding was finally dying down, or the lightly falling snow meant people wanted to be inside and not standing on a sidewalk. Either way, I was grateful it might be quiet enough for me to actually get a minute to speak to her.

A tribe of large moths (angrier and uglier than butterflies), were having some kind of civil war between my stomach and sternum as I approached the door. I greeted Brent, one of our newer security guards, and slipped inside. The Christmas vibe had been toned down since I was here last, in favor of one that was more winter wonderland meets disco. I dug it.

My eyes immediately found Chase behind the bar. Her hair was in a large knot on the top of her head, a yellow scarf tied in a bow around it. She smiled as she poured three cocktails and my heart kicked hard against my ribs. Fuck she was so beautiful. She looked happy, normal. Had she missed me at all? Did I even want to know?

I wiped my hands down my jeans and moved through the sea of bodies, doing my best not to stare straight at her, but keeping her in my peripheral vision. She moved through customers, checked on other staff members. She'd always been so good at this, even when she wanted to strangle every drunk idiot who leered at her. She was so good at it.

She moved towards the end of the bar as I approached. I didn't know if she'd seen me, if she'd be happy I was here, but I just needed her to see me. I needed to feel her eyes on me.

"Mack!" she said with a smile and wide eyes as I stepped in front of her before she could dart down the hall to the bathrooms and our office. "You're back."

I stopped breathing as she wrapped her arms around my middle and squeezed. She'd missed me, too, I could feel it, but was it like I had missed her? Like an essential part wasn't there? I let my arms go around her, enjoying the moment for as long it lasted. Her hair tickled my cheek and I sniffed it as subtly as possible.

Chase's arms released me and she put a step's worth of space between us. "It's great to see you. How was Nash?"

"A lot better. Still not ready to come home, but he'll get there." *I love you. I want you.* I need *you.*

She nodded, still smiling, eyes roaming over my face like she was trying to memorize it. "It really is good to see you," she said and nibbled her lip. "But you don't need to be here tonight, if you don't want to, we've got it under control. I gotta pee."

"Sure, yeah." I stepped aside and she darted down the hall. She'd made up her mind. Friends. She didn't need to say it again for me to know it. This was it. This was how it was going to be now. It needed to be enough. One day I hoped it would be, when I'd forgotten how she felt beneath me, when I'd forgotten the taste of her tongue, when I'd forgotten the way it felt to have her look at me like I was the only one she wanted. When I'd forgotten all of it, then I hoped that this would be enough.

Friends. Just friends.

37

CHASE

I ALMOST BLEW IT.

I saw Mack as soon as he walked in and I nearly swallowed my own tongue because he looked so fucking good. I'd tried to escape but he caught me and all I could think about was kissing him for the rest of my life, or at least the day, and telling him I loved him and I wanted him forever and ever, until we were old and wrinkly and I yelled at kids for having the music too loud in their ear pods—I couldn't wait to be old and crotchety. I almost did all that because, apparently, I had very little chill around him.

With a strength of will I didn't realize I possessed, I resisted the urge to kiss him and profess my love because I had a plan and I was sticking to it.

So, instead I forced myself to work and got through the night with minimal staring and absolutely no kissing.

A HALF NAKED Hunter Buchanan opened the door to Harley's apartment the following morning.

360

I stood mute and staring for what felt like ten minutes. I knew Hunter reasonably well, we'd been work related acquaintances for a few years, but I did not know him well enough for me to be seeing him without a shirt on. He had a gorgeous face, all twinkly eyes and devil-may-care smiles dented with dimples, but it was impossible to know what was going on anywhere else because he was almost always in loose fitting shirts.

Turned out he was hiding hotness under there. He was all long, lean muscles wrapped in warm olive skin and so many tattoos. He was a literal work of art from his collarbones to the top of his low hanging black sweatpants. Fucking hell. It was going to be hard to look at him with a straight face when I saw him next, knowing all of that was under his shirt.

"Hunter? Hi—ah—sorry, did I—do I have the wrong place?" I checked the number on the door. It was definitely Harley's apartment. Had I interrupted something? My cheeks suddenly felt very warm.

"All good, Chase, come on in."

"That's okay, I don't want to, um, interrupt anything," I said from my place outside the door. He'd moved a few steps inside, clearly in no rush to put a shirt on. I really needed him to put a shirt on. I tugged at the neck of my sweater.

"Chase!" Harley appeared next to him in pajamas. I was totally interrupting. I looked between the two of them.

"Sorry, have I—I didn't know you two knew each other. I'll just come back later so you can finish, whatever it is you're doing."

Harley laughed so hard she snorted. "You're not interrupting anything. Hunter is a friend, of forever-ish."

"So you're ... ?"

"Roommates," they said in unison, and I let out an awkward laugh.

"Right, sure, sorry. I just wasn't expecting—"

Harley looked at Hunter properly and immediately rolled her eyes. "Oh, God, will you put a shirt on. Your chest is distracting."

"In a good way?" He puffed himself up as he said it. She wasn't wrong, it really was distracting.

"In a *did they spell regret with two ts* kind of way." She poked out her tongue and he laughed. "Now, if you will excuse us, we have things to do." She grabbed my wrist, tugged me to her room and kicked the door closed. "Sorry about him. Okay, what are we thinking? Something that's going to make a statement, right? Sit."

I dropped onto the unmade bed as Harley pulled open her closet with a flourish. I had never seen so many things shoved into such a small space. Part of me had thought she'd been joking about the number of costumes she had. She wasn't.

When I went to Harley yesterday with the beginnings of my plan, the first step had been the hardest. But I told her that I was in love with Mack and that I'd probably fucked it all up but I needed to try and make it right. It took less than a second for her to tell me I would need the perfect outfit, which was why I was here.

She rubbed her hands together. "I have so many ideas ... are you opposed to sequins or animal print?"

Opposed was a strong word and yet for sequins, in particular, it did feel like the right one. But for today—"No."

"The correct answer. Time to get naked, sister. Strip."

For the next hour I was treated like a life-sized doll as Harley made me try on pretty much every item in her closet. Some of them weren't even clothes, as far as I could tell. One had been mostly pieces of string, she was disappointed when I called veto.

"I think the choice is clear," she said eventually, standing with hands on her hips in front of the three finalists laid out on her bed. I was still in my underwear, just in case she was struck by more inspiration. Although, I wasn't sure there was anything left I hadn't put on.

I stepped up beside her and surveyed our options. It was a lot of sequins. One was literally a gold sequined jumpsuit, which, despite her assurances I could pull it off, I was still very unsure of.

"The dress," I said because, of the three, it was the least bananas. The fact that a neon-pink, sequin mini-dress was the *least* out there was really saying something.

"Chase," Harley said my name like she was deeply disappointed in me. "Now is not the time to play it small, you're trying to make a *statement*. My vote is for the hot pants." Of course her vote was for the hot pants. The rainbow sequined hot pants that looked like they were pointing at my vagina. They covered less skin than my current underwear. Was that the statement I was trying to make?

"The jumpsuit," I said. Unlike both the mini-dress and the hot pants, it showed zero skin—but was so damn tight it didn't need to. I was terrified to wear it.

Harley grinned and I got the distinct feeling I'd just been played. "Jumpsuit it is."

"Can I get dressed now?"

I'D BEEN PLAYING it cool all afternoon but I couldn't take it any longer. Mack was at the other end of the bar, smiling and gorgeous, and I needed to stake my claim before someone else got him.

It was time.

During our planning session/costume carousel yesterday, Harley suggested it would be better to wait until at least eleven for the big reveal. The more eyeballs, the better. I think she wanted the whole thing to go viral. I understood her theory, but I couldn't do it. It wasn't even ten and already I was crawling out of my skin with the need to tell him. It had to happen now. And I rationalized that, because we were not quite at capacity yet, I'd be able to move around better on my skates.

I yelled to whoever was closest that I was taking a break and received a vague wave of acknowledgment. My stomach pitched and rolled as I made my way to the office and I swallowed against the panic crawling up my throat at the thought I might be too late. Or that he'd changed his mind. *Thanks but no thanks, Chase, you were right the first time.*

No, I had to believe that he was waiting me out, giving me space. He'd made his feelings clear, (and they didn't just go away after a week, right?), and I was the one who needed to catch up.

Even with my little pep talk, I was still dangerously close to emptying my stomach all over Harley's gold jumpsuit. But I shoved the uncertainty aside for the moment because, whatever happened, Mack deserved to know how I really felt and I was determined to tell him.

What I had not taken into account when agreeing to the jumpsuit, was the fact that Harley had been the one to wrangle me into it and zip it up. Doing so alone was a task. I was huffing and puffing, groaning and contorting by the time I finally got the zipper all the way up. Now for my skates, and no knee pads because I couldn't compromise the ensemble.

I sat in the office breathing deep for another five minutes. I knew I was going out there, bailing wasn't an option. I just needed a second first. And I needed to let the DJ know it was time. Because I had also lined up lighting and a musical accompaniment, which may or may not bomb—but a grand gesture was a grand gesture, so I was going all out.

The opening beats of *Sorry* filtered through the office door. Whether I was ready or not, it was showtime.

As soon as I was out of the hall the spotlight landed on me, reflecting gold twinkles everywhere and a murmur went through the crowd. A path opened, the spotlight following as I wove towards the bar, Justin Bieber crooning apologies over the sound system.

I could feel eyes on me, lots of them, but there was only one pair I cared about. The last few people stepped aside and there he was, staring at me with a bemused smile on his gorgeous face. I loved him so fucking much it was hard to breathe. I glided forward until I was right in front of him, the spotlight widening to encompass us both.

"Hey," I croaked. My mouth was so dry. Why was my mouth so dry?

"Hey," he said, eyes darting around before coming back to me. "What's up, Cheese?"

"I was an idiot."

"Oh, yeah?"

"Yeah, I was so focused on what might go wrong I didn't see everything that was going right. And I—" I blew out a breath and gripped the bar top to hide my shaking hands. "I love you, Mack, I'm *in love* with you, and I never should have tried to keep that, or us, a secret. I'm sorry."

He squeezed the back of his neck. "And you want to do this here?"

"I considered other options, but this seemed the most— um—dramatic."

"It is that." Was that all he had to say? Had I completely misread this situation? I'd gone full rom-com, grand romantic gesture and he was staring at me like I might have lost my mind.

My heart was in my throat. "Am I—am I too late? Is it too

late? I get it that I fucked everything up, but I wanted—I needed you to know that I love you, that I don't just want to be friends. I mean, you're still my best friend, obviously, but ..." I shook my head. "I was only risking as much as I was willing to lose, I think. The thought of losing you completely scared the ever living shit out of me. It still does. But you're my person. And I can't live with only half of you, I want all of you, Milton Alfred Carmichael Kent. I'm sorry it took me so long to figure it out." He wasn't saying anything, just standing there staring at me. How long was I supposed to stay here before I called it a night and went home to eat my weight in curly fries and cry myself to sleep?

He vaulted over the bar, making it look deceivingly easy, and landed beside me.

"Hi," I whispered, because I wasn't sure what else to say at this point.

His hands came up to cradle my face and my eyes stung.

"I would have waited for you forever, Chastity," he said, voice low and rough. The relief that swept through me made my knees wobbly. "Because you're all I want. You have been since you walked into the girls bathroom in freshman year. I think you might be my hero." He paused, his gaze roaming over my face. "And I fucking love you."

I laughed, a couple of rogue tears escaping down my cheeks. "I fucking love you, too." His lips found mine, gentle at first then hungry. I clung to his shoulders as his tongue sunk into my mouth and cheers echoed around us. *Oh that's right, we're in public.*

When we broke apart he took hold of my thighs and lifted me onto his waist to more cheers. I laughed into his neck, squeezing him tight as he walked us back to the office. He kicked the door closed, dropped me onto the desk and attacked my mouth. It was heaven. Had it really only been a week? It felt like an eternity since we'd been like this.

"Fuck I missed you," he said between kisses, fingers already finding the zip at my back and working it down.

"Me too, so much. I love you." I couldn't stop the smile as I said it. My cheeks were going to be sore tomorrow.

"Say it again."

"I love you." I kissed him. "I love you. I love you."

He groaned into my mouth as I squeezed him closer, my locked ankles holding him captive against me. I wasn't letting him go again.

"As much as I like this jumpsuit, I really need it off."

"Skates. Skates off first." I said as he peeled the sequined fabric off my shoulders and down my front.

"You are so fucking perfect." The words were low, reverent and sent goosebumps tingling down my arms.

"I am very far from perfect."

He shook his head, brushing kisses along my collar bones and down between my breasts. "You are fucking perfect for me." His lips continued their exploration over my stomach to the edge of the jumpsuit where it sat at my hips. "I'm sorry if I pushed you too hard," he said quietly and I tugged on his hair until he was looking at me.

"It was a shove that I needed. I'm sorry I refused to see how good we could be."

He dropped another kiss onto my stomach. "I meant it though, I would have waited as long as you needed me to."

"Seventeen years is probably long enough."

With a growl he wrenched off my skates, nearly pulling me off the desk in the process, then the jumpsuit was off and I was naked. In our office.

Mack kissed his way back up to my mouth as one hand slid between my legs. My hips rocked, chasing his fingers and the relief they would provide. I wanted him so desperately I could barely see straight.

"Please, Mack."

"I need you."

I nodded, flicking open his belt to free his straining cock as he sucked my nipple into his mouth. God, I'd really missed his mouth. I made a garbled sound and shoved his jeans down.

"Now."

"Yes," he groaned, sinking into me in one swift motion. My legs trembled against his waist and I kissed him, deep and slow, pouring everything I had into him. We moved together, panting, groaning, kissing. I pulled his shirt up and over his head, desperate to feel his skin against mine. I didn't know what the hell I'd been thinking, trying to keep this from both of us. He was right, we really were perfect for each other.

His hand slipped between us and he pinched my clit, sending me careening towards my climax with a cry.

"I love you," I said on a moan against his mouth. "I love you so much."

"*Chase*." He wrapped an arm around my back, hips meeting mine in hard snaps. "I love you—oh *fuck*." He came with my name on his lips and collapsed over me, breathing hard. "I love you."

"We had sex in the office."

He smiled against my neck. "Yes we did."

"We had a rule about that."

"Rules were made to be broken."

"It was a make-up sex exception."

"That might just tempt me to pick another fight."

I laughed as he pulled me up to sit, withdrawing with a pained sigh. I didn't like fighting, but if that was the result, maybe it wasn't so bad. His hands came back to my face, tilting it up to his and he brushed a tender kiss across my lips.

"We should probably get back out there," I whispered.

"Or we could just stay in here and I can make you come all night."

My thighs tightened at his hips. "I do like the sound of that plan. It's a shame there's no lock on the door." I nipped and licked at his chin.

"I might have to do something about that."

EPILOGUE
MACK

EVERY AVAILABLE SURFACE was covered in pie.

Ordinarily, this would bring me a fair amount of joy. Today, however, it caused a cold sweat to break out on the back of my neck and a nauseous feeling to swell in the pit of my stomach.

I paced halfway across the bar and back to the kitchen. Then I did it again. And again.

"Don't go pulling all those curls out, Milton, I'm quite fond of them," Chase said, circling me on her skates. I hadn't even realized my hands were in my hair until she said it. I paused my pacing long enough to watch her weave between the tables, smiling as she turned on a dime, and came back to me butt first.

It had been five months. Five months of life with her. Falling asleep tangled in one another, and waking the same way. Less than a week after the gold jumpsuit, Chase had moved all of her stuff into my place, which quickly became our place, and soon felt like it had always been that way. Because there had always been small touches of her everywhere. Now, there were just more. Like the clothes she left all over the place, or the ridiculous amount of curly fries in the freezer, or the hair that was constantly clogging the shower drain. I'd never been happier in my entire life.

She planted herself in front of me.

"You're going to wear a track in the floor."

I wrapped my arms around her waist and continued pacing, widening my steps around her skates.

"I'm going to be sick and it is all your fault."

She laughed, draping her hands over my shoulders. "I'm so sorry for being endlessly supportive."

I turned, her gold-flecked wheels making an awkward noise on the polished concrete floors as I took her with me for another lap.

"I don't know why the fuck I let you talk me into this."

"It was pie or becoming my figure skating partner. Pie was the right decision. We both know it, tell Lionel to take a hike." Her fingers slid into my hair, toying with the strands. I recognised that she was trying to distract me. It almost worked.

"This is not about Lionel, it's about the fact that my only two options were pie or figure skating." I sounded borderline hysterical but I didn't care. Chase made a noise somewhere between a laugh and a cough.

"Hey." She dropped her toe-stop thing to the floor, halting our progress, and I nearly took us both down. "Everything is going to be amazing, because *you* are amazing. You are *The Pie Guy*."

"Who the hell did I think I was, claiming that title?"

"You didn't have to claim it, I gave it to you. Anointed you, if you will. Although, I guess you did kinda claim it when you registered it with the city. Anyway, claimed, anointed, potayto–potahto." She grinned. "You make the best fucking pies in the state—if not the country—and it was rude to keep all that to yourself. This is your thing, Mack. Own it."

I knew she was right, but that didn't stop the anxiety from clinging to me like a cold, wet, suffocating blanket.

"You're right."

"I know." She reached up to press a quick kiss to my lips. I caught her before she pulled away, sinking my tongue deep into her mouth with a groan. If there was anything that was going to take my mind off everything today, it was Chase's mouth. Her fingers tightened in my hair, sending heat barrelling down my spine. I wondered if it would stop being like this, if I'd stop feeling like I'd never get enough of her. I doubted it.

"That's enough of that." Nash's laugh carried through the bar. "Time to open the doors, Pie Guy."

I was absolutely going to be sick.

"Tell Lionel to fuck off, Mack. You've worked so hard for this," Chase whispered.

"Still freaking out, then?" Nash asked, one arm draped over Jemma's shoulders. Before I could lie and say no, Chase answered for me.

"Uh-huh, but I give excellent pep talks, as you well know, Nashville, so it's all good, right?" She gave my chest a light slap.

"All good." And I almost believed it.

"It's going to be brilliant, Mack, honestly. Darcy and Harley said they can barely keep your pies on the shelf. They're gone by midday without fail," Jemma said as she stepped away from Nash and into Chase's hug.

Selling the pies to a few cafes and diners around Brooklyn —starting with Cream and Sugar—had been a soft launch of sorts for *The Pie Guy*. It was a good start, allowing me to settle into a routine of regular baking and get my head around what it would be like to do it full time. Was I still scared? Abso-fucking-lutely, but I'd come this far, and Chase wouldn't let me quit now.

I'd tried to tell her I'd still be available for bar shifts but she fired me. Then she promoted both Greyson and Micky to managers and hired more new staff, so she'd be able to step back a little. She was still here pretty much everyday but now some of that time was spent skating—our floors were apparently an ideal surface—or sitting in the kitchen watching me work. She was also taking her role as taste tester very seriously.

"Time to show the world your pies." She gave my ass a squeeze and I laughed.

"Okay, let's do this."

CHASE SHUFFLED INSIDE BEHIND ME, bumped the door closed with her hip and sagged against it. "I think I have a pie baby," she said, rubbing circles over her stomach and I imagined her belly one day round with our baby, not merely one from eating too much of my pie. One day, maybe.

She wasn't the only one to try a little of everything on the menu and, from what I saw, the reception to all of them was, as Chase anticipated, amazing. Now, I just needed to keep it going. I was excited at the prospect.

"You know, you didn't have to eat all of them." I dropped her skates on the couch.

"Of course I did, it's called being a supportive girlfriend. Something I take very seriously, I'll have you know."

She was so fucking perfect, I almost didn't have words. "None of it would have happened without you." And it wouldn't be the same without her with me.

She smiled and hooked her arms around my neck. "I just ate pie."

"You did a hell of a lot more than that."

One shoulder lifted in a half shrug. "Well, I would do just about anything for you..."

"Just about anything, huh?" I asked, pulling her into my chest.

"Yup. Any requests?" Her smile was sweet as she pressed herself closer.

"Don't tempt me." I dropped my head to the crook of her neck, letting my lips wander. She hummed.

"I might have one." Her fingers threaded into my hair.

"Mmm, what's that?"

"Marry me."

My head popped up and I watched her, waiting for a punchline that never came. "You're serious?"

"I am."

"You want to get married?"

"To you, specifically, yes." She grinned.

"But—but you don't—our parents, they—"

"It's true that our parents all made a royal mess of pretty much every relationship they've ever been in. But what I've realized, what it took me way too long to realize, is that we're not them. Nor are their mistakes ours. And, if there is anyone who makes me want to believe in marriage, believe in forever, Mack, it's you. So what do you think? You wanna be my husband?"

No question had ever been easier to answer. "You bet I fucking do."

Harley's story
coming in 2023

stay up to date at
www.erinthomsonauthor.com

ABOUT THE AUTHOR

Erin Thomson is a romance author based in Melbourne, Australia. After dabbling in writing for over 10 years she took the plunge and published her first novel, *The Wedding Planners*, in 2021. When she's not lost in the pages of her latest writing project, or wrangling her two kids, you can find her baking up some sweet treats in the kitchen.

instagram.com/authorerinthomson

One explosive night. No names. No numbers. No strings. And Jemma and Nash were never supposed to see one another again. Which is why being thrown together to plan a wedding is probably a recipe for disaster.

Can these two head strong chefs maintain their professional distance to get the job done, or will their simmering be too much to resist?

This is a work of fiction. Names, characters, places and incidents are either a product of the author's imagination or used fictitiously, and any resemblance to actual persons living or dead, business establishments, events or locales, is entirely coincidental.

Copyright © 2022 by Erin Thomson

All rights reserved.

No part of this book may be reproduced in any form or by any electronic or mechanical means, including information storage and retrieval systems, without written permission from the author, except for the use of brief quotations in a book review.

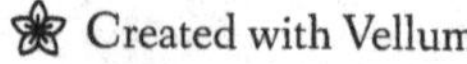 Created with Vellum